NORSKA:
A Viking Woman's Journey

**by Doris Meek
with Mike MacCarthy**

Published by   San Diego Writers'
                       Monthly Press
                       3910 Chapman Street
                       San Diego, CA 92110

First Edition

Library of Congress Cataloging in
Publication Data

Library of Congress Catalog Card Number: 95-92466

ISBN: 1-885516-01-0

Cover Design and Book Layout:
Sandra J. Welch and Christina Maule

Dedication:

To my husband and our two daughters.

"We are very blessed that it is the meek who are to inheret the earth, for they can be trusted with it."

—Madeline L'Engle
"Unifers" October-December, 1985
Publisher: First Unitarian Church of
San Diego

Acknowledgments

Grateful acknowledgment is made to the following women, men, and children. They were eager to participate in helping and learning along the way.

Karen Kish, News Director, KPBS; Jerry Bumpus, Professor of English, SDSU; Hope Shaw, Professor/Radio/Television, San Diego City College; Richard Harrison, Production/Program Supervisor, "Senior Lifestyles," San Diego County Office of Education.

Judith Meyers, Psy.D. Clinical Psychologist, Commentator on "Senior Lifestyles," cable TV show; Tom and Carolyn Owel-Towle, Parish Ministers, First Unitarian Universalist Church; Erling Nyhammer, Scandinavian English-Norwegian translator for book; Sigurd Stautland, Professor Emeritus, SDSU, Scandinavian-English translator for book.

First Unitarian Universalists Church members who are all eager to be the first to read *Norska*: Dona Foster; Darlanne Hoctor; Sue Manley; Dorothy Pannek; Bob and Betsy Stevens; Dorene Sulzer; Bill and Ruth Stockton; Sue Haskin; John Davis; Jon Fish; Isabel Mather, Writer, (R); Beverly Jay-Thompson; Betty Boone, Lawyer, (R); Betty Bange, Social Worker (R); Arthur Clark, Hospice Administrator; Maryann Blinkhorn, Health Insurance Broker; Michael B. Areta, University Administrator; Georganne Hoctor, Teacher; Leana Hosker, Exec. Assistant; Izetta H. Segal, Teacher (R); Barbara J. Rose, Physical Therapist; Jean Bruce, School Nurse Practitioner (R); F. Suzanne Moore, Writer/Artist; Charlyn D. Johnson, Nurse; Bonnie Tidd, Teacher; Deb Wilder, Educational Administrator; Ella M. Agnew, D.R.E. (R); Helen Burke, Teacher (R); Paul Bruce, Professor and Colleague (R); Bernice Clark, Storyteller; Wendy Fish, Minister; Erica Fish, Student; Wynne Hollinshead, Basketry, Knitting, Banners, Radio/TV; Martha Thomson, League of Women Voters, Pres.; Peg Tilford-Miller, Proofreading; Harry Miller, as needed; Callie Leef, Software Test Engineer; Budd Leef, Software Test Engineer; Caroline Clark, Library Worker; Elizabeth (Liz) Jones, Director of Religious Education; Bertha F. Crowell, Teacher (R); Helen Farrand Teagne; Janet L. Griggs,

Art Design; Mona Matthews, Social Worker (R); Jim Faris, Bookkeeper; Ruth Van Leeuwen, Author; Bridget Hanley, Hospitality/Community Bldg.; Colleen Wells, Church Administrator; Guy LaMothe, Intern Minister; Clarence Sevier Overstreet, Teacher, (R); Kg L. Farrer, Teacher; Francis Clare, Artist; Iris-Ann Decelles, Teacher; Alice H. Rathbone, Clerk; Angela L. Garner, U.S. Navy and Wiccan Newsletter; Wendy Bartel, Music Therapist and Recreation Activities Leader; Susan J. Olive Miller, Religious Education Assistant; Leonard Wener, Engineer (R); Connie diGirolanio, Procurement Specialist; Pete diGirolanio, Architect; Dory Scantlen, Teacher, Mother; Tomas E. Firle, Physicist; C.D. Becker, Instructor; Jorge Hinojosa, Research and Development Manager; Lynne Powers, Bank Trust Officer; Cynthia Thomas-Evans, Retail Management; Cheryl Sandquist, Nurse; Lynn Riggs, Manager of Operations; Sheila Marsh, Evaluations, San Diego Mesa College; Phyllis Kaplan, Disability Insurance Representative; Daryl Nees, Nurse Practitioner; Paul R. Marsh, Credit Union President, CEO.

Mitsuo Tomita, M.D., Southern California Permanente Medical Group, La Mesa, California — also participated in "Senior Lifestyles;" Denise Nelesen, President, City of San Diego Council on Aging.

Scandinavians in Denmark: Knut Amorsen (second cousin to Doris Amorsen Meek); Kaesten Norby, Danish Sisterhood. In Canada: Soren Thomas Amorsen (third cousin); Millie Amorsen; Maud Amorsen; Dave Dopp; Harry Curtis; Kate Amorsen; Reg Helliwell; Doreen Dopp; John Quaife; Christian Jorgensen; Luf Jorgensen; Hans George Quist II; Frederik Carl Christian II; Soren Christian Gronbeck.

Jean Stein, Former President, City of San Diego Council on Aging; David Pritchard, Ph.D, Associate Professor of Social Work, SDSU; Jim Dark, Radio, Television, San Diego City College; Tom Gripp; Telecourse Design Golden West; Jackie Collins Neal, County of San Diego, TV/Radio; Doris Steinman, Older Owls; Tom Reese, Senior Senator; Betty L. Springer, Newspaper Writer; Rachael Litonjua-Witt, Media Technology Services, SDSU; Sandra Welch, Art Director, Publisher (see cover design).

Lynda Palmer, Teacher (R), Reading Reviews; Anne Wall, Teacher (R), Reading Reviews; Joan Cudhea, Financial Planner; Janet Bowermaster, Law Professor; Ralph Devicaris, Engineer; Grace Duckworth, Social Worker; David Fountain, Television; Joy and Joe Combs, Apt. Broker; Juanite Harrell, Teacher (R); Michael Hoctor, Housing Administration; Susan Johnson, Nurse; Marilyn Kauffman, Word Processor; George Longstreth, M.D., Physician; Mary Maschal, Home Repairs; Ellie and Lou Stein, Writer; Mary Swedelius, Retired; Cherie Koss and Doug Waldo, Coordinator/Campaign Director; Everando Aguilar, Specialist A.F.S.D.; Marie Buckey, Retired; Keith and Janet Crosby, Reappraiser; Brenda Gipson, Orthalmic Assistant; Louise Karstens, Volunteer; My Luong Tran, Professor, SDSU; Elaine Elias, Secretary, SDSU; Leone McCoy, Professor (R), SDSU.

Resources: Laura Rodriquez, Logan Heights Family Health Center; Percil Stanford, Professor, Center on Aging, SDSU; Leonard Zonville, Chair, Advisory Committee, Area Agency on Aging; Shirley Weber, Afro-American Studies, SDSU; Prof. Ricardo Griswold, Mexican-American Studies; Daniel Whitney, Asian Studies; Union of Pan-Asian Communities; Daniel L. Laver, Director, Dept. of Area Agency on Aging; Angela Yang, Librarian, San Diego Public Library, Outreach Services; Ruben G. Rumbaut, Assoc. Prof. of Sociology; Kenji Ima, Ph.D., Assoc. Prof. of Sociology; Dianne Jacob, Chairwoman, Board of Supervisers, 2nd District; Dr. Charles Shockley, Ex. Dir. San Diego Minority Business Development Center; Maria Zuniga, Ph.D., Prof. of Social Work, SDSU; Margaret Wanaga-Penrose, Director UPAC.

"The Elderly Are Family, Too": Ray Schwartz, Area Agency on Aging, Senior Peer Counseling Program; Marjorie Howe, College of the Emeriti, City of San Diego Community College; Molly Drummond, Community Hospice Care; Dorothy Yomenitsu, Council on Minority Aging and Union of Pan-Asian Communities; Teddye Gentry, Episcopal Community Services, Mid-City Regional Recovery Center; Wanda Vevia, Lutheran Social Services; Jean Stein, President, Older Women's League; Jan Grossickle, Sharp Senior Health Care; Ann Sanderson, Southern Caregiver Resource Center; City of San Diego Council on Aging Education Committee: Kathy Boyd, Muriel Baze, Connie Curran, Carol Dentz, Kay Dennison, Margo Kasch, Todi Matthews, Lorrie McGrath, Pat Richardson.

Susan Chappellet-Metez, Ombudsman, SDSU; Erma Stoops, Teacher (R); Lester and Sybil Dray, Retired; Dick and Fran Thompson, Retired; Mary Lou Lyons, Homemaker; Gloria and George Ruhforth, Workers; Grace Lewis-McLaren; Administrative Assistant, Unitarian/Univeralist Church; Dr. Maria Nieto Senour, Professor, Counselor, Education, SDSU; Sylvia Wallace, Kaiser, Public Affairs.

Table of Contents

Chapter One

The Fisherman's Daughter

Even before she opened her eyes, the pungent stench of dead fish stung Anna's nostrils. Lying in bed, she wondered if she would ever take a breath without that bitter smell. As oldest daughter to Knud and Tuve Steffensen, she couldn't recall a moment in her life without that odor. "Times are hard," Papa would always remind her whenever she looked longingly at the horizon. "We're a Norwegian family and we fish. That's what we've always done. That's how we survive. It's the only way." Even so, if it weren't for Mama, she would have left months ago.

Anna rubbed open her eyes, rolled out of bed, and retrieved her faded work clothes. Today, like every other day, they still reeked despite her best efforts last night to wash them clean. She sat down on the edge of the bed, shoved her legs into the pants, then pulled on heavy boots and a warm sweater. Looking in a small mirror, she brushed her auburn hair and tied it in a knot so the winter winds wouldn't blow it into her eyes — big, piercing brown eyes.

She sighed and thought back to her high school days — now more than three years past — when she'd taken over Mama's job in the fish stall. She did it so Mama could take the warm corner. There she could sit down and collect money from customers. Mama enjoyed visiting with her friends when they came to buy fish. It was her only pleasure. But recently, she'd been coughing a lot and unable to work. Anna hoped Mama would feel better today. She missed working with her.

The young woman opened her bedroom window and looked down across the Voss valley and up at the surrounding mountains. It had been raining and looked as if it would be another cold, damp day. If only the sun would shine more often, she thought, maybe Mama would get well quicker. She studied the rolling waves in the *fjord* below to see if Papa had begun fishing. He always said that if he could get an early start, he would have a good catch. A few moments passed before she spotted the *Viking Star* and its distinctive hand-carved Viking on the bow, holding a star in one hand. With practiced eyes, the fisherman's daughter spotted heavy activity on deck — they were having a good catch. She sighed, thinking of the work ahead.

Anna straightened her bedroom and went to the kitchen. The sweet smell of coffee and homemade *fattigmanns* (doughnuts) made her realize how hungry she was. As usual, sixteen-year-old Gudrun was making breakfast. Although three years younger, she was already a half-foot taller, and prettier with long, glistening blond hair. Like Mama and Papa, Anna stood just over five feet and was plain to look at. Men didn't pay her much heed.

"Good morning, Fish Lady," Gudrun said, glancing over at Anna with a smirk. "Whatcha want for lunch? A fish sandwich?"

"No, thank you," Anna snapped. "I'll make my own." She sat down and began eating. "You think you can be on time for a change today? Looks like Papa will have a big catch. It's important you be on time to spell Mama. It's her first day back."

"Don't you worry about me!" Gudrun sneered.

"Well, I know it's hard for you to pry yourself away from Gunnar or Henrik or Frederik, but just remember Mama needs you."

Just then, their mother ambled into the kitchen. Anna noticed she was dressed in a blue wool dress and boots, her usual attire for work. She seemed to walk slower, though — shoulders bent, face pale, her once-blond hair turning to gray. Her round face appeared thinner, her blue eyes bloodshot and sad. She managed a slight grin and nodded at her two daughters.

"Good morning, Mama," Gudrun said, going to the stove.

Anna stood and helped her mother sit down. "Want some coffee and *fattigmanns*? They're good."

"Hmmm," Mama said, forcing one of her cheerful smiles. "They do smell delicious."

Gudrun brought her mother a cup of coffee, then left.

"We'll need warm coats today," Anna said, pouring cream and honey into Mama's cup. "Kind of icy and slippery out. I'll walk with you to the wharf. We'll get Nels to set up the shutters until the sun comes out so you can keep warm."

Mama nodded and chewed. "Hope Nels makes it."

Anna shook her head. "I don't know why you keep him. He's not a very good worker."

Mama smiled. "Anna, he's just a young . . . boy," she said, starting to cough. She strained to hold it back. A few seconds passed before she was ready to continue. "He reminds me of Grandma Inger helping in the stall when she was young. Give him time, honey."

Her oldest daughter held her by the shoulders. "Are you all right, Mama?"

"I'm fine. It was just a piece of the *fattigmann* — it went down the wrong way."

"You sure you're ready to go back to work today? Maybe you should stay home one more day."

"I'm tired of staying home while you and the others work twice as hard to make up for me. I'll wrap up tight in my wool coat, just like I always do. Don't you worry. I'll be fine."

"See you after school," Gudrun said, coming back into the kitchen, kissed her mama. She gave her mother a quick peck on the cheek. "Take care of yourself, Mama." She left.

Mama squeezed Anna's arm as they started down the mountain path to the marketplace on the wharf. Looking down at the *fjord*, they could see more boats setting their nets.

Anna held her mother tightly to keep her from falling; she seemed to be bending over too far. "Is the pain in your chest constant?" she asked. "You should go with me to see the doctor."

Mama shook her head. "It only hurts when I cough, but I'm going to be all right."

Anna thought she'd better talk with Papa. She hadn't discussed Mama's pains with him or her reluctance to go to the doctor. Papa's long hours on the boat made it difficult for him to spend much time at home. There was always so much to do.

Just as the two women arrived at the wharf the rain started again. Nels was waiting. "Good morning, Miss Steffensen."

Anna nodded. "Light the kerosene heater and keep the shutters up. Put Mama's favorite chair in the corner, away from the wind and rain. Then, help me set up the stall."

Nels was a sturdy fourteen-year-old who worked in the morning and attended school in the afternoon. He always dressed like a sailor, with his sailor cap perched on the back of his thick, blond hair.

It won't be long, Anna thought, until he'll be wanting to go out with the men and catch the fish, rather than stay here in the stall with the women.

The Steffensen family stall was constructed of wood painted green. It contained two long, wood counters, an ice chest, and two extra tanks for the iced fish. Also, there was a small table, two chairs, and a storage closet.

Anna checked the corner where Mama sat, wrapped snug in a blanket. "You taught me how to clean and prepare fish, Mama," she said. "Now, it's your turn to take it easy. You stay warm and we'll take care of the rest."

She and Nels fired up the wood heaters. Soon most of the old fish smell had blown away on the sea breeze, and they'd cleaned and arranged the stall. They were ready for the new fish. Suddenly, Nels took off his cap and waved out toward the *fjord*. "Look, I see the *Viking Star*. It's just docking."

Anna could hear Papa calling to tell her about the catch. She took a rubber apron out of the closet and wrapped it around her robust figure. "Nels, stay here with Mama," she said, running out into the wind and rain. "Coming Papa!"

Knud Steffensen was a short, stocky, tight-lipped man — always anxious to bring in the first load of fish; it gave his family an edge over the other boats.

Anna watched him open the tanks on deck, his back bent from years of lifting nets, his face weather-beaten and wrinkled. She was sure his deep blue eyes had never missed a single school of fish. His shaggy jacket and pants reflected his years of constant toil.

He waved back at Anna. "We're a winner today, honey."

Anna hurried back to check the ice chest, tanks, and trays. "Mama, we have a big catch out there," she said, sharpening her favorite knives.

Mama didn't answer and Anna didn't notice. Two handsome crew members rolled down the first containers of fish. "Wow, you're going to be busy," said one. His name was Ole Ludeman. He was a tall, young man with strong muscles who often helped on Papa's boat. "You're going to work today all right." He always smiled at Anna and smelled like dead fish.

Anna thanked the men, selected the biggest cod, and struck a vicious blow with a knife, chopping off its tail. She shook her head to keep stray hairs from falling down on her high forehead. Bit by bit, she sliced the fish and cleaned it, thinking about her grandmother working in a family stall, years before. "Mama," she asked, "did you help your mother like I do you?"

"Of course, Anna," she coughed and held her breath for a moment. "I worked with her starting when I was ten. But . . . ," she stopped again and leaned against the chair. "Thank God, the *fjord* always provided more fish."

Anna, after cleaning some of the fish, sloshed through the rain outside in her heavy boots and filled an ice chest with cut fish. Then she hurried inside and arranged trays of fish ready for customers. "Mama, you never complain about the odor. I smell it in my sleep."

"Dear, I . . . all do . . . ."

Her mother stopped talking.

"Mama, can I get you a cup of coffee? I'll get the canvas and spread it around your feet." She rushed out.

On the way, Anna noticed the other stall owners on the wharf who were preparing to open. Piles of flowers, produce, and fruits were arranged on their counters. The other fishing boats had not come in yet — only the *Viking Star* had. The Steffensens were going to sell a lot of fish today.

Anna hurried to the coffee house and brought back two cups of steaming coffee. She gave her mother one and held it for her until she was able to swallow a few sips.

"Thank you, honey," Mama said, leaning over and holding her chest with one hand.

"Can I get you anything else?" Anna asked, trying to conceal her concern. "I'm walking up to see Papa. Nels will be with you. If you need me, tell Nels to come and get me."

Her mother nodded, indicating she was all right.

"Come and stay with Mama," Anna called to Nels. "And stay here until I return from seeing Papa."

Nels nodded his agreement.

Papa doesn't realize Mama is sick, she thought, walking up the pier. It's up to me to make sure he knows.

Anna picked up the heavy hose to the *Viking Star* and, with much tugging and climbing, aimed the strong stream onto the deck, sweeping it clear of fish remnants. The rain was stopping now, making it easier to get about. She took a deep breath and climbed below. "Papa, I'm coming down," she yelled into the galley. "I want to talk with you."

Anna sat on the edge of the narrow berth and helped herself to a cup of coffee from his coffee pot. "I like your big cups, Papa," she said, warming her hands. Seeing Papa had no coat on, she said, "You'll be catching a cold if you don't put on a jacket."

"I'm all right. I'm trying to sort these tools," he said, on his knees with his back to her. "They fell down and slid all over the deck. You're worse than your mother worrying about my health."

"Mama hasn't been feeling well. She has bad chest pains. She should see the doctor. I can't persuade her to go because she won't admit she's sick."

"Mama ill? Why didn't you tell me sooner?" He turned to look at Anna. "What kind of pains? She's always been so healthy. Maybe I can talk with her and convince her to go for help."

"Papa, I think you should take her over to Dr. Guldvog's office right now."

He shrugged. "I'm sure Mama will be all right. I'll anchor the boat and go see her as soon as I can, Anna. "

She leaned over and gave him a hug, then climbed up the ladder. She loved her father and mother but they spent so little time together. The fish control their lives, she thought on her way back.

When she returned to the stall, Mama looked better and Anna went back to cleaning fish. Pretty soon Erna, a friend from high school, came by and bought some cod. She was short like Anna, but much heavier, wearing a yellow raincoat.

"Hi, Annie," Erna said. "Where were you?"

Anna smiled, pleased to see her old friend. "Working on Papa's boat. What brings you down here?"

"Remember Ingamor Gruhild?"

Anna nodded.

"Remember how you and she always talked about going to America some day?"

Anna nodded once more.

"Well, Ingamor wrote to me that Adild sent her passage money to go to Minnesota. They married, leased a farm, and now they're growing wheat and having a wonderful time."

Anna picked up a cutting knife and started to chop off another cod's tail. "Has anyone else done this?"

"Yes. Sig sent Elle a ticket to Minnesota, too."

Anna stared out into the cloudy morning. "Is any of your family going to America? I'm ready. It's 1883 and day after day, I stand here cutting the same fish, seeing the same people."

"Annie, do you know how much it costs?"

Neither spoke. Anna shook her head.

"If I have any more news, I'll let you know," Erna said, backing out of the stall. "You are so pretty. Your day will come."

Anna returned to her work, slicing the fillet for Mrs. Paulsen who always wanted just enough for two. Why do these customers poke at the fish trays? she thought. Do they think I have hidden a "special" under there?

She continued to watch her mother. "How are you feeling?"

"I just met . . . I forgot. My chest pains keep coming."

Anna knew that Mama enjoyed seeing her old friends — looked forward to it even. But right now, she was barely able to say hello. "What do you want, Mama? Do you want to go home?"

Mama emphatically shook her head.

The north wind blew through the skies during the rest of morning, but, before noon, the rolling white clouds came and the sun peeked through. Papa hadn't come yet, so Anna sat down beside Mama and got out her lunch bag. Mama didn't want to eat. Anna noticed how she was hunched over in an unnatural position.

"Mama, I must get Papa."

Mama shook her head, "I never could . . . oh, I feel that." She grabbed her chest again. "This pain hurts."

Anna helped Mama lie down on the canvas, wrapping her in a blanket. "Oh, Mama, you feel so cold and sweaty. I must get the doctor here. Stay right there." Anna ran out and called for Eric who had the nearest stall. "Please Eric, I can't find Nels. My mother needs help. Run to the *Viking Star* and get my father."

Eric turned and ran toward Papa's boat.

"Here come more customers, Mama. I'll take care of them. Rest right there. Papa is coming."

Anna didn't know what to do to help her mother. She tried to remember what she'd read in her health book.

Eric returned, panting. "He's coming."

Papa came running into the stall and knelt beside his wife. "Tuve, honey, where does it hurt?"

She pointed to her chest and tried to talk, but didn't have the strength.

He leaned down and kissed his wife. "Anna, I'm going to get Dr. Guldvog," he said and ran from the stall.

Anna brought a bucket of cold water and some towels and sat beside Mama, placing her head in her lap. She laid a cold towel on her forehead and held her mother's hand. Her mother didn't respond. New beads of sweat appeared on her ashen face.

Tears rolled down Anna's face. She wanted to hold her mother tight, but was afraid she'd make her worse. To think Mama was making change for the customers just minutes ago. Waiting for the doctor seemed endless. Couldn't Papa find him?

Anna took both Mama's hands and held them tight. Softly, she began to sing two of Mama's favorites: *"Norsk Bondevals"* and *"Ny*

Fiskervals." As she sang, she rocked gently side to side, just like Mama had done so many times for her when she was sick. Then, Anna hummed *"Den lille Ole,"* the song Mama used to sing to her when she was little. Anna kept thinking, Hurry, Dr. Guldvog! Hurry! Mama's eyes were filled with tears of pain.

Soon she heard running footsteps. Dr. Guldvog, his black bag in hand, rushed into the stall, Papa close behind. Anna noticed how his face tightened when he saw Mama on the floor. "Mama has been in pain on and off for the past month," Anna said quickly as Dr. Guldvog checked her pulse and blood pressure. Then, he listened to her heart. Mama seemed aware he was there. Anna noticed how carefully he examined her neck and chest, counting her heartbeats. Anna could feel Mama quivering with pain.

Papa gave Anna another cold cloth to put across Mama's forehead and knelt across from the doctor. Papa's face was pale, his clear blue eyes filled with tears.

"Her shortness of breath is getting worse," said Dr. Guldvog. "Her heart rhythm is unsteady. I'm wondering if she can withstand a trip to the hospital."

"I'll get a cart," Papa said, running off.

Anna and Dr. Guldvog looked at each another.

What would be best, Anna wondered, the trip down a bumpy road or the possibility of death in a fish stall? She felt helpless and futile, her tears streaming now. Her wonderful mother was dying before her very eyes in a fish stall and there was nothing anyone could do.

While Dr. Guldvog measured Mama's pulse and listened to her heart again, Anna could see she was losing consciousness. She leaned over and kissed her mother. "Breathe, Mama," she whispered. "Breathe!" She must live! Anna thought. How could we have ignored Mama's pain? We should have taken her to the doctor.

Papa came running back. "The cart's ready!"

Dr. Guldvog slowly shook his head.

Papa knelt beside Mama and held one of her hands. Her breathing had become slower and slower, barely perceptible.

Anna couldn't understand why Dr. Guldvog wasn't giving Mama medicine. Instead, he listened to her chest with his instrument and held her wrist. Suddenly, Mama was completely still. There was no breathing.

Dr. Guldvog looked up — eyes sad, mouth grim. "Knud, Anna, there is nothing more I can do. She is no longer with us."

Anna covered her face with both hands and began weeping.

Papa cried out and threw himself on Mama, wrapping his arms around her and pulling her limp body to his chest. His eyes were closed as if in a stupor and he began to weep. "Oh, my wonderful Tuve!" he sobbed. "I'm so very, very sorry. I love you so much. My wonderful wife, always working alongside me. I'm so sorry. It's all my fault. I should have taken you to see Dr. Guldvog. It's all my fault. It's all my fault."

Anna stood up, weeping out of control. Dr. Guldvog took her in his arms and held her tight. She couldn't believe her Mama was dead. Her own mother dead in broad daylight in a fish stall while, outside, the world didn't even notice — didn't even care. The market was open and nothing else mattered. They just kept walking about, wondering what they were going to cook for dinner that night while her own Mama lay dead on the floor.

Suddenly, she realized her Papa was still crying. She had to help him. He needed her. She wiped her eyes and separated herself from Dr. Guldvog, patting him with thanks. She went up behind Papa and took him in her arms. "No, Papa," she whispered, "it's not your fault. It's not your fault, Papa. You were a good husband. It's not your fault!"

Dr. Guldvog came up and put his arms around both of them. "It's nobody's fault. It just happened."

They stood that way for several minutes. Finally, Papa bent over and gently covered his wife's body with the canvas. He stood there staring at her, shaking his head and crying.

"Knud," Dr. Guldvog said after a while, his voice soft but firm, "I'll take care of your Tuve. You need to take Anna home, and don't forget you have another daughter. You'd better get her out of school before she hears the news secondhand."

Papa nodded and wiped his eyes. "Thanks, doctor," he whispered. He put one arm around Anna. "Come on," he said, kissing her head. "Today, the fish and the boat must wait."

Anna put one arm around her Papa as they walked away. She looked around the dirty-green stall where she and her Mama had spent so many hours, working so hard for so many days — for what?

In the months that followed, the friction between Anna and Gudrun completely vanished. They worked together in the stall so the family business could continue, but the ache in Anna's heart would not go away. Each day when she went there, the memory of her last moments with her Mama flashed across her mind. Whenever she walked near the spot on the floor where Mama died in her arms, she shivered. It was as if Mama was with her that very moment, and then, for the rest of the day, she would feel depressed and consumed with sorrow. She and Gudrun, although loving each other more than ever, could not bring themselves to speak of their mother's death.

One day, after another day at the stall, Anna carried groceries up the winding path to the family house on the side of the mountain. It was a clear spring day and for some reason she looked up and noticed how the setting sun made the houses on the hillside look especially graced. The rugged, stone-built homes with their red roofs and abundant firs struck an almost mystical cord in her soul. At that moment, she realized that was where her Mama should have died, not some smelly stall. The fact that her Mama had not died in her own home made Anna all the more sad.

She stared at the mountainside, then gritted her teeth. Someday before I die, she vowed, I'm going to have a house like that in America, and, so help me God, it's going to be far, far away from any fishing stall. Lord help any man who wants to marry me if he's a fisherman. I'll not die like my Mama.

She made a mental note to go see her friend Erna. Maybe she had more news from America about young men from Norway who wanted to send for a Norwegian wife.

Chapter Two

The Journey

Anna couldn't believe she was really going to America. Today was the day, and now, as Papa and Gudrun walked her toward *The Norwegian,* she was having grave doubts about her decision to leave her family. So, she thought, this huge vessel will carry me to New York City, many thousands of miles away. It was the biggest ship she'd ever seen. Its Norwegian flag snapped sharply in the brisk Bergen breeze. It seemed especially big when compared to the *Viking Star,* one wharf over.

Anna turned to her sister. "Do you know how much I'm going to miss you?" she said, hugging Gudrun. Her tears began to flow. "I'll write as soon as I can."

"We love you, Anna," Gudrun said, kissing her older sister.

Anna quivered inside, thinking how angry she had been with Gudrun when they were younger, now wishing Gudrun could come with her. Gudrun had certainly grown up these past few months, Anna thought. Papa needs her, though. A fierce knot seized Anna's stomach; she felt weak and sat down on her suitcase. Was she doing the right thing?

"Papa," said Anna, holding her forehead, "I feel sad going away without you and Gudrun. I wish I could take you with me."

But, she thought, she'd already given her word that she would follow the directions of the letter in her pocket and go to America and marry her new husband. It was the only way to get to a new world — away from the family fish stall, away from another lost existence like that of her mother, away from being just another free laborer in the family business.

"Remember, you are a Viking!" Papa said. "You all right?"

Anna stood and nodded, looking straight into her father's eyes.

For the first time she could remember, she saw tears in his usually clear blue eyes.

"Dear Anna," he said, "I love you and always will."

Anna wrapped her arms around his broad back. "Thank you, Papa. Me, too, you." How can you love someone and want to go away from him? she wondered. She gave him a big hug. "I'll always be thinking of you and will write as soon as our marriage date is set. Please keep up your spirits and let me know how you and Gudrun and all our friends are doing."

She held him close. The sorrow on his face made her wonder if it were too much for him, losing Mama and now his oldest daughter. If only Mama had lived to go on this trip . . . None of that, now Anna! she reminded herself. You must lead your own life.

She tried to hide her second thoughts by picking up her suitcase and starting toward the ship. Just before she reached the gang-plank, she turned to face Papa and Gudrun. "Let's join hands," Anna said.

They took each other's hands and bowed their heads.

"Anna," Papa said, "I'm sending you away to America with all our love. Give Mr. Ole Ludeman, your new husband, our regards. We'll be thinking of you having a lovely wedding and having a good, happy life. You will be in our hearts, always."

Anna squeezed the hands of her sister and father, then gave them both one last hug. Without a word, she picked up her suitcase and methodically, step by step, climbed the ship's gang-plank until at last she entered the open deck. There, she leaned over the ship's rail and looked for her family. When she finally found them, she waved frantically. Papa and Gudrun waved back, but Anna thought they looked small and lonely.

Sadness overwhelmed her. She wasn't going to see her sister and father for a long, long time. Who knew when, if ever? Tears came to her eyes. She realized how much she loved her family, but had to go away. How different life would have been if Mama had lived! But she didn't. There was no changing that. Anna would never forgive herself. Life in Norway was a constant reminder of Mama's tragic death and how she had been ignored and taken for granted by everyone, including her oldest daughter. That was Anna's fault, despite Dr. Guldvog's kind words. Her mother should never have been allowed to die in a windy fish stall. She should have been in her warm home. That's where she deserved to be. Anna should have sent for the doctor and stayed home with Mama. Whenever she thought of it, her stomach retched. Life in America had to be better!

The Norwegian was crowded with families and a few single people seeking their future in America. Anna was assigned to an upper bunk in steerage, the lowest deck of the ship. Children chased one another, laughing and crying. One mother with a boy about nine and a girl about seven, both dressed in sailor suits, ignored the noise and sat on a nearby bunk reading a storybook. They were all laughing over the pictures.

Anna liked the way the family stayed together and enjoyed each other's company. She noticed their mother was a tall, slender woman with blond hair tucked on top of her head and wondered where in America they were going.

Sitting on her top bunk, Anna could smell the musty blankets and the sweat from the rest of the throngs jammed into the steerage compartment. It was a worse smell than that of a city garbage heap, and there were no portholes for fresh air. Worse yet, the small lamps swinging above made poor light. She tried to look around the whole room, but it was impossible to see everyone. Some parents sat on their bunk beds while their children climbed up and down the sides, trying to amuse themselves. Some yelled after their children when they ran in the aisles. Anna couldn't understand parents like that: what else did those parents expect on a trip this long?

The sea was rough. They were already two weeks into their journey, and the constant pounding day and night by the Atlantic made it almost impossible for Anna to eat. It wasn't just the sea: too often, the diet of beans, mildewed bread, and tough meat tasted more like contaminated water. Resting in her top bunk, she thought of her family home high on the hill overlooking the *fjord*; she longed for a taste of Gudrun's *risengrøt* pudding. She shivered from the heavy cold air creeping into steerage.

The tall mother, who bunked just across the aisle from Anna, took her two children for a walk each day. Anna noticed the mother was very kind to her children, having books for them and playing simple games to keep them occupied. One day as they passed, Anna decided to speak to her. "Can you die of seasickness?" she asked.

"Not that I know of," said the woman, smiling graciously. "Is there anything I can do to help you?"

"I don't think so," Anna said, sighing. "It's just that this ship has been plowing through one wave after another for two weeks. Sometimes it comes down so hard, I'm afraid."

The woman nodded with understanding. "Is this your first ocean voyage?"

"Yes."

"Don't worry," said the woman. "These Norwegian ships are built to withstand this kind of pounding for the whole trip, if necessary. I'm sorry you don't feel well. Are you sure I can't do something to help you?"

Anna shook her head and the woman left with her children.

For two more days, the waves threw the ship headfirst into the stormy seas. The noise and Anna's fears caused her to cling desperately to the ropes on her bed. She finally decided to gather her warmest clothes. There was no more avoiding it —this ship might actually sink.

Through the next day, the ocean seemed to pick up the ship and smash it into the ocean. It made tremendous cracking noises and hurt her ears. When Anna was positive the sturdy hull was breaking apart, she hurriedly put on her heavy coat and shoes and held her purse. She waited in the passageway to avoid being tossed from her bunk by the force of another wave.

At that moment, a member of the crew yelled down the ladder, "Prepare to abandon ship!"

Anna rushed for the ladder where the crowd was fighting to climb up. Her hands were shaking and people were pushing and shoving to get up. Ice-cold water splashed down the steps, making the footing treacherous. She kept telling herself, You're a Viking, Anna. You can make it! You can make it!

Finally, she reached the deck where ferocious gale winds whipped and swirled the rain and sea. The guardrails had been swept into the ocean. Crewmen were helping passengers into lifeboats hanging alongside the listing ship. Huge waves swept over the decks periodically, soaking everyone and knocking some down. Anna knew her chances of survival would be small in one of these little boats, but it was her only chance. The boats were everyone's only chance.

With shaking hands and quivering knees, she accepted one crewman's strong helping hand. He had a rope wrapped around him and with each new wave he fought to keep his balance. Anna found a seat on a bench in the lifeboat and looked out at the mountainous waves. Other lifeboats were barely visible in the distance as they rose and fell across the howling seas. Each was crammed with passengers; the crewmen pulled bravely on the oars. Anna clung to her seat in the middle of the boat and thanked God for allowing her to be in one of the last boats. She wasn't sure if there would be enough for all the passengers. She noticed that the mother and children she'd met in steerage were sitting beside her; the children were dressed in heavy coats, scarfs, and hats. Anna also noticed a tall man sitting with the woman, but in front of her. Every bench was filled with six passengers; Anna counted thirty aboard. She nodded hello at the woman as the crewmen held the ropes and let the boat descend the long height to the ocean until it finally splashed into the roaring seas.

Anna had tied her scarf over her head but the water sprayed her again as the crewmen pulled out the oars. She closed her eyes and wondered if she would ever see Gudrun and Papa again. The waves continued slamming the boat up and down. Would she return someday? An angry wave washed over their crowded boat. Anna's coat, clothes, and scarf were drenched to the skin. How long can I withstand this? she wondered, thinking how much she missed Papa and Gudrun. Now, she felt all alone and small.

She looked back to see the last boat behind them fighting through the rain. One crewman used a huge oar as a rudder to direct it toward the other lifeboats. Anna felt the end was near. Who would rescue them in such a storm, especially with darkness of night quickly approaching? She sat with water dripping from her clothes. Each wave seemed to break on top of them. She gritted her teeth to stop the chattering. Crewmen handed out canvas to everyone to use to protect themselves from the waves breaking over them.

Anna turned to the tall woman. "What chances do you think we have?" she yelled through the storm.

"A good chance," she replied. "The waves will calm down. I'm Elsa Swensen." She extended her wet, gloved hand and nodded at the two children sitting beside her. "This is Hans and Lise. And my husband, Henrik, sits in front of us."

Although she was shivering, Anna took her hand. "I'm Anna Steffensen." As they were shaking hands, Anna saw a huge wave about to wash over them. "Look out! Here comes another one!"

Henrik reached out and grabbed Hans while Elsa, already under the canvas shelter, knelt down with her arms tightly around Lise. "Anna, come join us, quickly — under the canvas."

It seemed as if the storm would never stop smashing down on them. The crewmen kept shouting at each other to make sure they were rowing to the south, away from the storm. Anna hung onto the bench and closed her eyes as the wind and rain beat harder against the canvas. The winds were getting stronger; all the passengers huddled closer together. The cold meant some of them had already lost feeling in their fingers and toes.

Anna, Elsa, and Lise stayed under the big cover while Hans sat with his father on the bench in front of them; Henrik had wrapped his coat and one arm around the boy. Every few minutes another wave crashed down upon them and the man hung on to the bench and Hans to keep them from being washed overboard. Anna and Elsa fought their weakness against the cold by sitting close together and keeping Lise between them under the canvas.

In the middle of the night, the boat suddenly listed dangerously to one side. The crew leader yelled, "Get to the middle of the boat! We're taking on water." Everyone obeyed as best they could.

Anna called out to Lise and Elsa, "Put your arms around each other and cuddle up close! We'll have more strength!"

Each new wave brought more water into the boat. Anna wondered how long they could keep on like this. She heard water sloshing below their feet and felt as if she were becoming an icicle. Could she even move after the many hours spent clinging to the bench, trying to protect little Lise from the waves? Wet, soggy, cold clothes clung to her body; one shoe floated around somewhere under her bench.

Miraculously, the lifeboat kept moving all through the night. All the passengers worked hard to keep their weight in the middle. Anna's was afraid she might get sick, but kept putting it out of her mind; she didn't want to have to move to one side of the boat to throw up — it might cause the boat to capsize.

Finally, the long night was over. The first light showed itself in the east, then the wind and waves calmed. Anna joined the Swensen family in a prayer of thanks. Death had seemed too close. Henrik quoted Goethe: "Whatever you can do, or dream, you can begin it. Boldness has genius, power, and magic in it. Begin it now!"

"Good morning, Miss Steffensen," Elsa said, taking a deep breath and sighing. "Maybe we'll see some sunshine today. *Ja*?" She turned to Henrik. "May I present my husband, Pastor Henrik Swensen."

With unsteady balance, the tall, rugged man took Anna's wet gloved hand. He nodded at her and smiled. "Thank you for helping with Lise," he said. "What is your destination?"

"I'm going to Chicago. I hope."

"With a little sunshine, we'll all get there together. We're going to the same place."

Anna breathed a sigh of thanks. At last, someone to talk to for the rest of the journey. She watched in silent admiration as Henrik stood and gave a blessing to everyone on board.

The wind and high waves began to decrease. Lise asked to play a game with Anna; she nodded yes. She hoped playing a game would take her mind off her total discomfort. The lack of food, liquids, and warmth had left her weak and light-headed; being drenched to her skin from head to toe made matters worse.

"You want to play a finger game with me?" Anna asked.

"*Ja! Ja!*" both Lise and Hans shouted. They played with Anna for hours, each one trying to outdo the other and show Anna how smart they were. Meanwhile, the short Steffensen woman kept track of what was going on around her.

The skies were beginning to clear and the air was getting warmer. She felt a new ray of hope that a ship would rescue them. She'd come this far; she wasn't about to lose faith.

On and on, the crewmen worked on the oars, pulling harder to make up for the high waves. At the next nightfall the stars came out, but the winds kept blowing and the tall waves kept coming. Elsa and Henrik held their children tight and kept up their prayers. A few passengers started to sing "*Den lille Ole.*" Anna remembered when it was sung in Norwegian valleys. The tune began to move as a stream through the immigrants. Over and over again, they sang to the tempo of the rowing.

Anna was feeling better; she leaned over to Elsa. "Your family's faith is an inspiration for me. I now have a new ray of hope that a ship will rescue us."

When daylight finally showed with a rim of the sun, they all started to sing "*Den lille Ole.*" Anna recalled how she'd last sung this song on a canvas in a fish stall back in Norway, holding her mother in her lap and rocking her side to side as her Mama's life ebbed away right before her eyes. A tear rolled down Anna's cheek.

As Elsa hummed along in harmony, she watched Anna. She saw the tear, but said nothing.

The crewmen suddenly raised their oars, yelling, "We're here! Come and get us!"

Pastor Swensen stood up and far off in the distance saw another big ship in their path.

Anna saw it, too. "They're coming, they're coming!" she cried aloud and gave Lise a hug. "We're rescued at last!" She was so excited, she rocked her body to and fro, thinking it might help the crewmen, while she bent over and tried to find her lost shoe.

"You need to stop that, Miss," said one of the crewmen. "These waters are still pretty rough. We could still tip over."

Anna apologized and sat perfectly still until it was their boat's turn to board passengers onto the large ship. The whole group was so happy they joined in a circle of prayer and thanksgiving as soon as they were aboard. Afterward, they sang songs of joy and accepted clothes of any size so they could get dry. Unlike the other passenger ship, this was an old cargo carrier with canvas-covered boxes on deck and in the hole.

Anna didn't care about size. When pointed to her quarters, she quickly changed to oversized trousers and a jacket that immediately brought her warmth. She climbed into a bunk, pulled a blanket over her, and closed her eyes in utter exhaustion. As sleep overwhelmed her, she thanked God for helping her survive the vicious storm. Many who left Norway with her were now on the bottom of the ocean.

The rough seas continued to calm. Soon, the ship's hot food restored Anna's strength. A few days later, her clothes dried and she was able to return to her own suit, coat, and reunited shoes. She was feeling quite perky under the circumstances when she encountered the Swensens on deck.

"Welcome, friend," Elsa said. "Hans and Lise will be sad they missed you. They're off having a good time by greeting the crew with, '*God dag*' and '*God morgen.*' "

"Anna," Pastor Swensen said, "thank you for your help."

Anna reached out and shook his hand. In the light of day, his tall build, large nose, scarce hair, and undersized crewman's outfit surprised her. Her idea of a pastor had always been a man in church robes. "Helping each other was a way for all of us to survive," Anna said. "Thank you for helping me. Now I have to find out about going through customs."

"Anna," Elsa said, glancing at her husband. She was dressed in a dark wool dress and coat which the storm had stretched out of shape. Anna guessed Elsa to be about ten years older. "We'd be glad to have you walk through with us. Henrik will translate for our family."

Anna was completely surprised; it took a moment to compose her thoughts. "Thank you," she said, "from the bottom of my heart. I appreciate your kindness more than you know."

She looked around for the children. Not seeing them, she asked Elsa and Henrik if they would excuse her while she went and found them and gave them her thanks. They too had played a major role in her safe passage through the storm. Even though Elsa was a good mother, Anna thought she could return the Swensens's kindness by assisting with the children.

She found Hans and Lise playing hide-and-seek around the deck. Lise played by going indoors to see what was there. Hans took special interest in watching crewmen clean the dory that was tied along the side of the ship. Anna worried that they might need to use it.

A few days later, a warm day finally emerged. Hans and Lise were running about the ship's deck when Hans told Lise, "Go get Mother and Anna. I want to show them something."

When Anna came up from below and looked around, she couldn't see Hans. "Where is he, Lise? I can't find him," she said, her voice rising with fear. "I just saw him minutes ago. Let's walk up to the bow. Maybe he's up there."

Elsa came up on deck and she too began to worry. "You go north around the deck, Anna, and I'll go south. Look in every open door and then go down below."

Suddenly, the ship's horn blew three times. Three crewmen ran out and lowered the small dory into the water, attaching it on the north side of the ship. Two crewman jumped into the water, one with a long rope wrapped around his waist.

As soon as the horn blew, Anna and Lise came running back along the deck and looked over the rail. They watched as the two crewmen swam with a rope between them while the other in the dory began to pull it back toward the boat.

Anna suddenly realized that the rope was around a little boy. Elsa and Henrik arrived at the rail beside Lise and Anna.

"Help him!" Anna screamed, pointing at the crewmen. "It's Hans. I know that wet sailor suit. Save him!"

By that time, Henrik could see that the crewmen had Hans wrapped with a blanket. "It is Hans!" he said. "Praise God he's safe! How did he get in the water, Lise?"

Lise was so upset, she could barely answer. "Hans . . . talked about the fun in climbing on the dory . . . when it was attached outside the third deck, it was easy to climb aboard."

The crewmen opened the lowest exit deck and helped Hans up while his parents came racing down, Anna and Lise close behind. Anna kept wondering if he fell off or jumped off the dory.

Elsa and Henrik hugged Hans. Anna and Lise also put their arms around him. Anna thought he looked pale but was relieved he was safe. Henrik carried him to their cabin where Elsa changed his clothes. Anna wanted to yell at Hans, but didn't. The best thing was that he had been rescued. Praise God!

The ship kept on and Hans and Lise liked to play their hand games with Anna. She was becoming more and more comfortable with Elsa and Henrik. As the ship neared New York, however, she began to worry about how she would understand the immigration line. "Where do we go?" she asked Elsa.

"We'll stay together in line. They permit so many off the ship at a time or they are sent to Ellis Island. Werc you able to save your entry card?"

"I carried it in my brassiere but the ink ran so you can hardly read it."

"We have crumpled cards, too, but they'll have to accept them. Don't say anything, Anna. Henrik will talk to the men," said Elsa.

Anna was frightened when the ship had docked and the family had to wait until the office in Castle Gardens called their names. She thought, What if they don't accept me?

She watched each uniformed immigration officer take it upon himself to send some immigrants back to the ship or Ellis Island. Then others would have their documents stamped. Why? She closed her eyes and kept saying to herself, You'll make it!

When the immigration officer called for lower-bunk passengers, Elsa, Pastor Swensen, and the children walked with Anna up to the desk. Pastor Swensen said, "Here are our entry cards, soaked from the sea. We were rescued by this ship."

An officer spoke to Anna, "How much money do you have?"

She felt glaring eyes and a sense of helplessness. She felt herself shaking when Henrik translated. If she had no money, would they send her back?

Pastor Swensen spoke up, "Anna Steffensen is part of our family and will live with us. I'm pastor of the Lutheran Church in Chicago." The officer looked her over, holding the stamp in his hand. Anna felt faint. He was going to say no.

"Well, Pastor," he said. "She looks like a good scrub woman." He raised his hand and stamped Anna's card.

Anna looked at her card. She couldn't believe she held her own visa. She asked Elsa, "What do we do now?"

The older woman smiled and took her by the arm. Without another word, the Swensens and Anna walked through the office of Castle Gardens and down the ramp under the red, white, and blue flag; beside it hung a big sign that read: "Welcome to America."

They had made it. Anna and the Swensens were now in the heart of New York City where most everyone spoke English and she didn't.

Chapter Three

The Train Station

As they all walked through the exit out to the street, Anna couldn't believe the confusion: people crowding the stores and streets, horses pulling black carriages.

"Is this a holiday?" she asked Elsa.

"No, Anna. New York is the biggest city in America."

Anna and the Swensens huddled against the side of an old brick building, clutching their few belongings and watching the endless flow of people in all directions: newsboys hawking headlines; policemen in dark blue uniforms and tall hats directing carriages pulled by horses; young men in celluloid collars running from tall buildings, pushing racks of clothes down the street; vendors standing in the street or on the sidewalks, touting wares from neckties to fat sausages; and chubby women sweeping the sidewalk in front of dingy apartments. "How can people survive in all this rushing, pushing, and noise?" Anna wondered out loud in Norwegian.

"Most new immigrants have to settle in this city; that's why it's so big," said Henrik. "They have to search for jobs or become vendors. They aren't as lucky as we are, with tickets all the way to Chicago. Come on, let's catch an omnibus to Grand Central Station. That's where we must catch our train."

"I've never had a ride in an omnibus," Lise said.

"It's just a large wagon with horses," Hans observed.

At Grand Central, they were assigned seats on the train. Anna was exhausted. The strain of the past few weeks and months was beginning to take its toll. She collapsed in her seat next to Hans and Lise. "Aren't you glad we're on our way?"

Hans nodded. "I think we'll be in Chicago tomorrow."

Lise curled up next to Anna. "I'm so tired."

"Elsa," Anna wondered, reflecting on what she had just witnessed on the streets of New York, "have you ever been in a city of such constant action?"

Elsa smiled. "It's certainly more active than Bergen. Thank God we're on the last part of our trip. Hans and Lise, watch the Hudson River as we ride alongside the Palisades."

The track followed the cliffs along the river bank. Now and then they would have an unobstructed view of the river as it pushed downstream toward the Atlantic; small freighters struggled upstream in a northerly direction.

The view reminded Anna of Bergen's *fjords*. She wondered how Papa and Gudrun were doing at the fish stall and if they missed her. She knew she missed them. The maple and poplar trees on top of the cliffs weren't as pretty as the pines and firs on Bergen's mountains. Thinking of home reminded her of Mama, and, again, she couldn't hold back the tears.

Elsa noticed and again said nothing.

As the train lumbered on, Anna realized she hadn't seen any homes or farms such as could be seen in the Voss Valley. "Where are the people?" she asked Elsa.

"*Vaer talmodig* (Have patience), Anna," she said. "We'll be approaching Lake Erie and the lands of the midwest by nightfall. There you will see plenty of homes and farms."

The train made too many stops for Anna's taste, but she tried to hide her impatience with idle chatter as the train continued to discharge passengers and freight at one small town after another. "Is Chicago bigger than Bergen?" she asked no one in particular at one point.

"Yes," Elsa said, smiling at Anna's attempts to be pleasant. "I have a map of the city. It is the second largest in all of America, after New York."

Anna shook her head in amazement, sat back, and closed her eyes. There was much to plan for in her new life with her new husband-to-be. She hadn't forgotten that Ole Ludeman had been one of the young men who rolled the cart of fish into the stall the day Mama died. He'd seemed nice enough back then, always respectful and jolly and full of compliments. But after the funeral, Ole told Anna's father he wanted to start a new life in America. Knud was sad to see Ole leave because he was so strong and capable; it took two men to replace Ole. He'd only been gone three or four months before he wrote with his marriage proposal.

Still, Anna wondered what he would be like now, where they

would get married, and where they would live. Ole's letter had only included a marriage proposal and ship and train tickets. His letter also said he would meet her at the train station in Chicago, but didn't discuss the particulars. It was only after Anna, Gudrun, and Papa had gone to visit Ole's parents that Knud had agreed to let Anna go to America. She was still thinking of her last words to her family when she fell asleep.

Anna awoke with a start to find it was daybreak. Mile after mile of farmland stretched out on either side of the train. Rows of corn lined the fields and farmers could be seen working the land before the harvest. The roads were wider and there were more wagons and people. Anna rubbed her eyes; she wanted to see everything: all the people, all the roads, all the land. It was flatter than in Bergen or even in the Voss Valley.

"Elsa, look at that lake," Anna exclaimed at one point. "It's bigger than our *fjords*."

The train was slowing down as it passed through the suburbs. The houses were smaller, covered with shingles, and crowded alongside dirt roads. As the city itself came into view, Anna continued to be amazed by the tall buildings and the bustle of this new city. What would life be like living in such a busy place? she wondered. Where were the mountains and the pine trees and the parks? At least there was the big lake.

As they came into the Chicago station, Anna leaned out the window to try to pick out Ole. "Please, Elsa," she asked, "stay with me until I find Ole? I want to introduce you."

"Don't worry, Anna. Henrik and I will stay."

By now she felt so tight, afraid, happy, and scared — all at once. How should she greet her future husband? What if she found him looking like that filthy Viking crew that rowed their lifeboat through that horrible storm on the high seas? No, she reassured herself. That wasn't the Ole who had worked for Papa.

The train puffed into the station, then squeaked and ground itself to a noisy stop. Anna was the first one off the train, eagerly searching for her Ole. Henrik helped Elsa and the children down. "Stay here until I locate the baggage," he said gently in Norwegian to his children.

Anna wondered which man would be Ole; all the young men looked so much alike and Chicago's Union Station was bigger than the largest amphitheater in Bergen. And most everyone was speaking English. But there was no Ole.

Anna began to fret. "Elsa, why do you think Ole would not greet the train?" she asked.

"Maybe something held him up. We'll wait."

"Come with me, Hans and Lise," Anna said. "We'll have a walk around inside the station. Is that all right, Elsa?"

"We'll be right here sitting on suitcases," said Elsa.

Trains arriving, the shouting of salesmen, and the clatter out on the street echoed through the tall building. Anna wondered how Ole could ever find her among all these people. Why wasn't he here? She and the children walked back and forth until the children got bored and raced back to sit on their luggage.

Anna continued to walk around the station, looking to see if any young men came forward, but none did. The station house grew quieter and quieter. The afternoon light begin to fade. Where was Ole? Where could he be?

The children wanted to play hide-and-seek with Anna, but she couldn't get her mind off Ole. She wrung her hands, combed her hair, and rearranged her jacket. It had never occurred to her that Ole might not show up, especially since he paid all that money for her tickets to get to Chicago.

Henrik, too, had been checking on young men in the station. Dressed in his black suit, he reminded Anna of the pastor at home, ready to present a sermon when he came over to console her. "Don't worry," he said. "Ole may have obtained the wrong timetable. If you have his address, I'll try to locate him or a neighbor who may know what has happened."

"I can't understand it," she said. "Here's his address. My father wrote Ole to confirm when I was to arrive."

Henrik left.

Several hours passed. By now, Hans and Lise were racing around the luggage chasing one another and asking Elsa when the family was going to leave.

Anna was near tears and kept pacing up and down, walking around the luggage, sitting down and then getting up. Finally, she sat down on her suitcase, knees shaking. Why had Henrik not returned? Maybe Ole was in an accident or decided not to come. She was determined not to cry.

Elsa tried to reassure her, but there was no Ole and no Henrik.

"I have no money for a ticket home," Anna blurted in Norwegian. "I don't speak English and I have no place to live. What can I do?"

At that moment, Henrik returned. "Anna, I wasn't able to locate Ole. The desk officer and I went through the entire Chicago directory, but there is no such name or address."

Anna looked beaten. "I don't know what to do," she mumbled.

Henrik said, "If Elsa agrees, we will invite you to come to our parsonage. We can look for Ole from there."

Elsa held Anna tightly. "Of course, I agree, Henrik. We and the Lord will take care of you, Anna. We need you. We'll be happy to have you join us."

Anna smiled at her new friends. She thought of her father and sister in Bergen, of her months of trying to obtain passage to America, only to have it end up like this. She took a deep breath. "Thank you, Henrik and Elsa and you too, Lise and Hans. You have all been so kind to me. *Jeg er en Viking.* I appreciate and accept your generous offer. I only hope someday I can repay your many kindnesses."

Henrik asked Anna and his family to all join hands and form a circle. "We will have a moment of prayer," he said in their native tongue, bowing his head. "Thank you, our Father, for your many blessings. Thank you for getting us here safely. And now we thank you for our new friend, Anna Steffensen. Thank you for bringing her to us and we ask you for your continued help as we all enter into our new life and our new land. Amen."

Chapter Four

Searching in Chicago

Anna hadn't slept well at the parsonage. Most of the night she'd tossed and turned, asking herself over and over, Where was Ole? But it was morning now. She should get up, she told herself. Never mind how poorly she felt. She must send a wire with her new address to Papa. She paced the floor of her bedroom. Maybe Ole had sent a message to Papa. She heard noises downstairs in the kitchen and quickly put on her only dress. Most everything she'd brought with her from Norway had gone down in the Atlantic.

With an uneasy feeling of what her expected role in the Swensen home was to be, she entered the kitchen.

Elsa was busy feeding kindling to the stove and stirring cornmeal mush for the children. "Good morning, Anna," she said. "How did you sleep?"

"Not very well. I kept thinking about Ole. Let me stir the mush or get some more wood for the fire."

"You stir the mush and I'll get the wood. I discovered where they hide it," Elsa said triumphantly.

Elsa disappeared and Anna stirred. She wondered what else she should fix for the children and Henrik. It would take her a while to get to know their special eating habits. She pushed her hair back and thought how much she'd like a cup of hot coffee.

Elsa returned with an armload of wood and stoked the stove. "I washed Lise and Hans's sailor suits last night and hung them close to the stove so they would be dry for school. I'm going to get the children up, then we'll have a cup of coffee."

Only a few minutes passed before Elsa returned with both Lise and Hans, dressed in their sailor suits. "Hello, Anna," said Hans. "Are you going to school today, too?"

"No, I have to send my father a wire. Maybe first I could walk with you to your new school," she said, still stirring.

"Good morning, Anna," said Henrik, striding in, wearing his dark suit. He sat down and Elsa dished out the mush. "I heard you say you'd like to send a wire. You are welcome to walk with us to the children's school. After they are registered, we can go to the apothecary where Deacon Jensen said they send wires."

"I think I'll stay here and straighten up," Elsa said. "Anna, after you're done sending your wire, you can help me if you wish. I'd appreciate the help."

"Certainly, Elsa, I'll be glad to help," said Anna.

"Can I skip all the way to school?" asked Lise.

"Perhaps, Lise. We'll need to follow Deacon Jensen's directions."

The four walked down the dirt road, sometimes on the shoulder, and sometimes out in the street. Lise found skipping in the dirt kicked up too much dust and dirtied her Norwegian sailor suit. Her long braids swayed back and forth as she hopped from one foot to the other. Hans kicked rocks until Henrik asked him to stop; he might cause an accident.

The children took notice of the houses they passed and compared them to their new home at the parsonage. They noticed the clapboard siding, the little porches with flower pots bursting with bright red and orange flowers, and the well kept appearance and tidiness of the small yards.

"I like our house best," said Hans.

"Me, too," said Lise.

Other children passed and looked them over. One boy threw a rubber ball for Hans to catch. He smiled and returned the ball. "Oh boy! This school will be fun, but no one wears sailor suits around here," Hans said.

The two-story brick building on the side street had a big sign that read: Chicago Grammar School District Five. There was a six-step entrance to the double front doors, but the other children all walked around to the rear. Henrik, Hans, and Lise went up the stairs to the front door. Anna waited outside, watching the children enter the rear yard chattering and pushing and running with an energy level she envied.

While she waited, she counted the little money she had left. There was scarcely enough to send a wire. Carefully, she composed the words in Norwegian:

*Ole not in boarding house, missed train. I'm
staying with Pastor Swensen family at 630
Milwaukee Ave., Chicago.*
Miss you. Love, Anna.

"Come, Anna," Henrik said, bouncing down the school steps. "Hans and Lise are registered in their classes. The principal will take them to their classrooms. It is a nice school; they will learn to speak English right away."

The two walked down the road until finally they located the apothecary; Anna kept recounting her *krones*.

The clerk accepted the wire, but not the *krones*. "We only take American money," he said matter-of-factly.

Anna felt herself tighten up. How was she going to let her father know where she was? If she sent a letter, it would take a month or more to arrive.

Henrik leaned over the counter and looked the clerk in the eye. "I'm the new pastor at our local church. I'll stand responsible for paying in *krones* for this woman's wire. As soon as I exchange my *krones*, I'll bring the dollar bills to pay you." The clerk looked them both over again, finally saying, "I heard about your coming, Pastor. I guess I can trust you. Give me fifteen *krones*. I'll have it out today to Bergen."

Anna started to dole out her *krones*, but dropped the coins all over the counter and the floor. "Oh . . . Excuse me," she said, rushing to pick up her money and pay the clerk.

Henrik looked about the store and decided to purchase a newspaper. "This is *The Scandinavian,* Anna," he said. "It carries all the news about the Danes, Swedes, and Norwegians. It costs one *krone* — about five cents American."

"Does it carry an employment section? I must find a job."

"Don't worry. Ole undoubtedly will find you. In the meantime, you may help with the house and care for the children until you get settled."

A few days later, Anna dove into her new responsibilities at the parsonage. She helped Elsa clean the house and rearrange some of the furniture around the house. At the end of the day, she didn't feel as though she'd done enough.

"Now, Anna, don't worry," Elsa said one morning. "First, we need to get settled. Ole will write you. Things will work out."

"I have been living in a dream world," Anna said. "First my trip over here was a miracle — a dream come true — and now I face the possibility of no marriage. The few things I had for my hope chest went down with the ship." Anna brushed away a tear. "I feel so foolish. If it weren't for you and Henrik, I'd be totally lost and alone. I have no clothes. I have no job. I should never have left Norway. I was a fool."

Elsa took Anna in her arms and held her close. "Don't worry so much, Anna. God is with us. We are happy to have you here."

Just then the doorbell rang. Henrik was in his study working on his first sermon for his new parish.

"Please answer that for me, Anna," asked Elsa. "It may be one of the young men who promised to help us plant a vegetable garden. Tell him to start in the backyard."

Anna opened the door. It was Mrs. Jensen, the deacon's wife. A big container rested on the ground in front of her. Anna had met her at the welcoming party for the new pastor and his family. Mrs. Jensen was dressed in a beautiful coral green dress with a fitted waist and close-gathered skirt and a large feathered hat. She looked to be on her way to a party. Anna had heard from Elsa that the deacon's wife was the women's leader of the church and one of the best dressed.

"Mrs. Jensen, how nice to see you, again," said Anna. "Won't you come in? I'll get Mrs. Swensen for you."

"I have only a moment, Anna. This mock turtle soup," she said, pointing at the container, "is one of the deacon's favorites. Thought all of you might like some for dinner."

"Thank you, Mrs. Jensen," Anna said, trying to be as charming as possible. "We appreciate your kindness."

Mrs. Jensen nodded, smiled, and left.

Anna noticed how Mrs. Jensen looked her over as if still questioning what she was doing here with the Swensens. As she closed the door, Anna reminded herself that for the moment she was a maid. Of that, there could be no denying. Maybe Mrs. Jensen will give me a job. I must search everywhere for one.

That afternoon Elsa and Anna walked up to the school to meet the children. Hans and Lise came tumbling out of the door, each holding a book and anxiously looking for a familiar face.

"Here we are," called Anna.

All the way home the children practiced English words such as cat, dog, and ball; Elsa checked their pronunciation. Anna wished she understood what they were saying. She looked through Lise's primer and thought that she must learn English if she expected to be hired. Maybe she could practice at night with the children. As she listened to them curve their tongues around the new sounds, Anna realized what a task she had chosen for herself. "Let's go to the market," Elsa said to Anna and the children. "You can identify the produce while I shop."

As usual, Anna thought, Elsa's idea was a good one. It wasn't long before she and the children knew the American names for the various items for sale in the grocery store. Maybe with Elsa as her teacher, learning English wouldn't be such an overwhelming task.

"That was fun," said Hans. "Let's do it again tomorrow."

"Yes," said Lise. "Me, too. I want to do it tomorrow."

As the family settled into their new home, Anna worked hard to keep from fretting. Still, she knew she was running out of time. The Swensens had agreed to cover her board for the next three months, but it was the church who supported the parsonage. Anna worked hard on her English and diligently searched the daily want ads in *The Scandinavian*. Anna had Elsa translate those she thought she'd be qualified for, but she either didn't understand English or didn't know how to type and assist in an office. There were no other jobs.

Two weeks later, Pastor Swensen took Anna to the stockyards. He and Anna rode down to where Ole may have once worked. As they rode the omnibus into town, Anna took note of the houses they passed. She admired the large homes with the bay windows that looked out on Milwaukee Avenue. She dreamed of having a home like that, but realized how far away she was from that goal.

At 41st Street, Pastor Swensen stood up. "This is our stop. We will find the office and talk to the hiring boss."

The stench from the yards immediately filled Anna's senses. Heavy smoke and cinders from the many factories in the area spewed into the air and settled down around them like black flakes of snow. Henrik and Anna found the office and walked into a barren room with small windows along one wall. The windows were all shut tight, shades drawn. Henrik knocked on the glass of one. A window opened a small crack.

"No jobs today," said a young male voice in Norwegian.

"Please, just a moment," Henrik said. "We are inquiring about an employee who has disappeared. Can you trace Ole Ludeman's work record?"

"Don't think I can," said the sullen voice.

"Please, sir," Henrik said. "Ole sent for his bride and when she arrived, he couldn't be found anywhere."

"All right, all right. I'll take a quick look through the records. What was the last date of his work?"

"I think it was around March of this year," Anna said. "But I don't know for sure."

The window slammed shut. Anna and Pastor Swensen leaned against the side wall. There were no chairs. Dusty floors and dirty windows gave the whole room a feeling of deprivation. Anna wondered what Ole did in the yard. Was he in the meat cutting building or outside taking care of the cattle? How could anyone manage to work in such filthy places?

They waited so long, Henrik had to shift from one foot to the other. He finally leaned against the dirty wall in his good suit. "The smell in here is so bad," he said after what seemed like hours, "I don't think I'll be able to eat cattle again. Worse yet, it seems they treat the public like cattle, too."

After a good thirty minutes, the same window cracked open. "Can't find a thing, Mister. There's but one work card in for January and February, but nothing after that."

"Wait!" begged Henrik. "What was his home address?"

"Looks like it was over in the slum area, 47th and Ashland. Bums like him live in wooden two-flat houses." He shut the window with a bang, yelling, "That's all we know about that guy. Don't bother me again."

Henrik and Anna walked back to the bus stop filled with feelings of dejection. The cracked sidewalks, the few gas lights, and men standing on corners with bleary eyes and begging hands told of the low state of the economy in Chicago. Anna wondered how Ole saved the money for the tickets he sent.

"There is no need to visit the rooming house, Anna," Henrik said finally. "I already talked to the landlord. They have no further information."

Anna felt defeated. "There is nothing more I can do unless Ole's parents know his address and send it to me."

Their ride home was a quiet one. Anna's thoughts went around and around. Why did Ole take such a job with a packing house? Why did he quit? Why didn't he write to her and tell her where he was going? She kept thinking about Ole's bright smile and pleasant personality from when he used to work for Papa, and now he seemed to be such a man of mystery. What had happened?

When they arrived back at the parsonage, neither Henrik nor Anna were very talkative. She knew any slim hope she may have once held that she would be able to find Ole was now gone. She was all alone. She would soon have to find a job.

A few days later, Anna received a wire from Norway. Quickly, she ripped it open.

> *Dear Daughter:*
> *We feel terrible about Ole's disappearance. Contacted*
> *Ludemans. No news. If we get his address we'll wire.*
> *Thanks to Swensens for their kindness.*
> *Love, Papa, Gudrun.*

Anna felt better just reading the wire and knowing Papa supported her efforts to find Ole. She also knew that she must practice the English drills in Hans's book. It would take time.

"We liff in de midel vist," Anna wrote that night for practice. "Varm fogy, tunderstorm al night. Miels of hous her. Sum wete and smal farm hous here and dere."

Anna worked extra days for Mrs. Jensen. She was very thoughtful and after the house was cleaned, she prepared a little lunch for Anna and thanked her for coming. She paid her more than Anna had ever received for housework.

Now and then, Anna worked doing housework for other families and gave more money to the Swensens. But as the weeks and months dragged on, she still didn't know what to do. Odd jobs weren't enough to cover her food costs. Day after day she waited, hoped, and prayed, but there was no word about Ole. Neither was there any news about a new job.

Scanning *The Scandinavian* column by column, she read with Elsa's help of the skills most in demand: bookkeepers, accountants, and typists. She wasn't qualified. However, she wrote a list of household chores she could do, and added her ability to run a whole business selling fish, cooking, gardening, keeping up the house, and taking care of her own family when her mother died.

The pressure to find a job became more and more urgent with each day. Anna heard the deacon discussing the depression of 1880. It had affected church tithing, resulting in a tightening of budgets and restrictions on the ministerial fund.

Anna sat in her rocking chair one afternoon thinking about her dilemma. The answer seemed to be a loan for passage back to Bergen. Would the church advance this? Should she ask her father? Tears ran down her face. As much as she missed her family, she didn't want to go home. There had to be another way.

She walked around her room. She looked at her clothes. Except for two new dresses which Elsa had helped her sew from the leftover cloth of the Mission Sewing Club, she only had the stretched gray suit to wear. She looked in the mirror and studied her appearance. She was not pretty. She had a round face, pug nose, auburn hair, and dark brown eyes. Thankfully, there were no lines in her forehead. She wasn't tall but that was good. She looked like a good sturdy worker. She had to convince people of that. She pulled out an old clipping from *The Scandinavian* and went through it again line by line. There was nothing.

"Elsa, has the paper come yet?" Maybe the next issue would have a job for her.

One evening, she overheard Henrik and Elsa talking after the children had gone to bed. Anna was in the kitchen working on her English lessons.

"Elsa," Henrik said, "we can't support Anna any longer. What should we do?"

"Perhaps we should ask the congregation for help?"

"Yes," replied Henrik. "I'd thought of having a Silver Sunday to help with Anna's passage home."

"Oh, Henrik, we can't send her home after she has struggled so hard to stay in America."

"Elsa, there is no other way out."

"Let's give ourselves until the end of this month. Anna is such a good worker. Then we'll make a final decision. I will tell her that our ministerial funds have been cut. I wish there was some way we could help her find a job. I've read every paper, but Anna couldn't meet the requirements."

Anna fled to her bedroom and cried herself to sleep.

The next morning, Henrik explained the problem to their friend. Tears came into Anna's eyes; Elsa cried too and held her close.

Anna decided her only hope was *The Scandinavian*. She had a few more days. Monday, Tuesday, Wednesday came to no avail. On Thursday, Anna again went through the paper line by line. Suddenly, she let out a whoop. "Elsa! Elsa! There's a job to serve as a helper in a dry goods store! What do you think? Do I have a chance if I apply?"

The two women screamed for joy and hugged each other.

"Yes, you have a chance," Elsa said, coming under control. "Where is it?"

Anna had written down the address. Henrik got out his map. They located the address on the northwest side of downtown.

"Elsa, will you come with me?" Anna asked.

"Of course, Anna. What will you wear?"

"What about the dress we made from the material Olga Piersen gave me. Is that too dressy?"

"No, Anna. You look young and beautiful in that dress. They will hire you immediately."

The two women caught the omnibus into town at seven o'clock the next morning, arriving at the dry goods store before eight o'clock. Anna had tied her auburn hair back in a bun with a lavender ribbon. She was reminded by Hans and Lise to wear her "happy face."

As they approached the store, Anna grabbed Elsa's hand. "I'm scared. What if I am not hired?"

"Anna," Elsa said, patting her hand. "Trust in yourself. You are a hard worker. You have excellent references from Henrik. You are respected by our congregation. The store will be lucky to have you. Just go in and be your usual friendly self. You can do it. You are a Viking."

Anna looked through the entrance. The door was open. She walked in and heard the clerks speaking Norwegian. "Please," she said, "where can I find Mr. Hansen?"

She saw a tall, handsome young man with a neatly trimmed beard smiling at her. "See that door over there? That's where he is, but don't go in unless you see a coffee cup on his desk. He does no business until he has his morning coffee. Good luck." Anna walked to the office door and peered through its glass window. Hansen's coffee cup was there, but leaning to one side from being placed on a pile of messy papers. She looked around the office; it seemed to be filled with a collection of fabrics, books, and trash that needed to be placed in a trash can.

She knocked on the open door. "Mr. Hansen, I came to apply for the position advertised," she said in Norwegian.

"Walk in, the door is open," answered a deep, gruff voice.

You're a good worker, she told herself as she walked in. "Good morning, Mr. Hansen. My name is Anna Steffensen. I want to apply for the position you advertised."

Hansen looked her over. "Your references?"

"I have them here."

He took them from her and scanned the letters. "I see you've been in this country for less than six months. Do you speak English?"

Anna was shaky as she answered in broken English. "Yes, I spek English. I spek little."

Mr. Hansen took a swig from his coffee cup, spilling a few drops on her letters. He looked them over again. He scowled and looked at Anna. "Are you sure you want to roll the bolts, sweep the floor, run the errands, and tidy up at the end of the day? This is not an easy job."

"I've worked ever since I finished high school. I know how to work. I can do these tasks."

Mr. Hansen took out his pencil and began to scribble on a piece of paper. "Well, you look healthy enough to handle it. I'll pay you eight cents an hour for a ten-hour day."

Anna could hardly believe her ears. Mr. Hansen had been so abrasive she didn't think she had a chance. "Thank you, Mr. Hansen," she said, voice quivering. "When do I report?"

"Tomorrow. Eight o'clock sharp. And be dressed for work."

She was so excited she could barely contain herself, but managed to regain her composure long enough to look around the store. She wanted to know the size of the place. It was larger than the church social hall. Yards of colorful fabrics stretched across wide, flat tables. Up the sides of the walls ran shelves with rolls of cloth sticking out. These appeared to consist of the darker colors or those used for industrial work and not for usual domestic use. In addition, at the end of each row of tables was a cabinet loaded with all the necessities of a seamstress: needles, pins, buttons, buckles, threads in many colors, scissors, bias tape, beads in red, blue and orange, and feathers in white and black. In her joy, she imagined herself making an entrance tomorrow with a feather headdress.

The store's pungent smell of cotton and wool was accentuated by the dry air of a closed room. Two salesmen were engaged with two workmen, showing them fabrics of netting, canvas, and screening for a project they were doing. At this early hour, there were no women in the yardage department searching out the latest color or pattern. Anna noted that the big Butterick pattern books were readily available. In fact, she had used a Butterick pattern to sew the dress she was wearing.

She walked back and forth down the rows of colorful fabrics and let her hands feel the smooth texture of the cottons and the rough surface of the wools. I love to sew, she said to herself. She knew that her job was going to be one of pick up, clean up, sweep, and polish. There would be no time for sewing now, but maybe someday there would be.

As Anna was about to walk out the door, she took one more glance at the office of Mr. Hansen. He was watching her from the dirty office window that looked over the shop. Anna made a quick exit; she was embarrassed.

The minute she was hidden from Mr. Hansen's eagle eyes, she bounced down the steps of the store, calling to a waiting Elsa. "I am hired! I am hired!" Anna yelled, jumping up and down. "I earn eighty cents a day for a ten-hour day."

Elsa gave her a big hug. "I told you that you could do it."

That evening was one of festivity. The family celebrated Anna's new job by having *kjottboller* and *rødkål* for dinner. Elsa knew it was Anna's favorite dish. Pastor Swensen stood up and gave the blessing, and Hans and Lise sang *"Den lille Ole."*

Anna stood up and said, "Thank you all for your love and care. You've been such a support to me as I tried to find Ole and a regular job. I now can repay you in a small way for your generosity and trust. You are truly my American family."

Chapter Five

The Working Woman

Suddenly, there was a ringing in Anna's ears. It seemed to grow louder and louder. What was it? Her befuddled mind couldn't decipher the noise. Finally in desperation, she rolled over and squinted with one eye at the source of the noise. The alarm clock was banging its heart out. It read six o'clock. Time to get up. Today was the first day at her new job in the dry goods store. What was it going to be like?

After washing, she put on her work clothes and hurried to the kitchen. After firing up the wood stove, she cooked herself toast and a cup of coffee. She sliced off more rye bread and made liver sausage, and cheese sandwiches for herself, Hans, and Lise. Rustling around, she found some hard *hermits* and apples and tucked one of each in the three lunch bags.

As she worked, eating breakfast and packing lunches, Anna didn't notice the click of the kitchen door as it opened. A little face with sleepy eyes peeked in. Lise with her tangled blond braids, long flannel nightgown, and bare feet watched Anna scurrying about the room.

"Anna," Lise asked, "do you have to leave this early?"

The voice startled Anna. She whirled around to greet the owner of that small voice. "Yes, Lise dear, I have to. I leave on the next omnibus. Come here and let me hug you."

There was sadness in Lise's eyes as she wrapped her arms around Anna's neck and gave her a kiss on the cheek. "Goodbye, Anna," she said. "I hope you like your job."

"I will tell you all about it tonight," Anna said.

The little girl regretfully turned and left the room.

Anna selected a blue sweater off the clothes rack, reached for an apron in her bureau drawer, and gave her hair another brushing. She looked in the mirror and rolled her hair into a bun onto the back of her head. Seeing herself in the mirror gave her courage. You must succeed, she repeated to herself over and over. She kept an eye on the clock as she picked up her lunch, grabbed her heavy coat, and hurried out the front door.

At this early hour, the sun was trying to lift itself above the horizon while birds sang their morning arias. Horse-drawn coal and milk wagons hurried along the streets, making their morning deliveries. A newsboy stood by a bus stop hawking his papers. "Read it now or never!" he bellowed.

Anna walked to the corner of Milwaukee Street. Soon she heard the echoing clop-clop of hooves, the loud words of a driver, and the squeak and rattle of the omnibus. Its five passengers included four men dressed in business suits with ties held stiffly in place by celluloid collars. One bent old woman in an oversized coat carried a large shopping bag stuffed with rags. The omnibus ground to a halt in front of Anna.

"Come aboard! Hurry up!" Fats barked; she recognized him from her trip yesterday with Elsa. The driver snapped his whip at the two gray horses. The vehicle lurched forward.

Anna knew the horsecar traveled at five miles an hour. She'd allowed herself more than sufficient time to arrive before the store's eight o'clock opening.

As she waited for the ride to finish, Anna fiddled with her pocketbook and thought about Mr. Hansen. His abrasive manner worried her. To bolster her confidence, she remembered back to Norway and her original fear of big knives in the fish stall. She had beaten that fear. You can do it, she told herself. You can handle Mr. Hansen.

Anna arrived at the dry goods store before the salesmen; Mr. Hansen was in his office. She checked on whether his coffee cup was on the desk. It wasn't. What should she do? She walked back to the front door, opened it, then closed it with a big bang. This time she walked directly to Mr. Hansen's office and knocked boldly on the door.

"Good morning, Anna. I have been expecting you. Come in."

"Good morning, Mr. Hansen. I'm ready to start work."

"Sit down," he ordered.

His only chair was loaded with swatches of material. She tried to move the pile so she could sit on the edge, but the whole lot fell to the floor. Anna blushed and tried to pick them up. Mr. Hansen just sat there and stared.

He was wearing a dark brown suit with a celluloid collar and brown tie. It was held in place by a big pin in the form of an "H." The top of a white handkerchief peeked out of his left vest pocket. His hair had been combed, but he'd missed the cowlick. The dark brown hair at the back of his head stood up like a halo when he nodded his head.

Anna was taking too long to pick up. "Never mind," he said. "Sit down. Sign your name on these forms." He handed her two papers entitled "Work Agreement" and "Hourly Schedule."

She wrote her name. Although she had no real understanding of the papers, she felt too ashamed to ask. Was she signing away her paycheck?

"Now," Hansen began, leaning back in his chair, "I want you to realize that you are responsible for keeping the shop and the storeroom in order. Each day you will dust, mop, and rewind the bolts of cloth shown to customers. Keep the salesroom looking neat and clean at all times. It makes a good impression."

"Where is the mop and broom?"

"I'll show you. First, we'll walk by and meet the boys."

Anna felt a surge of excitement. She was looking forward to meeting the salesman who had pointed the way to Mr. Hansen's office. He was tall and handsome.

Hansen burst into the salesroom like a full-blown storm. "Hello, men. Come here. I have a cute little thing I want you to meet!"

The four salesmen gathered around while he introduced the tall man first. "This is Georg Amorsen — we call him Denny or Georg. Another Dane is Chris Christensen. Over here are two Norwegians: Jen Nygaard and Peter Gjerde. You're from Norway so the battle is three to two."

The men were dressed neatly in carefully pressed suits and colorful bow ties. They smiled and shuffled their feet. Georg knew what to do. He extended his hand to Anna and said, "Good morning and welcome." There was a twinkle in his eye.

Anna wondered, Why does Mr. Hansen act the fool? I'm no little thing. Wonder what Georg thinks of me. He certainly strikes a handsome figure. I hope he doesn't think me too short.

Hansen cleared his throat. "Did you bring your apron, Anna?" She nodded. He then took her arm and led her back to the storeroom. Its shelves contained bolt after bolt of colored fabric stacked high in the air. Long tables were covered with packages to be unwrapped and stored. Round wooden bins were stored along the four walls.

"I want you to start with these bins," he said. "Thoroughly clean the inside of each one and cover it with a lid. When you finish, report to me. Do you have any questions?"

"No, I have cleaned bins before."

Mr. Hansen patted Anna on the shoulder and tried to give her a hug as he left. "See me if you have questions."

Anna shook her shoulders free, her stomach whirling. She didn't want any of that!

Walking to the wall hooks, she hung her coat, then rolled up her sleeves and put on the apron she'd brought. She could see there were many bins waiting to be cleaned. This is not much different from cleaning out the fish bins back in Bergen, she thought, but the odor here is much better.

Anna could hear the voices and laughter of the salesmen as they gathered to drink their morning coffee. She was hoping to talk with Georg again. Where in Denmark did he come from; did he like to dance; was he married?

She started her scrubbing and soon realized there would be no chance to clean up the salesroom this day.

Mr. Hansen came by before the lunch break. He had taken off his coat, rolled up his shirt sleeves, and loosened his tie and the stick pin. "How is it going, Anna? Will you finish today?"

"I carefully cleaned out the lint as you suggested. I also wiped the sides. I am about halfway through."

"I was just making sure. Yes, they do look clean."

"Where can I eat lunch?" Anna asked.

"You can't eat in here. We don't permit eating in the warehouse. Come. I'll introduce you to Olga, our cutter."

Mr. Hansen again held her arm. He led the way through the storeroom by way of the rear exit which led to another room laden with materials and boxes. A large woman in a bright green dress was cutting a pattern while leaning perilously over the table's edge. On the top of her red hair rested thin, wire spectacles. She held a pencil in her teeth while her fingers quickly guided the scissors; she ignored them until she finished her task.

"Hello, Olga. I want you to meet our new employee, Anna Steffensen. She will clean and keep our shop neat and tidy."

Reflexively, Olga reached to the top of her head and put on her glasses. Examining Anna from head to toe, she nodded. "Welcome, Anna," she said. "Join me for lunch. You can bring it in here."

"Thank you, Olga," Anna said. "I'll be back in a few minutes."

She liked the big woman with the friendly smile and warm greeting. At last, another woman employee.

While they ate their sandwiches, Olga gave a brief history of the company. She told Anna the nickname she had given each salesman. "They like to tease me, and now they'll start on you, Anna, but ignore them. It is their way of being friendly."

"What do you call that nice, tall, young man with the beard?"

"Oh, he came from Denmark a year ago. I call him Denny."

"Do any of the salesmen join you for lunch?"

"You mean does Georg come by? He is the most friendly and will most likely be here tomorrow to get better acquainted."

Anna thought while walking back to her work how much fun it would be to go dancing with Georg. She imagined the feel of being in his arms. It had been so long since she had dated or gone dancing. She skipped about the store floor dreaming of being a beautiful butterfly.

By closing time, Anna's back couldn't take one more bin. The fabrics had been inspected, cleaned, and restacked. There had been no time to rewind the bolts. Anna wanted to work in the customer salesroom because it gave her the opportunity to feel and examine the many fabrics. Already, she had her eye on a purple blossom bolt. It would make a lovely new dress.

Anna took off her apron, put on her sweater and coat, repinned her tousled hair, and slowly walked through the main store. Again she was struck by the brilliant fabrics, the array of colors, and the variety of materials. A salesman was locking up as she went to the door.

"Anna, Anna," Mr. Hansen called out. "Come to my office before you leave."

Anna, weary and anxious to catch the bus, walked over to Mr. Hansen's office. The fabrics that had fallen off the chair were still on the floor. A dirty coffee cup sat on the desk on top of bills of lading. The grime-covered windows looking out on the store needed cleaning. Mr. Hansen seemed to fit into the office scene. His celluloid collar was unbuttoned and flopping around his neck, his hair in complete disarray.

"Anna, tomorrow I have to go over and meet with the buyer at Marshall Fields. I want you to clean up my office while I'm gone. Don't touch the papers on my desk, just dust and clean. Don't forget the windows. If you finish, you can fold the bolts before leaving."

Anna nodded acceptance of the new assignment. "Yes, Mr. Hansen, I will be glad to." She hurried from the office, through the front door, down the front steps, and across the street just in time to catch the omnibus loaded with passengers. She kept thinking about Mr. Hansen on the way home. He kept a strict eye on his employees and gave precise orders, but Anna felt uneasy with him. Why did he have to touch her every time he came by? She was not accustomed to such. Norwegian men never used to try to hug her; she was "The Fish Woman." How could she get him to stop? It was much nicer thinking about Georg.

Hans and Lise were waiting at the bus stop to greet Anna when she arrived home. "*Fortell oss!* Welcome! Tell us how it was. Did you have a good time?" asked Hans.

"Thanks for meeting me," she said, giving them each a big hug. "No, the scrub work was not fun. I cleaned out bins all day, and I'm glad to be home." She paused to look at their troubled little faces. "Tomorrow will be better. I get to fix up Mr. Hansen's office."

At dinner, Anna recounted the events of her first day on the job. Elsa began clearing the dishes. "Anna, sit and rest awhile. I'll take care of these. Lise and Hans will help. Will you have the opportunity to buy mill ends?"

"I don't know, but I already have my eye on a fabric for a new dress. It has a large poppy design and a purple background."

At work the next day, Anna felt better because she knew what to expect. The job of cleaning the office took considerable time. From its looks, it hadn't been cleaned in months. There was a note on the desk, which read:

> *Do not touch the papers. Lock door when you leave.*
> *Put key under door.*
> > *Theo Hansen.*

The day's work went well. Anna cleaned the windows first so she could look into the salesroom. It was fascinating to observe the customers and the salesmen. They resembled actors in a small play with their own special entrances and exits. She watched Georg greeting the customers and showing them fabrics. He was gracious and helpful. Once, he caught Anna watching from the window and waved.

At lunch, she joined Olga in the cutting room. "How could such a fussy man let his own office become such a mess?"

"You'll get used to Mr. Hansen," Olga said. "He talks a lot. I'm surprised he permitted you to clean his office. He would never let anyone in there before. I guess that's why it's so dirty. He must trust you, Anna."

"I cleaned the windows and watched the salesmen at work, but I keep forgetting their names."

"You'll learn them," Olga said, twirling her glasses. They slipped out of her hands and went flying across the room and landed on the floor without breaking. At that moment Georg came into the room and picked them up.

"Thanks, Georg," Olga said. "How about a cup of coffee?"

"Thank you, Olga." He turned to face Anna. "You can call me Georg, too, if you like. You've been doing a good job, cleaning that hole of his, Anna. May I call you Anna?"

"Yes, please do," she said, feeling her cheeks getting warm. "Cleaning Mr. Hansen's office is much easier than those bins I had to scrub yesterday." She paused to open her lunch bag. "May I ask how long you've been in Chicago?"

He smiled and bowed slightly, "I've been here a little over a year now. What about yourself?"

"It's about six months for me. I'm glad we Norwegians and Danes can understand one another. It will take me awhile to learn English. You speak English already."

"Yes, I was fortunate to have a grandfather who insisted I learn English. I wasn't interested then, but I am glad now. It helped me obtain this job as salesman."

The lunch break passed too quickly for Anna. After sixty minutes, Olga stood up in haste. "My goodness, our lunchtime is over. Back to work you two. I'll see you tomorrow."

Anna became used to the work routine and looked forward to her noon visits with Olga and an occasional visit with Georg. By each day's end, she was always weary, but her weekly check to the Swensens made it all worthwhile. It was drudgery, she thought, but I'm in America and earning my way. Soon, I will learn enough English so I can do other jobs and surprise Georg.

She arranged her work schedule so that in the late afternoon she could work in the salesroom rewinding the used bolts, straightening up the stock and the cabinets, and sweeping under the tables. Her reward for the day was that she was sometimes able to talk briefly with Georg.

When visiting with Olga each noon, Anna would discuss her job and talk about her favorite subject, Georg.

"Patience, patience," Olga urged. "He eats lunch here more than he has ever done. I think you're not here to visit with me, but to meet with Georg."

"Olga, I like to talk to you, too. Do you think someday he may ask me out?"

One afternoon when Olga and Anna were eating their lunch, there was a big bang on the door. Georg said, "Open it quick. Let me in, let me in."

Anna ran over and opened the door; Georg was holding three dripping bowls of ice cream. "Take one before I drop one. I brought your favorite flavor, Olga."

Olga looked at the bowls and at her wide girth. "Oh well, I may as well join you. Here, give me that chocolate one."

"How thoughtful of you, Georg," Anna said. "Thanks. I haven't had ice cream for months."

The three of them sat there like little children, licking their spoons. Some drips landed on the floor. Olga couldn't stand the mess and went after a mop.

"Where do you live?" asked Georg.

"By Humboldt Park, five miles from here."

"Do you like to dance?"

She widened her eyes. "Yes, I love to dance."

"Will you join me Saturday night? The Danish Lodge is having their monthly dance. I hope you can come."

For a moment, Anna couldn't talk. Going to a dance with Georg? It was only a dream. "Oh, thank you, Georg. I will be happy to go with you to the dance."

Olga came in waving the mop. "Out of my way. I don't want any sticky spots from the floor getting on my patterns. Do you two realize it is past lunchtime? Goodbye."

Anna walked back to her work thinking, He asked me, he asked me! What will I wear?

The remainder of the week couldn't pass fast enough. Although Mr. Hansen inspected her work in great detail, she accepted his inspection and comments. It distracted her, however, when he would come close and pretend to examine her work while staring at her figure with his beady brown eyes.

Anna had to continually think of new ways to avoid Mr. Hansen. One day, she got caught alone with him in his office.

"Excuse me Mr. Hansen, I need more cleaning supplies," she said, and rushed out the door.

She headed for the supply room and asked the clerk for a bar of soap and another refill for her mop. She delayed filling out the order forms until Hansen left the store for lunch.

Anna could not accept her boss's idea of employer-employee relations. Riding home that night, she tried to figure out a way to make him understand that she was not his little girl. His advances must be stopped without jeopardizing her job. She could not tell Georg or Olga or the Swensens. They would overreact. Besides, she could handle this challenge. She was a Viking woman, and there were already so many good things that had happened to her in America.

Each night, she gave a little prayer of thanksgiving. She gave thanks for the good health of her sister and father; for meeting Georg and the Swensens; for finding a job at Hansen's. Sometimes she thought of Ole and wondered about his fate, but her greatest worry was how to work out a strategy to keep Mr. Hansen from putting his hands on her again.

Chapter Six

Georg

Anna decided to dwell on happiness instead of that nasty Mr. Hansen. Georg had invited her to a dance. She'd seek Elsa's help in making an elegant new dress. She had the material; it had been a gift from the Church Circle women and, at last, Anna could use it. The two women worked together each night. "You're going to be the belle of the ball," Elsa kept telling Anna.

Her excitement intensified every time she thought about it. "Elsa, I haven't been dancing since I left high school. Those Norwegian boys were always stepping on my feet. I hope I can remember the polka, and the waltz, and the *Schottish*."

"As soon as you hear the music," Elsa said, "your feet will start going. You can always start with a polka."

"But Elsa, Georg is over six feet tall. He will have to bend down for me — I'm so short. How will I follow him?"

"You'll do fine. Just let him lead."

Lise and Hans, escaping from their evening studies, kept peeking in the room to see Anna. "Where are you going? Who is Georg? Do we know him?" they asked.

Anna, losing her patience, said, "Go back to your books. You ask too many questions."

When the big day arrived, Anna dressed early to be sure everything was just right. As she whirled and twirled herself around the living room, she felt sure the blue dress was perfect for dancing. Elsa had done such a wonderful job.

"You look wonderful," Henrik said. "Does he have a carriage?"

"Thank you," Anna said, her face turning red. "He never told me if he had a carriage, but the omnibus goes to the Danish Lodge where they hold the dances."

Elsa, Lise, and Hans all joined hands and danced around her. "Here's to our Anna," they sang.

Anna returned to her room for her coat. She looked in the mirror and saw an image she liked. I'm pretty in my own way, she thought. I'm not beautiful, but I am attractive. "Relax Anna," she whispered, "you know Georg. He said he likes to dance and so do you."

When she returned to the living room, Elsa wrapped her arms around her in a big hug. "You are a pretty young woman. Don't fret. You'll have a good time."

The doorbell rang and the whole family started for the door. Henrik grabbed Hans by his arm and told him and Lise to sit on the sofa. Then, he opened the door. There stood Georg, elegantly dressed in a dark blue suit with a blue tie, a white handkerchief in his pocket, and his hair and beard neatly trimmed.

"Please come in," Henrik said.

Anna introduced the visitor. "I want you to meet my friend and fellow worker, Hans Georg Amorsen. He is our star salesman." Lise giggled and Hans shook Georg's hand. Henrik also shook Georg's hand saying, "*Velkommen*, we welcome you."

Elsa smiled. "Anna has told me much about you. I'm happy to meet you. Won't you sit for a few minutes?"

"Thank you. What a lovely home you have. I live in a little flat which looks out on a brick wall. I guess it is just as well since I like to practice my clarinet."

"How long have you been in America, Mr. Amorsen?"

"Please call me Georg. I came here fourteen months ago."

Henrik spoke up. "We've been here a little over six months. We came from Norway. Do you like America?"

"Yes, what I've seen of it. My job keeps me inside all the time. I like the out-of-doors. I came from Denmark."

Anna sat demurely waiting for Georg to notice her new dress. Would he like it? Finally he smiled and looked over saying, "We'd better leave now so we can catch the omnibus."

Georg helped Anna with her coat, then shook hands with the Swensens. As he and Anna walked down the front steps, Georg waved to the children.

The Danish Lodge was crowded with couples dancing, talking, drinking, and playing cards. Georg commented, "These are the two biggest rooms on this side of Chicago."

The musicians took a break. Anna and Georg sat at one of the tables; Georg ordered Acquavit, Anna had a sarsaparilla. They sipped their drinks and looked over the crowded room.

"Do you know many of these folks, Georg?"

"No, I haven't been here very often. Now and then I'll meet this one particular customer. I always tell him how handsome he looks in his tailor-made suit from our store's fabric."

Anna noticed the variety of pretty silk gowns worn by most of the women. She decided hers looked equally pretty. The musicians returned to their instruments: a drum, piano, violin, and accordion. Anna trembled a bit, hoping she'd remember all the polka steps.

"Are we ready, Anna?" Georg asked. "Let's try this polka."

Anna had always loved polka music with its solid beat and vigorous steps. Georg turned out to be a good dancer and together they circled the dance floor. They made a graceful dancing team, even if Georg did have to bend over to lead Anna. Breathless after one whole set, they sat out the Norwegian *Schottish*.

Georg leaned over, close to Anna's ear. "Anna you are beautiful," he said over the loud music. "Your dress is so pretty and you dance like a feather."

Georg's comments touched her. She reached over and pressed his hand. "You look pretty wonderful yourself."

The two sat and looked into each other's eyes. Around them danced happy, laughing couples. Danish words flowed everywhere. Georg and Anna ignored the crowd until the band played a waltz.

"This is our dance, Anna. Come and join me."

She thought it was a lovely waltz and felt Georg's body close to her as they danced one, two, three with the music. They circled the floor with grace. Anna was ready to dance the rest of the evening, but the band stopped for a rest.

They found a table and Georg ordered another round of drinks. "Tell me about yourself," he said.

"What about yourself?" she answered quickly. She didn't want to tell Georg about her trip to America. How could she tell him she was a daughter of a fisherman? She couldn't reveal she had accepted an offer from a former crew member on her father's boat to come to America and marry him.

"I finished high school in Haderslev," he said, "and worked in the bank. My father used to be *bankdirektør* and *visekonsul* there. I'm sure you know that, since 1864, Germany has been in control of our government. The Danish have been excluded from the schools and from the businesses in the town of Haderslev. There was little opportunity there for me. My family encouraged me to sail to America."

Now Anna knew what to say. "I came to America also to search for new opportunities. It has been difficult for me to learn English, but I'm improving by listening to conversations at the store and studying at home. I use Lise and Hans's primers."

The music started again and Georg and Anna danced away, twirling and circling and laughing together.

It was a memorable night for Anna. She felt like the Fairy Princess one moment and the sorrowful Little Match Girl the next as she worried over how she could face Georg with her story.

Finally, the band packed up its instruments and the evening was over. Georg and Anna walked out to catch the omnibus. Georg put his arm around her as they rode to her home. "I had a delightful time, Anna. Let's do this again."

Anna was surprised and delighted by his sudden sign of affection. She snuggled against his shoulder and mumbled, "Yes. I too had a marvelous time. I love to dance; it was so much fun."

The omnibus stopped at the parsonage and Georg helped Anna off the bus. "Promise me you'll come next month." She nodded. He gave her a quick kiss on her cheek and ran back to the bus.

As she went to bed that night Anna wrote in her little Remember Book, "I love him, I love him. I could dance through life forever with him. Oh Georg, do you love me as much as I love you?"

By Monday morning at work, Anna was still reliving her evening of dancing and merriment with Georg. I hope he joins us for lunch today, she thought.

Over the next spring months, Olga played the part of hostess during their shared lunch hour. She often told Anna and Georg that she had an errand to do and left the room.

Georg loved to tease her, "Olga are you running another business at noon?"

Olga would shake her heavy head of red hair with glasses perched on top, wrap her big scarf around her broad shoulders, and saunter out the door. As soon as she was gone, Georg would move closer and put his arms around Anna. "Are you ready for another dance?"

"Georg, you're teasing me. If you go, I'll go."

Anna and Georg enjoyed their time together. They talked about their families and life goals. The noon hours were always too brief for Anna, yet she could never bring herself to tell Georg the truth.

Work progressed at the dry goods store with a surge of customers responding to the spring and summer sales. Mr. Hansen, busy with the crowds, did not have time to follow Anna closely about.

Georg enjoyed going to baseball games. Anna would regularly pack a picnic lunch, and they would ride out to Humboldt Park to cheer for the Chicago team. Anna had to learn about the game from Georg. The strikes, balls, and bunts were new to her. She often was in a daze about the score, but together they cheered the team. On Sundays, they would celebrate a win by going to Hook's Drug Store afterward for a soda.

The store was renowned for a drink made with a base of ice cream, syrup, and fizz, stirred until creamy smooth. Next, the soda fountain clerk would add soda and more scoops of ice cream, then whipped cream and a cherry.

Hook's Drug Store was also known for its patent medicines like Perry Davis Great Family Vegetable Pain Killer, Mrs. Winslow's Soothing Syrup for children, and Hosteller's Castoria. The shelves were also filled with sponges, straight razors, Prince Albert tobacco, plus plug slicers and pens.

Anna put a penny in the chewing gum machine. "Look, Georg, maybe I'll be lucky today." The reward was one cent or more of Wrigley's gum.

On the highest shelf rested a row of fifth-century glass jugs filled with old-time stick candy, cinnamon drops, wild cherry slugs, and root beer barrels. Some of the other jars were filled with powders, liquids, and pills.

"Doesn't it smell good in here," he said. "Let's buy some cinnamon drops for Lise and Hans."

When the weather was nice, Georg would sometimes take Anna to a concert in the park. The tall willow trees around the lagoon and the flowering bushes along the walks made it a romantic place for a Sunday excursion. One day, after a concert of rousing European marches, Georg asked, "Will you trust me to take you rowing around the lagoon?"

"Georg, this place reminds me of Bergen. I used to row the skiff around the harbor."

"Good," he said playfully, "you can row and I'll relax."

Once they'd rented the skiff, Anna took the oars and deftly rowed to the shade of the willow trees. "Crew, tie up," she barked, feigning harshness in her voice.

"Aye, aye, Captain," he said, playing along. "But you mustn't work the crew so hard."

He climbed into the back of the skiff, and they sat together watching the minnows darting under the shadow of the boat.

Suddenly, a gust of wind blew Anna's big hat into the water. Georg fished it out with an oar, but couldn't pull himself up once he had the hat in hand. He reached for balance from Anna. She grabbed him. "I have you Georg. Hang on!"

Georg pulled himself up and leaned against the plank seat. On his knees, he put Anna's wet hat back on her head saying, "Anna, dear, you're right. You have me." He placed his hands on her shoulders and kissed her firmly on the lips.

Anna closed her eyes. It couldn't be true. She clung to her hat with one hand and to Georg with the other as the passion of his kiss coursed through her veins.

Finally, he got off his knees, stretched his legs, and sat beside her. "You mean so much to me," he said, wrapping his arm around her and pulling her close.

They were so close she could see inside his big blue eyes; his soft beard felt like a small cushion to lean on. They were lost in each other's arms when a loud blast from a horn sounded across the water. It was the warning signal to return all boats. They clung to each other until the second blast.

Georg regretfully took the oars and rowed back. "Anna, dear, this day I will always remember."

Anna was slowly coming out of her trance. "I too will always remember this Sunday with you, Georg."

Anna moved through the following days, weeks, and months in an effervescent haze. In their spare time, she and Georg saw more and more of each other. At night, she dreamed of Georg, wrote little notes to Georg, baked cookies for Georg, and in the evenings before going to bed, would hold the little picture he had taken of them and talk to it. "Why can't I tell you the whole truth? Am I scared you'll desert me? I must be honest with you. I know you're the man for me. What can I say when there has been no word from Ole? I am certainly not betrothed to him any longer. He has disappeared into thin air. Yet, I wake up in the night with visions of me pacing at the train station, looking for an Ole who never arrived. I wish I knew what to do."

To make matters worse, Mr. Hansen started becoming more of a pest toward Anna despite her repeated warnings that she had no interest in his advances. One day, he asked her into his office and invited her to join him on one of his regular trips to Marshall Fields, the biggest store in Chicago. Hansen said he wanted her to "meet the buyer," and with that, he put his arm around her and pulled her close.

She tried to push him away. All she could see was his big nostrils, with gray and brown hairs hanging out. He was sweating from head to toe and his stench almost made her vomit. "Let go of me this instant, Mr. Hansen," she said, breaking away from his hold.

"Of course, Anna," he said smoothly, "you know I was just kidding. By the way, please call me Theo. This could be an important opportunity for you. I would like you to listen in on my discussions with the buyer and find out how we handle our orders, damaged sales goods, and bills of lading."

She realized this could be a wonderful chance for her to get to know about fabrics and the varieties of cloth. She reasoned that the buyer would probably be with them all day — that would be her protection against Mr. Hansen's advances. She would have to be very careful with him.

On the way to Marshall Fields, Hansen once again tried to force himself on Anna. He kissed her while they were waiting for the cabby to open the door at Marshall Fields. She felt Hansen's slimy mouth on hers. He held her tight and pressed himself upon her body as she wrestled to get free. Her purse fell on the floor. At that point, the cabby opened the door and announced: "Marshall Fields."

Anna pulled away. "Mr. Hansen, let me go! Don't you ever touch me again!" Her stomach churned and she almost threw up. She quickly collected her belongings from the floor and graciously accepted the proffered hand from the waiting cabby.

Hansen hopped down, walked on ahead, then turned back. "Well, Anna, are you coming? I haven't got all day. The buyer's waiting for us as we speak." He turned to walk away.

Anna ignored him while rearranging her hat so it wouldn't blow away in the howling winds. She considered returning to Hansen's store, but that would mean no job. She closed her eyes and tried to wipe Hansen's kiss out of her mind; she felt dirty and misused. But when would she have another chance to visit Marshall Fields? Probably never, things being as they were, and they were already there, so the moment of danger had passed. She wouldn't be alone with Hansen for the rest of the day. Anna followed him into Marshall Fields.

They stayed all day, and she did meet the buyer. Mr. Hansen introduced her as "his assistant." They spent the morning discussing invoices and concentrated on the spring fabric selections in the afternoon. She tried to pay attention to their conversations, but her mind kept wandering. She thought of what Georg would do to Mr. Hansen if he knew what happened. She kept wanting to wash her mouth, her face, and her teeth. She felt like a leper. What had she done to bring all this about? Should she tell Georg?

The meeting lasted for hours and hours. Anna wasn't able to follow all their conversation and didn't really care if she missed some. Her anger and resentment toward Mr. Hansen dominated her thoughts, but some of the words the two men used were familiar because of her work at Hansen's store. When it was finally time to go home, she noticed it was well past her normal quitting time. "I'll just take another cab home, Mr. Hansen," she said as the doorman hailed a carriage and driver.

"Don't be silly, Anna," he said. "You're perfectly safe with your boss. Won't you please ride home with me?"

She took a deep breath. "Thank you for your generous offer," said Anna. "I have a few stops to make on the way home, and it just wouldn't work out. But I want to thank you for this opportunity to learn more about the business."

"Your cab is waiting, sir," said the doorman.

Anna's smelly boss nodded and smiled at the doorman.

"Vood you please order me a cab?" she asked the doorman in her best English, securing her hat against the gusting winter winds.

"Yes, ma'am," came the immediate response, "Be a pleasure." The doorman went back outside to hail a second cab.

"You sure you don't want to ride home with me?" Hansen said. "Going to be awfully cold out there all by yourself. Those cabs are really freezing this time of year."

Anna slowly finished her preparations against the cold. "Thank you, Mr. Hansen, for your thoughtfulness. I think I'm well prepared for the cold. Remember I'm from Norway, too."

Just then the doorman returned. "Cab's ready, madam. Would you like some help?"

She gave the doorman a big smile and nodded. "Yah, yah," she said, "some help, please."

"Thank you for the wonderful opportunity, Mr. Hansen," she said and waved goodbye.

The doorman took her by the arm and escorted her to the waiting cab, Anna nodding and smiling the whole way.

The trip home was cold, but Anna didn't really notice. She was too busy trying to figure out what to do about Mr. Hansen. She felt hopelessly caught on a high wire with no safety net below. Had she already jeopardized her job by rejecting Mr. Hansen's advances? If she lost her job, where would she find another? It had taken her so long to find this one. She would probably have to return to Bergen, but she didn't want to leave Georg. And if she told Georg, he would have to do something, which meant he would probably have to lose his job as well. She couldn't tell Georg —she loved him too much to do that. And she couldn't tell the Swensens because then they would have to do something, which would mean she would lose her job.

When the cab arrived at the parsonage, Anna opened her purse to pay the driver. "How much, please?" she asked.

The driver shook his head. "No charge. No charge. My fee's already been paid."

At dinner that night, it was obvious to all the Swensens that Anna had had an unusually hard day. Her usual bubbly personality was absent and she barely said anything to Hans and Lise. Anna hardly touched her food, which was also very much out of character.

"Did things go badly at Marshall Fields?" Hans wondered.

Anna shook her head. "Everything's fine," she lied. "I've just got a lot on my mind."

"Did you have a chocolate sundae?" asked Lise.

Anna smiled. "No, Lise, I didn't. But I wish I had."

Elsa studied Anna as the young woman picked through her food. Elsa then decided to change the subject. "You know, Anna, Christmas will be here pretty soon. Do you have any plans?"

"No. Georg mentioned the other day that the Danish Lodge would be putting up their big tree next week. They have a big decorating party, and he asked me to go with him."

"Well, Anna," Henrik said, "we would like you to spend Christmas Eve and Christmas with us."

Anna took a deep breath and made a faint smile. Her eyes watered up and she swallowed hard. "I would love to spend Christmas with all of you. Thank you for inviting me. It means so much to me," she whispered, her voice cracking.

Elsa went over to Anna and gave her a long hug. "We love you, Anna Steffensen. We'd also like you to invite your friend Georg to join us with our Christmas Eve celebration."

"You would?" Anna said, her face brightening. "That's a wonderful idea. Yes, I will ask him. I'm sure he will enjoy being with us." She scowled for a minute, deep in thought.

"Be sure to ask Georg where Mr. Theo Hansen won't hear you," Elsa said. "He's a member of our parish and real funny about invitations. He gets upset when he gets an invitation that doesn't include his wife and their three beautiful little daughters. He never goes anywhere without them. So, if you want to invite Mr. Hansen, remember to invite his whole family."

Anna couldn't believe her ears. No one had ever told her that Mr. Hansen had a wife and children. Even Olga had never mentioned it. That was the answer. Now she knew what to do about Mr. Hansen and his roving hands. Suddenly, the day didn't seem to be so bad. She knew what to do to keep her job so she could be around her Georg. With any kind of luck, she might even learn more about the fabric business. She'd make the arrangements later.

Anna beamed. A big weight had been removed from her shoulders. She stood up and gave Elsa a big hug. "Thank you, my wonderful friend. I can't tell you how much you and all your beautiful family mean to me."

She looked over at Hans and Lise. "You two want to play a game, now? I think I've eaten enough!"

The two children ran to Anna and hugged her.

"Now our Anna is home," Lise said, smiling ear to ear.

Chapter Seven

A Scandinavian Christmas in Chicago

Anna was glad to see that the next morning brought white, billowy clouds into the sky. The wind lessened, and the sun tried feebly to shine from behind the clouds. The change in weather gave Anna a feeling of hope about Georg and her. As soon as the bus dropped her off, she waited for him by the stationery store across from work. She hoped he would arrive alone so she could invite him without others overhearing their conversation.

Soon he came walking fast down the street in his usual debonair manner. Anna caught up with him and hurried to keep up with his long strides. "Georg, the Swensens and I want you to join us at the parsonage for our Christmas Eve celebration," she blurted out. "Please come."

Georg stopped short and looked down at her. "Why, Anna, good morning," he said, smiling with joy. "How thoughtful of you and the Swensens. Of course, I would very much like to come. I would enjoy a real Scandinavian Christmas Eve. It would be my pleasure!" He leaned over and whispered in her ear, "You know I want to be with you."

Anna walked on air into the dry goods store. How exciting to have Georg to share Christmas with. Her mood changed abruptly however when she saw Mr. Hansen in his office. She knew what she had to do. What would his wife think about his behavior in the cab? She would go and invite him and his family this moment.

Anna walked over to his office and knocked. Theo was dressed in his brown suit with the big pin sticking in his tie. Anna stared a hole through him and wondered how she could stand to talk to him. How could he treat her with such disrespect and guile? Would he want his three daughters to be so degraded?

"Come in, Anna. How nice to see you. Won't you sit down?"

"No, I prefer to stand. Pastor and Mrs. Swensen, with whom I live at the parsonage, have asked me to invite you and your wife and three little daughters, Margrethe, Inger, and Kirstine, to our Christmas Eve celebration. Mrs. Swensen has sent you the invitation. It's coming in the mail."

Mr. Hansen's face turned white and then red. He took out his handkerchief and his hands shook as he blew his nose. He twirled around in his office chair, back toward Anna.

"Mrs. Swensen suggested that your children would enjoy playing with Lise and Hans," Anna added.

Mr. Hansen continued to blow his nose. He took a little calendar book from his pocket. "I didn't know you lived with the Swensens. That is very nice of them. My wife knows Mrs. Swensen from their church guild work together."

"Oh, how nice that the families can get together during this festive time of the year."

"No, Anna, I'm afraid we won't be able to accept the Swensen's . . . and . . and your . . . generous invitation. Our family will be gathering that night as well. I'm terribly sorry. . . . Maybe some other time."

"Thank you, Mr. Hansen. I will tell the Swensens."

Anna turned her back on Mr. Hansen with a smile on her face and walked out of his office. She felt sure that she wouldn't be having any more trouble with Mr. Hansen, his evil ideas, and his sweating body. Now she could turn her full attention to Georg. How did he really feel about her?

As Christmas approached, local merchants decorated the downtown streets with garlands of pine boughs. Scarlet poinsettia plants and Christmas lamps adorned the entrance to many a family shop. In their display windows were winter scenes, some with Nicoli and Nisses (Santa Claus's elves), sleighs, and Christmas trees loaded with ornaments and toys.

Hansen's Dry Goods Store's display room had red and green cloth strips wrapped around its support posts. A large tree in the corner sparkled with miniature dresses, aprons, baby clothes, and fabrics prepared by the wholesalers. The salesmen wore red or green ties with matching handkerchiefs in their upper pockets. Each day Georg changed his tie. Anna thought how handsome he looked in his carefully pressed suit and red tie.

Her anticipation of their Christmas Eve celebration together so delighted her, she felt as if she were walking on air. The thought of Georg coming to share the Swensen's family celebration filled her evening thoughts. She dreamed about his arriving dressed as Nicoli carrying a bouquet of a dozen red roses, then telling her how much he loved her.

At the store, Anna's work took on renewed vigor. "Why such energetic cleaning and sweeping?" Olga asked. "Are we expecting the mayor or is it Nicoli?"

"I'm getting ready to start the New Year right!" answered Anna. Every noontime, she repeated to Olga and Georg the same story. "Remember, Georg, you were the first person I met when I stepped into this dry goods store. You told me about Mr. Hansen's coffee cup, and here I am!" she'd say, triumphantly pulling a holiday cookie from her lunch. "Try a Christmas cookie, Olga. Tonight we are preparing *brune kaker, kringler, fattigmann,* and *knakkaker* cookies."

"Anna," said Olga, "please slow down a little. You'll be exhausted before the holidays arrive."

"No, Olga. I have even asked Mrs. Swensen to invite a parishioner who will come and take pictures of us with one of those fancy box-type, flash powder cameras."

One day, Georg walked into the cutting room with a sandwich. "Hi girls! What's the latest gossip?"

Olga had a response before Anna could answer. "Mr. Hansen has declared tomorrow a holiday."

Georg laughed. "That would be an event." He sat on the small stool where his long legs stretched out beyond the cutting table. His perfectly trimmed beard and immaculate suit gave him a touch of elegance. "Did you hear Theo may give us a Christmas bonus this year based on our sales or production increase?"

"I'll believe it when I see it," responded Olga, chewing on a chocolate cream tart. Her flowing dress wrapped around her large body like a small tent.

"You two have worked here long enough to receive a bonus," Anna said, chewing a liver sausage sandwich. "You're lucky!"

Georg smiled. "Relax, we don't have it yet." He looked out into the sales area. "One of my regular customers is waiting for me. See you later."

Anna returned to work, thinking of her past problems with Mr. Hansen. Since she'd confronted him about his family, he hadn't followed her in to the rear storeroom or tried to put his arms around her. The few times they had met during the day, he ignored her and made an effort to keep out of her way and go about his own business. If only I were sure he had changed, thought Anna. I don't trust him, but he knows I am a good worker.

These days, the omnibus didn't travel fast enough for Anna. The cold slush delayed it, and the cold was almost unbearable. She was anxious to get home to join the family in cookie making. Hans and Lise would greet her in the dark at the bus stop as she descended the stairs.

"Hurry, Anna," Lise said. "We're going to bake *pepperkaker* tonight."

After dinner, Lise and Hans would cut the brown wafer dough with molds into various shapes of hearts, stars, roosters, reindeer, and trees. As they baked, the cookies sent a delicious fragrance around the house. After they cooled, the children would decorate them. Hans's favorite color was red. He splashed red faces, stars, circles, and squares on himself, as well as the cookies. Lise painted trees on her cookies using only white and pink icing. She always had to eat one or two.

Fattigmann was a donut Anna especially like to make; they reminded her of her life in Bergen. She recalled how her mother and sister had baked *fattigmanns* just before Mama died. She realized this was to be her first Christmas away from home. She recalled images of all of them working together in the fish stall, or skiing out across the nearby mountains, or sitting down together for Christmas dinner. The memories made her sad. The next morning on the way to work in the omnibus, she wrote this letter.

My dear family:

Thank you for your letters. I'm sorry I haven't written more often. I've been busy in the dry goods store over the Christmas season. Mr. Hansen pays me eighty cents a day. I pay the Swensens for my board and room. They are a wonderful Norwegian-American family. I never could have managed without them. We are all having our Christmas celebration together at the parsonage. My new friend Georg Amorsen from Denmark, who also works as a salesman in Hansen's store, is coming too. Lise, Hans, and I study the school language primers each evening in order to learn English. Gudrun, start to study English. You'll need it if you come to America. My love to you, Papa, and my dear sister. I miss you.

Gledelig Jul, (Merry Christmas). Anna.

Elsa Swensen wrote a letter that evening as well.

Dear Mr. Amorsen:
We are pleased you can join us to share our Christmas celebration. We plan to trim the tree while the children are over at the Jensens'. You may arrive by 5 p.m. and join in the surprise for Hans, Lise and Deacon Jensen's children. They live just a short block from us. They offered an extra room in which you can stay overnight. We regret we haven't more space in the parsonage. We look forward to seeing you again.
Your friends, Henrik, Elsa, Hans, and Lise Swensen.

The preparations for Christmas proceeded with many secrets and giggles by Hans and Lise. "Look at my funny package, Hans," said Lise, wrapping one of her presents. "Do you think Mama will guess what it is?"

"I know what it is. You made it at school. I won't tell."

Elsa was checking the grocery list to be sure she could find the ingredients she needed for the Norwegian-Danish dishes. She asked Henrik, "Where can I find venison in this city?"

"It is not sold here according to the butcher."

On Christmas Eve day, Anna selected her one red dress to wear to work and the store luncheon party. She wanted to look her best for Georg. The four salesmen, Olga, and Anna had been invited by Mr. Hansen to a luncheon gathering. He closed the store at noon. *Danske smørbrød* had been set out for the employees in the decorated salesroom. Mr. Hansen enlivened the party with two bottles of Schnapps and bonuses for everyone, even Anna. She received a full week's pay.

"Raise your glasses, everyone," called out Peter. "A toast to Mr. Hansen."

Anna joined them, but only took a few sips of the fiery Acquavit. She was not used to drinking. They did not have liquor in the parsonage.

"Here's a toast to ourselves. *Gledelig Jul*," called out Olga. All responded with a cheer.

"Come and join us, everyone," called Georg as he stood up and put his hands out for all to join in a circle. Anna grabbed his hand to be next to him. He had on a bright red bow tie and a funny, tall, green hat. With the others, they walked around the little Christmas tree and sang songs of Christmas; "*Nu er det jul igen*" (Now it is

Christmas again) and *"Det kimer nu til julefest"* (The bells are tolling for Christmas). The old-time favorites brought out lusty voices. Even Mr. Hansen attempted to harmonize.

"Sing out," he ordered. Georg's tenor rang out in *"Aarhus Tappenstred Marsch "* (Danish March).

Anna found the right moment and whispered to Georg, "Try to come early tonight so you can help trim our tree. You are tall and can put the silver gilded wooden star — the star of Bethlehem — on the very top."

Georg winked and gave her hand a squeeze. "I'll be there, Anna. I don't want to miss a real Christmas this year."

Anna stayed after everyone was gone and helped clean up the salesroom, then hurried and caught the early afternoon bus home. She couldn't wait to get home and wrap the little gifts she had purchased from the bargain table at Marshall Fields. She hoped that Georg would like his present, she'd had no idea she'd be getting a bonus from Mr. Hansen. Maybe tonight Georg would even tell her that he loved her.

By the time Anna reached the parsonage, Elsa and Henrik had already started to decorate the tree with handmade ornaments. She had barely taken off her coat when Georg arrived with a large bundle, a potted poinsettia plant, and an overnight case. Anna ran to the door and helped him carry in his packages. She noticed he had on his best dark blue suit and a red bow tie.

The Swensens greeted Georg. "What a pleasure to see you, again," said Henrik, shaking his hand.

Georg was his usual gracious self as he gave the plant to Elsa. "It is indeed a pleasure to be included with your family for a Christmas Eve celebration."

"If you wish, you can put your coat in the study and your package under the Christmas tree in the parlor," said Henrik. "Thank you for such a pretty Christmas plant. I'll put it on the living table where we can all see it."

"You're welcome," Georg said. "I've been so looking forward to my visit with you and your wonderful family."

"Please excuse Anna and me," said Elsa. "We have to complete the dinner preparation. You and Henrik can finish decorating the tree. We've also invited the Jensens to join us for our *Juleaften* (Christmas Eve) celebration."

The two women returned to the kitchen filled with its delightful aromas. Elsa had *koldtbord* (cold board) dishes loaded with food and ready to serve. In addition, she had cooked a large bowl of *risengrøt* (rice pudding). Within the rice pudding, she had hidden an almond which when found, according to tradition, entitled the lucky recipient to a special prize.

"I wonder who will find the almond this year?" Elsa wondered. "Lise and Hans usually strain the pudding with their teeth to be sure not to swallow it."

Anna giggled. "I remember fighting with Gudrun when she found it because I felt she should share the prize," Anna said, stirring red cabbage. She inhaled its steam. "I really know its Christmas when I smell the *rødkål*."

"The *stekt julegås* (roast goose) is just about done," Elsa said, wide-eyed with excitement. "I can hear the crackling of the skin and smell the goose."

"It smells delicious," Anna said, cocking her head to one side and giving Elsa a warm and loving look. "It's so wonderful and exciting to be with special friends on Christmas." Suddenly, she paused, deep in thought. "I wonder what my sister and father are doing this holiday season. This is the first year we've ever been separated."

Hearing the sound of singing and ringing bells on the porch, Henrik opened the front door to greet the Jensen family as well as Lise and Hans. "Welcome! Come in!" he said.

By now, the family parlor had been closed off, so the deacon and Mrs. Jensen and their two teenage children put their coats on the sofa and turned to meet Georg.

"I want you to meet Georg Amorsen, a friend of Anna's and ours, too," said Henrik. "Georg, our guests are the deacon and his wife and children, Sigurd and Marie."

"Pleased to meet you," said Georg. He and Deacon Jensen shook hands.

Anna thought the deacon could well have been Santa Claus with his white beard, except he was wearing a black suit instead of a red one. Mrs. Jensen looked elegant in the lace dress trimmed with red bows. She was about Anna's height and had a red flower in her hair.

"I want to thank you for providing me with a room tonight," Georg said. "I don't know if you remember, Mrs. Jensen, but we've met before. I've had the pleasure to wait on you at Hansen's Dry Goods Store."

"I remember you, now," Mrs. Jensen said. "In fact, I'm wearing the dress I made from the fabric you sold me. Glad you could be here. You're certainly a long way from Denmark!"

Henrik escorted the Jensens, Georg, and the children into the front room. Everyone wanted to ask Georg questions about his home country and how he came to America. The well-spoken banker's son fielded questions with the grace and charm of an old pro. Hans and Lise took turns sitting in his lap.

Anna listened from the kitchen with one ear. She couldn't wait to join Georg in the evening's festivities, but first she had to help Elsa. How handsome he was, how tall, what a well-made suit, and an attractive bright red bow tie. But he was much more than that. As Anna listened to Georg and Henrik and Deacon Jensen exchanging points of view, it was plain Georg was no ordinary man. Here was a man of substance, a man to whom others would listen. Anna's buttons almost popped off her chest, she was so proud of her Georg. Her whole body tingled with excitement and joy; she was entering a new world of feeling. Her only fear was that Georg might not feel the same as she.

For the Swensons, the dinner was the important business. All seated themselves around the table in the dining room. Lise and Hans had made little name cards. Henrik gave the blessing. "May God bless you, everyone. In love and friendship, we join together in celebrating this special occasion."

First came the suspense of who would find the almond in the *risengrøt*. The children sifted the pudding through their teeth to be sure they wouldn't swallow the almond by mistake. Everyone swallowed their pudding with great care.

Lise stirred her pudding and rolled a small bite around in her mouth. "I found it! I found it!" she cried out and spit the almond into her spoon.

Hans said, "The prize is a piece of black coal."

"Hans," Elsa scolded good-naturedly, "don't tease your sister. The prize is a marzipan pear."

"Don't worry, Hans," Lise said. "I'll share the prize with you, Marie, and Sigurd after dinner."

After the *risengrøt* came the *koldtbord*: pickled herring in mustard, smoked eel with egg salad, and poached cold salmon. Special cold plates were provided as each selected their choices. In the middle of dinner, Henrik went in and lit the candles on the tree in the parlor and shut the door again. He went out to the kitchen to carry in the *stekt julegås* stuffed with prunes and apples. Loud applause greeted the baked bird, bedecked with Norwegian and Danish flags. Anna followed with *rødkål*, baked potatoes, and assorted vegetables.

Henrik expertly carved the goose while the children begged for pieces of crackling skin. Soon the plates were filled and silence descended upon those present. For dessert, Elsa served *Kransekake*, a delicate ring-shaped cookie pyramid of sixteen rings held together with delicate marzipan; more flags topped off this course. The cookies left a heavy almond aroma in the air while everyone sampled the pudding again.

Before the feast could end, Scandinavian custom required that each person walk up to Henrik, the head of the house, and say, "*Tak for mad*" (Thank you for the food) to which Henrik would reply, "*De er velkommen* (May good come of it)!"

Next came the excitement of opening the parlor doors. There stood the shining Christmas tree with lighted candles top to bottom. The decorations, the star, the small baskets, and chains of popcorn or cranberries brightened each branch.

Then came the presents. The children had a choice of opening one present. They crept on their knees under the tree in order to read the labels and feel the packages.

"Select the gift you want and open it, but do it so we all can see," Elsa reminded each child.

Lise was first. "I hope this is my new sweater," she said, struggling with the box.

Elsa smiled. She knew Lise had watched her knitting over the past several months.

"Hurrah, my blue sweater!" Lise put it on and danced around the room. "Thank you, Mama."

Sigurd, at age fourteen, looked a little bored but when he opened his gift and found a book on astronomy he let out a cry. "I've been wanting a book like this to identify the stars! Thank you, Nicoli!"

Marie opened her smaller package. It was a book of paper dolls with a full wardrobe for each. She quickly stood them up and dressed them.

Finally, Hans pulled a heavy box toward the center of the room and excitedly pulled off the cover. "Wow!" he exclaimed. "It is a big puzzle. Come on, Sigurd, let's start."

"Look, Anna," called Lise. "Here is a present for you." She pulled it over toward Anna. On the tag, it read, "To *Norska* (an endearing term for a Norwegian woman) from Georg."

Anna felt it, started to take the wrapping off, and stopped. She wanted to save this moment forever.

"Open it, Anna," Georg said. "I know you'll like it."

"Yes, I'm opening it." She tore more of the red wrapping paper off and lifted the lid. There was that beautiful, poppy-covered, purple fabric she had been admiring, feeling, and gazing upon during recent months. "Georg, how did you know this was my favorite color?"

"You always stop by that bolt, feel it, and stare at it."

Anna smiled, pleased that Georg was so observant. She pointed under the tree. "Now, it's your turn. There's a little box under the tree, Georg. Would you please open it?"

He picked up the right box, shook it, then pretended to listen to it. When finally he opened the present, out dropped two silver cuff links. His jaw dropped and eyes widened. "Oh, my, they're beautiful!" he said, giving her a wink. "Thank you so much, Anna. I can certainly use these. How did you know?"

"You roll up your shirt cuffs sometimes."

In the meantime, the families exchanged gifts of glasses of homemade jam. Lise and Marie were already dressing the dolls. Sigurd and Hans had put the puzzle together. In the middle of all this activity, there came a knock on the front door. It was Karl the photographer. Elsa went to the door and welcomed him.

"First would you like to sample our Christmas goose?"

"No, thank you. We're having dinner at my home soon. Now could you all stand in front of the tree?"

Hans, Lise, Marie, and Sigurd stood in the first row in front of the tree and the others grouped around them. Anna made sure she stood next to Georg.

Karl cautioned, "Don't look too serious. You were all laughing and having fun when I entered. Now smile!" After three attempts, smoke from the powder explosions filled the room.

"I'll have the pictures ready within the week, and remember I can take an outside picture later. *Gledelig Jul,*" Karl said, hurrying out the door.

Anna could hardly wait.

Too soon, it was time for Pastor Swensen to prepare for the Christmas Eve church service. He left them with the caution: "Bundle up, the church may be cold tonight. The temperature has dropped again and it is beginning to snow."

The parsonage was warm because of the fires in the stove and fireplace; Hans had brought in a good supply of wood. And to think, Anna reflected, we almost lost him in the cold and freezing Atlantic. The snow was coming down hard now, covering the church, homes, trees, and roads.

The Christmas Eve church services were for families and friends. Three Christmas hymns were sung. Henrik gave a brief sermon on

Jesus's birth. The service ended with the children's choir singing, "Christmas Has Brought Glad Tidings" in Norwegian. Hans and Lise stood in the front row of the choir singing joyously. The parishioners stood in a moment of silence during the benediction while the sound of church bells echoed through the neighborhood. All put on their heavy coats, muffs, scarfs, and hats, and then filed out, shaking Henrik's hand as he had one final word with each.

Outside, the falling snow covered the street and painted the landscape with a crisp and festive brush. The trees were laden with a thick white blanket of snow. Even the wheel marks of the omnibus were covered. *"Gledelig Jul, Gledelig Jul!"* sounded clearly in the stillness of the night as families and friends started walking home, crowding into farm wagons or waiting for the omnibus's last return trip to the city.

Georg thanked Henrik for the Christmas message and for the joyous evening. He then held Elsa's arm and helped her down the steps. "Thank you for my wonderful visit with you and your family and the delicious dinner," he said, turning to Elsa. "I felt as if I were home again."

Elsa smiled and accepted his thanks.

Turning to Anna, he took her hand and they stopped walking. He looked down into her smiling round face as the heavy snow drifted down through the darkness. "Goodnight, *Norska!*" he said with tenderness. "Thank you so much for inviting me. I can't tell you how happy I am to be with you. Thank you for a real Christmas. It has been a wonderful evening."

Anna felt weak in the knees as she looked up to his blue eyes and glowing smile. "Thank you for coming, Georg. You made my first Christmas away from my family so wonderful. I'm happy you could be with us. I'll see you in the morning. *Gledelig Jul.*"

"Gledelig Jul, Norska."

Both smiled, turned, and hurried to catch up to the family with whom they would spend the night. The Jensens walked quickly down the center of the street where the snow was less deep. Sigurd and Marie jogged alongside Georg for the one short block to their home; they were sleepy but bubbling about the evening and their new gifts.

At the church, Henrik extinguished the lamps and the candles and locked the door. The Swensen family and Anna then walked across to the parsonage. Anna was ecstatic with how things had gone this Christmas Eve. She thought of the fragrance of the cookies, the pine boughs, and the crackling goose roasting in the oven. How beautiful their Christmas fir had been with the candles aglow, and then there were the lamps burning in the church during the service. How inspiring the sounds of laughter and voices singing the Christmas songs! The image of Georg and the Swensens joined together in celebrating Christmas would remain in her memory forever! Still, she was surprised Georg hadn't said something more about how he felt toward her. Maybe he was hiding something, too.

Chapter Eight

The Salesman

For Anna, the rest of the holiday season was equally joyful. She spent Christmas Day with Georg and the Swensens. The young couple spent hours and hours walking in the snow, laughing, holding hands, and kissing during the week after Christmas. On New Year's Eve they spent the night dancing polkas at the Danish Lodge. When she arrived at work following New Year's Day, she was surprised to see Mr. Hansen waving a letter in his hand.

"We both received letters today, Anna. Here's yours."

She thanked Mr. Hansen and glanced down at the address. Yes, it was for her and, like a bolt of lightning, she recognized Hans Georg Amorsen's name as the sender. Yes, it was his handwriting. She hurried to the warehouse wondering why he'd send her a letter. They had parted just a few hours ago after a perfect evening of dancing and laughing with his friends. Her fingers were all thumbs as she opened the letter:

Dearest Anna:

My father had a stroke. Mother wired me a ticket to catch the Helga out of New York. In order to arrive in time to board the ship for Copenhagen, I had to catch the midnight train to New York. There was no way to let you know so I put the letter to you and one to Mr. Hansen in the store's mailbox. Please forgive me. Until he is able to take over his work at the bank, I will have to help out in the bank. Anna, I will always remember our days together. Jeg er en Viking. Med Kjerlighet.

Georg

Anna couldn't believe what she read. How could he leave Chicago without coming to see her? Her heart ached. She recalled her last hours with Georg at the Danish Lodge as they whirled and circled, laughing and having fun, the feel of his tweed suit as he put his arm around her, the time they rowed out in the lagoon and let the boat drift as they shared their dreams of the future, and the beautiful Christmas they had celebrated just a few days ago with the Swensens.

She started to cry as she tried to picture his return, but another image jumped into view — that of Ole. She could scarcely recall how he looked from the times she had seen him in Bergen. She felt a chill go through her. Was her life doomed to sorrow? And then there was the haunting question: what happened to Ole?

Anna sat down and put her head on the yardage table, sobbing. She felt she had been struck a blow from which she could not recover. She mumbled to herself as if her message would cross the Atlantic. "I love you, Georg, and you love me. Please write and tell me what's in your heart. I'm lost without you." If only Papa and Gudrun were here to lean on. What would they think of Georg leaving so abruptly?

Finally, weak from her sorrow, she dried her eyes, got up, and put on her apron. There was nothing she could do. She might as well get started and drag herself through the day's chores.

Shortly before closing time, Mr. Hansen came back to the store room. "How are you, Anna? Georg certainly left in a hurry. He wrote that his father had a stroke. He didn't say when he would be back."

"I'm all right, Mr. Hansen. I can't understand why he couldn't contact one of us. Are you employing a new salesman?"

"No, Anna. We will manage with our same crew. Georg may return sooner than we think."

"Thank you, Mr. Hansen," she said. He could certainly be a nice man when he made up his mind to do so, Anna thought. She put on her coat and walked toward to the bus stop for the new cable car; she was in a daze. What would she tell the Swensens? Maybe Georg didn't want to tell her he was not coming back. The whole turmoil over Ole's disappearance kept going through her head. What if the *Helga* is hit by an iceberg? What if Georg disappears? Anna shook her head. She couldn't relive it all again. It made her feel faint and weary.

At dinner, Elsa noticed that Anna was quiet and withdrawn. Usually the family shared funny stories or talked about the day's events. "What's the matter, Anna?" she asked.

The younger woman started to answer, but her eyes filled with tears. "Georg had to return to Denmark," she mumbled. "His father had a stroke."

"Oh, Anna," Henrik said. "We're so sorry. Is there anything we can do?" The Swensens exchanged worried looks. Anna's silence was understandable. "I'm sure he'll return."

Anna couldn't eat. She excused herself and went to her room. She sat in her rocking chair and stared at the moon shining on the trees — the same moon watching over Georg, she thought. If he loved me he should have taken me with him. Maybe his parents wouldn't accept me. I don't want any part of this unpredictable world.

She climbed into bed and pulled the blankets over her head. After a night of tossing and turning and repeated nightmares, she pulled herself together and sat up on the side of the bed. What was she dreaming about? A vague picture of Georg stranded on an ice floe in the Atlantic, but to her horror she recalled another figure in her dream. It was Ole disappearing under the iceberg.

The days at work became drudgery. Often Olga would come by seeking to join her for lunch. "Come on over and eat with me, Anna. Jen or Peter will come by and we can catch up with what they've been doing."

Anna would shake her head. "No thanks, Olga. I just can't bring myself join you right now. Maybe if I hear from Georg I'll be in a better mood."

At home, she marked the days on the calendar since Georg had left. Then, in little print, as if she didn't expect it to happen, she wrote the earliest possible date a letter could arrive from Denmark. It would take about five weeks. The days passed slowly. Once in a while, she'd try to tease the salesmen, but her spirits weren't in it; they stopped teasing her as well. At home she was quiet and morose.

Finally, Elsa had seen enough. "Anna, let's go for a walk after supper and visit a bit."

They walked up to Lise and Hans's school and sat on the benches overlooking the barren school yard. In the twilight, the playground was empty, dry, and bumpy. Just like my life now that Georg is gone, Anna thought.

"Tell me, Anna," asked Elsa. "What can I do to help you feel better? Georg's sudden departure was an emergency. He undoubtedly will write you as soon as he can."

"But, Elsa. Why didn't he send me a wire when he arrived? I feel so abandoned . . . as if I don't matter."

Elsa shook her head. "Where is all your laughter and buoyancy? What a different picture you are now when just a month or so ago you were riding on a big white cloud. You are the same person if you want to be. How can Henrik and I help?"

Anna shrugged and shook her head. "I can't sleep at night. I keep having nightmares of Georg and Ole on an iceberg. I feel a chill go through me as if another tragedy is ahead."

"You're worried about your future. Ole's disappearance has hung over you for nearly a year. Now Georg has had to leave on an emergency and you feel sad again. When you left Bergen, you were feeling sad about your mother and what you should have done in the past. You can't spend your life looking backward and thinking sad thoughts. Let's think what you'd like to do with your future, what makes you happy. Once you told me you'd like to be a salesman at the store. Why don't you follow up on that? It would give a boost to your feelings about yourself and provide a new challenge."

Anna perked up a little. "You're right. I have thought about applying for the salesman's opening, but I just haven't had the enthusiasm."

Elsa took Anna's hands and held them; she looked her in the eyes. "You have been too hard on yourself. Think about the job and maybe you'll decide to apply. We all love you, Anna, and want to see you happy. Georg will write you as soon as he can."

Anna mulled over Elsa's words. "I really must get out of this morbid mood. Maybe Mr. Hansen will let me fill in on Georg's job until he returns."

"Good, Anna, think about it. You could try."

One morning when Anna was ready to leave the parsonage, Anna raised the question with Elsa. "Do you think I really have a chance to apply for Georg's job?"

Elsa looked at Anna as she stood there in her bright, colorful woolen dress she had sewn for herself. "Anna, just look at the lovely dress you are wearing. Of course you have the ability to sell. Just ask Mr. Hansen. He owes you a raise after these months of paying you eight cents an hour for a ten-hour day. You haven't missed a day, have you? Also your English is much better."

Anna took a deep breath. "Thank you, Elsa. On my way to work, I'll practice what I'll say to Mr. Hansen. If he's in a good mood, I'll ask him about the job."

Hansen was already in his office when she arrived. He had a big cup of coffee half-filled, so Anna decided to ask him immediately before the other salesmen arrived. "Mr. Hansen, may I please have a word with you?"

He took off his coat and tossed it on the chair. As usual, he had on a celluloid collar and brown tie held in place by his tiepin. Anna hadn't been in his office since their meeting shortly before Christmas when she invited him to bring his whole family for Christmas Eve. Mr. Hansen had been a perfect gentleman ever since.

"What brings you into my office so early, Anna?"

"Would you consider me for temporarily filling Georg's salesman position? I sold fish in our fish market in Bergen for four years. I get along with customers and I have learned much watching Georg sell fabrics."

Mr. Hansen looked stunned. He stood up and walked around his desk. With his back to Anna and looking out at the salesroom he said, "We never hire women for salesman positions."

"Please, Mr. Hansen, more ladies come in to buy yardage than men. I have followed the fashions. I know what colors are popular. I also sew; therefore, I can be of help in selecting patterns from garments to curtains."

Mr. Hansen went to his desk, sat, and started scribbling figures on his paper pad.

Anna felt this was her last chance to persuade him. She stood and said, "Please give me one month's trial. If I don't sell my quota, I'll return to my old job."

He looked up at Anna. "All right, Anna," he said nodding. "I'll accept your offer, and I'll raise your pay from eight cents to ten cents an hour for a ten-hour day. If you are successful, I'll consider another raise later on."

She was stunned. "I thank you, Mr. Hansen," she mumbled. "I'll reach my quota, and I appreciate the opportunity to meet your customers and sell your beautiful fabrics."

Mr. Hansen smiled. "Good!" He extended his hand and they shook hands. "We have a deal."

As Anna walked back to the storeroom, she worried to herself. Now you have a new job Anna, one you've been wishing for since you came. Can you really reach these quotas in one short month? She looked at herself in the restroom. There was a glint in her brown eyes that hadn't been there before, and a determined set to her jaw. At last she had something on which to concentrate her energy.

Returning to the parsonage that evening she reported her success. Elsa rushed to give Anna a hug while Lise and Hans circled chanting, "Hurrah for Anna."

Henrik shook her hand. "You don't need to worry, Anna. I'll encourage the Church Circles to ride downtown and examine your fabrics. I'm sure they will purchase yardage."

Returning to her room after dinner, she sat on the side of her bed looking at the picture of her father and sister. She knew they would be proud. If only Georg would write. Maybe his parents disapproved of me. I wonder what he told them?

The next day, Mr. Hansen called a brief meeting of the three remaining salesman and Anna. "Chris, Jen, and Peter, we all appreciate the fine job Anna is doing for us. Now she is going to move into sales. I expect your full cooperation which I'm sure you'll give her."

The men looked at one another, speechless. Jen registered a half-hearted complaint. "I guess we can't tease you anymore or you'll take away our customers."

Anna smiled. "No, I won't. I'm planning to build up my own clientele." As she left the room, she overheard Chris whispering to Peter, "Oh boy, has she got a lot to learn."

She went home the first night wearier than when she cleaned the storage bins her first day of work at Hansen's. The tension of the job, the learning of inventories, the handling of sales, the variance of money from American dollars to Danish *krones* to Norwegian *kroners* kept her busy. She fell asleep reminding herself to greet each customer with a smile and always have the latest patterns artistically displayed.

During Anna's second week, Elsa encouraged two of the Church Circle groups downtown to go shopping at the store. Many purchased yardage from Anna. Others sought her advice on the pattern selection and on the choice of color and materials for their varying fashions. The Circle Groups often divided their time in making clothes for needy children and sewing their own dresses. Many times, they returned for more fabrics. As the fourth week ended, Anna was sure she had reached her quota. She went home feeling that she had passed another milestone. If only Georg were here to share with her.

Mr. Hansen put Anna on the regular payroll. The salesmen were more than surprised. Chris said it best in front of all the others: "Anna, we were hesitant about your abilities, but we have to give you full credit for your dedicated work and your ability to get the Church Circles to come shopping in our store."

A few days later, Anna was greeted by Lise and Hans as she walked up the road toward the Swensen home. They came running to meet her, each carrying a letter in both hands. "Anna, these are all for you!" exclaimed Hans.

Her joy about things at work was immediately forgotten. All she could think about was that there had to be a letter from Georg.

Without reading them or the handwriting, she thanked Hans and Lise, hurried to her room, and shut the door. Spreading the envelopes address-side-down on her bed, she closed her eyes and selected one. It was from Norway:

> *Dear Anna:*
>   *It's been nearly a year that I've been selling Papa's fish. My friends come and hang around a bit so I don't get lonesome. How goes all those Danish Socials in Chicago? We miss you.*
>   *Your sister, Gudrun.*

Papa wrote:

> *I have had good catches and repairs on the* Viking Star. *Here's my love to you.*

Anna gave the envelope a hug. How she loved her family! If only someday she could bring them to America. She picked up the second letter. It was a thank you note from the Church Circle for helping them select patterns, fabrics, and color. She crossed her fingers as she reached for the third letter. It had to be from Georg. As she turned it over, there was his handwriting. She couldn't wait to tear it open. Big letters leapt off the page:

> *I WANT TO MARRY YOU! PLEASE SAY YES! MY FATHER IS BETTER. I WILL RETURN THIS SUMMER!*

There was more news in the letter, but she couldn't contain herself. She dashed from her bedroom into Elsa's waiting arms. "He wants to marry me!" she blurted, sobbing out of control.

"Oh, my Lord, how wonderful!"

Elsa called to Henrik who came out of his study to find out what all the noise was about. He beamed when he heard the news. "When, my dear young woman, is this wedding to take place?"

Anna stopped her weeping and ran to fetch the letter. "It says he'll return this summer and hopes that Pastor Swensen will marry us at the end of July or the first of August."

At the end of the letter, Georg apologized for his abrupt departure. He had caught the *Helga* arriving in time to find his father much improved:

We made arrangements to lighten his load at the bank.
My mother believes they can manage. She hopes you and I
can return to Denmark. She is eager to meet you.
Med Kjerlighet. *Georg.*

Anna whirled about in a daze. After weeks and weeks of worry and sorrow, it was as if a load of bricks had been taken off her back. She hugged Lise and Hans and ran out into the yard to pick a blossom for her room. It was too good to be true, she told herself, singing song after song.

She'd forgotten about the last letter as she moved with joy helping prepare dinner and discussing plans for the wedding with Elsa and Henrik. It wasn't until she started to bed that night that she saw the other letter lying face down on the bed. She turned it over to find that it was from Deacon Jensen's wife. She invited Anna to come to an afternoon tea party next Sunday in appreciation of the arrangements and enjoyable visit the woman had had at Hansen's Dry Goods Shop.

Anna smiled to herself as she read the letter. As a janitor she had been overlooked, but as a fabric salesman, she was welcome. Mrs. Jensen's letter caused her to reflect on Georg's mother. Would she accept Anna as a salesman? She reread Georg's letter, kissing the first page where he had written his proposal. She put the letter under her pillow and began pacing the floor. She had to plan how she should act when she met her new in-laws.

Chapter Nine

The Wedding

No matter how hard she tried, Anna had trouble sleeping since receiving Georg's letter. There was much to think about. She'd been so busy worrying about Georg's disappearance that she'd never really thought about being his wife: Mrs. Georg Amorsen, part of a family of bankers. But now that Georg had actually proposed marriage, she wondered if, as his wife, she would embarrass him. She looked at her hands. Five years of cutting and selling codfish on the wharf in Bergen had left her hands weather-beaten and rough. Georg had never said anything about them. Maybe he didn't notice.

What would it be like to visit Georg's home? She recalled the pictures he had shown her of his home in Haderslev with rows of large wooden two-story houses. Georg had told her they were painted in a variety of colors. His green home had huge windows opening toward the street, a slate roof, a tall brick chimney, and a garden in front encased by a wrought iron fence.

He told her how Haderslev had been under the rule of Germany since 1864. Danish could not be spoken in the schools or in business. The principal building in town, the cathedral, built with beautiful baroque fittings, was their house of worship and only there could they speak Danish and practice "high church." Reverend Swensen's church was a small wooden church with seating for less than 100 parishioners; Anna didn't even know what "high church" meant.

All she wanted was a little cottage built on the side of the hill like the one she'd shared with her father, mother, and sister Gudrun. It was only one-fourth the size of Georg's home. Yet, Anna thought, how warm it was on a cold wintry night with the snow falling and the wind howling. After a day at the fish stall selling the fish Papa had caught on their *Viking Star*, it was such a snug, cozy haven.

Her anxiety continued to grow and she longed for the comfort of her family. She loved Georg and wanted to marry him, but the thought of meeting Georg's father, Soren Amorsen, *Visekonsul, Bankdirektør,* or his mother, Anna Christine Amorsen; the whole idea made her feel small and insignificant. If she only could bring her father and Gudrun to America, but there was no money for passage. What would Georg's mother think of Georg marrying a fish peddler? As daylight seeped through the shades, Anna fell asleep still grappling with her feelings of inadequacy.

"Wake up. Wake up, Anna," Lise repeated. "If you don't hurry you'll miss your bus." Lately, the young girl had taken it upon herself to be Anna's caretaker, following her around at home and practicing English with her.

Anna scrambled out of bed and gave Lise a hug, emotions from her sleepless night still in mind. I am a worker, she thought, how can I relate to the *visekonsul* and *bankdirektør*? On her way to work, she asked herself if she felt right saying "yes" to Georg without talking with someone about her own feelings. If only Georg were here; he was still waiting for her answer.

Anna arrived at work in a quandary. She walked by a display that she had designed of summer fabrics: voiles, ginghams, and cottons. With her head down, she brushed against it with her arm and the cotton bolt fell off and rolled on the floor. She perfunctorily went about resetting the display.

"Where are the linens?" a woman asked.

Anna ignored her, lost in her own thoughts. She didn't notice Mrs. Jensen, the president of the Church Circle. She always dressed in the latest fashions and had come in to purchase material for a summer dress. "Oh, Anna, Elsa told me the good news about your getting married. When will Georg return?"

Anna was in no mood to respond to Mrs. Jensen's words of cheer. "Thank you," she said, forcing a smile. "I'm afraid we haven't set a date yet."

She made a mental note to tell Elsa of her second thoughts. How could she discuss the wedding if she had doubts about marrying Georg? What if the Amorsens didn't accept her? Yet, Georg had written that he was eager to return home with his bride and "show her off."

That night, Anna reread parts of her diary to reassure herself. In it, she read the fantasy love letters she had written while waiting to hear from Georg: "Hold me tight and caress me. I see your blue eyes looking deep into mine. Can you read my mind across the ocean? I love you — always."

She picked up the pen and wrote about her feelings of being a salesman: "Which of my feelings will your family honor? Can I trust you? Olc ran away from me — will you do that?" On and on she scribbled trying to find the answer. Finally she decided to talk things over with the Swensens.

That evening, she asked Elsa and Henrik to hear her out.

"Come into the study and sit, Anna. Of course we would like to help. What is the trouble?" asked Henrik.

Anna bluntly forced out the words. "I, as you know, am a fisherman's daughter. I have worked five years selling fish on the Bergen wharf. I have had to work hard to learn to speak English and learn the dry goods trade here in America."

"You are the best salesman they have, Anna!" said Elsa.

"But my mother and father did not complete grade school, and while I went to high school, I didn't learn any job skills. You can see why I feel very inferior to Georg's family."

She couldn't go on. She started to cry, then made herself stop. "Georg wants me to marry him. He wants us to return to Denmark to visit his folks. What if they don't approve of his marrying a former fish peddler?"

Henrik reached over and took hold of her hand. "Anna, you have riches within you."

"What do you mean?"

Elsa responded carefully. "Your childhood in Bergen has built within you the love and caring that you are able to give to others. I'm sure that Georg's family will be eager to meet you and treat you like one of their family."

Henrik added, "The Lord said 'As you sow so shall you reap.' You have been a ray of sunshine and love for our family. You do fit in, Anna, you really do."

Elsa put her arm around Anna. "Look at yourself. You are the only woman dry goods salesman in Chicago, and he doesn't even know that. He proposed thinking you were still working at your first job at Hansen's. Georg will be proud to introduce you to his parents. They are so fortunate that Georg found you."

Anna's brown eyes opened wide. She twisted her handkerchief in her hands, which by now was soaking wet; she was overcome by their kind words. "Thank you, Elsa and Henrik. I've tried to do the best I can. You have such faith in me."

Elsa said, "Anna, Georg loves you. He wants you to be his wife.

He wants you to meet his folks. They love their son and respect his choice. They will love you, too."

Anna reached over and hugged Elsa. She turned to Henrik and shook his hand. "Thank you very much. You see, I have never told Georg about how I promised to marry Ole."

Henrik nodded and spoke with wisdom. "You did everything you could to find Ole. He owes you a full explanation and apology. You were never in love with Ole — he is just another insignificant part of your past. Your heart belongs to Georg. However, it would probably be wise to tell him about Ole. I'm sure he will understand."

That night Anna slept fitfully with visions of herself back on the wharf selling cod to her future in-laws. She woke up trying to erase the scene in her head. She must decide.

While combing her hair before the mirror the next morning, Anna tried brushing it up to add a bit of height and then combing it down so it fell around her shoulders. Who am I, she thought? She finally rolled it in a bun at the back of her head as she usually wore it. She looked deep into her intense brown eyes, thinking, I love you Georg. I know I can trust you. I can feel your strong arms around me. I will send you the answer today.

Chris noticed the difference in Anna when she arrived at the dry goods store. "What's going on, Anna. You look happy today."

"Georg and I are going to get married."

"Hey, Jen! Peter! Did you hear that? Our Anna's going to marry Georg."

"What's going on?" asked Peter.

"Georg and I are getting married at the end of July. You are all invited to the wedding."

"Say, when did all this happen? Did he return?"

"He sent me a letter. His father is better and he will return soon."

At lunchtime, Anna walked around the block twice thinking of what her new life would be like. I have overcome the difficulties of making a new life in America. I was able to work my way through Ole's disappearance, I learned to work in the dry goods store. I made a home with the Swensens. I can do it, she finally decided. She went to the cable office and sent a cable of five words. "Yes, I love you, too!"

Within the next week, Elsa rode with Anna to the dry goods store to select the material for her wedding dress. First, they went through page after page of Butterick patterns. Finally, Anna found the one she liked. "Look, Elsa, it has a blouson bodice over a fitted slip, nice long narrow sleeves and a natural neckline. I have a rather short neck."

"A dirndl waist with soft ribbons will add height beside Georg," said Elsa. "What do you want for a headpiece?"

"I'd like a small floral wreath. It will be more appropriate with my small veil."

"Good morning, ladies," greeted Mr. Hansen as he came out of his office.

"My friend Mrs. Swensen is helping me select the material for my wedding gown."

"Congratulations, Anna, I just heard the news. Take a ten percent discount on whatever you buy."

Unlike his usual blustery self, Mr. Hansen joined them as they looked through the fabrics. "What about chiffon or organdy?" asked Elsa.

"No, I think I like that roll of ivory satin. Here let me hold it up and you can see how it looks, Elsa," she said, draping the smooth material across her body. It brought an image of herself walking down the aisle. To be married — it seemed a dream.

Mr. Hansen looked at Anna holding the satin. "Anna, make that a twenty percent discount," he blurted. "You'll drum up a lot of business."

Elsa started sewing the bridal gown within the next week. Each evening, when Anna came home from work, Elsa would fit the gown on her. "Oh, it is beautiful, Elsa. It gives me such a feeling of elegance. I may only be five feet tall but your design and the fabric does make me look taller."

When Elsa finished with the gown, Anna took it into her room where she could admire it daily. One night, however, she had a horrible dream of marching down the aisle with Ole. Anna awoke with a start. What if Ole should return and now claim her for his bride? She shook all over recalling the days of loneliness spent hoping he would find her, but now she shook with fear. What if he appeared? He was the last person she wanted to see.

She remembered how close her body and Georg's were that day in the park when he kissed her in the rowboat. His kisses had seemed like sweet drops of dew, his long arms and legs enwrapping her. It was a warm sensuous feeling; she hungered for more.

Georg wrote he had booked passage and would arrive on the 30th of July. Anna wished away the days in her eagerness for the wedding. Her worrying over acceptance in the Amorsen family had almost disappeared. If only Georg would arrive sooner.

Hans and Lise were having an exciting time preparing for the wedding. Hans was chosen to be the ring bearer but fought having to wear the long pants suit his mother was making for him. "Do I have to wear this in the wedding?"

Elsa scowled. "Hans, we all are getting dressed up for Anna's wedding. You can't wear summer knickers."

Lise enjoyed every moment of being fitted with a new dress. "I can swirl my skirt. Do I look like a ballet dancer?"

Anna smiled, "Lise, you'll be a perfect ballet dancer."

Elsa not only sewed their wedding apparel, but in cooperation with Mrs. Jensen, organized the Ladies Auxiliary of the church to prepare the wedding smorgasbord. All the church members were invited to the wedding.

"Anna, unlike our Christmas Eve dinner, guests expect to sit for three or four hours enjoying the wedding dinner."

"Are the Circles preparing all the dishes?"

"Yes, they are happy to join in the celebration. The Sigurd Nelsons, who own the local bakery, are making the wedding cake as their gift to you and Georg. It will have white icing, many layers, and a cascade of flowers as the crowning delight."

"Elsa, what more can I do to help you? This sounds like a tremendous amount of work."

"Anna, you are part of our family. We want you to have a beautiful wedding. It is our gift to you. We'll do the same for Lise someday."

The day before Georg arrived, the Circles gave Anna a wedding shower. They held it as a surprise party at Mrs. Jensen's large home which was decorated with white wedding bells and summer flowers. Elsa took Anna over on the pretext of borrowing some dishes. They walked into the house and there were the women with a huge heart-shaped cake with the words "Georg and Anna" inscribed.

The young woman could hardly talk. "Thank you all so very much. I hope you all plan on coming to our wedding."

Mrs. Jensen spoke up. "We made a few useful gifts to get you started. The twenty women sitting in this room are delighted to welcome you to our Circle Group. Now, do open the packages."

Anna was nearly in tears of joy as she started to open the many gifts. She thought of the times Mrs. Jensen had seemed a little snobbish but now realized she had been really greeting her in her own way. Anna was overcome by the kindnesses of the women of the church. Finally, it was time to cut the cake and visit with her new friends. She had met many of them at the dry goods store as well as church. They really liked her and wanted to be her friend. Later, she stood by the door as they left saying, *"Mange takk!* Thank you. I thank each and every one of you. Do come to the wedding."

At last the day came for Georg to arrive. The Swensens and other church members joined Anna as she anxiously waited for him at the train station. When she finally heard the train's whistle, she thought of her arrival at the Chicago station expecting to see Ole. What if it happened again? What if Georg didn't arrive? The train gradually came into sight and slowly ground to a halt. She felt faint. Pull yourself together, she thought. It seemed as if an eternity passed while she searched for Georg's face. Finally she saw him. "I see him. The second car. He's standing on the steps waving." She was jumping up and down. Everything was going to be all right.

The train was still moving when Georg jumped off, raced toward her, and picked her up. "Oh, Anna, I love you. It's been so long." He gave her a big hug and kissed her repeatedly before putting her down. Anna didn't want to let go. Clinging to him, she whispered, "I have waited so long for this day." She stood on tiptoes and kissed him again. Neither noticed the others around them.

Finally, Henrik couldn't wait any longer. "Congratulations, Georg," he said, interrupting the couple. "Thank you for your invitation to perform the wedding ceremony."

Elsa gave Georg a hug. "We've all missed you, particularly our Anna. Welcome home."

Hans and Lise grabbed hands and danced around him reciting, *"De er velkommen."*

Soon they were on their way to the parsonage. The Jensen's invited Georg to stay with them. The wedding was to be held the next afternoon.

Georg and Anna spent the rest of the day catching up on their lives and making arrangements to rent a small flat in Georg's former building. At one point, he confided some important news. "Anna, I promised my family I would return to Denmark with you. We'll leave within three months or as soon as we can afford passage on the *Helga.*"

She wasn't sure if she should share with him her concerns. Finally she said, "Georg, I'm worried about how I will fit in with your family."

"Anna, they are eager to meet you. They are so excited to add a daughter-in-law. My mother and father have fixed up one of the upstairs rooms for us."

"But they don't know me."

"Yes they do. I told them about the good times we had together and all the fun we had at your Christmas celebration. They thought I would never marry, but I was just waiting for you, my beautiful *Norska*."

She gave him a big hug and sighed with relief. "Yes, my wonderful Georg. I will always be your *Norska*."

The parsonage was awhirl on the wedding day. Parishioners arrived with delicious foods for the smorgasbord. Small tables covered with light blue and pink cloths were put up in the rear garden. Flowers were tied to the lower tree branches, and a single red rose was put in a vase on each of the tables. In the backyard, a large table was covered with a white tablecloth and was already filled with wedding gifts. Inside, the dining room table was loaded with food.

Henrik preached his regular sermon at eleven o'clock and concluded by saying, "You are all invited to join us in the wedding celebration at two o'clock. Please take care not to knock the flowers from the pews."

Hans and Lise were eager to put on their new clothes and prance around the house. "Lise, my dear girl, will you marry me?" asked Hans as he brought his sister a pillow on which he had placed a dead snail. Lise responded by offering Hans a posy. "Here you are, my good man, a real flower for the wedding." She gave him a raw onion she had pulled from their garden.

Elsa rushed around attending to last-minute details for the wedding while church members trekked in and out of her kitchen bringing food or preparing more. Ushers set up chairs for the reception in the garden area.

Anna sat in her room hearing the turmoil all around her while she arranged and rearranged her curly auburn hair to fit the flower crown. She looked in the mirror at her wedding dress and thought, I do look beautiful. I am worthy of Georg and he will be a good husband. Don't ever start belittling yourself again. She whirled around to take a full view of the wedding dress Elsa had made with its beautiful lace bodice, full circular skirt, and long train. Anna closed her eyes for a minute and said a little prayer. "Thank you, God, for the strength, courage, and perseverance you have given me. I'll be faithful to Georg forevermore."

Before two o'clock, the church was filled. The white satin bows, colorful flowers, and green ferns added a festive air to the rather plain wooden interior. Hans and Lise, dressed in their new outfits, were eagerly waiting in the foyer. "I wish they'd hurry up," said Hans. "If I lose the rings, they can't get married!"

Anna walked across from the parsonage in her resplendent hand-sewn wedding gown. She carried the train under her arm until she entered the foyer. Elsa had found time to sew herself a new dress and looked young and happy as she waited for Mr. Jensen to escort Anna down the aisle.

The organist played the first chord of Wagner's wedding march. The congregation stood and Lise, in her sparkling white voile dress, new white slippers, and a bouquet of flowers, marched toward the pulpit. Hans, in his long blue pants and jacket to match, carefully balanced the pillow with the ring case. Elsa, serving as Anna's matron of honor, entered.

Then, Anna and Mr. Jensen walked in together. The congregation "oohed" and "aahed" at the beautiful bride and the Swensen children. Anna held her breath as she got close to the altar. Where was Georg? Did he change his mind? There he was. He entered through the side door looking majestic in his carefully tailored striped pants and dark blue coat with a white bow tie and a little white rose on his lapel. Anna thought he looked as distinguished as a *visekonsul*, although she had never met or seen one.

As they came together in front of the altar, Georg gave Anna a wink as if to say, "It won't be long."

Henrik stepped forward to begin the ceremony. "Today is a very special gathering. Anna Marie Steffensen and Georg Quist Amorsen have found each other and have determined to share with one another their future lives."

He then opened his Bible and slowly read the ceremony. When done, he had Georg repeat, "I take you, Anna, to be the wife of my days, mother of my children, and companion of my home." Anna repeated. "I take you, Georg, to be the husband of my days, father of my children, and companion of my home."

Hans offered the rings to his father. "Take these rings," said Henrik. "These wedding rings are a visible sign of love and symbolize your union for life, a symbol of unity — lives joined in one unbroken circle." After putting on the rings, Henrik pronounced Georg and Anna man and wife.

Georg gently lifted Anna's veil, kissed her, and whispered, "I love you."

Anna felt his strong arm around her. She closed her eyes as he kissed her and brought herself closer. The words "father of my children" echoed in her mind. She visualized herself pushing a little Georg Junior in his baby buggy.

Later, a photographer took pictures of the wedding party; each picture was marked by a big flash and puff of smoke. "Wait so we can get a little closer!" Georg told the man behind the camera. Anna beamed.

She was too nervous to sit down and eat. "Georg, let's just walk around and talk to the guests. I don't know all of them, but I'm sure they know us."

"By now I do believe your whole neighborhood knows of our wedding. I really think they are all here. I wonder why Mr. Hansen and his wife came."

"I invited them, Georg. I have only one regret and that is that our families could not be at our wedding."

"Soon we'll be visiting our folks. We'll bring them some photographs. I wonder what science will think of next."

The garden scene outside the church was one of joy. "Look at all the little children excited and happy," said Anna.

Georg leaned over and whispered in Anna's ear. "We'll have our own children someday."

"I can hardly wait. During the ceremony, I had a picture of little Georg in his buggy!"

The couple went over to the Swensens. Elsa greeted Georg with a hug. "You are taking our Anna away, but we couldn't have asked for a better husband."

"Elsa and Henrik, thank you for this lovely wedding," Anna said. "We want your family to visit us."

Georg smiled. "As soon as we settle in our new flat, we'll invite you to dinner. Anna is such a wonderful cook."

Chapter Ten

The Visitor

Anna awoke as the sun streamed through the window into their small, dingy bedroom. It was their first morning together in their small flat — the same building where Georg had lived when they met. She looked around their apartment. No, it wasn't a fantasy, she thought. It was real. There was Georg, her own husband, beside her — yawning, stretching his arms, and reaching for her.

"Come over here, my *Norska*," Georg said, pressing his body against her and kissing her tenderly on the mouth. She could feel the excitement and passion of their wedding night returning. Suddenly there was a loud sound of tramping boots out in the hallway. Anna stiffened. "What's that?"

"Don't bother about them," Georg said. "They're just part of the street crew going to work. They have a flat upstairs and like to wake up everybody."

"What time is it?" she asked.

"Time for some coffee?" he said, giving her a quick kiss on the cheek and heading for the kitchen.

She put on her robe and threaded her way through the boxes and their clothes tossed about the room. Her wedding dress was half falling off the bureau. She picked it up and held it before her and tried to dance around the boxes. She sang the song her mother sang when she was small.

"Den lille Ole med paraplyen, han kjenner alle småfolk i byen."

Without her noticing, Georg had maneuvered himself to where he could see her dancing and singing and holding her wedding dress up against herself. A warm smile lit his face and he tiptoed back into the kitchen. "What are you doing in there?" he called. "I found the coffee. Want a cup?"

"I'm coming. I'll be there in a minute." She hurried to the bathroom, dashed water on her face, combed her hair, and looked in the mirror. A smiling face greeted her. "I love him. I love him," she said to the mirror, and continued her song.

As she tried to walk through the living room strewn with paper, boxes, wedding gifts, and flowers, she grimaced at the dark green sofa and the two high-backed chairs loaded with unpacked clothes. Through two windows, the sunlight shone on the barren walls and dull brown carpeting. This place is ugly, she thought. I wonder what I can do to brighten it up?

As she looked at all the gifts, she remembered the many friends from Hansen's store and the church who had come to the wedding. How lucky she was to have met the Swensens. A twinge of sadness swept through her mind as she thought about her father and sister. Maybe they could visit Bergen after they visited Georg's home in Haderslev.

"Come on, Anna," called Georg. "We can open the other presents after breakfast. Want a muffin?"

By noon, they had opened their presents from their friends and co-workers: Chris, Jen, Peter, Olga, and Mr. Hansen. Anna guessed, "I'll bet he sent us a bolt of cloth — see, here it is. What a pretty yellow color with daisies on it, just right for a tablecloth or curtains. I'm glad he offered you a job. When do you think we'll go to Denmark?"

"We'll have to work for two months to pay for our passage. My father has offered to buy our tickets, but we'll work for them. I'll tell Mr. Hansen of our plans. I wouldn't want to take the job without being honest."

"Mr. Hansen sure has been nice to us," she said, glad she never told anyone about her troubles with him. "What are we going to do with all this stuff and all this food? Our friends were so generous."

"Give it away? Storage? I don't know."

"My dear husband, you're going to help write all these thank you notes, aren't you?"

Georg groaned. "Enough of that." He picked her up and carried her toward the bedroom. "We have more important things to discuss right now."

Olga and all the other workers were at the entrance to the store when Anna and Georg walked in on Wednesday morning. Streamers reading "Congratulations," "Happy Day," and "Welcome Back" hung in plain view. The whole staff sang "Here Comes the Bride."

Later, Georg explained their plans to Mr. Hansen who said he wanted Georg to begin work anyway. That would give him a chance to give some of the other staff some well-deserved vacations before the newlyweds left for Denmark. On this happy note, everyone quickly adjusted to their positions. Anna served most of the women searching for patterns and dress materials while Georg filled in wherever needed.

Soon, the new couple had settled into a routine. They finished writing their thank you notes and packaged the wedding gifts they planned to leave in storage. Anna brightened up the flat with the daisy curtains and tablecloth she had sewn.

Finally, they were ready for the promised dinner party for the Swensens. Anna knew she couldn't match Elsa's expertise; she prepared roast chicken, mashed potatoes with creamed carrots, and cabbage. Georg asked to bake the cake.

"Whenever did you learn to make a cake?"

"I used to help my mother, I know what I'm doing. You'll see."

Anna put the new tablecloth on their one table, moved it into the living room, and found a few yellow flowers on the bush outside to brighten up the room.

Georg, after much stirring, placed the cake in the oven. "Just wait until you eat this. It's my mother's recipe. I hear them on the steps. Help me take off my apron, quick."

Anna had her mind elsewhere. She ran to the door and beamed as the family walked up the stairs. She hugged Elsa and Lise and shook hands with Henrik and Hans.

Georg came in from the kitchen, wiping his hands on the apron. He shook hands with everyone. "Welcome to our small home. I hope all of you will be comfortable."

"You've really brightened it up," said Elsa.

"It's only temporary," said Georg. "We hope to go to Denmark and visit my folks in a few months."

"We're trying out our first dinner party on you," said Anna. "I hope you don't mind. The chicken will be done any minute."

"Going back to Denmark, eh?" said Henrik. "I hope you won't forget your old friends. We want you to come home to us when you come back."

"Thank you very much," said Georg, forgetting about his cake. "We'll plan on doing that very thing."

The dinner was a success except for the cake; it turned out a bit lopsided. Georg, a little chagrined, said, "Let's have our coffee now and wait a bit for the cake to cool off."

Anna and Lise cleared the table. Then Anna took Elsa into the bedroom to show her some of the wedding presents. Suddenly, there was a heavy knock on the door, then another. Georg looked surprised as few knew their address. Perhaps it was the street boys again. He opened the door.

In front of him stood a weather-beaten man about six feet four inches tall with a rough stubble on his face, a seaman's knit cap on his head, and a satchel in his hand. His trousers were wrinkled and his sea jacket had a tear in the sleeve. In a gruff voice he demanded, "I want to talk to Anna Steffensen."

Georg scowled. Who was this disorderly person requesting to see his wife? "Please give me your name and I'll get her."

"Oh no, you won't. I want her right now. My name is Ole Ludeman. She promised to be my wife. I've looked everywhere for her. If it hadn't been for that Jantzen at the Mission, I would never have found her."

Georg was beginning to get angry. "You are mistaken. Anna Steffensen is now Anna Amorsen. I'm Georg Amorsen. She is my wife. Please leave us alone."

"Out of my way, I must see Anna," said Ole, trying to push Georg aside. Georg blocked his way and kept him out.

The loud voices brought Anna. "What's the matter, Georg?"

"Oh, this fellow is all mixed up. He thinks you're to be his bride."

Anna felt faint. It couldn't be Ole. They had given him up for dead. She didn't want to go to the door. Her knees were weak. What could she say? Could it really be Ole after all this time? She steadied herself by the sofa and walked to the door.

The man didn't look at all like the fisherman who had worked on the *Viking Star*. "I hardly know you. Are you the Ole who was supposed to meet me?"

Ole stared at her. "You're prettier than I dreamed. Of course you know me. You took my money to get here."

Anna couldn't think of what to say. "Ole," she finally stuttered, "I'd like you to meet my husband Georg."

The visitor ignored Georg. "You can't marry anyone else. You were promised to me."

Anna's mind was awhirl. "Won't you please come inside and have a cup of coffee or a piece of cake. We were just having a little dinner party. You can tell us where you've been."

Clutching his satchel, Ole stepped into the room. Henrik Swensen stood up. Anna introduced Ole to her pastor. The clergyman shook Ole's gnarled hand. "We searched everywhere for you when you didn't meet Anna."

Anna was still trying to figure out what to do. "This is Elsa Swensen and the Swensen children, Lise and Hans."

"*Ya*," said Ole. "I knew from my folks that Anna was connected to that church somehow."

"Do sit down, Mr. Ludeman," offered Georg, looking confused. "Anna will bring you a cup of coffee and a slice of cake."

Anna went into the kitchen. Her stomach had tightened into a knot and she leaned on the sink. It was Ole all right, but he looked older, more weary than in the days when he worked on her father's boat. Why did she ever accept those tickets for passage to America and promise to marry him?

Anna took a drink of water. Then, she poured a cup of coffee and cut a piece of cake for Ole. She berated herself for never having told Georg about Ole. What must he be thinking of me? She forced herself to go back into the living room. It was time to face Ole with the truth.

"Here's your coffee and cake," she said. "Tell us what happened to you, Ole. Pastor Swensen and I searched all over this town for you when you didn't meet me at the train station."

Mouth stuffed with cake and spilling coffee on his faded shirt, Ole sat down. The fragrance of the coffee and cake was overwhelmed by the smell of mildew and fish from his clothes. "I'll admit I was fired from the stockyard job," he began. "Goddamn place treated us like slaves. I couldn't find new work. There was no way I could meet my room rent, buy a ring or a suit, or do justice to our wedding. I just had to get away.

"An Alaskan fishing company was recruiting Norwegians. I applied and was hired. They sent me to Valdez where we went after herring and salmon in season. I took the job to earn enough for us to live on. Unfortunately, we were promised more than we received. I started gambling. After a year, I had barely enough to return to Chicago, but I did and I've been looking for you ever since."

Anna reached out to his calloused hand. "Ole, the Swensen family took me in. I too had no money and no job. I couldn't speak English and was without job skills."

"Why didn't you save your wages?" asked Georg.

"I wagered on the catch, but I just wasn't lucky."

"Why didn't you write?" asked Anna.

"I expected to earn enough to come back to you."

"Why did you think you could marry me now?"

"You promised. You accepted the money to come here."

"Yes, but we spent weeks and months searching for you. I wrote my father and yours, but no one knew where you were. We thought you had been killed."

"You still owe me for the passage money."

Georg paced the floor. This conversation was beginning to get on his nerves.

"Why do you think that? I tried to meet my part of the arrangement," Anna replied.

The Swensen family sat in tense silence.

Georg held up his hand. "Please! Mr. Ludeman. We were having a nice dinner party until you arrived. Anna and I are married. This is our home. Please get out!"

"Like hell I will," barked Ole. "She promised me. She owes me the money."

"Ole, that was a long time ago," said Anna. "Your claim is not valid now."

"Oh, yes it is. I'll go to the magistrate and get my money back one way or the other."

Georg was getting angrier. He wanted to throw the visitor down the stairs. While he had never heard of Ole, he was firm in his love for and faith in Anna. "Get out, Mr. Ludeman, I tell you. We've had enough of this!"

"If I have to leave here without the money due me, I'll get even with you both," Ole shouted.

Henrik stood and looked into Ole's eyes. "Why do you want to hurt Anna and Georg so much if you love her? Maybe we can work out a way to help you."

"I want it right now! No foolin' around."

"We don't have the money to pay you," Georg answered.

"When can you get it?" Ole sat like a block of cement.

Georg angrily said, "Stop harassing us and threatening us. Get out of our home or I'll put you out!"

Ole stood up ready to fight. He looked as angry as a wild bull. Georg took his arm and pushed him toward the door. Ole swung his satchel at Georg but missed. Pastor Swensen opened the door and Georg shoved him out on the porch.

"I'll get you if it's the last thing I do," bellowed a red-faced Ole. He slammed the door so hard the curtain fell down. Everyone could hear his heavy footsteps going down the stairs.

The Swensens and Anna sat in stunned silence while Georg stood, watching through the window as Ole walked away. Anna's hands were shaking, her face ashen with tears welling up. "Georg," she began in a quivering voice, "I'm so sorry about this. It's all my fault. I wanted to get to America so badly I accepted Ole's written offer of marriage and passage. We barely knew each other in Bergen. On the boat from Norway, I met the Swensens. They were coming to Chicago as well. When we arrived, there was no Ole. Please forgive me."

Georg paced the floor.

Henrik added, "We took Anna into our home. We searched and phoned everywhere, but there were no clues to Ole's whereabouts. We all know the agony and hurt she went through."

"Anna helped care for our children," Elsa said, "and finally found a job in the dry goods store where you two met."

Georg kept pacing, arms behind his back.

Anna's tears crept down her face as she realized Ole's intense anger and her own regret in withholding the story from Georg. She felt ashamed that she had arrived in America to get out of being a fish lady.

The room was silent except for Georg's pacing. "Anna," he said finally, "did you sign a contract with Ole?"

"No. He wrote my father. He worked on my father's fishing boat, but I hardly knew him. We never had a single date. When his letter came, my father suggested I go and visit his family. They convinced me and I wrote accepting his offer. He had already sent the tickets when he wrote my father."

Georg nodded and stared out the window.

"I was so lucky to meet the Swensens," she said. "I would have been completely lost without them."

Henrik nodded. "It was lucky for all of us. We have been greatly blessed by Anna's presence our household."

"Georg," Anna pleaded, "I should have told you, but my past was very painful for me. I couldn't get myself to tell you about it. That was a big mistake. I'm so sorry."

Georg walked over to Anna and sat beside her. He then put his arm around her. "Dearest," he said, drawing her to him, "do not blame yourself. I love you. We'll just have to reach an agreement with Ole, whether we want to or not."

"Yes," said Elsa, "I think that is the best solution. Ole is serious. He might become violent."

"I will write his family," Anna said, "and ask for his address. They should know if he has one."

Georg took a deep breath and stared at the floor. He churned over in his mind the fact that he and Anna would have to work at least three extra months, depending upon the amount of their bonuses, in order to purchase three passages to Bergen or Haderslev. A gloom descended upon both families. The festive occasion had been burst like a balloon. The children sat wide-eyed, still shaken by Ole's threats.

"Would anyone like another cup of coffee or piece of cake?" Anna asked, trying to capture the earlier mood.

"No, thank you, Anna," Elsa said. "It is time we go home. Don't worry, dear, we'll work out a way to help. Thank you for the delicious dinner. You're both wonderful cooks."

Henrik shook Georg's hand. "You are a lovely couple. Don't let this intrusion upset you. Anna and I did all we could to locate Ole. Unfortunately, the man sounds desperate. The sooner you can work out a solution with him, the better. Would Mr. Hansen advance your wages for a month?"

Georg grasped the cleric's hand. "Henrik, you are a true friend. Thank you for your advice and help to Anna. I love her no matter what happened in the past."

Lise and Hans ran over and put their arms around Anna. "We love you, Anna. Don't let that bad man in."

As they waved goodbye to the Swensens, Georg and Anna stood arm in arm on the porch steps. Just as they shut the front door and locked it, something crashed through the front window. Shards of glass flew in every direction. Georg pushed Anna into a corner of the kitchen. A big rock lay on the living room floor, and big chunks of glass covered the couch where they'd been sitting until just a few minutes before.

"Georg, I'm scared. He could have killed us."

"That fool is already carrying out his threat. He's blackmailing us, that's what he's doing," said Georg.

Before leaving for work next day, Anna and Georg double-checked the locks and boarded up the windows. They hoped their security would be enough to keep Ole out. As they walked to work, both wondered if Ole would throw rocks at them. Once there, Georg went directly to Mr. Hansen's office with great trepidation in his mind. "May I come in, Mr. Hansen?"

"Yes, Georg, sit down."

"We've run into some unusual expenses which we have to meet. I'm here to ask for a loan against my wages."

"A loan? You've hardly started back to work. What for?"

"We need enough for a ticket to Bergen."

"Is Anna going home?"

"Oh, no. We promised a ticket to an individual, and he wants it right now."

"I see," said Mr. Hansen, studying the younger man. "Can I depend upon you to stay here till it's repaid?"

"Yes, sir."

"I'll think it over. See me at the end of the day."

Georg left the office with a heavy heart. He winked at Anna when he walked by the Butterick patterns, but felt discouraged. That night, they sat at the kitchen table, figuring a way to survive for a month on a very limited income.

"Georg, I don't see how we can do it."

"We'll have to sell some wedding presents. I have a small amount in my bonus account, but it won't meet all our needs."

"How will we find Ole?" Anna worried. "You think the church janitor may have his address? Can you go see the janitor after work tomorrow? I'll write the Ludemans tonight."

"I'll go right after work tomorrow. Let's hope we find him before he does more harm. We'll have to call the police."

The following day Anna walked home alone. Sunset hadn't come yet and she hurried to get to the flat while there was still daylight. Georg had taken the cable car to meet with the church janitor. With shaking hands, she unlocked the front door to their flat, entered, and quickly relocked the door. She didn't notice the unlatched window.

As she crossed the room and went into the bedroom, she stopped with a gasp. All of their presents, both those packaged for storage and the ones stacked in the corner, lay scattered throughout the room. Some had been torn apart; others were untouched, but strewn across the floor.

Nervously, she checked the closet and bathroom. No one else was there. She saw the open window in the living room and unsuccessfully tried to lock it. The damaged hardware was dangling from the frame where it had been pried off. Finally, she pulled a chair to the protected corner of the flat and huddled there in the growing darkness, tears flowing while her mind raced through recent events.

You should never have accepted Ole's offer, she told herself. But then you wouldn't have met Georg.

With trembling hands, she twisted her handkerchief and dabbed her eyes. What if Ole forced his way into the flat right now? If only she had told Georg the whole story before all this happened. "Oh Georg, please hurry home. I'm so sorry."

Another hour passed before Georg returned. He knocked on the door. "Anna, turn on the light. Are you there? Open the door, please. What's happened?"

She rushed to the door, unlocked it, and fell into Georg's arms, weeping out of control. When finally she calmed down, he could see what had happened. "Oh, Anna, my darling," he said. "I should never have left you. I'm so sorry."

"Georg, we're going to have to get away, somehow."

Georg nodded his agreement. "I've been thinking about that on the way home. My family has been wanting to see you. Instead of waiting the two months, I'll wire my father for a loan."

"What about Mr. Hansen? He's been so good to us. We can't walk out on him."

"You're right, but our lives are in danger. I hate walking out on him, but we have no choice."

"How will we pay off Ole?"

"Mr. Hansen owes me a bonus I didn't take when I left so unexpectedly last January. I'll give it to the Swensens and have them purchase a ticket for Ole as far as the money will take him. When he discovers we're gone, he'll go see the Swensens."

"Will your father cable you the money?"

"Yes. I've always paid my debts to my father, although I've only borrowed in an emergency. This is an emergency."

Georg made reservations on the first ship to Frankfurt, then went to explain the situation to Mr. Hansen. A deep scowl furrowed his forehead as Georg shared the details of Ole's terror against them. "When are you returning?" Hansen asked when Georg had finally finished.

"I'm not sure," Georg said, "but we can't ask you to hold our jobs. This is an emergency and we feel badly about having to leave on such short notice. You've been extremely good to both Anna and me, but our ship leaves in a week." He sighed. "For our own safety we just have to leave. We both want to thank you, Mr. Hansen, for the wonderful opportunity you gave us by allowing us to work in your dry goods store. We will always remember you."

Hansen scratched his head, still staring downstairs. "You sure haven't given me much time. However, I do owe you a bonus and Anna, too. I'll have your final check ready within the week." The two men shook hands.

Georg told Anna the good news as he returned to the floor. "He is a shrewd boss, but he promised us our bonuses. We'll most likely have enough to pay off Ole. I'm buying his ticket as soon as we receive the bonus. Pastor Swensen will give Ole the ticket."

Within a week, they had boxed the bulky wedding gifts, stored them at the Swensens, and cleaned up the dingy flat. They bid goodbye to their upstairs friends, "the street boys," who stood guard over them until they left.

Many goodbyes and hugs and tears enveloped Anna and Georg on the day of their departure from the train station. Elsa insisted they promise to return to Chicago. The children clung to Anna's hands. Olga and some of the clerks took time off to say goodbye to the couple at the train station. Many church members came carrying flowers and signs that implored Anna and Georg to return to Chicago.

They waved to the crowd as the sound of the train came closer. Tears ran down Anna's face and she hugged Elsa while the train hissed to a stop. "I'll always think of you," she said the Swensens. "You've been my dearest friends. I love you all."

Quickly, their luggage was loaded. Anna and Georg stood in the rear of the train, waving to their many friends as the train lurched and bellowed out of the station. As the giant machine built up steam and moved away, Anna recalled her first trip to the Chicago station with the Swensens just a few short years ago. She hadn't been able to speak English, had no money or American work skills, and didn't know anyone except the Swensens.

Look at all these wonderful people, she thought. You didn't get this kind of a send-off when you left Norway. What a wonderful place America is. If only Ole hadn't messed things up. It's really your own fault though, Anna; you should have told Georg about Ole before you got married. Now you've got to go to Denmark to try to find a home. Anna, how could you have been so shortsighted? That's not what Mama would have done.

As the train station faded into the distance, tears still streamed down Anna's face. Georg pulled her close and kissed the dampness on her cheeks. "It's going to be all right, my *Norska*," he whispered. "We are Vikings and the north wind makes us strong. Our journey has just begun."

Chapter Eleven

Denmark

For the newlyweds, the trip to Denmark aboard the *North Star* became their honeymoon. Anna tried to sleep late each morning, but still found herself waking at first dawn — her habit of getting up early was hard to break. One night, she dreamed the ship never docked. She saw herself and Georg spending the rest of their lives in an idyllic wonderland, laughing, eating, dancing, and making love all day long. When she awoke, she pondered the meaning of the dream: maybe she was still afraid to meet Georg's parents.

One day, Anna noticed the sea was getting rough. She tied a neckerchief around her curly brown hair and put on her heavy winter coat. "Come on, Georg," she said, taking his hand, "let's go for a walk. I love this kind of weather."

On deck, the ship pitched and rolled before the swirling seas. Georg put his arm around her. "These waves are getting too dangerous," he yelled above the howling wind. "We're running into a storm. Let's go into the lounge." A wave crashed into one side of the ship; the impact threw them against the bulkhead. Anna remembered her trip to America with the Swensens, but now she felt safe with her husband.

"Georg," she shouted, "this wind and the rolling of the ship bring back memories of fishing with my father. When I was little, he would take me along and tie me to the masthead. He gave me a stick and a little string and I'd pretend I was fishing."

"This is no place for memories," he said. "Come, Anna — it's too rough out here. Let's go inside."

Anna clung to Georg's arm. The roar of the waves made conversation almost impossible. They huddled against the bulkhead. "Come inside, Anna! It's too risky out here." He tried to pull her toward the door, but Anna felt exhilarated. She was a Viking woman going through a hurricane.

Georg forcefully pulled her toward him. "Come, dearest," he said, struggling to open the door against the wind. Finally, he got the door open, but only with Anna's help. Inside, she removed her neckerchief and directly walked across the lounge to the bookshelf. She picked up a book entitled *Tivoli Gardens: Twenty-five Years.*

Georg stroked his beard and cocked his head with puzzlement.

"Ever since I was in grade school," she said, "I've dreamed about going to the Tivoli. It's the first place I want to visit in Copenhagen. I want you to tell me all about it."

Together, they looked through the library and found several guides on seeing Denmark. Georg pointed out that the train trip ahead from Hamburg to Copenhagen passed through the flat farm lands of his native country. "It is a very pretty trip, quite different from the mountains and *fjords* of Norway."

Their remaining days aboard ship were filled with happiness. When the seas became calmer, Georg taught Anna to play shuffleboard. "Lean into the stroke, Anna," he'd call out when she pushed the disc toward the target.

Anna would laugh because she did so poorly in the beginning, but she kept practicing. By the time they arrived in Hamburg, she actually had beaten George once or twice. He noticed how intense her big brown eyes became during their matches, and how loving and warm afterwards, especially when she won.

En route to Copenhagen through the green fields of lower Jutland, Anna spent her time staring out the window and comparing these rolling flatlands to the high peaks of Norway. The farm houses were made of warm, red bricks or white plaster with thatched roofs that overhung the edges. At times, they flashed by tall, red brick and sandstone churches with green verdigris on their copper roofs. She saw Jersey and Holstein cows in the fields of the dairy farms while the vanes of the windmills whirled from the wind blowing in from the ocean. In some fields, the crops looked ready for the fall harvest.

Something puzzled her. "Why are there big nests up on top of so many of the farm houses?" she asked. "Many are built on top of the chimney."

"Those are nests the storks build. According to folk tales, storks also deliver newborn babies."

Anna began counting the nests. She wondered if she and Georg would need a stork nest in their future home. Later, she imagined herself in their small compartment on the train, holding a baby as they traveled north. Finally, she grew restless and tried to encourage

Georg to get off for a minute or two when the train stopped at each little station, but he wasn't interested.

She decided to do it by herself. She would stand in the vestibule whenever the train stopped and she would peek out at the far horizons. She loved feeling the wind blow sand against her face and inhaling the fresh earth and pungent animal smells from the barnyards.

Anna stared in awe and fear at the burly, uniformed German soldiers guarding each station while a German flag flapped overhead. More and more, she became aware of the military on the roads. I hope my papers are in order, she told herself. She was beginning to feel uncomfortable because she was so accustomed to the many freedoms of America and Norway.

Once in Copenhagen's Central Station though, she forgot all about that. She hurried them across *Bernstorffsgade* to a small hotel where Georg had reserved a room. She insisted that their unpacking be delayed until they read the Danish newspaper *Aktuelt* which included Tivoli's schedule

"I found it," she exclaimed. "The main events occur in the late afternoon and evening. The *Commedia Dell'Arte* theatre will have mimes and dances of *Harlequin*, *Columbine*, and *Pierrot*. And they're opening the dance hall!"

"Anna, I found something better. The *Belle Terrasse* faces the Tivoli lake and offers lobster and chicken."

"We'll do both!" they said together.

And they did, and much more. At first they just walked around, admiring the crowds and their bright festive clothes. Something caught Georg's eye.

"Let's follow this path over to the lake. Look, they have rowboats, and there must be over one hundred paper lanterns around the lake."

"Do you want to take me for a ride in a rowboat like you used to at the Humboldt Lagoon?"

"You're just teasing me because I kissed you while kneeling in the boat and nearly tipped us over."

She laughed.

In the distance, they could see and hear the riders on the high roller coaster. Right beside the merry-go-round, an organ was pumping out a Danish March. The sounds echoed and became louder off the lake. Anna was getting more excited. Soon, they found a restaurant and had their delicious dinner. As they were leaving, her eyes lit up.

"I hear a dance band." There was a pavilion filled with dancers. They were playing "*The Borghild Reinlaender*" a Norwegian

Schottish. "Come on, Georg," she said, taking his hand, "let's go dancing. Remember our first date at the Danish Lodge Dance?"

"I'll always remember that night. We danced until dawn."

They walked to the pavilion and elbowed their way into the crowd. By the time they got there, the band was playing a rollicking *Hambo* with arms and feet getting in everyone's way. "This is too rough, Anna."

She just smiled. "We are Vikings. This is nothing."

After dancing, they went to the Little Mime Theatre, the shooting gallery, and the Casino. Georg played Blackjack a few times, but he rarely beat the dealer. When he did, he reluctantly gave Anna the small change. Later, they went back to the lake and sat at a table lit from above with colored paper lanterns. They provided an oriental effect.

"Isn't this romantic, Georg?"

He had a long face. "Sitting outdoors on a hard bench in the wind isn't my idea of romance."

She walked around the table and sat beside him. "Here's a kiss, you sad little boy. Look at all the children jumping and rolling on the lawn. They are full of laughter and fun."

Georg gave Anna a big hug. "It just makes me angry to be so short of cash. I love you, my *Norska*, and I'm embarrassed I don't have more money to spend on you."

A huge boom echoed across the lake and deafened their ears for a moment. Anna sprang to her feet thinking the German military was shooting.

Georg laughed, "Those are just the fireworks, Anna. Move out to the lawn and we can see better."

Stars, rockets, and circling fire flames filled the sky. All the crowd stared upwards.

"The fireworks mean Tivoli Gardens are closing," warned Georg. "Here comes the final rocket. Hold your ears!"

The crowds slowly thinned. Georg and Anna walked back to the hotel hand in hand. It had been a marvelous evening.

Next morning at breakfast, Anna could see Georg had something on his mind. "Here's a nice place to sit," he said as they walked down the street. "I want to talk to you."

They sat down. She had an idea of what was on his mind.

"I've been thinking, Anna, about trying again to find a job as a teller so we can remain in Denmark. Maybe the next time we visit Copenhagen we can afford to go shopping."

"Whatever you decide is all right with me," she said. "I want you to be happy. We'll just hope that a teller is needed somewhere. Once you find a job, then we can start saving for a house."

"I'm going to read the ads and walk around some."

"Notice, Georg, how many are here are from other countries. They have found jobs. Just look at all the bags people are carrying, filled with toys and wrapped gifts. It doesn't look as if this economy is failing."

Georg nodded agreement and kissed her on the cheek. "Thank you, my wonderful *Norska*. You truly are a Viking woman."

Next morning, they took the train across Zealand, the ferry to Nyborg, then the train down to Haderslev. Anna paced in the small train compartment, sat down, stood up, combed her hair, and straightened the hem of her new dress. She became more nervous as the train traveled the final miles. How would the Amorsens greet her? What should she say? Did she look all right?

Georg held her hand. "Sit down, Anna. Don't worry. My mother and father are friendly people."

The train's whistle screamed as it chugged into the station. Anna looked out the window and pointed. "There they are, standing by the carriage. I recognize them from your pictures."

"Uh, oh, my father has a cane."

Anna noted his elegant clothes; he was even wearing a top hat. "Except for the glasses, Georg, your face is a copy of your father's. He is tall like you and stands very straight."

Georg's mother wore a well-fitted light blue suit that reminded Anna of Mrs. Jensen at the church who always wore the latest fashions. Mrs. Amorsen was just about Anna's height and that made her feel good.

The train stopped, the conductor opened the door, and Georg and Anna stepped off the train. Two German soldiers stood guard by the exit gate inspecting each person's papers. Anna was a little frightened. The two heavy-set soldiers in gray uniforms inspected their visas and returned them with a, *"Danke schon."* Georg crossed through the gate, ran to the other side of the station fence, and grabbed his father's hand. "It's so good to see you. You look great. You're able to get around! This is wonderful."

Before his father could answer, Georg gave his mother a big hug, then announced: "Here's my Anna, Mother and Dad."

Soren Amorsen reached out and shook her hand. "We've been anxiously waiting for you to arrive. *Velkommen!*" Anna Christine

Amorsen gave Anna a warm hug. "Welcome to Denmark," she said. "We're so delighted to meet you. With two Annas in our family, we'll have a great time."

Anna beamed. "I've been hearing so much about you from Georg all these months, I feel as if I know you both. I'm so looking forward to our visit with you."

Soren drove the carriage to their home. He stopped before a big two-story house surrounded by an iron picket fence and a flower garden in front. It was Anna's dream house. "What a beautiful home. It looks just like the pictures Georg showed me."

"Anna, this is your home, too," Georg's mother said with a smile. She put her arm around Anna. "Come in and make yourself comfortable. Georg, you and Anna can have your old bedroom. We painted it since you left. We even saved your old skates."

"I feel like a little boy again," Georg told Anna. "I haven't skated since I was in the fifth grade." He carried the luggage upstairs. "See that dent on the banister?" he said to Anna. "I tried to run my skates down the railing."

"Did you make all of these marks?"

"No. My older brother Frederik used to do it. When we were growing up, we always tried to outdo each other, especially on skates." Anna noticed how carefree and happy Georg was to be home. He grabbed her and kissed her. "We're here at last."

Before they finished putting away their clothes, Georg's mother called up the stairs to let them know dinner would be ready in thirty minutes. Anna hurried to clean up and put on a pretty red dress Elsa had made for her. She ran downstairs to see if she could be of help. Anna Christine had on a red and white apron and was taking the chicken out of the oven. "Thank you, Anna. Would you like to set the table? The silverware and dishes are in the cabinet."

The dining room overwhelmed Anna with the *Toiles de Jouy* wall patterns depicting eighteenth-century hunters and forest scenes. A solid cherry armoire stood against the inner wall. The wood had a deep richness in the delicately hand-carved dining table. Anna kept feeling as if she were in a castle.

After a sumptuous dinner of baked chicken, *rødkål*, and *kartoffels*, Georg finished off five cookies. "What a feast. The red cabbage and mashed potatoes were delicious, and these macaroons are wonderful. It's great to be home. Thank you for such a good dinner, Mother.

"And Dad, we were able to pay Ole the money he thought we owed him. We used our bonuses. Thank you so much for sending us the money to come here. I'll pay you back as soon as I get a job."

Soren proudly looked at his son and new daughter-in-law. "We are delighted to have you with us. That must have been a harrowing experience you went through."

"Yes, he was trying to blackmail us," Georg said. "He made it impossible for us to live there."

"What do you want to do, Georg?" asked his mother. "Back to the bank again?"

"Yes, I'd like to work in the bank. I've been a salesperson for the past two years, but I prefer banking."

Soren shook his head. "Our bank has cut positions. We have nothing there. Business is slow because the German economy regulates so much of what we can do."

"Maybe we'll have to move to a smaller town," said Anna.

"Georg and Anna," said Anna Christine, "enjoy yourselves for awhile. Georg, take some time to show Anna our city. You'll find a job soon enough."

"I'll meet with the Bank Commission in two weeks," said his father. "Of course we hope you won't settle too far away."

When Anna fell asleep that night in Georg's arms, she felt so much at home she slept more soundly than at any time since they'd left Chicago. She realized her fears about Soren and Anna Christine were groundless. In her dreams, she was in her little Bergen home. She was decorating the house with roses, tulips, daffodils, and daisies while Gudrun was baking a cake to celebrate her visit.

"Wake up, Anna," said Georg. "Let's go out and see the town. I found my old bike and Frederik's. I have already had breakfast. Mother's made hot sconces."

Anna sleepily pushed herself out of their feather bed. "Can't we just sit for a day?"

"It's not raining today. The weather gets cold quick here. We'd better take advantage of this good day."

Anna's eyes got big and a big smile lit her face. "Can we find the cathedral you said was built in 1682? I've never been inside one."

"It's right where its always been — on *Hambrosgade*, the main street through our town."

"Let's go there. I've heard a lot about high church and I want to know what it means."

"You'll be seeing it quite a bit. It's where my family attends church. Our ancestors helped found it."

The tall steeples overwhelmed Anna as they entered. The bold but harmonious interior with its beautiful baroque fittings impressed her. The stained glass windows portrayed pictures of Christ on the cross. The pulpit was ten feet in the air so the pastor could speak and be heard by the whole congregation. Curved wooden figures representing the disciples lined either side of the church. Clean white pillars reached up to the roof. Anna sat in a pew, closed her eyes, and thought of all the many parishioners who had worshiped in this holy place since 1682. Chills of happiness filled her. Suddenly, she felt directly connected with two hundred years of Viking history — two hundred years of joy and sorrow, struggle and triumph, life and death, long journeys and short. How lucky, she thought, Georg and I are to be starting our journey with such a wonderful people and such a wonderful family.

Sunday came and they attended the cathedral. For Anna, it was a service of solemn music and prayer — a tone quite unlike the informality of Pastor Swensen's church. She whispered to Georg, "Someday we'll have our children baptized here."

He pulled her closer. "I love you," he whispered.

She snuggled closer and let the sound of the organ serve as background for a scene she was imagining: she and Georg walking toward the pulpit with their new baby to be christened. Anna sighed. She wanted a home and a baby. Was that asking too much?

As the weeks rolled by, Anna helped Georg's mother with meal preparation whenever she could. She liked Anna Christine's directness and friendliness.

"You are an excellent cook, Anna," Georg's mother said one day. "Where did you learn?"

"After my mother died, I did the cooking for my sister and father. Later, in Chicago, Elsa Swensen taught me many new dishes. Anytime you wish, I will be glad to cook for us."

"Thank you, Anna. The hardest part is going to market and finding what you need. The produce is poor. It has been very difficult under German rule, since they make us speak German."

Georg began to look for a job. They had spent all of their savings; paying back the borrowed passage money from his father hung heavy on his mind. He walked the streets of Haderslev, read the daily paper, and checked with old friends.

One day an old high school friend told him, "This is a poor time to look for any job. We do not have a big company here. Most of our classmates have moved north to Jutland or sailed to America to get away from the Germans."

Soren met with the Bank Commission, but there were no teller jobs or any other jobs at the Bank of Haderslev.

After another long day of searching, Georg told Anna, "My feet are tired, I've read every newspaper in town, I've talked to my friends — there is nothing. I feel useless. I may have to take a job fishing for six months."

"Georg, there must be a job somewhere closer. I can't live alone here for six months while you go out fishing."

"I don't want to go, my dear, but I feel indebted to my folks. I need to make a living for us."

"Georg, please don't leave me."

He held her close. "Anna, I must find work. They're signing up crews now. Six months won't be that long. We'll find a little home when I return. I love you, *Norska*."

Anna broke into tears. "Georg, please try some more around the town — just one more week. Please?"

Georg wiunkal his anns an outl her. "T lule *Norvka*, going fishing for six months is the last thing I want, but we can repay the loan and find our own home when I return. I will look around here for one more week, then I must sign-up."

Anna clung to her husband, "Please, don't leave me, Georg. Please! I love you, but couldn't bear to be without you."

Once day, Georg borrowed his father's carriage and asked Anna to join him on a trip to Rodding. "I heard they just opened a job for a teller. I'm sure I can qualify. It is about three hours from here in southeast Jutland."

"I'll pack us a lunch."

As Gotrot, the family horse, pulled them along the country road, Anna noticed how immaculate rural Denmark was. The square, red brick farmhouses with thatched roofs and white plastered walls had an inner courtyard and large barns. Every farm had a pig sty filled with fatted pigs. The dairy herds roamed in lush green pastures surrounded by stone fencing.

Rodding came into view with its small inlets and estuaries intersecting the hills. The town had a small business section composed of brick buildings and the usual military station with the German soldiers on guard.

Georg drove the carriage under a shady tree on the *Hambrosgade* and took out his paper with the address. "Here we are. The bank must be the one with the cupola on top. Will you be comfortable here?"

"Of course I will. Here's a hug and kiss. Good luck!"

Georg carefully straightened out his suit, put on his coat, and brushed off the dust. He combed his hair, tied his tie, and stroked his beard and took a big breath. "Bye, see you soon."

Hours later, when Georg came bouncing down the stairs from the bank, Anna was sitting under one of the trees, face pale. Georg saw her and sauntered over. "I got the job!" he said, a big smile on his face. "We can move here within the week."

Anna's hands were shaking. "Hold me, Georg," she whispered. "Gotrot ran away with me. I thought I was going to be killed. I couldn't stop him."

"What?" exclaimed Georg, running to her side. "My God, Anna! Are you all right?"

"Yes. He finally ran into a farmyard and found a water trough. Between the heat and some big dog barking and nipping his legs, I guess he'd had enough. Before I could do anything, he was galloping down the main road; it was all a blur. I was lucky to hang on until he stopped."

"I'm sorry I was so long, Anna. I had to meet with two other officers of the bank." He put his arms around her, and they sat there in silence for several minutes. Finally, he asked where the carriage was.

"Down the main street where it turns into a lane." She gave him a big hug. "I'm so happy you got the job. Now we can start saving for our own house."

The ride home was slower than the one going north. Gotrot moved as if he had won his last race. Anna's bones felt every bump, but she was happy. They talked of their plans to move.

"I've really enjoyed getting to know your parents, Georg. They are lovely, kind people. Why was I so fearful?"

"That's what I tried to tell you before we were married. I knew they would like you, too."

Dinner at the Amorsen's was over by the time the young couple arrived. Georg ran into the house shouting, "I have a job!"

Soren limped out of his study. "Congratulations, son. Tell me more. Where and when?"

"Within a week I start work in Rodding. We have to find a place to live near there."

Anna Christine came downstairs. "You have the job? Congratulations. We will miss you. I hope it's not too far away."

Days later, Georg and Anna drove a carriage with their belongings to a rental apartment near Rodding. The three rooms were bright, sunny, and clean.

"This is just a start," said Georg as he carried her over the threshold for the first time.

The warm days of summer soon disappeared. The fall rains and snow reminded Anna of Bergen. She devoted her time to reading, cooking, and writing home to her father and sister. One day they sent her a box of china that Mama had saved for her; they also sent some family pictures. The package reminded her of those days out on the wharf in the bitter cold. She wrote back:

> *How fortunate I am. Georg and I hope to come and visit you, but it will be a while before he has any time off.*

Georg worked extra hard at his teller's job. He made friends easily with his co-workers and the bank's clientele. The weather improved during the Christmas holiday; the couple took the train to Haderslev for Christmas with Georg's family. He had a furtive air about him as they ate Christmas dinner. Anna also seemed to have an expectant look. Finally, Georg could keep the secret no longer. "I have a wonderful surprise for you."

"*We* have a surprise for you," Anna corrected.

"Tell us! Tell us! What's happening?"

"We're going to have a baby!" Georg said, beaming.

"Our first grandchild born in Denmark!" shouted Anna Christine. "How wonderful!" She jumped up from the table and hugged Anna and Georg. "When is the baby due?"

"August," they chorused in unison.

Soren smiled proudly. "This calls for a drink. Bring in the glasses, and we'll toast the new little one."

Anna and Georg settled into their new life. They met other couples whose husbands worked in the bank. They shared sleigh rides, recipes, and baby books because most of the other employees already had two or three children.

Anna used her time to sew and embroider little outfits for her baby-to-be. She sought advice and finally felt as if she were ready, but the spring and summer days began to drag. She felt the baby kicking and turning, getting more and more fidgety. Each day, Georg would ask, "How are you feeling today?"

"Georg, please relax. The baby is alive and kicking and isn't expected until August."

"But with all its moving around, it acts ready."

"But I'm having the baby, not you, and I'm telling you it's not ready yet. I'll let you know."

Toward the beginning of August, Georg would hurry home at noon to see how she was feeling. "Any news?"

"Georg, the doctor told me to send for him as soon as the contractions start. Everything is fine."

On August 12, 1887, Georg came home to find Anna flat on their bed. "I think it's getting time," she said. "Call the doctor."

Georg ran to the doctor's office down the street. "Help, help," he knocked on the door. "We're having a baby!"

The old doctor smiled. "Don't rush so. It will be awhile. Go get Hildred."

Georg rushed home and called for Hildred. She lived next door and had volunteered to help. The doctor finally arrived and, after checking on the rate of contractions, told Georg, "You can go back to work. This will take some time."

At one minute past midnight on August 13th — Georg said he would always remember that time — their first child was born. It was a girl. The first thing Anna thought as she held the baby was that they hadn't picked a name.

"Anna, my love," Georg said proudly, "she must have a beautiful name, after a Greek goddess. Let's call her two names. Thea Christi."

Anna thought the name over for awhile and decided it did sound very elegant. "Yes, we'll baptize her Thea Christi Amorsen. We'll go down to Haderslev as soon as I'm better and show her to the family. We can spend Sunday there and have her baptized in the Cathedral."

Georg nodded his agreement.

Soon the hot days of August passed, and the cooler winds of fall began. Baby Thea would cry at night until Anna took her in bed and nursed her. Georg would get up half-awake in the morning after a night of walking Thea. He made a point of telling everyone at the bank, in the stores, at the barber shop, "I have the most beautiful baby. She's named after a goddess."

As the holiday season approached, the political pressure by the German government gradually begin to slow Denmark's economy. The Rodding bank deposits decreased. One morning, Georg was called into the manager's office. The old gentleman had a sadness in his eyes. "Georg, this is very hard for me to say, but we no longer can employ you. I realize you recently had a baby girl, but we just don't have the resources. Times are bad."

Georg left the bank feeling the weight of the world on his shoulders. He and Anna had saved some money to buy a home, but their main source of income had just disappeared. He had sailed to America the first time because there was no work in his German-controlled Denmark. He should have known better. Now, once again, the same thing had happened.

When he came home that evening, he threw his shoes against the wall, poured out two glasses of Acquavit, and sat dejectedly at the kitchen table.

Anna sat down at the table across from him. She didn't know what to expect. Georg hardly ever took a drink. "The bank laid me off; there's no business."

Anna got up and hugged him. "I'm so sorry, Georg. You were their best teller." She picked up her glass and in silence they both sipped. "So, what are we going to do?" she asked finally.

He shrugged. "I don't know . . . but I do know one thing. I'm not going to worry about it this minute. It's Christmas in Denmark. We're surrounded by people who love us. We've got a new baby and a wonderful marriage and I plan to enjoy them both this holiday." He paused and took another sip of his drink. "We'll work out something. Maybe it's time we thought about going back to America."

Chapter Twelve

Dangerous Journey

Early Christmas Day, Anna and Georg took Thea to see the tree and light the candles at his parents' house. Her eyes got big and she cried for Anne Christine, who rocked her in the family rocking chair.

Over breakfast Georg had an announcement: "I've been up half the night figuring out what to do. Now I know. We'll go to Victoria and visit Frederik and his family."

Soren and Anna Christine scowled. They didn't believe Georg would leave again. "What will you do there?" Soren asked, trying to conceal his displeasure.

"I've heard there are jobs. Many people are going west. I wrote Frederik a month ago, and he sent a card inviting us."

"Do we have enough money for passage?" asked Anna.

"Yes, my dearest. We've been saving for a house, but we'll use it to get to Victoria and make a new start."

Anna Christine wiped her eyes. "I'll so miss little Thea and all of you. Why do you have to go that far away?"

"Think it over for a day or so," Soren said.

The following morning they caught the train back to Rodding. By the time they had a chance to talk that night, Anna was more upset. "Are you sure you want to return to America? What did Frederik say about the availability of jobs? Did he actually say there were teller jobs?"

"Anna, we've been through this. I told you he said, 'You, Anna, and Thea are welcome.'"

"Your folks are very upset. Thea Christi will soon be four months. She is their only grandchild in Denmark."

"For heaven's sake, Anna. We have to live our own lives. We told them we were leaving. I'm going to go buy the tickets tomorrow.

We can stop in Chicago and see our friends."

"And I suppose we don't have enough money to see my family, just enough to get to Victoria?"

"I'm sorry, but that is the situation. We barely have enough to get to Victoria. As it is, I will have to borrow from my father. Anna, my dearest, I will work as hard as I can so we can come back and visit your family. What else can we do?"

She began to cry. He was so determined. "What about Thea Christi? Is she strong enough for such a long trip?"

"Anna, we've decided; we're going. Let's get on with the packing and not discuss this any further."

She felt defeated. He hadn't even looked for another job in Denmark. They could have lived with his folks while he was looking. Would he really settle down in Victoria? She sometimes thought Georg enjoyed traveling more than homemaking. Would he always be this way?

Grandma Amorsen's eyes filled with tears as she waited for them to board at the Haderslev train station. She held little Thea close. "Give your grandma a smile," she said. Thea turned her head and Grandma gave her a big kiss.

Grandpa Amorsen came over and patted his granddaughter's curly hair. "Remember your Danish grandparents, Thea Christi," he said. "You're very important to us."

Georg paced. "Our leaving is not easy for any of us. You have been so good to us, Mother and Father. It is very hard for me and Anna to say goodbye."

Anna put her arm around her mother-in-law and gave her a hug and kiss while tears filled her eyes. "I love you both so much. I'll send you pictures of Thea once we get settled."

When Georg reached over to take Thea from her grandmother, she yelled and squirmed. Grandma soothed her, "Little girl, we will send you pictures of Denmark. Maybe someday you can come back and visit us."

Georg embraced his father, then kissed his mother. "Georg," she said, "we send you with all our love. And give all our love to Frederik and his family."

As the train slowly pulled away from the station, Anna thought what a forlorn picture Georg's parents made as they waved farewell. They had taken not only Anna but also little Thea into their hearts. She wondered how she would feel when it was time for Thea and her husband to leave home.

Elsa and Henrik Swensen and the Jensens greeted Georg and Anna at the train station in Chicago. The children's choir from the church sang, "Hello, Hello." They all waved and shouted, *"Velkommen!"*

Anna looked out at the joyful crowd as Georg held up their baby. She wondered what they would think when they found out they were on their way to Victoria, British Columbia. She wished he would look for a job in Chicago. These are our friends, she thought. I want to be with them.

Cheers went up as they stepped down from the train. Hans and Lise ran over. "Hi, Anna. Hi, Georg. Can we hold the baby?" When the two children came closer Lise said, "Gosh, Anna, what a cute little baby."

The Swensens and Jensens greeted them with hugs and enthusiastic hand shakes. "I've saved your little room for you," said Elsa. "Lise will sleep on the couch so the baby can have her room. It is so good to see you! Oh my, what a beautiful little girl."

They rode out to the parsonage in Jensen's carriage. It barely held the five of them plus the luggage. Thea sat on her father's lap, staring at the bluebird on Mrs. Jensen's hat.

"No, no, Thea. Don't touch," said Anna.

With the bird bobbing right in front of her, Thea could not be stopped. She reached out, grabbed its feathers, and started to put them in her mouth. Mrs. Jensen nearly lost her hat before Anna could break Thea's grip on the bird.

Anna felt as if she were returning home. Even though she'd been born and raised in Norway, she realized her real life began in Chicago with the Swensens — her life as an independent person, not just another fisherman's daughter or wife like her mother had been. The years she spent with the Swensens meant a lot to her. She wondered what the far west would be like. The atlas showed nothing but forest around Victoria. What will I do in a forest? I've lived in cities all my life. I wonder what it costs to live in a forest and can Georg find a job there?

They arrived at the parsonage where Elsa invited them all in for dinner. They sat down at the table while Thea rested beside them in a bureau drawer, kicking and cooing.

Henrik gave the blessing and concluded with, "We welcome our dear friends and little Thea Christi Amorsen."

Several courses later, everyone was full except Georg. He filled his plate again, and then, with his mouth nearly full, proclaimed,

"This dinner is delicious. The ship's food wasn't very appealing, and this is so good!"

"We're not through yet," said Elsa. "I made *rullekage* for dessert."

"What a party," cried Hans as his mother returned from the kitchen with a beautiful cake decorated with whipped cream.

After dinner, Henrik asked Georg, "Are you planning to return to the dry goods store?"

For a moment Georg didn't know what to say.

Anna spoke up. "We'd like to stay in Chicago, but there are more chances for jobs in the far west. We're going to visit Georg's brother in Victoria."

"Well," said Georg, squirming in his chair, "I am a bank teller and I'd like to find the same kind of job in the west. With all that gold they're mining and more Scandinavians migrating to the Northwest, I feel a bank teller position will be easier to find there."

"When do you plan to leave?" asked Elsa

"I wrote my brother we'd be there this spring." He then explained their route: St. Paul to Winnipeg and later the ferry across the Strait of Georgia to Victoria from Vancouver.

"We looked up the route on the ship's atlas," said Anna.

Elsa shook her head in disappointment. "We certainly will miss you. We were hoping you'd stay here in Chicago." She sighed. "Anyway, at least we have time to visit and get acquainted with Thea."

One evening Anna summoned her courage and asked Henrik how he dealt with Ole. "Did he accept the ticket back to Bergen?"

"Yes, Anna. He was the same pugnacious fellow who came crashing into your home. He took the envelope and stormed out of the house."

"Well," sighed Anna as she stood up and walked around the living room, "I feel a great relief."

"He certainly was a big, strong guy," said Georg. "Seemed to have a bad temper; it was a little scary. He could have killed us if we'd been sitting near the window when he threw that rock in the house."

Too soon, the day of departure arrived. They repacked the wedding presents they'd stored in the Swensens's attic. The suitcases were ready. The Jensens drove up in their carriage to take them to the train. Everyone was bundled up: little Thea in a red and white hand-knit outfit with cap and mittens, Anna and Georg in heavy Danish winter coats, hats, and scarves. Overnight, a February blizzard had swept down on Chicago from the north with a biting wind and heavy snow.

The Swensens hugged Georg, Anna, and Thea with tears in their eyes. "Do write us," was all Elsa could think to say. She knew this would probably be the last time she would see Anna.

"Send us pictures of Thea," said Hans, his voice cracking.

"Big ones," Lise added.

Anna didn't know what to say either. "Thank you for your gracious hospitality," she said, trying to be brave. "Maybe someday you can come and visit us. We will send pictures and keep in touch."

Inside her heart, she was doing her best not to be angry with Georg. He hadn't even tried to look for a job in Chicago as a teller, and now he was forcing her to leave her wonderful friends and go to a colder place where they didn't know anyone except his brother. It didn't make any sense.

"Thank you," said Georg, shaking Henrik's hand and hugging Elsa, Hans, and Lise. "You are all our true friends."

"God bless all of you," added Henrik, waving goodbye.

The trip to the train station and getting aboard was one big blur for Anna. They were going. There could be no doubt about that, but she didn't have to like it. They'd left Denmark against her wishes, they didn't stop to see her family, and now they were leaving Chicago and she didn't know why.

She tried to get her mind off her feelings as she stared out the train window at the passing countryside. The driving snow covered the barren trees and brown grass with an inviting soft, white blanket that made her want to run out into the storm and yell where no one would hear.

Georg was holding Thea and trying to leave Anna alone so she could deal with her own thoughts. She knew he felt bad about taking her away from all that she loved and cared about, yet he believed in what he had decided. He didn't know what else to do but what he thought was right. She decided to break the silence between them.

"I read that as we go west," she said without looking at him. "We cross the bleak northern prairie where only a few years ago the Indians used to hunt buffalo."

Georg smiled. "Yes," he said with a note of irony, "it's unbelievable how quickly things can change in America."

The train's haunting whistle echoed across the barren stretches of the provinces of Manitoba, Saskatchewan, and Alberta. Its only stops were for coal and water.

Anna and Georg huddled into a small sleeping compartment with two bunk beds. She slept in the lower one with Thea, and Georg's long legs hung over the top edges. The clatter of the wheels and the sameness of the snow-covered land made time seem almost endless as they sped west.

They took turns caring for Thea. She was now able to sit up, barely. Georg used a baggage strap to tie her to the bunk so she wouldn't fall. Sometimes, he would play "horsey" with her, bouncing his little daughter on his knee; she would squeal with delight. Other times, they played peek-a-boo and sang songs. He often carried her up and down the aisles.

One day, Anna and Georg met the Talbots, passengers in the next compartment. They were traveling to Port Angeles from England. He had a contract with a construction company. Each morning, he and his wife would wear heavy wool sweaters in matching blue and green colors and greet them with, "Good morning, what a jolly day." The two couples began sharing a dining table. Mrs. Talbot would ask, "May I hold Thea?"

"Of course," Anna would say. Thea was happy to have another playmate and enjoyed being the center of attention.

"What are you heading west for, my friend?" asked Mr. Talbot one morning.

"I'm in banking," said Georg in his booming voice. "We're visiting my brother in Victoria."

After that, when they entered the dining car, the waiter would lean down to Thea and say, "Welcome, little homesteader."

Anna would poke Georg. "Please tell him to call us by our names. We are not homesteaders."

"Never mind," Georg would say. "We may be."

Anna would give Georg a dirty look.

During the coal stops, Georg would occasionally get off and walk alongside the train. As they approached the mountains, he told Anna he liked the dry smell of the sage on the lower levels and the pine and cedar at the higher altitudes. "Besides," he said, "I need my exercise."

One time when he went outside, she watched him from the train window. He walked vigorously but every now and then picked up a handful of snow, fashioned a snowball, and threw it as hard as he could at the nearest tree. As he threw, his face contorted into an ugly sneer — one she'd never seen before.

Why couldn't he tell her what was bothering him? Anna realized Frederik had not promised Georg a job. Just then, the conductor passed through the train, checking off his report. Anna stopped him and asked, "Sir, when will we arrive?"

"We're almost to Kicking Horse Pass. We have to go up a four-percent grade with nine miles of switchbacks through all this snow. It's a long, slow pull and usually takes about eleven hours. But in this weather, who knows?"

Georg came in from his walk and took off his wet coat. It was still snowing hard outside. He stretched out in the leather chair in the observation car. "I walked up to the front and looked over the engine. They've added a wooden plow on the front reinforced with steel to clear snow from the tracks. They'll need it soon if this snow keeps falling."

As evening came, the train was moving with great effort. Slowly it climbed the Continental Divide. It twisted and turned on the switchbacks, forcing its way up through the pass. Just before Anna and Georg and Thea fell asleep, the storm turned into a blizzard with snow and wind beating against the windows.

All three were sound asleep when the train stopped with such a jolt Georg bumped his head; Anna and Thea were nearly thrown from their bunk. It was pitch dark.

"What is it, Georg? Turn on the light."

Georg climbed down rubbing his head and went over to the windows. "I can't see anything," he whispered. "Snow seems to be glued to the window pane and the compartment lights are blinking."

"Georg, listen. The train's stopped. We're just stuck on the track. It's so quiet. What shall we do?"

"I'll go and find out," he said, rubbing his head. "It's getting colder. You'd better bundle up! Is Thea asleep?"

"Like a log. Come back as soon as you find out."

Georg had hardly stepped out of the compartment into the aisle when he met Alfred Talbot, who for once did not repeat his "jolly day" routine.

"What's happening, Georg?"

"I guess the snow is piling up so fast the plow on the front can't handle it."

Soon the aisle was crowded with people wrapped in robes, blankets, or overcoats. They were all talking to one another as if by doing so they could protect themselves.

"Ladies and gentlemen," announced the conductor. "We regret the sudden stop. Snow drifts have covered the track. We have wired for help and two snowplows are on their way. The heat has been turned down to conserve the boiler's capacity. Also, please limit your use of the lights."

"What are we expected to do," shouted a man from the rear of the car. "Stand around here waiting?"

"Don't worry," replied the conductor. "Wrap yourself in a blanket and go back to bed. We expect to be moving within the next twenty-four hours. I'll give you a new report first thing in the morning."

The passengers grumbled and returned to their compartments, feeling their way along the aisles as the lights blinked.

Anna had overheard the conductor. "What about food?" she asked, the moment Georg returned. "I'm scared. I have to have food so I can nurse Thea. If I don't eat, I won't be able to feed her and she could die in this cold."

Georg put his arms around her and held her tight. "Anna, we're in this together. I understand you need food. We'll work it out. Help is on the way."

Anna felt his body against hers and clung to him, feeling safe and warm in his arms. She thought how good it was to have him close; he'd been so distant since they left Haderslev.

"Georg, I love you so very much," she said. "Our love and strength will keep us going."

"Shhhh," he whispered. "Give Thea to me. I'll tie her in the upper bunk."

When he finished, they squeezed into the lower bunk even though his feet hung out in the cold. Anna snuggled up into his arms and they kissed and made love the rest of the night.

In the morning, they dressed in their warmest sweaters and walked toward the diner. The snow had frozen on the windows making it hard to tell morning from night. The Talbots came out at the same time and they all talked about the storm.

Just then, the conductor came through. "I'm bringing you good news. The first snowplow is here and clearing the tracks. It will take at least two days. In order to obtain food, it is necessary to have a food ticket which you can get from me. More food is coming. We'll be on a short ration until then."

"Give me your ticket," Georg whispered in Anna's ear, "and I'll go down right away and get our share."

He returned sooner than she expected, a worried look on his face. "They insist that you come down yourself," he said. "I didn't see much except for crackers and bread."

Anna left Thea with Georg and walked to the diner. She knew she had to remain calm. There is no way to get out of this snow, she thought. I must keep up my courage. But if I can't get enough juice or food, how can I nurse Thea?

At the diner she spotted a waiter. "Please sir, I have a five-month-old baby and need some juice and crackers."

"Let's see your ticket," he demanded. After a thorough inspection, he handed it back. "All right, you may take a box of crackers and one orange."

"But that's for my baby. I must eat, too. Otherwise, I can't nurse her."

"Sorry, lady, that is the best we can do. We don't know how long we'll be stuck here. That orange is my last one."

Anna returned slowly. The darkness of the cars, the grim view of snow against the windows and the sound of the wind howling outside greatly disturbed her. What if they can't break through within the next day? What am I going to do? I can drink water, but my breasts will dry up without nourishment.

Back at the compartment, she quizzed Georg, "How long do you think it will really take for the food to get here?"

"Depends if the storm stops. Snow is covering the rails. The conductor told me it would be longer than two days."

"Are there any little towns anywhere near here?"

He shook his head. "We're on the crest of the Cascades. There are no villages. We just have to hope the rescue crews can get us out in time."

Anna fought to control her temper.

Thea spent much of the day rolling around the bunk and playing peek-a-boo with Daddy. Toward the end of the first day, she began getting restless from being confined in such a small space and began to cry.

Anna put a little of the fruit juice in a glass and carefully held it. Thea hadn't mastered drinking from a glass yet, but kept sticking her tongue down into the glass for more.

"Here, Anna, let me take Thea outside for a walk down the aisles. She likes to be carried and see all the people. I'll take her big blanket. It's really getting cold."

The day passed slowly. As the weather became colder, more and more passengers hibernated in their bunks. Thea finally went to sleep after Anna had sung to her for hours.

Georg paced the aisles but soon became bored. He put on two layers of clothes, his heaviest shoes, and a snow hat, and wrapped a big blanket around his shoulders, Indian style. He then followed the aisles to the coal car and carefully lowered himself into the snow. He walked close to the car to avoid sinking over his head in a high snow drift. Icicles hung from under big boulders where streams once flowed. Tree branches laden with snow bent down as if ready to break. Finally, he arrived where the engine stood. It looked like a Christmas toy all wrapped in white tissue paper. There was no evidence of another snowplow. The biting weather was beginning to freeze his nose; he quickly retraced his footsteps and climbed back aboard.

Night fell. The snow and wind decreased. Georg picked up his rations: two pieces of bread and a package of crackers.

Anna was crying when he got back.

"Here, share my food," he said.

"No, Georg," she sobbed, "my stomach hurts, and I'm starting to have trouble nursing. What are we going to do?"

He tried to console her, but couldn't think of anything to say. The situation was becoming serious. The image of the frozen engine and the lack of any action or crews working left him with a feeling of utter despair. He knew they couldn't last much longer. Anna and Georg didn't get much sleep that night.

The following morning the conductor reported, "Food is due in today. They're sending it up on sleighs. They haven't been able to clear the rails yet. Be patient it will arrive."

Thea was becoming more restless and cranky. Songs, stories, and piggyback rides didn't interest her.

Anna drank water but it didn't help the flow of her milk; she was almost out of food for Thea. Her mind raced. She thought about walking for help, which she knew was foolish, or storming the dining car in search of juice and solid food. That wouldn't work, either. With nothing else to do, she nestled Thea in her arms and sang Danish and Norwegian songs.

Georg checked with the conductor at noon. The news was encouraging. They had cleared the tracks and the snowplow was on its way to batter away the snow piled in front of the train. "Anna, we're soon going to be free," he blurted, bursting back into their compartment.

But by evening, there was no snowplow. They turned in for the third night, sleeping in their clothes and rolled up tight in their blankets.

"Let's pray this is the final night," Anna suggested. "I don't think Thea and I can last another twenty-four hours. We're both very weak. My stomach is really bothering me."

"I know, I know," he said. "You've both been very brave. If I knew where to go, I'd dig my way through for you. Just one more night and we'll have food."

Again, the Amorsen's spent a restless night. Thea kept waking up, wanting more food.

Next morning, the news was good. The conductor came through the cars and said, "Come down to the diner when you are called. Think of bacon and eggs, juice, and hot coffee." Anna's faith in the future was renewed. She bowed her head and said, "Thank you, God." Her stomach couldn't deal with all the food she'd ordered, but Georg made up for it.

He came running into the compartment after lunch. "The engine is on. We'll be starting soon. It will be a slow climb, but we'll be moving." Georg gave Anna and Thea a big hug. "Don't worry anymore. Everything is going to be all right."

Around three o'clock, the train started to move, but couldn't develop any traction. The slope and the weight of its load was too much for the engine. The passengers held their breath while the train tried again and again.

Anna broke into tears. Georg tried to comfort and reassure her, but she couldn't stop. She had all these emotions and thoughts swirling through her mind, but she knew she couldn't share them. Coming west was a mistake. They should never have left Denmark or Chicago. There wasn't going to be any work for them in Canada, and who knows how long they were going to be stuck in this horrible snow storm.

She was still crying when the Talbots came in from their compartment. Anna stopped her crying, and the four of them just sat in silence, staring out the window. Thea had finally fallen asleep. The two couples understood how the whole situation could become life threatening at any moment if there were an avalanche or another serious mechanical breakdown. No one dared speak of it.

Suddenly, the sound of the conductor's bell echoed down the aisles. "Now hear this. Now hear this," he announced. "We're hooking onto the snowplow engine at this very moment. It will give us a pull when we start this time. Patience, folks. Patience, folks. We're nearly on our way."

A few minutes later, Georg and Alfred stood between two passenger cars and strained their necks to see what was happening at the front of the train. At that moment, a blast of steam shot from the engine's boiler into the cold winter afternoon, then another, then another. The train moved. Another blast, and the train moved again, ever so slowly. Another blast and another. They were moving.

The two men cheered and soon they were drowned out by a mighty roar of approval from the other passengers as the train kept moving. Everyone began clapping and cheering and pounding each other on the back. Joy and happiness filled the train. Some laughed, others cried or shouted or hugged whomever they met.

Georg and Alfred dashed back to their wives. The couples exchanged hugs and tears of delight and profound thanks.

"May we always remember this day," Georg said. "May we always remember to thank God for His many blessings, especially his answer to our prayers on this day."

"Amen!" said the Talbots.

"Amen!" said Anna, putting her arms around Georg. She decided that God really intended for them to be going to Victoria. Why? She had no idea, but she wasn't going to worry about that right now. All she knew was that she and her Georg and Thea were going to be safe. They really were going to see Frederik . . . and lots more snow.

Chapter Thirteen

Victoria

It was almost dark when the ferry pulled into Victoria from Vancouver across the Strait of Georgia. A tall, slim man rushed toward Georg and Anna. He was the same height as Georg and, although older, he and Georg could have been twins. He was six feet tall, with an angular face just like Georg. He also wore a short beard with a mustache that seemed to curl up to his nose. He had on a lumberjack's dark blue jacket, a tight wool-knit cap wrapped down around his ears, and boots covered with mud.

The man and Georg gave each other a husky hug. "Brother, Georg! *Velkommen!*" he said. "Am I glad to see you. We were so worried over the news of your train being stuck at Kicking Horse Pass. Each day we've been expecting to hear you were on your way. Welcome to Victoria!" He gave Georg a slap on his back.

Georg pulled Frederik to where Anna was holding Thea. "Here is that big brother of mine, only now I'm as tall as he is."

"We've been waiting for you, Anna," Frederik said, extending his hand. "Pleased to meet you."

"Thank you," Anna said, forcing a smile. She was exhausted. Frederik turned to Thea and tickled her under the chin. "So, young lady, you've stopped crying for the moment, have you? You must know you're in the Queen's town."

Anna tucked the blankets around Thea. The cold wind of the Pacific Ocean tore through the straits. She pulled her snow cap down over her ears and pulled Anna Christine's hand-knit wool cap over Thea's ears. It felt as if a big storm were building up.

She sat leaning on her hands and thought about sharing Frederik's home. His wife Karen had sent pictures of the cabin and it looked rather small. Karen and Katy, their little girl, stood in front. How can there be enough room for all of us? Will we settle down and stay someplace? I just want to sleep in a warm room with a big fluffy comforter.

Frederik's horse carefully picked his way along the unlit dirt road that led through the center of town. The older brother motioned to the shadowy shapes of buildings on either side of the road. "We have over seven thousand people in and around Victoria. This is our main shopping center."

As they passed through the town, Frederik pointed out the Hudson Bay Company lantern hanging in front. "The other white building is the former Fort Victoria. It is now used as a community church."

Frederik didn't bother to hold the reins. "Nappy knows his way," he said as the horse avoided mud holes while the wagon wheels drove right through them. Anna gritted her teeth as each bump shook her tired body. Thea had fallen asleep.

As they entered the forest, Anna immediately noticed the stillness and it bothered her. The darkness from the overhead wine pines and firs and the wisps of fog that began to settle along the road made it seem like an airy, strange land afloat somewhere. It was so small. If only Frederik could help Georg find a job. What can he do? Anna closed her eyes, trying to control her desire to scream. Why did they come here? Seven thousand people? Bergen was bigger than that.

Nappy stopped before a clapboard cabin surrounded by the tall pines and firs. The house was constructed of knotty pine and old barn wood. From the two front windows a warm glow shed light on the entrance stoop. The smell of pine smoke from the chimney beckoned them. Around the front porch the bushes had withered from the winter freeze, yet the house offered a feeling of welcome and warmth.

Anna handed Thea to Georg. Her body was stiff and cold as she eased herself to the ground. At last, they had arrived. All she wanted was warmth — a hot tub and a warm bed.

Frederik led them up the path to the cabin. "I built this myself from the old barn and the pines I cut from out back."

The door opened before they reached the stoop. Little Katy stood in her nightgown. "Come on in," she said, smiling ear-to-ear. "We've been waiting and waiting for you." She had golden hair like her mother's and freckles; she jumped up and down with glee, then ran into the house, calling, "Mother, they're here with a baby, too."

Karen glided out of the kitchen. She was a tall woman somewhat on the rotund side with blond hair rolled in a bun at the nape of her neck. A small white blossom from an indoor plant was tucked above one ear. "Welcome to Victoria, Anna," she said, giving her a hug. "We have followed the *Victoria Press* for news. Thank goodness you're safe." She took one look at Anna. "You must be exhausted. Have a seat and take off your coat and boots."

"It is wonderful to be here," said Anna, sinking into the chair nearest the fireplace and closing her eyes. I made it, she thought, loosening her heavy coat and wet, muddy shoes.

Georg brought Thea over to Karen and Katy. "Thea is ready for entertainment now. She is wide awake, and I see that she is watching Katy's every movement."

Katy held her hand. "Will you play with me?"

Georg put Thea on the sofa surrounded by a wall of pillows. "Katy, Thea doesn't talk yet, but she likes to pretend. You can sit beside her," he said. He took off his overcoat and cap and lowered his big frame to the floor. "These last few days have really sapped our strength."

Karen leaned over Thea. "What a pretty little girl. She even smiled at me."

Anna felt not only the warmth of the room but the kindness of Frederik and Karen, her only sister-in-law. What gracious people to take us into their home, she thought.

Frederik came in from the barn where he had stored their extra luggage. He was carrying an armload of wood. He walked into the kitchen and found a bottle of Aquavit. "Here's the warm-up you need, Georg. Let me pour you a glass."

"Thanks, Freddy. Remember when I'd call you that?"

"I cooked a big pot of soup so it would be ready for you. May I serve you?" Karen asked. Her bright blue eyes and rosy complexion matched the long blue dress and the handsewn Nordic apron she wore.

Anna stood up to examine the reindeer design. "That's a very pretty apron. Did you embroider it?"

Karen smiled. "Yes, this is my home business. I sell handmade Nordic garments. Please, Anna, rest. I'll bring you soup, or would you rather wash up first?"

"Yes, I'd like to wash. A cup of soup would be fine later." Anna followed Karen down the hall to the bedroom. "What a pretty room," Anna said as she noticed a delicately-embroidered comforter on top of the double bed.

"This is your bedroom. We have a baby bed over there in the corner for Thea and we moved Katy in with us. Please make yourself at home. I'll bring in a basin of hot water. Here are some towels. We are delighted to have you. It is lonesome with our families so far away."

As Anna soaked her face in the hot water, she wondered what life would be like in Victoria. Would they too live in the country? Would Georg find a job? What would they do when their money ran out? The cheery pine room with colorful curtains brightened her thoughts.

Refreshed, Anna returned for a cup of soup while she watched Thea, Georg, and Katy play together. Katy had an elfish little smile and a twinkle in her eyes. Anna sipped her soup, looking around the living room. Behind the door to the hall, Anna noticed a map of the world with two big circles. One was around Victoria, the other was marked Haderslev. In looking at the distance they had traveled, she thought to herself, No wonder I'm exhausted after such a long trip —halfway around the world.

Katy had to go to bed and, shortly after that, Thea became grumpy. Anna picked her up and said good night. She carried her into the bedroom, washed her, changed her, and put on her nightgown. She sang *"Den lille Ole"* as she nursed her and then put her down in Katy's old crib.

Anna gratefully climbed into bed. Nothing had ever felt as good as she snuggled under the comforter in the feather bed. Georg could come whenever he wanted. Anna was asleep before she had a chance to think about the future.

The storm blew over during the night and the cabin was covered in the sun's rays as Anna tiptoed out of bed after a refreshing night's sleep. She gave Georg a poke, but he just turned over. Thea was asleep too. Anna dressed and went to the living room. The fireplace had been stoked and had burned all night. Anna added a few logs from the pile in the basket next to the hearth, and soon a bright blaze started up.

The house was quiet. Anna went into the kitchen and looked for coffee and a kettle. She found a kettle that looked as if it hung on the hook in the fireplace. She filled it with two cups of water and two tablespoons of coffee and watched it come to a boil as she enjoyed the warmth through sun-lit windows. She poured herself a cup and thought about how she loved the feeling of the warm coffee mug in her hands and the aroma and steam as she leaned over the cup. Settled by the fireplace with the beauty of the tall pines waving slowly in the light early morning breeze, Anna felt she faced the new day with renewed vigor.

She heard Thea fussing and went back to get her.

"Get up everybody, get up. We're going on a picnic today,"

announced Frederik, starting a fire in the kitchen stove. Soon Karen was scrambling eggs, and Georg eagerly sat down at the breakfast table, drank a cup of coffee, and started in on a big plate of eggs with toast. Anna and Katy had hot cereal and toast. Frederik, eager to get the group started, began making the sandwiches and packing the picnic basket. Blankets, snacks, and Katy's red wagon were included.

First, they followed the old road to the garden plot where they could see a few little green sprouts pushing through the ground. Karen pointed out the variety of produce they grew: cabbage, tomatoes, celery, spinach, rhubarb, berries, squash, and melons. "We sell all our produce to the local market. We're the only wholesaler on the Island."

Frederik drove by the woodlot where cords of neatly cut wood were stored. "We sell the cut wood to many of the settlers. They don't want to cut it themselves."

After completing the ride around the farm, they drove past the Navy lighthouse on the point. The sun shone through the trees on the road to town and Anna eagerly watched the other travelers. Farmers in wagons, loads of cut wood pulled by a team of horses, school children playing in the grammar school yard during recess, and glimpses of the ocean's brilliant blue color brightened the day.

Approaching town, Frederik said, "Let's take a walk through town and afterwards we can go to Victoria Park for our picnic."

The first store they stopped in was the magazine store. It was small, but crammed onto the shelves were books, cards, stationery, toys, candy, dry goods, and the newspaper the *Victoria Press*.

Georg bought a copy. He wanted to look over the job section. The two brothers walked back to the wagon. "Where is the bank? I missed seeing it," said Georg.

"We didn't go by the post office, yet, but the bank is located right next to it on the main street by the Hudson Bay Company. I know Bill Nelson, the manager."

"Do you think they need another teller? I sure would like to get a job there."

"Georg, I really don't know. If you wish, we can drive down tomorrow and you can talk to him."

"Thanks, brother. I really appreciate your help."

They untied Nappy and drove to Victoria Park. It was in the center of the town — a nice lawn with two cows grazing at the north end. They unloaded the wagon and sat in the sun to eat their sandwiches and nibble popcorn.

Karen told Anna, "I like to sit on the bench and watch all the goings-on and who is out shopping. Often I come along with Frederik when he delivers the produce. I bring along my Norwegian aprons to spread out on the bench. They are for sale and I also offer a sewing club for learning."

The next day they again drove into town. This time Georg was dressed in his best suit as he was going to talk to Bill Nelson, the bank manager. They tied Nappy to a tree and Anna waited in the wagon for Frederik and Georg to come out of the bank. Over an hour before Karen had taken Katy and pulled Thea in the little red wagon down to the beach. Nappy restlessly swiped flies with his tail and scuffled his feet as if to say, "Let's go."

Anna finally dozed, and in that suspended state, heard Georg and Frederik's voices as they walked out of the bank.

"I told you, Georg, to keep quiet and let me do the talking. I know Bill Nelson. He's a fidgety old guy but acquainted with all the business owners on the island. He holds the mortgage on our land. After my introduction if you had kept quiet, he would have provided you with some leads. You don't get anywhere by coming in and telling the bank manager that you are an experienced bank teller in your father's bank, as if you were some gift from heaven."

"Oh Frederik, you're wrong," said Georg. "I'll bet Nelson would be glad to have un up-to-date teller to help his business."

"Well, his bank handles all the military accounts as well as those of the local businesses and townspeople."

As they climbed into the wagon, Anna shook her head after hearing Georg's last sentence. "You just wait and see if he doesn't contact me."

Turning to Anna, Frederik took the reins and asked, "Where are the girls?"

"They are down on the beach playing in the sand," said Anna.

"I'll drive by and pick them up. Don't blame me for the delay. Georg tried to out-talk Nelson, the bank manager."

"Frederik, that's not fair. I know the business — you don't."

Anna wondered how Georg could be so courteous with his dry good customers and act like that with the manager. Perhaps it was his eagerness to get a job that overcame his good sense.

Nappy, pleased to be moving, nimbly pulled the wagon down to the ramp by the harbor. Thea was sitting up in the small, red wagon while Karen and Katy struggled to pull her up the hill. Already they had developed a language without words.

Evenings around the fireplace were spent with Karen showing Anna how to embroider the Nordic aprons. Frederik was usually busy bringing in the wood from his wood lot for the next day. Thea and Katy liked to play on the floor with a fluffy soft ball. Georg often took an evening walk through the woods.

Anna kept thinking about Georg's restlessness. Nelson did not contact him about the teller position or any other job. Why did he have to separate himself from the family? If only she and Georg could talk together.

One Sunday morning when Frederik, Karen, and Katy went to church services in the former Fort Victoria, Anna and Georg sat in the living room drinking their coffee while Thea investigated the carpet by picking up each little spot of dirt, bugs, or paper and putting it into her mouth. They watched her in silence.

Anna decided to face Georg. "You do not look very happy here. What are you going to do?"

Georg looked surprised at Anna's blunt question. He went over to the kettle and warmed up his coffee, then poured more into Anna's mug as he answered, "I know we can't stay much longer depending on Frederik for food and housing. He has been very generous. When Nelson didn't respond, I sent Alfred Talbot, whom we met on the train, a letter asking him about chances for jobs in Port Angeles."

"Port Angeles?" said Anna. "That is across the straits in the United States." She stood up and picked up a log. "What next?" she asked, as she threw the log onto the fire.

Georg shrugged his shoulders. "Have patience, Anna. We'll find a way."

Anna turned on him. "I'm tired of moving from place to place, as you try out job after job. I want to settle down and have our own home. Why go across to Puget Sound?"

"There are too few people here. I want to work in a bank."

"Face it, Georg. Nelson never responded. Did you go back and see him? That's what I mean. You have to persevere. You give up too quickly. I don't want to move to Port Angeles. Did you look through the *Victoria Press* for ads?"

"Anna, I'm not a janitor or a typist. I'm helping Frederik in the garden. He needs an extra hand now and then. But if I don't hear from Albert, I'm still going to go across on one of the fishing boats and meet with him and look over the town."

"I told you, Georg, and I'm saying it again. I want to settle here. Please, first go out and visit on Vancouver Island. I'm out of patience. Take care of Thea. I'm going to bed."

That night Anna couldn't sleep. She counted sheep and counted numbers, but her thoughts were being forced back to their arrival in Victoria with the expectations of hope, wonder and excitement. Scenes flashed through her mind. What to do?

Days passed too quickly. Anna kept asking Georg, "When are you going to go down and see Mr. Nelson?"

"Anna, I've told you already that Frederik and I went by to see him, but he is too busy right now during tax time. I know how it is. I'm waiting until the rush is over."

"Why not run an ad in the *Press*? I read through it and some jobs were listed. Georg, our visas will soon be up. Maybe I could help?"

"You take care of Thea. I'll find what I want. Trust me, Anna. I'm keeping busy with the produce and log deliveries until I go across the straits and find Albert."

Anna wished she could hold in her anger when she tried to address Georg's job search. He wanted a teller job and apparently wasn't going to look for anything else. Anna yanked at the embroidery thread while she followed the apron pattern as if she were pulling Georg's head right off. We need to do something, she thought, but felt boxed-in over a situation in which she seemed to have no control.

Chapter Fourteen

Lost At Sea

Anna loaded Thea into the little red wagon and, with Katy's help, pulled it down the rough path to Frederik's vegetable garden. The smell of the pines warmed by the morning sun, the song of the black and yellow spotted oriole, and the scolding cries of the blue jays gave witness to the clear spring day. Oh, what a beautiful day, thought Anna. She inhaled deep breaths of air and felt the sun on her face. The smell of the rich earth, the scent of the wildflower blossoms, and the rows of celery, corn, and green beans yet to break though the ground reminded her how much she loved the outdoors.

As she hoed the weeds, Anna thought of her farewell with Georg over a week ago. She hadn't wanted him to go to Port Angeles, but he wouldn't change his mind. She remembered how sad she felt waving goodbye and watching him sail off in Mr. Bates's fishing boat. What can I do? she thought. He doesn't listen to me. I hope he finds Alfred since he didn't respond to Georg's letter. When, oh when, Georg, will we settle down? If you don't find a job there, will you please try again here in Victoria? There must be something available on this large island.

Anna continued working. She thought of her developing friendship with her sister-in-law Karen. Both had come across Canada from Denmark with their babies. Karen told Anna of having to live in a tent that first summer while Frederik worked to rebuild part of their present house. Anna admired Karen's strength and good-natured attitude toward hard work.

Frederik had asked Anna to pick the ripe lettuce. She and Katy knelt and selected round, smooth heads. The sight of curly-haired Thea in her red play suit sitting in the wagon watching them, of Katy in her blue overalls, and herself in her green blouse and light blue skirt, reminded Anna of a painting she'd seen in Denmark entitled, "Joyous Welcoming of the Gifts of the Earth."

It certainly would be nice to have a painting to put on the walls of our own home, she thought. Maybe someday. In her mind she had pictures on the wall of the Amorsens, her in-laws, and those of her father, mother, and sister. But as always, her thoughts turned to Georg. When would he return? Did he find a job or a place to live? A scream from Thea brought Anna out of her daydream as she ran over and grabbed her out of the wagon. "Katy, what happened?" "I don't know. I think I saw a big spider on her."

Anna looked over Thea's arms and noted a bright red spot on her right arm. "Here, here, honey. Don't cry. We'll go home and put cold water on it," she said as she kissed and hugged Thea.

Anna rocked Thea. The baby still sobbed and kept squirming in Anna's arms.

By noon Thea didn't want to nurse any more and she felt feverish. It was time to take her to Dr. Christensen. He immediately examined the swollen arm and took Thea's temperature. "It certainly looks like a spider bite," he said. "Her temperature is nearly 102 degrees. I'll use this antidote. Now take her over to Queen's Hospital. For the next twelve hours she needs to be under surveillance. I'll come by this evening."

Anna looked down at Thea, lying listlessly in her arms. Would the injection prevent spread of the poison? Why did I take my eyes off of her? Anna kept turning over in her mind what she should have done. If only my baby's temperature would drop, she kept repeating to herself.

They arrived at the hospital and Anna, with Frederik's help, signed the admission papers. The nurse took Anna and Thea to the children's section and helped settle Thea in her crib. She just lay there without a cry. Anna slumped down in the chair beside her crib. She felt as if she had a brick tied around her neck. She couldn't stop blaming herself for not taking better care of Thea. She peeked through the crib rails and then leaned over to be sure that Thea was still breathing.

Anna leaned back against the chair and a few tears fell as she longed for Georg to be beside her. If you knew what happened, Georg, she thought, you'd swim across the straits.

Dr. Christensen came later in the evening. "How's our baby doing?" he asked as he picked up Thea, then examined her arm and re-took her temperature.

Thea didn't want anything to do with Dr. Christensen. She started to cry and reached out for her mother. Anna took her and held her close whispering, "Mama's here, honey."

"Her temperature should be down by morning," Dr. Christensen said, his voice confident. "Don't worry, Mrs. Amorsen."

Anna didn't sleep all night. She paced the room, wondering if the doctor meant what he said. She checked on Thea's breathing. She seemed too quiet. Should she call for the nurse? Her head nodded and she had to fight off sleep.

When Anna awoke early in the morning, Thea was smiling and kicking her feet. "You look like you're ready for action today. Are you hungry?" She picked Thea up and nursed her, then checked her arm and forehead. The temperature was down, the redness fading.

Later that morning, after the doctor finished his examination, he gave her back to Anna. "She's fine. We caught it in time. Just keep her as quiet as you can today."

Anna rinsed her face and felt her anxiety leaving. Now, if Georg would just come home.

Soon Karen, Katy and Frederik arrived. After Anna and Thea were finally discharged, the couple helped Anna into their wagon. "Thank you for your kind help," Anna said. "Thea's fine now, thanks to all of you. I'm sorry I caused you so much trouble."

Thea was sound asleep in Anna's arms.

"No bother. We are part of a family, Anna," Karen said. "It is such a joy to have all of you with us. Georg will be home any day. Bates is an able fisherman. He won't cross the straits if the water is too rough."

Anna sighed and looked Karen in the eye. "I hope he returns soon. I really appreciate your patience while we try to settle down, but I'm beginning to lose hope."

"Your time will come, Anna," said Karen. "Maybe Georg will return and decide to search for a job here. Port Angeles is a very small town just beginning to grow."

Later, Anna carried Thea in her arms as the whole family went for a walk into town. Just as they walked into the grocery store, a dark cloud passed overhead. "Why does the weather change so quickly here?" Anna asked. "The day started out so sunny."

"We often have clouds blowing in with the west wind," said Frederik. "Come with me, I want to show you something." He led the way to one side of the store where a barometer hung on the wall. "It looks as if the mercury is at 29.5."

Anna understood. "My father used to show me how to read the barometer in his boat."

"Usually when we have such nice weather and the mercury is falling it means a storm is coming," Frederik said.

"Thank you, Frederik," Anna said as she walked to the front door of the store. "Let's get a paper."

They walked to the magazine shop and Anna bought a copy of the *Victoria Press*. She found the weather report and read it aloud. " 'A storm is sweeping in from the Pacific and will bring heavy rains all across the Island.' " Anna closed the page. A terrible feeling of danger suddenly swept over her.

On the ride home, she was very quiet. Finally Karen said, "Anna, please don't worry yourself. Thea's arm is healing. Georg certainly won't try to cross the straits in a storm. Why don't you get out for a walk before the storm comes. I'll keep the girls and you can follow the path home."

"Thanks, Karen. I do need some time to pull myself together. I hope I'm not a burden to you."

"Anna," said Frederik, "you're never a burden. There is a good spot. It is about a mile or so from our home."

Anna stepped off the hard wagon seat and started home, walking along the path through the woods.

As she felt the solitude envelop her, she heard the breeze rustling the pine needles and the faint hammering of a woodpecker. The sounds reminded her of Papa and how much he loved the outdoors. To think that she once thought she'd remain in the fish stall to the end of her life. The sweet pine scent reminded her of the joy of smelling the sap instead of being entrapped with smelly fish in a harbor stall in Bergen like her Mama.

As Anna walked along, she pondered Georg's decision to go to Port Angeles. Both Karen and Frederik had warned him of the pioneer stage the town was going through. She shook her head, thinking about his determination to find work in Port Angeles. When was he going to realize that an inside worker such as himself would find almost no job opportunities in an outdoors kind of town? Poor Georg. How she wished she was in his arms in a home of their own.

Someday we'll have one, she thought. I love you, Georg. Maybe you'll renew our visas and have us stay on Vancouver Island? I'm so lonely and worried. If only you would send me a cable. I don't want to lose you.

At breakfast the next morning, the sky was overcast and a breeze was beginning to build up in the tree tops. Anna asked Frederik, "Do you think Bates will try to outrun the storm and come across today?"

"It depends upon the catch and the waves. Remember his

livelihood depends upon fishing, just like your father's did. Bergen is protected by high mountains; our strait acts as a funnel entrance to the storm, causing huge waves. Maybe Georg is waiting till this storm passes. Certainly he would send us a wire if he were going to be delayed."

The morning became darker as heavy rain clouds gathered. Anna saw flashes of lightning, then heard the first boom of thunder. Her body tensed and she wanted to curl up like a little baby. The deluge came with such force that the house creaked and swayed like a ship on the seas. Georg, she thought, I hope you're not out there in this storm.

Karen was calmly ironing embroidered aprons and brought them into the living room to show Anna. "Why, Anna, you look ill," she said. "What's the matter?"

"I have a headache. Will you watch Thea while I lie down for a little while?"

"Of course. The storm should pass by this evening. Maybe tomorrow we can get outside."

"Save the aprons for tomorrow, will you? I do want to learn more about the Nordic patterns."

The storm did not let up. It poured day and night until the road was a quagmire. Both Katy and Thea became restless and cranky from being kept inside. Katy started to pile all her toys under her bed just to keep them from Thea. Finally, by the end of the week, the storm dwindled and the sun came out. The whole family went out and stood on the porch to face the east, so happy to see the sun.

"I've got to get to town with our produce," Frederik said. "What's left of it."

"If it's convenient," Anna said, "would you buy me a newspaper. I want to keep track of the weather."

"Sure, Anna. Their reports are usually a day behind, so I'll check with my fishermen friends as well. These springtime storms soon wear themselves out. I don't expect another."

Anna tried to do her embroidery but found herself pacing. She took Thea out and put her in the red wagon. If she kept busy, she kept from thinking about Georg. After lunch, when Anna put Thea down for her nap, she heard Nappy clip-clop up the road. She walked to the front door to greet him as he came in from the barn.

"Hello, Frederik. You're early today," she said, trying to sound casual. "Did they have a paper?"

"Yes," he answered as Karen stepped out of the kitchen and joined them. His face was grim. "The *Victoria Press*. I read the news and went down to the wharf and talked with my friends. Apparently, the report is correct. Anna," he handed her the paper with trembling hands. "Bates's boat was found capsized near the entrance to the strait. They found no survivors."

Anna stood staring at him. Her breath wouldn't come, and she couldn't talk. Her face turned pale, eyes dilated.

Karen put her arms around her and held her tight. "Anna, we don't know that Georg was on the boat."

"I sent a cablegram to the Port Angeles Post Office, attention of Alfred Talbot," Frederik said. "I asked for his assistance in locating Georg, if he were in the town or nearby, and to tell Georg to send us a cable."

Anna closed her eyes and staggered to the sofa. "No! No! It can't be!" she whispered, supporting herself with one arm. A small cry came and then a big sob as if she were catching her breath. Suddenly, she fell down on the sofa, weeping and shaking her head, unable to listen to any more.

Karen brought a glass of water, but Anna wouldn't take it. She just lay there, crying and crying. Karen carefully patted her hair and stroked her back. "Anna, dear, we don't know for sure. Please try to believe we will find Georg in Port Angeles. He wouldn't cross in the storm."

Frederik knelt down beside her. "My dear sister-in-law, we are all Amorsens. We are Vikings. Please don't despair. That brother of mine is very cautious. He'll be home within the week. Wait and see."

Another day passed. Anna was frantic. Her face was flushed, body quivering. She couldn't eat. The hours passed slowly. Should they wire the sheriff of Clallam County and have him make a search for Georg? Maybe Georg hadn't located Alfred. But she always came back to one thought: If Georg were alive, he would contact someone.

Frederik decided to send a cable to the sheriff in Port Angeles, asking for help. Afterwards, he went to the wharf and tried to locate those who knew of the accident. The information was sparse. The storm had forced the boat on the reef. No bodies had been found.

Frederik and Karen continually tried to reassure Anna. "I still believe," said Karen, "Georg is safe somewhere. For some reason he's been delayed."

"How can you say that?" Anna snapped, staring out the window at the woods. "Surely he thinks enough of his family to send a cable. How long do we have to pretend he's still alive?"

Frederik had another thought. "He could be on some other boat, you know. There may have been a last-minute change and his boat hasn't docked yet."

Karen brought out some aprons. "Let's work on these together," she said to Anna. "Look, I already started one. Don't you think it's turned out well so far?"

Anna continued to stare out the window, her face immobile and still as if she were made of china. "I can't sew," she said, barely moving her lips. The pink in her cheeks had been replaced by an ashen pallor. "I can't think. I can't go on like this anymore!"

Just then, Thea let out a cry from her bedroom. Her nap was over. Anna walked toward the bedroom as if in a stupor. Tears streamed down her cheeks while she changed her daughter's diaper. When done, she picked up the baby and held her close. The feel of the child's warm body against hers, the gurgles of glee, the kicking of little feet and the sunny smile which lit Thea's face brought a fresh warmth to Anna's thoughts: This small person needed her; this little human being trusted her and loved her.

I must have faith and hope, she told herself. Yes, I am a Viking. I must go on. She remembered how she had worried once before about Georg when she was in Chicago and he had gone to Denmark. He had been fine then. Why should it be any different now?

Another week passed with no further reports in the newspaper or by cable. Frederik noticed how troubled Anna was and how she was trying to hide it from everyone. "Come with me to town, Anna," he said, "while I deliver this load of produce. While we're there, let's see if we can find out anything more."

On the way, he told Anna how he started his garden and, without being aware of it, became the main produce supplier on the island. "The work is never-ending, but it has provided us with a satisfactory life. If you want to join us, we'd be happy to have you."

Anna just sat, staring ahead and saying nothing.

The magazine store had no cables for Anna or Frederik. The *Victoria Press* had a small insert about the effort to salvage Bates's boat. Frederik drove Nappy down to the docks. There, he hailed an old friend who owned a fishing boat. "Do you know anything more about Bates and his crew?"

The tall, robust man had weather-beaten features and a rough voice. "No, I ain't seen nothing. It's odd. The tide would force the bodies to float, but we ain't seen none."

Anna turned away, fighting the urge to vomit. The thought of her Georg lying face down in the water was more than she could bear. Frederik took her by the arm and helped her into the wagon. "Come along, Anna. We'll drive home. I told Nels in the magazine shop that if a cable came to have Eric bring it right away."

The end of the third week laid heavily upon Anna, Karen, and Frederik. A dull cloud of gloom suppressed their usual laughter and joy. Katy took to teasing Thea to hear her cry and had to be banished to the bedroom. Frederik lost his optimism regarding Georg, but couldn't imagine losing his only brother.

Anna felt as if she needed to think ahead. "What shall I do?" she asked her hosts one evening. "Shall I return to my father and sister in Bergen, visit your parents in Haderslev who love their little grand-daughter dearly, or stay in Victoria?"

"Stay with us," Karen and Frederik answered together.

"Thea and Katy have fun with one another," Karen added. "As Thea gets older, it would be nice for her to have an older cousin to play with."

"My folks would love to have you and Thea," Frederik observed, "but their economy is still suffering." He paused as he noticed Anna's scowl. "Oh, let's not talk this way. Until they salvage Bates's boat, we won't know the truth. So much of what has been said is conjecture."

On the fourth Sunday, Karen invited Anna to bring Thea to church with them. They all dressed in their finery. It had been a long time since Anna had dressed up. She looked at herself in the mirror. Yes, you have lost weight, she thought, noticing the puffy bags under her eyes. Smile. She tried but it wasn't much of a smile. She still felt without any hope.

Their church was built inside the Fort. It was a copy of a Danish village church with its white walls, red roof, and painted gables. In the sanctuary, there was an altar painting of a Danish boat at sea. A model of a ship hung suspended from the ceiling above the nave.

Pastor Johan Hambro was a small man with a face disappearing under a bushy beard. He came out in his clerical robe and after a few hymns which he vigorously led, he launched into his sermon, "Life after Death." Anna covered her face with a handkerchief as the tears started to flow. It was too much to hear more about death and the life hereafter.

At the end of the service, Pastor Hambro asked everyone to pray for the souls of the drowned men from Bates's boat. All Anna could think of were coffins bobbing on the sea. She clutched Frederik's arm, suddenly realizing all the pain he must feeling about the loss of his brother.

On the way back home, Frederik suggested they stop at the magazine shop and buy the Sunday edition of the *Vancouver Times*. He said, "The late Saturday boat brings in a small supply of them each Sunday. Maybe it would have something more about . . . the accident . . . ." He swallowed and remained silent until they arrived at the store. With few words, he purchased the paper, bought a bag of popcorn for everyone, and returned to the wagon. Anna sat in back, searching the pages while Karen held Thea on her lap. All at once, Anna let out a scream! " 'FISHING BOAT CREW RESCUED BY JAPANESE SHIP NIJIYA,' " she read at the top of her lungs. She jumped and began dancing for joy. "They've found the Bates's crew!" she shouted. "They've found Georg!"

As she feverishly read the article and turned to the last page, she saw a picture of the crew. In the background was a tall man with a mustache and beard. "Look! Look!" she yelled. "It's Georg. It's Georg. Look at this picture. It is blurred but I know it's Georg!"

Frederik brought Nappy to a halt. "Let me see, Anna," he said, his voice trembling with emotion. "I'd know that crazy brother of mine anywhere." He carefully studied the picture. "You're right, Anna," he said finally. "It is Georg! It is Georg. He's really alive!" A tear rolled down one cheek.

Karen placed Thea on the floor and threw her arms around his neck, then reached for Anna to join them. The three of them stood there, hugging and crying and sobbing. Thea just cooed while Katy stared up at the three adults. "Why are you crying, Momma," Katy kept asking.

No one knew quite what to say, so Frederik picked her up and kissed and hugged his beautiful little daughter. "It's all right, Katy. We're just happy." Suddenly, he got an idea. "Let's go send a cable to the paper and the ship and hope they take it to Georg," he said, his voice breaking.

Anna and Karen nodded, wiping their tears.

Frederik shook his head. "Can you believe that Georg? I told you that brother of mine would return."

Anna picked up Thea and Karen read out loud. " 'The Nijiya rescued the crew who were found clinging to the damaged boat at the entrance to the strait. The Nijiya was sailing to Port Townsend for U.S. customs clearance, but did not obtain clearance due to a rash that developed among the crew. The U.S. feared scarlet fever, and the whole ship was quarantined.

" 'It wasn't until the ship crossed into Canadian waters and docked in Vancouver that the men were free to leave. However, since it was a communicable disease, the Vancouver Health Department insisted they remain aboard until examined.' "

Karen folded the newspaper and put it on the floor. Then, she took Katy from Frederik so he and Nappy could finish taking them all home.

"No wonder we didn't hear from him," said Frederik. "I hope he's all right. Our cable should reach him and keep him from worrying about us. I hope he can come home soon."

"Thank God for this blessing!" exclaimed Anna, sitting down. She wanted to dance with joy, to squeal with delight, to laugh and shout and proclaim to the universe, but she was holding Thea. She would dance later, alone in the woods.

"Georg is coming home!" she announced in an affected public voice as if she were the emcee at an important public event. She reached over and picked up the newspaper. With one hand, she found the story of the sea rescue, and kissed Georg's picture. She could hardly wait to see her Georg. There was something she had to tell him, something she was pretty sure would make him very happy.

Chapter Fifteen

Isabel

ARRIVING HOME TOMORROW ON EARLY
MORNING FERRY.
GEORG.

The cablegram was pasted on the Amorsen's kitchen cabinet. When Frederik, Karen, Anna and the children arrived at the dock, they could see the morning ferry coming around the edge of the bay and moving slowly toward its berth. They waved and jumped and shouted as the boat got closer.

Suddenly, Frederik let out a piercing whistle; Anna slapped hands over her ears. "Sorry," he said. "When Georg and I were little, we used to signal one another by whistling when we played in the woods in back of our home. He'll recognize it."

At last the ferry was moored at the dock and the passengers disembarked. It seemed forever as they stood anxiously waiting. Suddenly, Georg appeared and practically leaped down the gangplank. He threw his arms around Anna and Thea, then hugged Karen and Katy and slapped Frederik on the back. Anna cried with joy as she clung to one arm.

She thought he looked more like a gold miner than a bank teller. His beard was unkempt, and he had on a strange mustard-colored jacket that was too small and trousers covered with stains and dirt. He looked a lot thinner, too.

"You certainly had us worried," said Frederik as he gave his brother a big bear hug.

Georg picked up Katy and swung her around. She giggled with glee. When he went to pick up Thea, she turned away and cowered against her mother. Georg shook his head and took a deep breath. "A month is a long time for anyone, especially a baby." He wrapped one arm around Anna. "It sure is good to see you, my *Norska*," he said, pulling her to him. "I've really missed you." He gave her a big kiss.

Karen suggested they start home. "Don't you have any boxes, Georg? Did you save anything?"

"I lost all my belongings. What a tale I have to tell you. Almighty God saved us. It was a miracle that the Nijiya picked us out of the cold water. We couldn't have held on much longer."

Home was a raucous place with Katy excitedly running through the house. Thea was rolling on the floor in her pretty pink dress while her mother tried to take it off and put on her play clothes. Anna was singing, "*Den lille Ole.*" Karen was in the kitchen beating eggs for an omelet while Frederik warmed up the fire. Georg just sat in the chair by the fireplace with his jacket and shoes off.

"Tell us what happened, Georg," said Frederik.

Georg was silent for a moment. "The blizzard and huge waves caught Dale's boat in a trough," he said softly, "and it started to take on water. He lost control and it smashed against the rocks. We all clung to the boat, praying for someone to find us. The boat tossed and turned and our hands and bodies began to turn blue."

Anna came over and gave Georg a kiss and a hug, then put Thea in his lap. The child grabbed his beard. He took his daughter and held her high above his head. She squealed with delight. "Well, fairy princess," he said, smiling with love, "I'm glad you're finally playing with me again."

"So, did you find Alfred Talbot?" Anna wondered.

"Yes. He helped me understand the founding of Port Angeles by the Puget Sound Cooperative Colonists. However, that democracy has fallen apart. Alfred said that the 651 colony settlers were distraught and some were leaving."

"Were there any jobs available?"

"Yes, Alfred was recruiting skilled carpenters. They were constructing buildings for the expected grocery and butcher shop, the hardware and lumber store, and a government building to house the post office. But the work was moving very slowly and Alfred didn't think there would be any employment until some of the unrest settled down. He told me to try again next year."

"Well, what about finding a job here?" suggested Frederik. "With spring here now, there is an upsurge in business."

Anna took Thea back while Georg and Frederik talked about how things were going in town. She wondered what plans he had. Maybe he could see the banker, Mr. Nelson again, or even

Mr. Sturtevent, the grocery store owner. He knew the Amorsen family, and his business was booming. She sighed and put Thea down on the floor. She decided now was not the time to be a pest.

As they cuddled up in bed that evening, Georg said, "Anna I'm so grateful to be home. I thought I was going to die."

She gave him a big hug. "It's so good to have you home. How terrible for you to know every moment could be your last." She studied his face for a moment in the dark. He still looked tense. "How did Bates end up in such a situation?"

"We started out early that morning so we could be back here at daybreak. It was barely raining when Bates started the motor and threw off the ropes. As we came out into the straits, the storm had built to gale strength with constantly changing winds. Bates thought he could turn us around and return to shore, but in the process the boat took on water, the engine died, and we were thrown up against the rocks at the strait's entrance. The boat cracked like an eggshell.

"We each grabbed something to hang on to. I thought of you, Anna, and Thea. How would you manage? I blamed myself for going to Port Angeles. I thought of my mother and father and how I had probably hurt them. I felt as if my life were at an end, but I hung on, vowing that if I lived I would try harder to be more considerate of others and to tell you every day I love you."

"Georg, I love you, too. I missed you so much. Thea was bitten by a spider and put in the hospital. I felt for awhile that I was going to lose both of you."

He gave her a big kiss. "My poor little *Norska*. I'm so sorry. I didn't mean to cause you so much worry."

She smiled and gave him a big hug and kiss. She wasn't quite ready to tell him her big surprise. "Just remember this," she said. "From now on, no matter what job you have or where we live, if you're happy, you can count on my support. We're never again going to quarrel about that. That's my promise to you!"

Slowly, he shook his head side to side. "I'm so lucky and I love you so much." He pulled her close and gave her a long, warm kiss. Anna melted. Now she felt whole; they were one. Soon they began making love, and it was the best it had been for many months. Later, they fell asleep in each others arms.

Several days had passed. Georg carefully put on his white shirt and the one good suit he had left. He had trimmed off most of his beard. He carefully combed his mustache. A tie and a handkerchief in his breast pocket completed the attire.

"Turn around twice, Georg," said Anna, nodding approval. "Yes, you do look like a bank teller. Now keep your voice down when you talk to Mr. Nelson and concentrate on your recommendations and experience at the Rodding bank."

Georg put his arm around Anna and gave her a strong hug. "I will, don't worry. I really want this job, Anna. Look, I even borrowed Frederik's hat. I don't know what I can ever do to thank him for arranging this interview."

His brother dropped Georg at the bank and then went on to make his usual delivery at Sturtevent's grocery store. Karen and Anna rode along, too. Their curiosity wouldn't allow them to stay home. One of the neighbors stayed with the children.

After his delivery, Anna could hardly wait for Frederik to flick Nappy's tail and make him move faster while they bumped their way back toward the bank. Standing in front of the combined post office and bank building, Georg saw them and waved. He ran at them. "I've got the job!" he yelled. "Mr. Nelson wants me to work three days a week and handle all the military business." He leaped into the wagon. "You were right, brother. I just presented my recommendations and answered his questions. It worked. Thank you for all your help."

The whole family celebrated that night. Karen prepared *frikadeller*, and Katy helped decorate the table with pictures she had drawn. Anna had a new bounce to her step. She sang *"Den lille Ole"* as she stirred the flour into the eggs for a *dansk lagkage*. Her heavy burden had been lifted. She recalled how happy she was when Georg obtained the first Rodding bank job, and now he would work again as a teller. That wasn't the only thing she remembered about Rodding.

Frederik took out his bottle of Acquavit and shared a glass with Georg. *"Skal,"* he said to Georg. "We wish you great success, brother."

As they sat around the table that night after putting the children to bed, Georg asked Frederik, "What is available for rent in town? We appreciate your hospitality but we must find ourselves a home."

Frederik quickly replied, "You're welcome here. Don't feel you have to move right away. Why don't you wait awhile and see how things go. You can help pay for your food by working two days a week with me in the produce garden."

Anna spoke up, "Thanks, Frederik, but we do need to find something. Maybe in another month or so."

Karen interrupted Anna. "Excuse me, Anna, but there are very few rentals in Victoria. Most of the settlers build their own homes."

Anna shrugged. "Well, we'll see. I love being with all of you, but we don't want to impose."

Frederik laughed. "You are no imposition. We've had a great time together. If you move out I'm sure Katy would want to go with you."

In the weeks that followed, Georg came to love his new job. Each day, he came home lighthearted and full of fun. "Here, Thea, give me a hug," he would sometimes say, holding her and pretending they were dancing across the carpet. Anna could feel his renewed sense of joy and love, especially when he kissed her.

She and Karen kept busy sewing the Nordic aprons. They put some in Sturtevent's store and they sold out immediately. Anna felt happy because she was making a contribution. "Anna," Karen said one afternoon, "you've really learned a lot and you sew so fast. You've helped triple our sales."

One morning after the men had left for work, Anna asked Karen to sit a moment and share a cup of coffee. "I want to tell you something very exciting."

"Anna, please tell me quick. The suspense is too much."

"I'm pregnant. Well . . . I think I am."

"Praise God!" said Karen, jumping up and giving Anna a hug. "Have you seen Dr. Christensen?"

"No. Can Frederik make me an appointment with him? Tell him not to tell Georg. I want to surprise him."

Karen smiled. "Of course. He'll be so excited."

Several days passed. Anna was waiting for Georg as he walked through the front door after work one day. "I know something you don't know," she said coquettishly. An impish smirk lit her face.

Georg grinned, noticed Karen and Frederik pretending to be busy in the kitchen, then gave Anna a quick kiss. "Is that right?" he said louder than usual, his eyes darting around the room for clues. "You're a very smart woman, Anna. There's much you know that I don't, but when you get that smirk on your face, I know I could never guess your surprise. What is it?"

Anna grinned triumphantly. She really did know something he didn't. She loved the feeling. "I'm pregnant," she announced. "We're going to have another baby."

"Yikes!" Georg yelped. He lifted Anna off her feet and twirled her around and around. "Frederik, Karen," he shouted, "Anna is going to have a baby!"

Frederik laughed. "Calm down, little brother. You're going to need all that energy now that you're the father of two!"

On August 13, the family celebrated Thea's first birthday. Anna baked a cake, Katy made paper hats, and Karen sewed her a beautiful embroidery-covered dress. Georg and Anna bought a new buggy to push her in when they went to town. It would be nice to have another daughter, thought Anna. Thea could play with her. If we had our own home, I could decorate the baby's room with a new crib and colored quilts. Someday, someday, she kept promising herself. We are saving money to buy a home later. But it is more secure right now being here with Karen.

The end of the summer days were hot. Karen and Anna took the girls down to the beach. The bumpy road soon became too rough for Anna. Each bump bounced the baby and increased her nausea. However, they loved the deep blue of Puget Sound with its big waves rolling in one after another, crashing against the sand. The girls usually ended up covered with sand but at least Thea learned not to eat it.

One cold early morning in February, Anna was seized with terrible cramps. "Georg," she nudged him, "Wake up and help me. It hurts; hold my hand."

The pain lasted all day and night. Dr. Christensen had spent the whole night at the Amorsen's. As daylight broke, Anna could scarcely move her head. The continuous pain was burning up her energy. "Help me, Karen," she said. "Hold my hand - oh, oh, my water just broke. I feel it running down my legs."

"You're on the final thrust," said Karen. "I'll get towels."

"Breath deeply," said Georg, "bear down. Remember, Anna, you brought Thea into this world."

Anna pushed and pushed. She began to feel the movement downward. "Get Dr. Christensen right now!"

"Come on, Anna," said Dr. Christensen, walking into the bedroom. "Stretch, breath deeply,"

He listened to the baby's heart beat, observed the abdomen, stood up, and smiled at Anna. "We're nearly there. Now I'm going to count and you breathe in," he said. "Then, hold it to the count of ten. Are you ready?"

"Anna, let's give it one more try," said Karen. "I'll hold your hand and squeeze as you contract. We're both going to help you."

With two on either side of her, Anna pushed and pushed. Slowly the head appeared. "Good, Anna, keep at it. Here comes the head." Dr. Christensen reached for the baby, gently holding it by the shoulders. "It's a girl! It's a girl!"

Georg looked at the clock. It was 6:00 a.m.

"She looks something like a greenish fish, but don't worry — it's just the meconium," said the smiling doctor. He skillfully cleared the baby's throat, then clipped the umbilical cord. Working quickly, he sponged off the baby with warm water, then wrapped her in a blanket and put her in Anna's arms.

With a look of complete exhaustion and satisfaction on her face, she beckoned Georg to take the baby and said, "Georg, let's call her Isabel."

Chapter Sixteen

Farewell

Isabel's birth brought many changes to the Amorsen household. Georg and Anna's bedroom got more crowded after they added a pink-ribboned basket balanced on two heavy wood stumps beside their bed. The new baby turned out to be a quiet, smiling child. She quickly took to nursing and seldom awoke more than twice during the night. But it was still a big adjustment for everyone.

"Why won't she stay awake and play with us?" Katy asked.

"You've forgotten, Katy," Anna answered, "that you're six. When you were little you slept a lot, too."

Thea, a year and a half old, seemed confused. She peeked in the basket and, copying her mother, would say, "Baby?"

Anna realized Thea was used to being the "baby" of the household and tried to reassure her. She would pick her up and hold her tight. "You are my big girl, Thea," she would say. "Later on, you can push the baby in the buggy."

Dr. Christensen advised Anna to rest each afternoon until she regained her strength. Consequently, the Amorsen household became a quiet place in the afternoon while Thea and Anna napped. Katy rode with her mother and father on their daily trip to sell the garden produce and Karen's embroidered Nordic aprons. While she slept, Anna often dreamt of Norway, and the beautiful home with red-shuttered windows she used to admire on the Bergen Mountains across the bay from her parents' home.

Georg worked only three days a week at the bank. He spent his other days gardening and stacking fresh vegetables and fruits for Frederik to sell to the Victoria grocery. Georg would often kid his older brother, "You're trying to make me into a farmer. " He and Anna worried about their long stay with Frederik and Karen. It had been over a year now.

Georg tried to find a small house for rent, but there were practically none to be had. The number of new colonists increased each day. "Even if we found a place," he told Anna, "we hardly have enough money to rent it. I like my teller job, but it has no future. It's just a small branch of the main Vancouver bank." Anna felt for Georg. "I can embroider more aprons," she offered.

Georg leaned over and gave her a hug. "You have two daughters to take care of, Anna. I'll keep trying."

At dinner the next night, Frederik and Karen both repeated their previous discussion. Frederik said, "We want you to stay with us." "Yes," said Karen. "We have a wonderful big Amorsen family. The girls are fascinated by Isabel. They also enjoy playing with one another."

Anna thought how kind they were. Maybe some day Georg could find a better job and our own place to live. They need their own home just as much as we need ours.

Spring passed into summer. Anna took over the household work. Karen started an embroidery circle whereby she provided the material and the women completed the Nordic embroidery scenes. Karen sold them to tourists, and she paid the women on an hourly rate. Frederik could hardly fill the demand for his greens and fruits at Sturtevent's grocery.

One day Frederik jokingly told Georg, "You should give up your part-time job and cultivate the land on the west side of the house. Within a year we could ship produce to the north island because the colonists are gradually moving there."

Georg just smiled and kept up with his weeding. "No, maybe the bank will expand."

"Why not risk it?"

"Well, I like to work with people, too. Out here you just talk to the vegetables."

One fall day when the leaves were turning brown and falling to the ground and the last of the pumpkin crop spilled over the garden, Frederik returned from his daily trip to town with a letter for Georg.

"Hi, little brother," he called out as he drove the wagon up to the barn. "The magazine store received this a week ago."

Georg shook his head. "A week ago. What happened?"

"I haven't stopped by all week. They don't operate a delivery service."

"Thank you, big brother." Georg took the envelope and noticed it was from Alfred Talbot, his friend in Port Angeles.

Georg walked into the house and opened the letter and started to read it. Suddenly he called, "Anna, Anna come here!"

She was in the midst of making bread; she slapped the dough, rinsed her hands, took off her flour-sprinkled apron and went in to see Georg. Karen and the girls were outside.

"What is it?" she asked, wiping her hands.

"Come into our bedroom. I want to talk with you."

"My, this must be a check for a thousand dollars," laughed Anna.

"Just about as good. Alfred sent me this letter to invite me to join him in a plan to buy out the Port Angeles grocery store. The owner died and his widow wants to sell out."

"How much will it cost? You know that our savings would never cover the purchase of a grocery store."

"Wait, Anna, before you decide. Alfred is offering to share the investment with us. He wrote that we could pay back at a rate we could afford."

"What's in it for him?"

"Anna, all these matters will have to be agreed upon. The best part I haven't told you yet. Upstairs above the store is a two-bedroom apartment with a kitchen and a living room. I saw the framework going up when I was there last year. It has big windows looking out over the harbor and the mountains. He sent me a plan of the building."

"Why do you think he wants to invest?"

"We had a number of long talks when I was there. I longingly said I'd give my right eye for a home of our own. I think he and his wife would like us and little Isabel. Remember how he used to hold Thea so we could eat when we were in the dining car? They have no children."

"A home of our own." Anna's dreams shone in her eyes, but she felt she must find out the costs. "How much, how much?"

"Alfred wrote out the costs. Here, you can read them. He says that with the license, the mortgage, and taxes, we need about $500."

"Georg, we've only saved $370."

"I know my father will lend us the remaining amount. We can do it, Anna. I know we can."

"What are the sales? Is it an active store?"

"Anna," Georg hugged her as he answered. "I will have to go over and talk with Alfred and find out about these details. Please, honey, this is our chance to live our own lives in our own home."

Anna looked up at Georg. He was so tall and she always had to look up to him. "I don't know how I can stand another crossing of the Straits of Juan de Fuca, Georg, but if you believe so heartily in this, I guess that you'll have to go over and meet with Alfred."

"I knew you would support me. I'll write him a letter telling him I'm coming and I'll return with all the details. I'll be gone four days because I can take off one Friday at the bank."

That evening Anna and Georg discussed with Frederik and Karen the possibilities of a successful grocery store in a town of 300 colonists.

"I read," said Frederik, "that they are heading for a land boom. Port Angeles has great potential in both logging and in fishing. They have the first protected harbor as the ships enter the straits from the Pacific Ocean."

Karen spoke up. "Mrs. Neilsen, a member of our church, just returned from a visit to her daughter there. She said the town is bustling with activity."

"I heard that most of the settlers are Scandinavian," said Georg. "I met a number of Alfred's friends from Norway."

Within the next week, Georg arranged passage on Bates's new boat to Port Angeles. As the days passed, Anna kept repeating to Karen, "Do you think Georg is there now?" The horror of his rescue at sea filled her mind every minute he was gone.

"Anna, he'll be all right. The storms of winter are not rolling in yet," said Frederik.

When Erik came up to the house the next day to deliver Georg's wire, Anna grabbed the letter feeling such a relief to know her Georg was safe. She read it to Frederik and Karen.

Dear Anna:

Alfred took me through the market, going through the stock. It is in excellent shape. Mrs. Peerson, the owner, showed me around her upstairs home. It is quite sunny, and has about as much space as Frederik's house, and has a beautiful view of the mountains and Puget Sound.

Alfred will accept $370 as a down payment until we receive the rest from my father. We can take possession as soon as Clallam County's recorder clears the title.

Georg

"Oh, Anna!" cried Karen as she tried to dry her eyes. "What are we going to do without you?"

Katy looked puzzled. "Can I go too, Momma?"
Frederik took her on his lap. "There are boats that cross the
strait regularly. It is only a three-hour trip. We can easily visit one
another."
"But, Daddy, I want to go with Thea."
"We'll plan to visit as soon as they get settled."
Anna asked, "What do you think of Alfred's offer?"
Karen nodded her head. "It sounds like you'll have a home,
Georg will have his business, and the girls can go to the first kinder-
garten Port Angeles started in Washington state."
Frederik agreed. "We will miss you so much, Anna, but I do
agree with Karen. When Georg returns, if he is satisfied and you
too, then it is a good beginning."
"Well, we'll wait until Georg returns," said Anna.

As she went to bed that night, Anna realized how much she was
torn between her love for the Amorsen family and her desire to have
her own home and have Georg happy with his work. To be able to
settle down and live in one location for over a year would be wonderful. Of course, she wondered how she would get acquainted with
the other women. Where will the children play if we're next to the
harbor? Anna walked up and down the bedroom. She looked down
at Thea and Isabel who were sound asleep. What will your lives be
like as citizens of the United States? As she tried again to go to
sleep, she muttered, "This must be the final change."

Frederik drove all the family down to welcome Georg when he
returned Sunday evening. Anna kept walking to the end of the wharf
and peering down to the harbor entrance. Georg's crossing the straits
brought up all the sorrow she experienced when Bates's boat floun-
dered. She could hardly stand to wait.

Finally the boat arrived. Katy and Thea waved but Georg didn't
come down the gangplank with the other passengers. She began to
feel faint.

"Frederik, please go aboard and find my husband."

Anna and Karen stood there in the cold wind, smelling the fishing boat docked nearby and watching the waves slap against the shore.
"Anna, relax. He must have a reason. Maybe they had to recheck
his passport."

Just then Frederik appeared at the top of the gangplank carrying
a large box. He hurried down and yelled, "He's O.K. They just have
to verify he was working for me. That brother of mine forgot to
renew his visa. But, he brought up a whole box of Dungeness crabs.
Come and sit in the wagon. He'll be here in a minute."

Georg, at that moment, came running down the gangplank as if he were shot out of a cannon. He circled Anna and baby Isabel in his arms and kissed Anna saying, "I love you."

Anna wiped tears of happiness off her cheeks and said, "Oh, Georg, I worried so much over you. How glad I am to have you home."

That evening they boiled the water to cook the crabs. The kitchen began to smell like Rudy's fish stand. "I fought those crabs all the way across. They kept getting claws outside the boat as fast as I could stuff them in."

After the children were in bed, Georg began to tell Frederik, Karen, and Anna about his trip. "I used every moment to find out about the grocery business and the town. Alfred accepted our down payment. Mrs. Peerson is moving to Tacoma to live with her daughter and said we could have the furniture except for her desk, China chest, and sofa.

"Anna, you'll like the apartment. It is roomy and has plenty of cupboards."

"What about the title, Georg?" asked Frederik.

"Alfred said he would take the papers over to the county office Monday morning.

"I stayed with the Talbots. Alfred is in charge of his own construction company. A land boom is making house-building a very profitable business. He built his beautiful home up on a hill at Second and Lincoln. Here, I brought you a copy of the *Port Angeles Times*."

"Well," said Frederik, leaning back in his chair, "if the rest of your groceries are as tasty as the crabs, we'll be over to see you often. So, you've decided to leave us, Georg. Don't say anything to your bank manager until you have the title in your hands."

Karen spoke up. "Take the basket with you, Anna. Isabel will need it. What more can we do to help you?"

When Anna and Georg went to bed, Anna asked, "Georg, you are sure this is what you want to do? Remember how hard you had to work at the dry goods store? Of course, you spent your time charming the ladies to buy fabrics."

Georg leaned on his elbow and looked through the darkened room at Anna. "Don't worry, honey. I already have another idea to attract the townspeople. I want to talk with Frederik tomorrow. There are few green vegetables in Port Angeles. Their climate is colder than Victoria's. I'm going to ask Frederik to ship a supply of greens and fruits over each week. Hudson Bay has a boat that regularly crosses to the Port. 'Fresh from the garden.' Can't you see the house-wives rushing to buy fresh cabbage, celery, tomatoes, carrots, and fruit fresh from the garden?"

"Georg, you're always thinking. How clever! Stop your planning for a while and pay some attention to me."

The next two weeks were spent in sorting their usable items from the many packages they had stored in the barn. Katy followed them around with a forlorn look on her face. "Please, Aunt Anna, take me with you."

Anna felt sad to have Katy and Thea's friendship interrupted. "You wait a while, Katy, and we'll have you all over to visit our new home."

What a task to pick up and pack all of our belongings while waiting for the recorder's report, thought Anna. To settle in a strange town is much like our first little home in Rodding where we stayed ten months. Everyone spoke Danish. I wonder if my English is good enough since I've added some Canadian expressions. Georg is so excited, but it is harder for me because I have to take care of the two children. I expect that he will also want me to help him in the store.

The second week came and no letter arrived from the recorder. Within the next day, however, Georg received the deed and a letter from Alfred.

"Anna, Alfred writes that a claim on the property had to be cleared before the recorder could sign it. Everything is all right now. He has the key to the property."

The last few days were filled with packing and talking. Karen and Anna put together a plan for Anna to take the material to Port Angeles to start a circle of women to make Nordic aprons. Georg and Frederik worked out a deal with Gunnar Henrikson, who had the largest fishing boat, to bring the produce across the strait. Katy even parted with her special rag doll so Thea could play with it before she came.

Frederik had to make three trips to the wharf with all the boxes and luggage of Georg and Anna. He hired Gunnar to take them over so that there would be plenty of room for little boxes, big boxes, baskets, clothes, kitchenware, and packages of food for the first day.

As Anna walked out of Frederik's home for the last time, she picked a flower from the bush at the front window and carried it with her. "Karen and Frederik, you must come over and see us soon. You have been our dearest friends and relatives."

When they reached the wharf, Gunnar was waiting to catch the morning tide. The brothers hugged and slapped each other on the back. The mothers both wept as they clutched each other to say goodbye. Katy lay down on the wharf and wouldn't move until her father picked her up.

Anna said, "Katy, come now. We'll see you at least by Thanksgiving."

"*Mange takk*," said Georg. " I thank you all."

Gunnar released the rope and the boat started down the harbor to cross the Juan de Fuca Straits. Anna sat outside holding Isabel and Thea and longingly looked at the fading figures of her family. She wiped away her last tear and told herself, You can do it, Anna! She hugged her daughters.

Georg came over and sat with them. "We're on our way to a new adventure," he said.

Chapter Seventeen

The Port Angeles Years

Anna opened wide the window shades of her new home. She could see the clear blue ocean water to her left and the tall firs of the Olympia forest along the mountain to her right. Somehow, the beautiful view calmed her disgust. Hands on hips, she stared back around the inside. This was really no place for little children, she thought. Her dreams of how their new home would look had been quickly dashed when they arrived at the grocery store. The living quarters looked worse than the storage shed for the store. The two-story building had space for them upstairs, but the dark woodwork was filthy and had kept her busy for the past week. Boxes, suitcases, wedding gifts, and clothes were still everywhere; the crib and the bed had been squeezed into the children's tiny bedroom.

Anna couldn't believe the way things had turned out. This was no home. It was a cracker box.

She kept working at going through the boxes and putting things away in what little available space there was.

Thea brought a book and sat down beside Anna. "Read?" she asked in a tiny voice.

"I'll finish with these clothes, then I'll read to you," Anna replied. Wish I could let her out in the yard, she thought. She's not old enough to stay away from the water.

The waves from the strait often rolled up to the edge of their lot. She was glad Georg had put a lock up high on the door at the top of the stairs so the children couldn't reach it, but wished he had more time to be with the children. He spent most days and half the night downstairs in the store, sorting items and checking inventory.

He told her that the customer count was getting better. Many just came out of curiosity — they wanted to meet the new owner of Peerson's Grocery.

One of his first visitors came dressed in a suit and tie, leaning on a cane, and wearing a felt hat at a jaunty angle. He pushed his hat to the back of his head and saluted Georg with, "Well, young man, are you going to stay with us or go bankrupt like the Cooperative Colony?"

Alfred had told Georg and Anna that Wilbert Abernethy was the first property owner in the town site of Port Angeles in 1864. He would most likely be one of the first to find out who had taken over Peerson's Grocery store. He had opened the first lumber mill and hired workers who were a tough breed of men known as loggers.

"I told him that Mr. Talbot and I own the store. When he heard Talbot's name, he said, 'Take my advice. Don't give these rascals credit. Cash on the barrel! Then you won't have to sell your cows, and other assets like the Puget Sound Cooperative Colony had to do. What's your name?' "

Two months after they arrived, Georg came up for his quick lunch one afternoon and said, "Alfred came by, and he and Elizabeth invited us over for dinner to meet some friends next Sunday. He said he'd send his driver for us. If it rains, it would be a haul to get to his place on the hill."

"Who are the friends, Georg? Shall I wear my Nordic apron with all its pretty colors over my blue dress? It will be a chance to urge the women to become Nordic seamstresses."

"Sure, wear whatever you like. I'm wearing my suit. I didn't get the names of the friends."

Sunday came with a rainstorm. Mr. Talbot sent Rudolf, his handyman, over to pick them up. As the horses struggled to climb the muddy and slippery hill, Rudolf pointed to the house ahead. "There it is."

Anna's eyes grew big. "Georg, you didn't tell me they lived in a mansion.

Elizabeth and Alfred met them at the door. "Welcome to Port Angeles. We're happy to have you here," said Elizabeth.

"Let me have your coats," said Alfred. "Thea, you have grown up since I last saw you on the train."

Thea ran over and clung to her mother's Nordic apron. She was too little to remember when Alfred used to hold her on the train to Victoria.

"Wait and see, Thea, I have something for you," he said.

Elizabeth said, "We will never forget when we were stalled on Kicking Horse Pass. So this is the new baby?" Isabel looked at the lady. Sometimes strangers made the child cry but something interested her this time. Elizabeth had on a tight-fitting suit with the jacket sprayed with sparkles. She reached out for one and tried to pull it off.

Anna grabbed her hand. "No, Isabel."

The doorbell rang and Alfred opened the door for other guests, Harry Smith and his wife, Ethel. "Welcome. Come in and let me take your coats."

They followed Alfred into the living room while Anna stepped into the vestibule with Isabel. The large wall mirror caught their reflection. Look at my dress, she thought. I really look thinner and my apron with the red embroidery is colorful. Why, I look pretty.

As she started to the living room, Anna noticed the ceiling's hand-painted rose border and the beautiful shiny hardwood floors. Also the sliding doors were open to the dining room, and there was a highchair for Isabel. A huge Tiffany lamp hung from the ceiling over a table set with silver goblets. She walked back to meet the guests.

"What a beautiful home you have," she told Alfred.

He brought out two brown fuzzy teddy bears. "One for Isabel."

She immediately tried to put the little bear in her mouth.

"Thea, here is another little bear for you," said Alfred.

Thea wasn't sure about the gift but she took the bear, cuddled it in her arms, and gave Alfred a shy smile.

Mr. and Mrs. Abernethy arrived and Alfred hurried outside to greet them. "Welcome friends, come in," said Alfred as he took their coats and led them into the living room and introduced them to the others.

"Georg, I know you have met Wilbert and this is Winifred, his wife. Anna is Georg's wife and these are their two little children, Thea and Isabel."

Anna smiled. "Pleased to meet you." Within her mind was Georg's tale about Mr. Abernethy's visit to Peerson's Grocery. He looked nearly two-hundred pounds with a potbelly, a brown suit, and a silk shirt which he periodically stuffed within the belt around his waist.

Anna was more pleased with Winifred who wore a fashionable dress undoubtedly hand made. It was a flowering pink shirt and skirt cut just to fit her.

"That's a lovely design," said Winifred, pointing to the bright colored apron.

"Are you ready, folks? Let's eat," said Alfred.

Georg and Anna savored every bite. They had not eaten so splendidly since they stayed with Georg's parents in Haderslev. The aroma of marzipan reminded Anna of their last Danish Christmas — the whirls of marzipan cake into the shape of a pyramid with the icing dripping out between each circle and a little flag on top. This time it was the United States flag.

After dinner, Alfred lit a cigar and offered one to the men and everyone but Wilbert refused. Elizabeth invited the two girls to build a block house for their teddy bears and took them to the living room. Ethel, Winifred, and Anna went to the den so Anna could teach them about the Nordic aprons.

The men sat together and Wilbert asked, "Well, Georg, how's it going?"

"We feel good about sales and the interest of the townspeople; some of the homesteaders have little money."

"I told you to watch cash on the barrel. That crowd is a bunch of squatters we need to get out of here."

Georg shook his head. "They are just trying to make a living. Times are hard."

Abernethy then interrupted and took charge of the group to avoid an argument. After that Georg kept quiet.

Anna liked the rest of the evening because Isabel went to sleep in Elizabeth's arms and Thea was busy building castles over the heads of the teddy bears. She gathered up her sewing bag and brought out samples of Nordic aprons. Ethel and Winifred watched while Anna took the thread and said, "First watch my hands as they work, and I'll show you how to get started."

The evening ended with Isabel waking up and crying for her mother. Anna looked in on Elizabeth and her children. "I don't want these beautiful little dolls to go home," Anna's hostess said. "Thea is an expert castle builder. You must come and visit us again. We have no children."

Anna thanked the other women for letting her show them how to make the Nordic aprons. She promised to help them whenever they needed it.

The men came out and shook hands while Abernethy kept talking about getting rid of the land jumpers.

The Amorsen's thanked Alfred and Elizabeth for the lovely dinner and said their goodbyes to the others. As they rode down the hill, Georg turned to Anna and said, "Alfred had the dinner party to introduce us to the main business men in Port Angeles. Harry is a quiet man but smart. I can't stand that Wilbert. I tried to tell him how my brother is transferring his produce and fruit on Gunner's boat to our market and he didn't give me a chance."

One day Anna pushed the girls in the buggy over to a meeting of the Lutheran Women's Fellowship in a home about three blocks away. She was hesitant as she stood at the door and rang the bell. How would they greet her, she wondered. What if they don't accept me? A very large woman welcomed her in. "Hello, I'm Eva Brown. What two pretty little girls you have. Our little girl Melody is at school but will be home by noon. They can play together." Anna smiled and said, "I'm Anna Amorsen. This is Isabel and our oldest is Thea. My husband, Georg Amorsen, recently purchased Peerson's Grocery along with Mr. Talbot." "I'm delighted to meet you. Come and put your things down in the hall and then we'll meet the other women."

Eva introduced each of the five women who nodded their heads with a polite, "Hi llo." They continued with their plans for the coming festival. Anna listened. One lady said, "What cute little girls," but otherwise the conversation centered on how to raise funds for the festival.

At lunchtime, they shared fish sandwiches, cookies, and coffee. Anna decided to speak up. "I've brought some samples of Nordic aprons. We used to raise money at church by embroidering them. The women liked them because the funds supported the Children's Survival Overseas Fund."

"Stand up," said Eva, "so we can see the design. It doesn't look too difficult."

Anna did and walked around the table giving sample designs to the ladies. "You'll enjoy making them." She felt slight resistance at her new ideas at first, but before she left they had agreed to give her embroidery a chance.

As she maneuvered the buggy along the wooden sidewalk, she thought about friendships and her need to talk with other women. They seemed to accept her living above the store. Of course, when she mentioned Mr. Talbot's name, that seemed to make a big difference. Not only that, but Thea made a new friend.

Melody Brown came over to play with Thea within the next few days and the girls seemed to get along even though Melody bossed Thea around. Anna was just happy that Thea had a friend.

With Thanksgiving coming, the store became busier and busier. Georg had to hire Eddy, a friend of Rudolf's whom Alfred had recommended, to work weekends and when needed.

"Eddy's the kind of worker," Georg told Anna, "who goes ahead and sees what has to be done. A fine young man. This extra help gives me time to pay the bills and send out orders to meet the needs of special customers."

Anna and Georg had invited Frederik, Karen, and Katy to come over and spend Thanksgiving. Georg sent the invitation with the check for payment of the produce.

The day after Thanksgiving, they all walked down to the dock. It was hard for Anna to see Karen leave. They hugged and a few tears fell. "Thank you for coming over. We do miss you. You have been such good friends."

Frederik kidded Georg, "You have certainly boosted my produce business. If you want to switch jobs, let me know."

Little Katy waved back and their boat slowly left the wharf, then disappeared around the harbor entrance. Anna wondered when she would see Karen again.

The grocery store, with Georg's promotional talents, caught the town's fancy. Another handyman was hired to meet the customer demand. The produce supplies that had become a bit scant over the winter multiplied as spring came. Customers stood in line to buy the fresh produce.

On the Fourth of July, Port Angeles held a parade to celebrate the incorporation of the town into Port Angeles. Everyone with a wagon decorated it to be in the parade. Georg decorated his grocery wagon with American flags.

Anna dressed the girls in red, white, and blue dresses, but wore a worried expression.

Georg noticed. "We're in the parade to support the homesteaders," he said. "Look, Anna, they now can stake a claim. Would you like to live in a tent?"

"If you don't maintain good relations with the town leaders, we may be in a tent," she replied.

He angrily drove the wagon to the starting line of the parade. While waiting, Harry Smith came over and asked, "Who are you supporting, Georg?"

"I'm advertising my grocery store, Harry." He didn't mention that he had a homesteaders sign in front of the wagon.

"Remember, we don't want these claim jumpers in our town," Smith said.

"Harry, the homesteaders have to live. Why can't we share our land? According to the law, the land is open to settlers."

"They haven't earned the right to the land. They're a burden to us," yelled Harry as the line started to move. Anna was seated beside Georg on the front seat of the wagon. "You heard what he said. How can you support the land jumpers?" "I'm celebrating the incorporation of the town. I feel for those in need. I'll support them in my own way, but I won't raise the wrath of the town's fathers."

With the band playing and alongside the many other decorated wagons in the parade, Georg felt like another proud citizen of Port Angeles because of the town's new status. Georg had big signs on each side of his wagon that read: "Support Port Angeles. Trade at Peerson's Groceries."

The following morning he stopped by the backyard shed where he kept his wagon. He was greeted by a stinking smell and thick clumps of mud picked up from the sewage line running to the ocean. It was all over his wagon.

"I can't believe it " he told Anna. "门......... knew me well enough to find the luck to the shed and to carry buckets of this smelling seashore mess to cover the wagon. It stinks. Besides that, I have to clean off all the stains."

"Georg, did you talk to anyone else about the homesteaders besides Harry?"

"Not that I can think of. Would Harry do such a thing because we don't agree? I doubt it."

"Did you notice any of the city government people following you up to the mountains when you've been bringing leftover produce and stale bread to the land claimers?"

"Oh, Anna, stop sticking with me pins! I just don't know. I'll ask those I can trust around town — maybe find out who was paid to do such a dirty trick."

"Someone who has compassion for people will support you. I told you to be careful in dealing with the business crowd."

"Anna, leave me alone! I'm not going to stop helping the homesteaders. I'll just do it more quietly. We won't talk of this any more."

In 1891, The *Port Angeles Times* celebrated the opening of a steam-operated plant to produce electricity. Primarily it was a trial experiment, but Anna told Georg, "Just think how wonderful it would be not to have to run around to light the lamps."

Anna was gradually able to free herself from the burden of worrying about making ends meet or about having a place to live. She often wondered, however, what happened to Georg's search for those who threw the mud on his wagon. He would not discuss it. Georg put a bigger bolt on the shed, and it didn't happen again, but Anna knew he was still bringing scraps to the homesteaders.

In the afternoon, she'd look out the windows at the blue Puget Sound on one side and the high Olympic Mountains on the other. She felt as if she were home. Georg and his new promotional ideas were doing well at the store. The best, Anna thought, was that he had time to spend with his family. They often walked to the nearby park so Thea could swing on the bars and Isabel walk and run on the grass. Yes, it was wonderful to have settled down to a real home.

Melody became Thea's best friend; she couldn't wait to follow her everywhere. They got along fairly well except when Melody began bossing Thea. If Isabel was awake, she had the role of baby. The older girls would use leftover clothes or fabric to play dress-up, draping them as if they were all kinds of garments for queens, princesses, or witches.

One rainy Friday afternoon, Anna was on the back porch washing clothes, and the garment box was out. Once again Isabel was to be the baby.

"Let's put this little hat with a veil on Isabel, and this red piece we'll tie around her waist," said Melody.

Thea found a bright orange fabric. "Look, I'm the queen."

Melody had just started to make a paper crown. "No, you can't. I'm the queen. You're the witch."

"No!" said Thea. "You're the witch."

"Oh, come on, Thea. Next time you're queen."

As Isabel sat up to find out what all the yelling was about, her veil flopped down over her eyes. She gave it a few swipes, but it didn't move. She clutched a rag doll to her chest.

"Melody, no. I'm the queen!"

"Thea, I'm going home!"

Melody had often watched Georg open the door and decided this time she could do it. She took the highchair, put it by the door, and carefully stood on her tiptoes, just reaching the key. "Now, you'll see. I'm going to walk out of here."

Thea yelled, "Go, witch!"

With that Melody opened the door and said, "I'll show you. You're no queen anyhow." She started down the steps.

Thea stood on the landing and watched her friend leave.

At that same moment, Isabel was stumbling around the room, holding Thea's rag doll and trying to pull the veil from her eyes. She walked in the direction of the noise.

Thea watched Melody reach the bottom of the steps, hoping she would come back.

There was a bang and a bump. Before Thea could bend down to catch her, Isabel was rolling down the steps. Thea started after her, but the steps were too steep and Isabel was rolling too fast. Melody was gone. There was no one to stop the baby's fall. Thea screamed, "Mama, Mama, quick! It's Isabel. Come!" Then louder, she yelled, "Mama!"

Anna heard Thea's call and ran into the living room. Aghast at seeing the open door, she rushed to the top of the stairs and looked down. There was Thea in tears at the bottom of the steps, kneeling over the rag doll and the quiet body of her baby sister.

With hands still wet from soapy water, Anna raced down the stairs yelling, "Thea, go get Daddy. Hurry!" She lifted the dress-up veil from the child's bloody face. There was a big gash in her forehead. Anna knew she needed something to apply pressure to the wound. In desperation, she placed her wet hand over the wound, hoping to stop the flow. If Georg would only come and get a bandage and a blanket. Isabel's face was white as a sheet; Anna feared for her life. Hurry, Georg!

He came running with Thea trailing after him. "Thea said Isabel went out the door and fell down the steps."

"She has a head wound. Get bandages. Dampen one in cold water and bring a blanket. She's as cold as ice."

"Oh, Isabel, my darling," he said, his voice cracking. "I'll be right back."

Anna gently stroked Isabel's arm. She leaned over her to be sure she was breathing. Every breath made Anna tighten up and say, "Dear God, please save her!"

The blood continued to gush onto Isabel's face.

Georg ran back. "Here's a blanket and bandage. Can you stop the blood flow? Shouldn't we move her?"

"No, some of her bones may be broken. I'll hold the bandage against the wound. Go get Doc Butterworth."

"I'll get him here the minute I find him," Georg said.

He ran down the street in his grocery apron.

Thea looked at Isabel and started to say, "I didn't do it," but began to cry. Anna reached up and pulled Thea to her while she kept her other hand on the bandaged wound.

"Thea, honey, it's not your fault. Don't cry. Mommy loves you. The doctor is on the way."

Georg ran to Dr. Butterworth's office which was about six blocks away. A note on the door said, "Return in an hour." He jotted a note: "Emergency. Isabel bleeding. Come fast!"

He turned and started back down the steps. Suddenly, there was Doc walking straight at him, head down.

"Doc!" Georg called, "come with me. Isabel's dying!"

"What's happened?"

He quickly explained.

"Go home, Georg. I'll get my satchel and be right there." Within minutes, Doc was at the door. He rushed to Isabel, still at the bottom of the steps. He took her pulse and checked for broken bones. "She has a fast pulse and is unconscious. We need to bring her up to her crib."

Anna rewrapped the blanket.

Once in her crib, Doc cleaned the wound and stopped the blood. "Keep the window shade drawn and her head low until consciousness returns, then raise it on two pillows. Check every hour to see if she is conscious. If she isn't conscious in twelve hours, come and get me. Keep the bandage on her head."

Anna watched and listened. She wanted the doctor to tell her how Isabel was right now. She couldn't stand the suspense. "Doc, will she be all right?"

"We'll know more later."

"What can we do?" Georg asked.

"Head injuries bleed a lot. The bleeding has stopped now but you need to watch it so it doesn't start again. We may need to stitch it." He sat on Thea's bed. "I'll stay awhile."

Anna kept standing, looking down at Isabel. "Her face is so pale. Is she breathing? What more can we do?"

"Keep her flat. Watch and hold her head if she moves."

Anna was ready to scream. My daughter, my daughter, you must live, she kept repeating to herself. I will sit up all night and watch you. Why did I ever leave the children alone? She blamed herself.

Georg stood there looking at Isabel. "She seems so small. I'm going downstairs to put up the closed sign in the window."

Thea came in to look at her sister. "Isabel, wake up. I want to play with you."

Georg picked up Thea and held her on his lap. "Honey, this was an accident. We know you would have stopped her. It is not your fault. I must nail that key much higher."

Doc gave Thea a hug. "You'll take good care of your sister. I have to go now but I'll be back tomorrow."

Georg looked down at his little daughter and all he could wonder was how soon she'd be well, if ever. There was no answer. He shook Doc's hand. "Thanks for your help."

The next morning, Isabel was still unconscious. Doc came at dawn and examined her. Her condition hadn't changed. Anna and Georg were frantic. Each had been up all night, sitting watch. Both blamed themselves. Doc came again before noon. "I met with Dr. Schmidt and he said we should wait a little longer before moving her to the hospital."

"Please, Doc," Georg said, "maybe you should take her now?" Dr. Butterworth looked at Isabel's pale face. He reached into the crib and gently lifted her out and walked around the room with her. He held her head firmly and walked back and forth. He put her back in the crib and told Anna and Georg, "I'll go and meet with Dr. Schmidt again and see if we have any other solutions. As soon as we decide, I'll be back." He picked up his satchel and walked down the stairs.

Doc's suggestion to operate on Isabel sent cold chills down Anna's back. She beat her fists against the mattress. This can't hap pen. She remembered Isabel playing with Katy. She recalled her first smile and what a happy little girl she was. Lord, what can we do? What can I do?

Georg picked Isabel from the crib. "Come, Anna, why don't you hold Isabel awhile."

Anna reached out her arms and Georg carefully laid Isabel there. Anna sat quietly. She could hear her baby breathing but her eyes were closed and her face more drawn than before. Anna hummed "*Den lille Ole.*" There seemed to be no change. Time was running out. She started to put her in the crib when a small little voice called out, "Mommy, Mommy."

Anna clutched Isabel close. Tears began to flow. She kissed the child. "Isabel, dear. We're right here."

Georg bent down and carefully looked in the child's blinking eyes. He too cried. "We've been waiting for you to call us, honey. Are you hungry?"

"Here is your rag doll," said Thea. "I've been taking care of her for you. Look, she can dance and turn over. I know she'll dance for you."

Isabel just stared and seemed to snuggle down in her mother's arms. Anna felt as if she were reborn. The terrible battle was over and Isabel had won.

Georg sent Eddy to tell Doc that Isabel was awake. He soon arrived with his satchel. When Thea saw him, she said, "Isabel is awake. We don't need you."

Thea awoke with excitement and energy. It was the day marked on her calendar — September 7, 1892. Thea was going to the first grade. Watching Melody going to school had made her eager to attend. "Get up, get up, Mama. You said you'd walk me to school, today. Hurry."

Isabel turned over sleepily to watch Thea pawing through her dresser drawers to find the pink socks she wanted to go with her pink dress. "Isabel, do you have them?"

Isabel shook her head. "The socks are on my teddy bear."

Anna couldn't convince Thea to finish her oatmeal. She kept asking, "When do we leave? We can't be late."

Anna pushed Isabel's buggy to the gate of Cleveland school where Melody met them. "Mrs. Amorsen, I'll take Thea to her classroom. You've already turned in her papers."

"Thank you, Melody. Go ahead," she said, giving Thea a quick kiss. Already, Anna felt lonely for her oldest. She watched her go in room five on the first floor with Melody and later Melody came out and waved. Anna waved back, turned Isabel's buggy around, and started home.

Georg greeted her at the store. "Anna, you can't believe what happened. Wilbert told me when he came by the store this morning that he's sold his mill to a financier, Gilbert Lauridsen."

"Georg, he's the richest man in town," said Anna.

"Wilbert said he was tired of keeping the mill running without modern equipment," Georg said. "He also told me Mr. Lauridsen arranged for a boatload of men from the Grand Army of the Republic (GAR) — over a hundred of them. Lauridsen convinced them to start a new life in the west."

"He undoubtedly paid their passage and promised them jobs in the mill. Where will they live?"

"All we've been hearing about lately is the declining economy," Georg said. "Our homesteaders are having a rough time. Lauridsen may have put the new fellows in tents."

One Sunday afternoon Georg and Anna took the girls for a walk in the park. It was a lovely sunny day; Isabel and Thea hurried to the sand box to build mountains and animals. Finally a tired Thea called, "Daddy, help me make the swing go up and down." Then, Isabel had to have Georg hold her in his lap so she could swing too. Georg and Anna were taking turns pushing when Harry Smith came by and sat on the bench.

"Good afternoon, my good friends. I haven't seen you for some time. Have you heard about Wilbert selling his mill? He was glad to get rid of it. He told me he was going broke." "Business has slowed down here and in Vancouver," Georg said. "Our main sources of income are the forest and the fish. The Northwest is beginning to face an economic slow down," said Smith. "Don't get caught in an overload. I heard our bank may close."

The local bank closed the first of the year. The *Port Angeles Times* printed headlines about Gilbert Lauridsen taking over the role of broker for practically all the county lumber mills. He flaunted his success with the GAR Colony Mill by turning out Lauridsen paper bills and metal coins. His employees nicknamed it the "Grand Army Mill" and were paid with his new currency. Georg held the paper up for Anna to see. "Look at that scoundrel. He's taken over the town. My customers have been bringing this stuff to pay their bills. I won't accept it."

Later that week, Georg came upstairs one day with anger in his voice. "I found out from Harry why none of the mill employees come here to buy any more. They're required to accept that damned Lauridsen money and then buy flour, sugar, bread, and meat over at a store Lauridsen has just opened."

By the next month Georg's customers became fewer and fewer. He had to cancel his brother's contract. He rearranged the shelves and tried to sell bargain merchandise, but there were no customers.

Georg invited Alfred to meet with him and Anna at his home one evening to discuss their assets. Alfred put the papers before Anna and Georg. "Here's the account books, the bills of lading, and the paper work concerned with the overall status of the loan. It means we sell out and divide what's left."

Anna didn't want to accept the thought of selling. "Maybe we can go over and talk to Mr. Lauridsen."

They agreed to have Alfred work out a satisfactory price around $1000 and set a date to talk with Lauridsen. Within the next week Alfred drove them over to Lauridsen's office.

"Mr. Lauridsen will be with you," said the secretary. "He told me to tell you he'll pay $500 in paper money."

"Oh, no," said Anna. "It can't be. We've had the best grocery in town. Look at all the work Georg did to the shelves and our home upstairs. It has to be worth more."

Georg reached over and put his arm around her. "Honey, we'll do our best to work out a way."

When Mr. Lauridsen walked in the room, he acted as if they

should stand up. "Well, what more do you want out of me?"

"What's going to happen to us?" asked Anna. "We've cut down every way we can. We've taken good care of our store."

"Isn't there some way you can buy this building and pay us according to its value?" asked Georg.

"Give me that list of figures again."

Alfred handed him the list of figures.

Anna watched him look over the figures as she worried about the children. *How would they find new friends in a place where we haven't been, and where we don't know anyone? Maybe we should go back to Victoria and live with Frederik.*

"What do you expect for this place?"

Anna looked up at him, "We have two small daughters. We have to find a new home somewhere. We're not squatters. We need your help, sir, please?"

"What do you think I should pay?"

Georg spoke up, "We expect to receive at least the money we invested. I've redone the store and the upstairs."

"You mean you want American money?"

Alfred answered, "Yes we do. It is worth $1000. We invite you to come over and see what a good building it is."

"We welcome you. You can meet our daughters. They are well behaved. Come and see the house is not scratched," said Anna.

Mr. Lauridsen's face became red. "Maudie," he barked at his secretary, "get in here and open the safe and give these people $500. Have them sign the sale certificate."

Anna spoke up. "You have a successful mill. Why can't you help us by offering us a fair amount?"

The room was silent.

She sat there as tears dropped one by one. *Where could they go? What would they do? Why couldn't this millionaire offer them a fair deal?* "Mr. Lauridsen, I beg of you to give our children a chance for the future. We need the money."

He looked at Anna, Georg, and Alfred and said, "Maudie, make it $750." Then he walked out of the room.

For the next two weeks, Anna began boxing their belongings. One day a special delivery letter from the Superior Court addressed to Georg Amorsen arrived at the door.

What had he done? thought Anna. Fearful of its contents, she shoved the letter in his pocket while he was in his office, paying bills.

"I'm afraid to open this," he said after dinner. "But I must face whatever it is." He broke the seal and read. "It's an invitation from A.A. Richardson, County Clerk of Clallam County," said Georg. "It is a notice to appear at a ceremony to become a citizen of the United States of America.'"

Anna felt weak with relief. "Oh, Georg, how wonderful!" "It's to be November 23, 1893, at the Superior Court."

The grand occasion brought forth the Talbots, the Abernethys, the Smiths, the Browns, Frederik and his family, the church Guild, and friends from the grocery business. Twenty men stood up and were sworn to citizenship. Georg stood tall and proud. His Van Dyke beard, gold-rimmed glasses, and dark blue suit made Anna want to run up and kiss him.

Afterwards, friends came to their home. Before he put the certificate on the wall he read a sentence: " 'As appearing to the satisfaction of this court, Georg Amorsen, a native of Denmark, has resided under the jurisdiction of the United States for five years. Georg Amorsen is hereby admitted and declared to be a citizen of the United States of America.' "

"Here's to Georg Amorsen," said Alfred as he poured glasses of champagne.

Anna's spirit soared. Now they were both citizens and Georg could vote. But, she felt sad because this would most likely be the last gathering of their friends. She looked around the room at the children playing and Alfred puffing his pipe and turning the room blue with smoke as he and the other men talked business. She looked at the women in the kitchen: Elizabeth, what a good friend she had been; Melody Brown's parents bringing up their daughter with love and laughter; Ellie, the president of the church Guild, a hard-worker at keeping the Children's fund alive; Karen, her dear sister-in-law; and good old Frederik, who was helping in the kitchen.

That night she asked Georg, "Where are we going to go?"

"San Francisco," he said. "The newspaper calls it the financial and social center of the West — the Gateway to the Orient. And they have horseless carriages."

"That's fine but what about the people, the schools, churches, and jobs?" she blurted.

"My old friend Christian will write me, Anna. Let's wait."

"To move to a big city isn't my idea of home," she said. "The quietness of Victoria, the lovely mountains, the blue Puget Sound surrounding our home. Being able to walk to schools, parks, church, and friends is important to me."

Georg leaned over and gave her a kiss. "You know we'll find

what we need. Let's wait until I hear again from Christian."

"I'm tired of waiting," Anna said, pacing. "I think of the mountains of my old Bergen and our quiet family home on the *fjord*. I wish we were there now. Of course, my father is too old to fish now and my sister Gudrun is married. Maybe they could come to America one day." Suddenly, she became quiet and shook her head. "How silly I am sometimes. We hardly even have enough money to move to San Francisco."

She walked around the house, admiring her photographs of the family on the wall. She smiled at the picture of Frederik's family. Katy was now up to her mother's shoulder. She went into the bedrooms and admired all the Nordic-design comforters she'd made. Our sixth move, she thought, and started to cry. She lay on the bed and sobbed. Will we ever settle down?

Georg received a letter from Christian within the next week. He read it to Anna:

> *We're glad we moved to San Francisco. It's a fascinating city. Something is happening every minute. We've had a depression here too but I've kept my job as a cabinet maker. I'm sure if you decide to come, you'll have no trouble finding work. Here's how to find our home. We welcome you, anytime.*
>
> *Christian and Martha.*

Anna asked for the letter and reread it. "They sound as if they're happy there. How thoughtful to welcome us to stay with them. Did you tell them we have two girls?"

"Anna, we'll write again. Are you ready to return to a big city?"

"Not really. But will you agree, Mr. Citizen, that this will definitely be our final move? You promise me? Seal it with a kiss."

"Of course, Anna," he said, then hugged and gave her a big kiss. "This is it."

Chapter Eighteen

San Francisco

With so few days left before their departure, Georg and Anna invited Frederik, Karen, and Katy to celebrate Christmas with them. Georg wrote:

> *This will be Christmas like no other. In one week we'll be on the* Halsingborg *ship to San Francisco.*

The Frederik Amorsen family crossed the Juan de Fuca Straits from Victoria in the now familiar Bates's fishing boat. Georg greeted them at the wharf. He hugged Karen and Katy and gave Frederik a big slap on the back. The two men embraced. "It's so good to see all of you," he said, grinning ear-to-ear. "Besides," he said with a twinkle in his eye, "we knew you'd want to help us pack."

Everyone laughed.

As they climbed the stairs to the flat above the grocery store Georg added, "Anna has been busy sorting out what to bring and what to leave. Boxes are everywhere. We have little space. In fact, we look like a post office station."

"This place does need some help," said Frederik as Georg opened the door.

Anna greeted them at the door, giving each of her guests a warm hug. Her mind raced, realizing this would be their last visit. A cold chill covered her body as she thought of leaving her dearest friend. "It's so wonderful to see you again, Karen," she whispered, wiping a tear from her eye.

When the time finally came to sit down for Christmas dinner, which by tradition was eaten on Christmas Eve, Georg had the children sit between the parents. He looked around the table and, when

171

all conversation finally stopped, he said, "Please, hold hands while we say a silent grace."

The minute seemed like an hour to the children, but the adults thought about how they had lived together in Victoria for almost five years. They had kept up their friendship by visiting two or three times a year. Now, this was the final farewell.

"Amen," said Georg, and all the children's heads popped up like so many bouncing balloons.

Frederik and Karen felt the emotional drain of losing their only close relatives. They knew it would be almost impossible for Anna and Georg to return to Victoria from San Francisco.

"What are you planning to do, Georg?"

Anna spoke up, "Our first thing to do will be to look for a flat near the Andersens. They have invited us to stay with them for awhile. Christian wrote that their neighborhood is a small Scandinavia."

After Georg and all her guests and children had gone to bed, Anna couldn't sleep and went out to the kitchen. She looked around at the bright yellow room that now seemed like an empty shell. What will life be like in a big city again? Chicago was only a sample. She thought of her six years of house moving. She recalled the days when the girls would paste childish drawings on the ice box, and the two sailor suits she made like those Lise and Hans had when they sailed across the Atlantic Ocean. The girls must keep me going, she thought. Will we never settle down? My whole life until I left Bergen was spent in our little house on the *fjord*.

After the opening of presents, Christmas Day became a work day. Bit by bit, the kitchen silverware and utensils and even clothes were sorted. The table and chairs, beds and boxes of tools and kitchenware were sold. By the time they walked Frederik, Karen, and Katy to the wharf for the boat ride to Victoria, a silent sadness hung heavy between the two families.

"Goodbye, my dearest, Karen," said Anna as she hugged her tightly and tried to hide her tears. "I'll write to you regularly. You do the same." She still felt the chill within her bones and tried to smile. The anxiety of being separated from their only close relatives in America made it more difficult. The winds from the sea added to her distress. Yet, the cold wintry weather served as a beacon of hope as she remembered what her mother and father always said during the stormy months: "The North Wind makes the Viking strong."

Georg and Frederik slapped one another on the back, but didn't want to admit that they might never meet again. Anna knew it was a difficult moment for each man.

"Don't look back," Frederik said, "just look ahead. We'll keep up with one another."

Georg gave him a friendly push and another hug. "We couldn't have made it out here without you and Karen and Katy. We'll keep in touch. Sometime in the next year, we want to have a reunion. And we can go visit folks together."

Little Katy climbed aboard, clutching her doll and waving tearfully to all. Karen wiped away her own tears, gave Georg a hug, then kissed Anna and the girls. Frederik gave Anna a hug, but decided to whirl Thea and Isabel around. He and Karen sang "Farewell and Goodbye" as the fishing boat headed out of the harbor and disappeared around the point.

Anna broke down and cried and cried. Georg tried to comfort her. "She was like a sister to me," she sobbed. "And I haven't even seen Gudrun since 1885."

Georg put his arms around her and held her tight. "We will find a home and stay there this time. I promise. We'll work it out together, Anna."

Later that night, she felt exhausted but couldn't go to sleep. She climbed out of bed; Georg was sound asleep. She needed to pull herself together. What will life be like in that big city? Will we find a home? How much money does Georg have to keep us going until he finds a job? At times it is so difficult to figure out what Georg is thinking. He likes to get everything arranged and then include me in his dreams later. Life seems to be a series of hurdles. You are so proud when you jump the first one, but each time they grow higher and higher. She yawned. She had no answers.

Anna awoke to the rat-a-tat of hail on the roof. Where am I? she wondered, and started to awaken Georg who was sleeping beside her. Suddenly, she realized they were in the Andersen's guest bedroom in San Francisco. Now she remembered. She had been sick. The tossing of the ship had given her another case of seasickness and made her weak. She couldn't afford to be sick. There was too much work to be done.

In her head, she began making a list: enroll the girls in school; find a place to live; locate the Danish *Sotersambrung* lodge so I can introduce my Nordic embroidery to the women of the Sisterhood; find out about the demand for dress-making.

Christian knocked at the door. "Get up, Georg. I want to take you to meet our building supervisor. He may have a job."

Georg pulled his lanky frame from the bed. "I'm not much

interested in this visit," he said to Anna, "but Christian is trying to help me."

"Don't turn a job down until we get on our feet."

"Anna," Georg laughed. "You never give up, do you?"

After the men left, Martha, Christian's wife, offered to help Anna enroll the girls in school. She was an inch or two taller than Anna with blond hair, a pug nose, and big brown eyes.

When breakfast was over, they were all ready to go to school. The three Andersen girls (Grace, nine; Lena, eight; and Mary, six) walked with Thea and Isabel along the narrow edge of Sixteenth Street. Martha showed Anna the way until they reached Valencia Elementary school on nearby Valencia Street.

Thea jumped and sang on the way, "Hurrah, I'm going to school." She liked to be doing things and was always ready to try anything new. Isabel clung to her mother's hand. "I don't want to go to kindergarten again," she whispered. Mary heard Isabel and took her hand. "I had your teacher. You'll like her."

Anna often visited Valencia's classrooms and was pleased with the teachers. She felt the girls would continue to feel good about their school.

Georg went out with Christian's wagon to work as a tile layer, but wasn't able get the hang of it. Christian came up to Georg's chin, but could carry a lot more weight. His blond hair still had a little wave in it and his blue eyes would twinkle as he talked. He and Martha had a lot of energy. Both had served as officers in their lodges.

"Don't worry, Georg. You'll find something. It takes time," Christian said.

Anna asked Martha, "When does the Sisterhood meet? I'd like to bring my Nordic embroidery to show the women."

"I'll be glad to take you."

Day after day, Georg's job search continued. He walked through the neighborhoods hoping to find a help wanted sign in one of the grocery stores. If after another week of frustration there would be no signs in the windows or ads in the Danish newspaper, Georg and Anna agreed to list an ad.

"Expert manager of busy market, salesman, and accountant looking for position. Can do all three. Experience."

In the meantime, Anna read *The San Francisco Bulletin* and the *Danish Bien* regularly to locate a flat in the Valencia school vicinity and within the Sixteenth Street area of their Scandinavian friends.

Martha asked all of her friends to help find a prospective rental for the Amorsens. One Sunday, Martha returned from her American

Lutheran Church with excitement in her voice. "Anna, Georg," she called, "I've found it! There's a flat coming up for rent over on Sixteenth. You'll have to go over right away before someone else beats you to it."

Anna was excited. When the couple returned an hour later, Martha and Christian knew from the smiles on their faces they had found an acceptable flat.

"When are you moving in?" asked Christian.

"Next Saturday," said a beaming Georg. "It has a little view of the Bay, two big bedrooms, a bathroom, a kitchen with room for a little table, and a living room."

"It also has a porch on the south side," Anna said, "and the place is clean. They have just finished painting it."

"We put a deposit on it," Georg said. "Now all I need is a job. Any more miracles up your sleeve, Martha?"

The following week Christian helped them move. He used his horse and wagon from the till business. Most of their boxes were untouched and stacked in the basement of Christian's home.

Anna worked at arranging things in their new home. It was late afternoon when Christian, Georg, and Anna drove back around the Valencia school. They had taken a different street. The three of them were looking at the Victorian homes when they passed a neighborhood market. They all saw it at the same moment: A "Help Wanted" sign.

Georg jumped to his feet. "Wait here. I'm going in — even in these work clothes."

Christian drove the wagon around the corner to a shade tree. They could see the entrance to the market. Anna and Christian sat there, silently praying Georg would be hired. She told Christian about Georg and his partner Alfred Talbot. "We were forced out of our market by the ruthless behavior of that millionaire Lauridsen. Georg and I put five years into that market to make it a success. Georg is having a hard time starting over."

The horse restlessly pawed his hooves and swatted flies with his tail. Christian and Anna waited and waited. "He's either getting the job or is already telling the manager how to run his market," Anna said.

Finally, he came out and looked up and down the street for the wagon. Christian slapped the reins on the horse and when Georg saw them he sprinted down the street. "I have the job! The manager is Kristian Hvidt; he knows his business. I'm the produce manager and I open up the store each morning at seven."

"What about the pay, Georg?"

"Well, Anna, it's not what I want but it is a start."

That night at dinner, the two families celebrated. Christian stood and toasted, "To our dear friends, we wish the best of life, as they settle into our great city, San Francisco." Christian took them to their new home after dinner. The girls brought along packages of drawings, homework, and stories from just the short time they'd been in school. Georg brought his suitcase of tools. Again the wagon was full as they drove up to the flat.

After the children went to sleep on blankets spread on the floor, Anna and Georg sat on the floor surrounded by half-opened boxes and bags spilling their contents. "It feels so good to be in our own home," she said, stretching her arms. "We have more space than we ever had at Port Angeles. We'll watch the ads and gradually add the furniture we need."

"Anna, I love you. Without you I don't know what I'd do. Here we are with a home and now I have a job." He leaned over and pulled her to him, grabbing her around the waist and kissing her passionately. Anna, caught within his long arms and lengthy kiss, forgot her resolve that this must be their last move.

By the end of the year, Anna and Georg had made many Scandinavian friends. Anna's Nordic embroidery apron patterns were a new design which attracted the Sisterhood's sewing circle. Martha confided one day, "You certainly are well liked by the women in our lodge."

As the years passed, the girls grew much older and entered high school. Family life for the Amorsens had become more stable and predictable. Georg kept receiving salary raises and the family was able to buy dresses, school books, and artist materials. Now the children could afford to join clubs such as the Girl's Guide, and Anna had more time to help the girls with their homework. She also had time to attend the Scandinavian lodges and sewing club meetings. Besides the school work there were school programs of drama, speech, and chorus.

Anna helped Thea practice her writing. She received an invitation to submit a weekly column to the *Valencia News*. Isabel concentrated on drawing in beautiful colors. Anna was proud of her daughters and did all she could to keep them active and learning new things. She was happy to have settled in an area surrounded by Scandinavians. Family life moved within the areas of school, work, church, and lodge. Anna was elected to the position of treasurer of the Sisterhood. Georg joined the Danish Brotherhood, and the whole family enjoyed the social picnics, dances, and special day celebrations. One morning, Georg came running up the stairs of their flat. "Anna! After all these years, Kristian Hvidt is retiring. He offered me the opportunity to buy the grocery!"

Anna cried with delight. "Yes, do it! We have saved and will have enough for a down payment. We don't have our own house yet, but I know we will, one day soon."

"We've done it, my little *Norska*. We've done it!"

They hugged each other and laughed with joy. Life in San Francisco was indeed good. They had made the right decision.

The years passed quickly. Thea finished high school. One day in 1906, she came home from her typing job at the *Bien* newspaper and threw her purse on the sofa. She tossed her jacket on a chair and collapsed in the rocker. "I'm sick of that place. I type the copy and then Hann, the editor, makes changes and I have to do it all over again."

Anna brought in a glass of lemonade. "Thea, the editor has to meet deadlines with the latest news. You're doing just fine."

"Well, someday I want to do more than type."

Just then, Isabel came home, lugging a drafting board and sketching materials. "My teacher is taking a few of us on a field trip to the wharf. I can't wait to sketch one of those sailing ships."

Anna brought her a glass, too. "Remember when you were little and told me you how you wanted to be a great artist."

"Thanks, Mom," said Isabel, taking the glass. "And now, I'm really doing it. It's hard for me to believe, too."

Anna smiled with pride. "Lately, I've been pasting pictures in the family album." She reached over to the coffee table and opened the book. "Look. Here you are, Thea, at graduation, and here you are, Isabel, receiving the first place award in the tenth grade for drawing the carousel in the park." She turned a few more pages. "And here the three of us are at the beach, playing in the waves."

"Oh my Lord," said Isabel, sitting beside her. "Look at those old-fashioned black swimming suits down to our knees."

Thea joined them. "There's the two of us with Dad in front of the grocery store," she said. "Look at my hair!"

"Here's a picture of us riding in our wagon in the Valencia school parade," said Isabel. "We both had on red, white, and blue streamers to celebrate the Fourth of July. I was in the sixth grade and didn't want to be in the parade at all."

Anna shook her head and closed the book. "These years in San Francisco seem to have passed too quickly. We'll have to finish this at another time. I've got housework to do."

Isabel and Thea exchanged a puzzled look.

The next morning Isabel and her friend, Ilse, rode the street car to the bay. Ilse was in Isabel's class and wanted to be an artist, too. She had long red hair that hung down her back. Isabel teased her by telling her someday she'd paint her picture wrapped in red hair.

Isabel felt particularly confident for some reason. "I'm going to draw a sailing ship — you know, one of those old wooden kind that have been written up in the *San Francisco Bulletin*."

"You can have it," said Ilse, staring out the window. "I'm drawing the Market Street Tower at the wharf."

As soon as she arrived at the pier, Isabel walked directly to the *Skandinavisk*, took out her bag and drawing board, and started to sketch. The ship's sails billowed from the masts, making a wonderful scene. Isabel worked as hard at sketching as the sailors did their climbing. That evening when she returned home, Isabel greeted her Mother with, "See what I sketched."

"It's beautiful but it needs some background," Anna said.

"You're just like the sailor who came down to see my sketch. He asked, 'Aren't you going to finish it?' He was interested in my work, but he didn't look much like an artist. Ilse came by and said he couldn't be an artist with such dirty hands and fingernails."

On the second trip to the wharf, Ilse had finished her tower and followed Isabel, helping her set up her incomplete sketch of the ship. "I need to shadow in parts of this, but look how I've captured the elegance of the ship."

"Isabel, you are such a big talker. It's a ship. So what?"

"Ilse, I don't make fun of you or your work."

When Isabel returned that night, she told Anna, "The same sailor came down to watch and asked me where I learned to sketch. He also read my name on the sketch. He shook his head and then asked Ilse for her school address."

"I hope she didn't answer," said Anna.

"Ilse said our high school was on Polk and Fifteenth Streets. He looked at us and mumbled something about knowing someone with the same name. He looked more like a bum than a sailor but I saw him working on the ship."

Anna shook her head. "You shouldn't give your address out to strangers. It's not safe." She was glad the waterfront sketching sessions were over.

Isabel was proud of her artistic efforts. She put her sketch up on the sofa so everyone could see it and slipped the easel stand under the sofa.

Anna remarked, "That ship comes alive. Excellent!"

"Yes," said Isabel, "the same sailor who came back to watch me said I was an expert. Guess he was bored with deck duty. He spent his time spitting tobacco all around the harbor."

Isabel proudly went off to school, carrying her drawing the next day. She felt sorry for Ilse. The Market Street Tower looked like the top of a squashed hat.

Anna spent part of that morning organizing her patterns for the women's sewing group. Martha came over to share a cup of coffee. They were neighbors now. Anna, who had been elected treasurer, always tried out ideas on her. It was like having a sister again.

A loud knocking sounded on the door.

"Who could that be so early?" Puzzled, Anna opened the door.

A man with a heavy black beard, wearing a dark blue cap, dirty dungarees, a dark blue jacket, and carrying a sea bag stood before her. "About time you opened the door. I have business with you." He pushed Anna aside, walked into the house, and just stood there looking around the room. "I've waited a long time."

Anna leaned against the door, legs weak, brain unable to digest what this man was saying. What kind of business was it? She held onto the knob — maybe she could run out for help.

He turned, pulled her from the door, and slammed it shut.

Martha sat at the table near the kitchen without moving. Who was this rough-looking man? One of Anna's relatives?

Anna carefully moved across the room and sat down on the sofa. She didn't trust herself to stand. There was something about this man she recognized. It suddenly struck her. No, it couldn't be. It was over 20 years ago since Ole broke windows and tore up their wedding gifts. Was this the Ole who paid her passage to America to marry him and didn't show up when she arrived? This man looked so old and weather beaten.

He looked around the house, out at the Bay, and said, "Pretty nice place you have here."

Anna asked, "Who are you? What do you want of us?"

"I told you I'd get even. That flimsy little return ticket to Norway didn't stop me. I've spent most of my life with the Alaskan fishing fleets, but when I returned to Norway this year my family told me that you had moved to San Francisco a long time ago. I deliberately signed aboard this ship in order to get to San Francisco."

"Ole!" exclaimed Anna. "It is you. Why, oh why, do you carry this grudge? We settled with you 20 years ago. Why are you bursting into our home now?"

"You know why." He turned to Martha, "Lady, you'd better listen, too. I sent this woman passage from Bergen to Chicago. She promised to marry me and ran off with another man."

"That's a lie, Martha. I waited for Ole at the Chicago Union Depot for hours. He never showed up. A year later, I met Georg at a dry goods store where we both worked and we were married. After we were married, Ole forced us out of Chicago."

"Anna, you owe me two hundred dollars. You're taking a walk with me down to the bank and you can pay me."

"Ole, we've paid our debt to you. We can't pay again."

"Do you call one ticket to Bergen payment?"

Anna tried to keep herself under control. She recalled how ferocious he could be when he lost control of his temper. She thought of ways to stop him. She'd grab the big end of Isabel's easel which was stored in back of the sofa and when she would shout at Martha he would turn his head, and she could knock him down. No, she wasn't that fast. How could she stall him?

"Why don't you return when Georg gets home, and we can talk this over?"

"I don't want to look at that stuck-up husband of yours."

Anna started to get up. "Would you like a cup of coffee? Martha, turn up the fire on the coffee pot."

Martha was afraid of this sailor. Why did Anna want her to light the coffee pot? Maybe that would give Martha time to escape down the rear steps?

"Yes, I'll get it for us," said Martha.

"I don't want any of your shitty coffee. Sit down!"

As Ole turned to Anna, she pretended to pick up a book.

"Sit there. Don't move!" he yelled again.

Martha was close to the kitchen door and scooted around the corner, quietly locked the kitchen door behind her, and crept down the back stairs.

Ole ran to the door, but couldn't force it open. He picked up Martha's chair and crashed it against the door. "Tell that woman to get back in here." He shoved and swore, but couldn't break the door. He finally turned to Anna. "I won't stand for this. You pay me or else you'd better watch that little artist of yours. Any moment I want, I can find her. I know her school and her friends. I bet she'd make a nice date."

"You keep my daughter out of this. So you were the one that was watching her draw your sailing ship."

"Yes, she's quite a looker. I'd take her dancing and have a few drinks at the bar, and we'd really get to know one another."

Anna held her breath. If only she could keep him talking a while longer. Maybe he didn't realize there was a back way off the porch, and Martha could go for help.

"Will you be here a few more days? I really would like you to see Georg," Anna said.

"Shut up! I'm telling you for the last time, open up your bank account or you can expect trouble. I'll go find Isabel right now."

Anna felt the edge of the easel. Could she reach it and hit him? He was getting angrier by the moment. Oh, if only help would come.

Ole must have sensed something. He reached into his belt and pulled out a small revolver and pointed it at Anna.

"For the last time, I'm telling you. You have that money and I'm going to get it. If not, your daughter will pay!" Anna felt her skin tighten. He'd never pulled a gun on them before. There was no way she could grab the easel and prevent his pulling the trigger.

Ole smiled. "So, you're gonna get that dough, aren't you?" He kept his eye on Anna, but leaned over to pick up his sea bag, then backed to the front door. "We'll walk out real nice, won't we? I have the gun so don't yell or I'll put a hole in you."

Anna's knees felt like jelly. She got up and grabbed the railing as they went down the steps. Nobody was in sight.

"I already checked on your bank. Turn right at the corner and down the hill."

Anna breathed in fast gasps. Every moment she thought she might be able to outrun him. Can I stop abruptly and trip him? Can I swing my purse in his face? It all seemed futile.

They reached the Scandinavian Trust and Savings and walked inside. She walked up to the window with Ole at her heels. If only one of her teller friends were there, she could get some help. But the teller was a trainee and seemed unconcerned about Ole.

Anna wrote the withdrawal slip for two hundred dollars to be dispensed in ones. Ole would need more time to count them, she thought. That would give her a chance to think what to do.

Before the teller had verified the withdrawal, Ole leaned over the counter, scooped up the bills in his left hand and shoved them in his pocket. He whispered in Anna's ear, "Just walk up to the door in front of me. When I open it, I'll be out in a flash and don't you yell! I can still find your daughter."

When Ole carefully maneuvered Anna to the front door, they suddenly found no one was available to open the door. Ole jabbed his concealed gun against her back. "Is this some of your monkey business? Tell them to open the door."

The manager, Erik Grundtvig, walked over to them. "Excuse us for a moment," he said to Anna. "We've had trouble with the door sticking shut. We've phoned for a locksmith."

The man's tall rigid posture and abrupt manner alarmed Ole. "Why in the hell do you lock your doors if you can't open them?" he asked. "Is that how you treat your customers?"

"Excuse me, Mrs. Amorsen, I believe you just withdrew $200?" questioned Grundtvig.

Anna wanted to yell, "Grab him! Grab him!" but with a gun in her ribs, she just nodded.

"Why don't you folks sit down over here and be comfortable until the locksmith arrives?" the manager invited.

She noticed that Ole was itching to get out of the bank. "Where's the back door?" he asked. "That must work."

"Please sir, sit down here. We only use this door."

Anna sank in the upholstered chair. She closed her eyes and prayed for help. Was Mr. Grundtvig actually telling the truth or was he aware of the gun Ole carried? If so, how could the manager stop him when they repaired the door? When will all this end? His words about Isabel kept echoing in her ears.

Time dragged on. The locksmith didn't come. With the locked door, there were no depositors or counter transactions. A deadly stillness descended upon the bank.

Ole was getting nervous. "Where are all the tellers in this rotten place? Why can't we get out of here? Let me give it a few pushes, and I'll bet I can open it."

Grundtvig smiled. "Why, that's a good idea. Come over with me, and we'll both see if we can open it."

Anna watched Ole gulp. He hadn't planned on being taken up on his suggestion. "Sit here," Ole told her. "Don't move."

Anna couldn't understand what Grundtvig was up to, but she nodded her head and pretended to be in agreement. If she was only brave enough to run up to the counter.

Grundtvig and Ole started pushing on the door. With no success, they tried using a file to spring the latch. Ole did not see three policemen moving up on him from the rear. With a command from the sergeant, the three man jumped Ole. His gun dropped out of his belt and within a minute, his wrists had handcuffs around them.

Grundtvig shook the sergeant's hand. "Thanks. We appreciate your getting here so fast. This sailor kidnapped one of our depositors, Mrs. Amorsen, and forced her to take money out of her account while he pointed a gun at her."

"Glad to take over, sir. We checked with his ship. Ole Ludeman has been trouble since he signed on. He was planning to jump ship and to live off Mrs. Amorsen. He told one of the crew he had found the end of the rainbow. We'll take him downtown for tonight and they'll take him back to Norway tomorrow."

Anna sat in a chair, unable to believe that her feeling of being on the edge of death or the death of her daughters was past. Her hands were still shaking and she couldn't stand up. She tried to catch her breath. The horrible picture of Ole kidnapping Isabel wouldn't leave her mind. She wiped tears from her eyes and gritted her teeth. "It's over," she whispered out loud, again and again. "It's over . . . ."

Martha came running into the room and engulfed Anna in her arms. "Relax, Anna," said Martha. "Thank God, I got here helping you. You are will all right!"

Anna nodded. Martha helped her up.

"You are my dearest friend," Anna mumbled, the room seeming to swirl. "I feel as if you have been carrying our lives in the palm of your hands. Oh Martha, how can I ever thank you?"

Chapter Nineteen

The Quake

Anna awoke to the sound of deep rumbling, unlike any she had ever heard. The bed was shaking. What could it be? Another shock jolted the room. She knew. Anna leapt from bed, shouting at Georg, "Wake up! Wake up! It's an earthquake!"

By now, Georg realized the house was swaying. He jumped up, yelling, "Thea, Isabel, quick, grab a coat and run down the front steps. Go to the center of the street as fast as you can!"

Anna ran to the living room, holding her heavy coat. Another jolt knocked her to her knees. The big picture of Georg's mother and father crashed to the floor, glass flying. The sofa lamp toppled and ripped its shade. A china closet wobbled, fell over, and flattened the lamp. Anna's prized Danish blue dishes smashed into minute pieces, shards spraying across the room. "Mother's treasures!"

Thea and Isabel had grabbed their coats and tried to open the front door, but it wouldn't budge. "Papa, we can't get out!" Thea called.

"Hurry, Papa, I'm scared," Isabel cried, as the living room window shook loose and fell out to the street below.

Georg was holding onto the wall to keep his balance as the rumbling and vibrating continued. With his coat half-on over a long nightgown, he jiggled the key in the lock. "It won't work," he exclaimed. "It's jammed."

He attempted to pull out the door's hinge pins. "They won't come out. Here, girls, push on the door while I give it a big heave." Thea and Isabel ran to the door. "Ready? Push." The door wouldn't move. "The house has settled. Use the back door. Remember those stairs are narrow."

"Papa, the door won't open!" Isabel screamed.

"Keep calm, we'll open it," Georg said as he grabbed a hammer from the tool box and slammed it against the lock. The old wooden door was too solid. Georg couldn't make it move.

"What are we going to do?" Isabel cried. They heard another deep rumbling. "There is no way out! We'll be killed!"

Anna threw her arms around Isabel in a tight bear-hug. "We'll be all right, honey. Your father will open it."

Georg frantically pawed through his tool box and found a heavier hammer and wrench. "Here, take one." He handed each of them a tool. "When I lunge against the door, everyone hit it in the middle as hard as they can."

"Make sure you don't fall down the steps!" Anna shouted, as she took Georg's hammer and aimed for the middle panel.

Before they could move, the house shook again, this time with a sharp up-and-down motion that had the four of them hanging on to one another. The girls screamed.

Anna fell to her knees, again. "Oh my God," prayed Anna. "Please, save us."

"Get ready. When I say hit, do your best. One, two, three, hit!" Everyone did their part, and the door broke apart. All four of them ran down steps covered with wood debris, branches, broken glass, and pieces of yesterday's wash.

As they ran into the rear yard, the noise of wood splitting hit their ears. With a resounding crash, the cornice of their next door neighbor's house hit the ground, breaking into small pieces on the sidewalk between both buildings.

Anna said a silent prayer of thanks for the warped door. If not for it, their whole family would have been crushed.

"Hurry!" Georg yelled. "Everyone get out to the middle of the street, and watch out for falling bricks!"

Pieces of red clay lay everywhere. Anna stumbled, but the girls grabbed their mother and helped her to the center of the street.

"I'm all right," Anna said as she wiped her eyes. "My strength has been shaken out of me." She looked at their apartment building. "We are so lucky."

Georg picked up two apple boxes near the steps and placed them in the middle of the street for Anna. Tears flowed down her face as she looked at what was happening around them. The fog and cold enclosed them in a damp cocoon that deadened noise from around the city. The thick cloud made those few neighbors she could see look like ghostly blurs against the surrounding landscape. She felt disconnected from the rest of the city.

The four Amorsens looked around, shivering. What would happen? Each wondered when the next shock would come. Thea sat next to her mother and stroked the back of her neck. She wrapped the heavy coat tightly around her. "We love you, Mama. Everything's going to be all right. We're all safe!"

Isabel leaned over and kissed her mother. "Don't cry, Mama. We're all alive and well. That's all that matters."

Georg gave her a hug. "Thank the Lord, we got out in time. We'll manage, Anna."

Anna tried to regain her composure. She held on to Georg's hand, trying to rid her thoughts of what might have been. Each time she closed her eyes, all she could see was the huge cornice smashing to the ground. She forced herself recall all her photos: the good times with the neighbors when they had a street party with the Danish band; the Women's Sewing Club embroidering Nordic aprons to raise money for the Children's Fund; the laughter together over the antics of both children; the pride she and Georg shared in watching their two daughters grow into beautiful young women.

Anna began to feel better. As the four of them huddled together like frozen statues, the sunrise began to burn off the fog and the shadows of the neighbors began to come alive. Georg pointed. "Look at our neighbors. I hardly know who they are. Did you ever see such outlandish costumes?"

Thea laughed. "You should see yourself, Papa. You can outmatch any of them with your long nightgown hanging out under your church coat. You didn't even grab a pair of slippers."

They giggled at Papa and then began to laugh as they examined one another: Isabel in an orange short coat, scarcely covering her sheer night-gown, and wearing a pair of red boots; Thea with her black suit coat matched by a long skirt; Anna in her night-gown and heavy coat buttoned to her chin.

As the sun rose, it was like a picture unfolding. Up and down their block little groups of families, dressed in the most outlandish attire, clustered together in the middle of the street. Some leaned on one another for support, others just sat on the street, crying.

"Hello, hello, nice day, nice day," squawked somebody's parrot.

They could also see the damage done to nearly all of the chimneys with mounds of red, shattered bricks on the street. Broken glass from the windows lay scattered along the sidewalk. Georg noticed that the chimney on the Andersen's house leaned as if it would fall any moment. Georg ran over to warn them yelling, "Get away from the building; the chimney is ready to fall. Hurry!"

The Andersen family ran and reached the street in time to turn around and see the bricks at the top of their chimney tumbling down onto their front porch. Christian grabbed Georg's shoulder. "Thank God, Georg, you got us out of the way just in time."

Anna folded Martha into a hug and Thea and Isabel put their arms around Lena and Mary. They all sat down on the street shaken and unable to talk.

Finally, Martha said, "You saved our lives, Georg. We had the front door open to leave when we heard your voice. We would have been killed."

Both families just sat on the cold blacktop, each thinking how close they had all come to death.

Georg in his flopping gown and coat was shivering along with the others. "Christian, let's build a fire. We can use some of the whole bricks, and we'll get twigs and loose lumber. We can at least warm ourselves. That is, if anyone has matches."

By now, all of the neighbors were out of their homes, restlessly milling around and trying to keep warm. Disheveled and shivering, many still trembled in fear of another sharp shake that would destroy their homes.

Christian walked up with an armload of bricks. "Everyone is dressed in such peculiar outfits," he said to Anna. "It makes it possible to laugh with one another while we're still shaking. It helps relieve the tension." He noticed a strange look in her eyes. "Are you all right, Anna?"

She wrapped her arms around herself and nodded. "Yes, thank you, Christian. We had a terrible time getting out of our house, but the delay kept us from being under Nielsen's cornice. It crashed down where we would have been."

Martha Andersen came over and put her arms around Anna. "I know what you mean. Oh, Anna, Georg saved us!" The two women hugged, but Anna had her mind elsewhere. She looked over Martha's shoulder at the house she and her family had just left.

Christian dumped his bricks. It startled Anna. She watched as he went from one person to another, asking for a match. She noticed that both her girls had their eyes on him, and Georg was still getting more wood.

Finally, Christian recognized old garrulous Peerson with his everlasting pipe hanging from his mouth. "Just what we need, your pipe," he said. "Would you lend us a light?"

Peerson looked him over. "What for?"

"I want to start a fire in the little red brick stove we just made."

"Ah, sure. I'll give you a light if you'll let me warm up. I'll even tell you my story of how I got out of the attic."

Christian walked with Peerson to the stove and watched him as he leaned over and lit the twigs with the red ash from his pipe. The fire took hold and the twigs crackled. Thea and Isabel crowded close to the bright flame. Peerson leaned over and warmed his hands. "Oh, how good this feels. I'll save my horror story for another time."

Isabel sat down by the edge of the bricks and took a big stick and stirred the red-hot twigs. "At last, I'm warming up."

Thea raised her eyebrows. "If you had grabbed your long coat, you'd be feeling warmer."

"Don't preach to me, Thea. I get tired of being corrected."

"But you don't listen," said Thea.

"Just leave me alone!" said Isabel as she threw some more wood on the fire.

Mary added, "Gosh, Thea, you and I won't need to go to work today. First, we haven't any clothes, and second, most likely the *Bien* Newspaper Publishing Plant is unsafe."

"Who wants to sit out in the middle of the street all day?" Lena asked. "Not me. I'd rather be in school. Do you think we'll even have school?"

"I doubt it. The building's most likely collapsed," Thea said. "Thank goodness the earthquake came before sunrise."

As everyone stood talking and warming by the fire, Georg noticed that Anna had disappeared. "Have you seen Anna?" he asked the others around the bright red and yellow flames.

Anna's obsession with the loss of her mother's heirloom dishes and the *Sotersambrung's* books and money box gave her no time to chat. As soon as she saw everyone around the fire, Anna headed for the house. She picked her way through the rubble and held her breath as she climbed the stairs.

She found a bag in the kitchen and sat down on the living room floor to pick up the pieces of the rest of the teapot and the cup. It was useless. The blue-rimmed dishes were smashed beyond repair. Tears streamed down her face. "Oh, Mama," she said out loud. "I'm so sorry! I'm so sorry!"

Still crying, Anna went into her bedroom and put on a warm dress and shoes and stockings and re-buttoned her coat. Then, she leaned under the bed for the Sisterhood's books and money box. She couldn't reach the lodge's records and had to squirm under the bed. With both in her hand, she started to back out when suddenly the third aftershock struck. Plaster broke loose from the ceiling. As it fell, the ceiling supports fell with it. The slats and spring couldn't hold the weight and the bed collapsed on Anna.

Martha looked up from the fire at Georg's last question. "Have you seen Anna?"

"Yes," she said, "I last saw her walking toward your house." Georg's eyes grew big as he turned to look at their building with the chimney partially destroyed and the cornice rubble from Nielsen's house spread over the entrance way. Except for the red bricks, everything was a dull gray: the sky, the broken cement, the pavement. A pang of fear shot through his stomach as he ran toward their home. What was his *Norska* doing?

"Anna," he called. "Are you up there? Anna, come down right now. Another shock could destroy the house. Get out."

There was no sound. He could see no movement. Maybe she had walked down to the end of the block, he thought, and found some of her Sisterhood friends. He started down the block but something held him back. At that moment, a small after-shock rumbled down their street. The street crowd ran away.

Georg ran to the back steps. Anna must be upstairs. Was she hurt? With his long legs he climbed over the debris, calling, "Anna! Anna! Where are you?" He entered through the rear porch, but she wasn't in sight. Cabinets and pictures and crockery were scattered in pieces on the carpet.

"Anna, answer me. Anna?" Silence hung heavy in the air. Georg ran through the kitchen, into the bathroom, and to the girls' bedroom. His breath came in short gasps. When he glanced in his and Anna's bedroom, he saw her two legs stretched out from under the bed. He scrambled down on his knees and tried to get underneath, but found that the plaster, slats, and mattress had fallen on her back. He tried to force them up, but couldn't. He got on the floor beside her and saw that she was unconscious, blood draining from one ear. By her side lay the Sisterhood's big record book and the treasurer's money box.

Georg ran down the stairs, shouting, "I need help! Anna is trapped in our bedroom." He spotted some neighbors. "Ignacion! Christian! Hans! Come. Martha, please find a nurse or doctor."

Ignacion crossed himself before he entered. Christian and Hans took a big breath and scrambled up the steps. In the bedroom, the men threw big chunks of plaster to one side and held up the slats and mattress while Georg moved Anna out from under the bed. Blood was crusted in her hair.

The men pulled one of the girls' mattresses as a litter. Georg tucked a blanket around her and tied a rope across her body to keep her from falling off the litter. He placed the Sisterhood book and box beside her feet.

In the street, Thea and Isabel started to cry when they saw Anna's face so white and the blood on her face and hair. "What happened?" sobbed Thea.

"Why your mother had to risk her life for some damn records and a half-filled money box is beyond me," blurted Georg.

Isabel tried to kiss her mother. "I love you, Mama, please open your eyes."

Anna lay there without a sound.

"Where's that nurse?" Georg wondered.

Just then, running down the street toward them came Martha and a man in his pajamas, carrying a satchel. He leaned over Anna's face and held a small mirror to her nostrils. The fog on the glass showed she was breathing. He took her pulse and then held up her eyelids. "Force of the blow knocked her out. Her ear's bleeding only slightly now. I'll clean it out and put a bandage over it."

Georg knelt down besides her and stroked her forehead.

The man patted Georg's back. "She is going to be all right and will soon regain consciousness. I'm over at the first aid station. Call me as soon as she awakes. Don't let her sit up. I'm Dr. Stautland."

Georg and his friends moved the mattress closer to the fire to keep her warm. Thea sat on one side and Isabel the other. Each held a hand. Anna's eyes remained closed, although her breathing was regular now.

"Why did Mama have to go after those books?" asked Thea.

"Would the Sisterhood have held her responsible, even though there was an earthquake?" questioned Isabel.

Georg looked down at his wife and two daughters and thought that he'd give anything to see Anna conscious again. He looked at Isabel. "That's your mother," he said in a daze. "She is determined and when she says she'll do something, she does it. Although this time, she put her life in serious jeopardy."

The sun fought its way through the fog. The warmer rays helped raise the morale of everyone in the neighborhood. The news spread that the earthquake had started a fire which now was burning inside the Palace Hotel.

Christian came back with bad news: "I just talked to the safety patrol officer. He said no one may move back into their home until their chimney has been inspected. They're afraid of fires. We'll have to cook and sleep outside."

The sun begin to shine brightly. Georg fixed a shade over Anna's head. He held her hand and hummed her favorite little Danish tune, *"Den lille Ole, med paraplyen."*

Hans Nielsen came by and asked Georg, "Why don't you go get dressed? We're going in after clothes and food. Of course, the officer told us it was at our own risk."

Georg looked down at the hem of his nightgown, full of dirt. His feet were scratched and swollen. "I wonder how we're going to stay clean? Will they bring us water?"

Nielsen shook his head. "I don't have the answers. Just think, we are only one block. What about the others?"

Anna moved ever so slightly. Georg leaned over and kissed her on the cheek. "Wake up, my sweetheart," he pleaded. She turned her head slightly and let out a little moan.

"Then Isabel Came Your mother is waiting."

With another slight turn of her head, Anna opened her eyes and smiled at her daughters who by now were kneeling by her side. "Where am I? What happened?"

"The plaster, slats, and mattress . . . ," Georg said. "They fell on top of you when you were under the bed."

Anna looked surprised, then suddenly tried to sit up. "Where are my Sisterhood records and treasury?"

Thea held them up. "Right here, Mama. You saved them."

Anna leaned back on her bed and smiled. "Oh, I feel so much better. I couldn't let those women down."

Isabel went after Dr. Stautland. Shortly, they returned. This time he wore his suit. "How do you feel, Mrs. Amorsen? Can you turn sideways?"

Anna carefully turned to her right side.

"What about the left side? Can you manage that?"

Anna turned all the way over although she wrinkled up her face. "It hurts but I can move."

"Can you sit up?"

Anna pushed herself up with her hands. "I think this heavy coat of mine protected me."

"Thea and Isabel," said the doctor, "keep an eye on your mother. She needs something to eat and drink, but keep her here until later this afternoon when she can get up."

George shook Dr. Stautland's hand. "Thanks so much. I was worried she may have broken her back."

Georg knelt beside his wife. "Anna, my dear, I was so scared when I found you under the bed." He leaned over and kissed her. "Can we get anything for you?"

"Yes, a cup of hot coffee."

Isabel leaned down to her and caressed her face. "Mama, you sure are a sturdy Viking."

"If it will be safe, Papa, we'd like to go up and put on our clothes and bring out the coffee pot and some food to eat," said Thea. "The ice box won't keep the food long without our iceman."

"I can't have you go up there," Georg said. "There may be an aftershock. I'll get your clothes. Tell me what you want. After that, we'll fix some lunch. We can boil coffee and cook on this grill top I found from our brick stove."

The girls told him what they needed, and Georg left. Exhausted from their tension and fears, the girls sat on the apple crates. Isabel turned to Thea. "It's scary to have Papa go up there. I hate this. I hate earthquakes!"

Anna leaned up on one arm and looked around. "When I see all this debris on the street, I'm just glad to be alive."

Soon Georg came back with his daughters' clothes. They found a private place and changed while he went back.

"Coffee will soon be ready," Thea announced.

When each of them had a warm cup of coffee to hold, the girls began telling Anna about some of the happenings.

"Mrs. Andersen told me," said Isabel, "that the officer said fires started in at least a dozen locations because people built fires in their stoves without realizing their chimneys had fallen. With all the twisted and broken water mains, there's no way to control the fires. We're surrounded by the Bay, yet there's no water for fires."

"I'm supposed to work tomorrow, but the newspaper is close to Market Street. I wonder if the fire will go there?" said Thea.

"Thea," exclaimed Isabel, "how can you think about your job? Our job is to take care of mother!" The teenager glanced over at Anna. "Can I get you anything, Mama?"

"No thanks, Isabel. This coffee is wonderful. I can see that we're going to have to camp on the street. The Jorgensens have already moved their kitchen stove out to the street."

"We want you to rest now," said Thea. "Soon, Mama, you'll be feeling fine."

Georg came out from the house dressed in his workday blue pants and white shirt. "Now, are you satisfied?" he said to his family. "I even put on shoes."

Anna shook her head, frowned, then felt her bandaged head. "Goodness, that hurts. Georg, would you get me a pillow?"

"Certainly," he said, searching among their things. He held up the lodge's book and treasury box. "I can understand why you went after these, but why the cracked teapot and cup?"

Anna smiled. "They're the only heirlooms I have left." She studied her tall, handsome husband for a moment. "I didn't know you came after me. You must have saved my life."

He pulled one of the apple crates over and sat beside his wounded wife. "You don't know what a panic I was in when I realized you had returned to the house. When the aftershock came, I was scared the roof had fallen on you." He kissed her forehead. "Oh, my little *Norska*, I'm so glad you're okay."

As night descended, more and more mattresses and blankets appeared on the street. Most of the neighbors had also carried out iron stoves and stoked them with wood or coal to keep them warm all night. Georg got out boxes from the store that he had saved under the back porch and used them to hold their pots, pans, dishes, and food. He also brought out a big kerosene lantern to light up the area.

Christian, Martha, and their girls came over to sit and share their day's experiences with the Amorsens. Christian couldn't forget what had happened: "You saved our lives, Georg." Then, he looked at Anna. "When we pulled you out from under the bed, I never thought I'd see you alive."

Anna shook her head, "In another minute I would have been out of there, but the aftershock knocked me out. Thanks for helping Georg carry me out. Martha, thank you for finding Dr. Stautland. The two of you saved my life."

"How about a cup of coffee?" asked Isabel.

"Where did you get the water?" questioned Christian. "The water mains in the city are broken and the sewer lines destroyed. The gas and the telephone lines are useless."

"We had a gallon jug of drinking water in our ice box," said Georg. "I hear they are going to bring a big tank of drinking water for us tomorrow."

Martha pointed at a fiery glow in the dark sky. Ashes were beginning to sift down onto their heads. "Do you think the fire will cross Van Ness and Market?"

"Let's find a security officer," said Georg. "Maybe he'll know. Come along Christian."

The officer shook his head when they asked about water and

sewage facilities. "The city can't promise anything. We don't have enough water to put out the fires. Right now, they're roaring through the streets burning everything in their path."

Christian asked, "Do you think the fire will get this far?"

"Sorry, sir, I can't answer that. I heard some talk about blowing up the houses to make a fire break."

The Amorsens, Andersens, Nielsens, and Jorgensens grouped together around the red brick stove. They couldn't believe that the city would blow up their homes to stop the fire.

Helplessly, they looked at one another. "Let's wait until tomorrow," suggested Christian. "I've had enough for one day. As soon as Thea and Isabel were settled down for the night, Georg told Anna he had to go visit his market. "I'll be back within an hour. Don't worry about me. I'll tell you how it is as soon as I return, if you're still awake." He put out the lantern and carried it during the four-block walk to his store.

When he finally returned, Anna was waiting. "I was so worried. I kept thinking what might happen if we had another shock . . . How do things look at the store?"

"Let me tell you. I knew I wasn't supposed to be out after 10 p.m., but the market is our income and I had to check the damage. I skirted around the police patrol and saw the fiery glow along Market Street. The clouds above looked as if they were welcoming a sunset with their pink and red glow. The air smelled as if a chimney was spitting out heavy smoke and ashes. The pitch dark streets were covered with sleeping bodies.

"I found the market standing, unlocked the door, then stepped on a nice squashy orange. Lighting the lamp, I held it high to see the corners of the market. What a mess. The floor was covered with produce, canned goods, broken bottles, and leaking liquids that smelled like vinegar and chlorox. One whole shelf had collapsed, dumping bread, cakes, and cookies — all my years of work turned into garbage. It will take a long time to rebuild and clean up the place. I filled two bags with whatever food I could find."

"Oh, Georg, our lovely store," said Anna. "How terrible. Maybe tomorrow, we can start to clean it up. Come to bed, Georg. I need you beside me. We're both so tired the whole world looks like a nightmare."

For more than three days and nights, the soot and ashes rained down on their heads. The fires couldn't be controlled. At night, the sky was as bright as a fireworks display. The fires swept up the street, completely eliminating the wooden tenements below Market Street. The only help the Amorsens and their neighbors received from the city was a water tank drawn by two big horses and a soup line which was set up the second day.

Anna felt useless. The doctor had told her to walk just a little, but she wanted to help. "I can peel potatoes like the rest of you. Give me something to do."

Isabel shook her head. "Mama, take care of yourself. Here, I'll read to you from my history book." Soon smoke from the approaching fire blocked out the sun and she had to stop.

On the fourth day, the police called all of the block's residents together. "I have been ordered to read you the following statement:

" 'Due to the need to contain the fire and make a fire break, as of six o'clock tomorrow morning, you will take what possessions you can each carry in a suitcase or a duffel bag to the north corner. Army trucks will move all of you to Tent Cities at Fort Mason or the Presidio, where you'll be housed. ' "

"You can't do that," said Georg. "These are our homes."

"Oh, the only way to fight the fire is to dynamite rows of buildings. Tomorrow morning the Army will set off the dynamite. Arrest awaits those not out."

Anna began to cry. Already she had lost her blue Danish dishes, treasured for over 20 years. The picture albums of their wedding, the girls in school, the big picture of Georg's Amorsen family and the one of Anna's father and sister had already fallen and cracked. But, the furniture, their clothes, and Isabel's school books had survived and could be taken with them. Each time they moved, Anna felt sure it would be the last. Now they had to go from their nice home to a tent. Georg knew what she was thinking; he leaned over and hugged her. "Anna, dear, we'll manage. Remember, our family is together."

They spent most of the night trying to select what they would most need. Using the lantern, each packed a duffel bag. Georg helped Anna pack her Sisterhood records and the treasury box as well as the broken crockery.

"I can't part with these after what I went through to get them," she said. "They are my only keepsakes."

"Anna," said Georg, "fill a little hand bag, and I'll fill a second duffle bag and carry it for you. I don't want you to strain your back. Tell me what you need."

"Don't worry about me," she said. "I feel fine. I'll make my pile right here."

However, as much as Anna tried to fill her bag, she found saying goodbye to the memories of a lifetime almost more than she could bear. The lantern cast shadows on broken crockery and glass scattered throughout the room. Anna pulled the pictures of their Danish and Norwegian families from their broken frames, rolled them up and put them in with her clothes. She also included one of their family photos when the girls were in elementary school. Tears rolled down her cheeks as she tried to sift through a lifetime.

The others cleaned out drawers, made their choices, and left the rest. "Isabel," said Georg. "You cannot put your drawing pad in your bundle. It's too big. Carry it yourself. Put in your clothes, books, and what you will need. Wear your heavy coat, not that thin yellow thing."

"I'm trying, Papa. I'll put the box of sketching charcoal in my pocket. I want to keep up my art work."

Georg decide to take his market and legal papers. He remembered something he'd heard: "Anna, they're going to pay for dynamiting our home. I do not know when they'll let me open the market, but I've started cleaning. There are no major cracks. When we get settled, whether we're allowed on the rubble-strewn streets or not, I'm walking over there to go to work."

Thea was calmest of all. She methodically folded underwear, blouses, and dresses suitable to wear to her newspaper job. "Mama, shall I take this pink fabric you bought to make a dress?" Thea had just been employed on the paper and they both went out to celebrate by finding a beautiful light pink fabric for a new dress. "If you have room, take it. I'll make that dress. I'm bringing my sewing."

When daylight shown through the windows, they all went through each room thinking of the good times they'd had. "Let's form our family circle," Georg called. "It is time to go." They joined arms and stood quietly a moment, each with their own thoughts. "Thank God, we are safe," he said. "We can build a new life again."

Anna tried desperately to keep from crying any more. Her hands were shaking and she had to hold both of them over her mouth as George finished his prayer.

Afterwards, they all lugged heavy bundles to the corner where they stacked them until the trucks arrived. The Nielsens, Jorgensens, and Andersens were waiting. There wasn't much anyone could say. "This is a day filled with sorrow for all of us," said Georg. "Where do you want to go? Fort Mason or the Presidio?"

Christian spoke up. "I've been to the Presidio. There's lots of room. If we have a choice, it is the best place." The Nielsens and

Jorgensens agreed. "You tell the driver, Georg," said Hans. "Since we all agree on the Presidio, he should take us there."

They climbed into the first truck, lugging their bundles and trying to get comfortable on the hard benches. Between the luggage and the families, they filled the wagon.

Anna sat between Thea and Isabel and kept twisting her handkerchief, trying to hold back her tears. What would their lives be like living on a military base? She took one last look down the street to see their home standing there with the collapsed chimney and broken windows, surrounded by a wreath of red bricks. She closed her eyes thinking of how it had once looked. Would they ever have a place of their own?

Georg climbed up beside the army driver. "Our families talked it over, and we all want to go to the Presidio."

The driver flicked the reins and off they rattled down the hill. "We're headed for Tent City," he said.

Anna couldn't stop her tears as they silently flowed down her cheeks. At this moment, she wished she could have found a quiet place to curl up in and be left alone until this nightmare was over. She thought about her mother and how she had died in her arms. That was her first living nightmare. Maybe she and Georg should have gone back to Bergen after Port Angeles. At least there wouldn't have been earthquakes to worry about, and they would always have had some place to call their own. Her tears kept flowing.

Chapter Twenty

Letters

Anna opened the tent flap and peeked out into the dawn. The thick fog cloaked all the tents, causing them to look like rows and rows of grey-white ghosts. The heavy mist clung to their tops, and she knew rivulets of cold water were running down their center poles, just like hers, causing more water and mildew to accumulate inside. The whole sight made her stomach churn, and a brief shiver coursed through her body. How long, she thought, can I stand this crowded tent, the miserable fog, and the long lines for food?

Nearly three months had passed since the earthquake had brought Mrs. Georg Amorsen and her family to this military complex, and none of the city officials could give them a time when they could expect to leave Tent City. But this was not her main worry this morning. A greater problem loomed.

She let the tent flap fall back in place and quietly put on a heavy sweater. She had to go see Martha this morning before the girls awoke. Anna put on her raincoat and checked to see if the girls were still sleeping; Georg had already ridden his bike over to their store, she slipped under the flap and out onto the wet grass. Through the heavy mist, she made her way toward Martha's tent.

How could they fit five human bodies in that size tent? she wondered. The four of us can't even fit in ours.

"Martha," she whispered through the Andersen's front flap. There was no answer. She didn't want to wake everyone, but made one more try. "Martha, Martha."

It was important to Anna that she and Martha talk before the rest of the families in the complex awoke and took over the limited space in the Day Room. There were no other meeting places except under a dripping tree.

Anna turned and started for the Day Room to keep warm while waiting for her friend. Just then, she heard Martha's soft whistle. Anna stopped and waited. Soon Martha came out of her tent in a raincoat and hurried to catch up.

"Hi, Anna! Whatcha doing out here so early?"

Anna grabbed her arm as if she were the last life raft. "I'm so glad to see you. I need to talk to you. Let's hurry over to the Day Room and warm up."

Martha nodded and they walked on in silence.

Anna wasn't sure how much she should tell her best friend. Last night she had tossed and turned, feeling herself going deeper and deeper into a new and scary unrest that permeated all aspects of her being. If only she could sleep and let go. But the chill and terror she had felt when they tore apart their Port Angeles flat had returned. The brutal earthquake followed by the dynamiting of their 16th Street flat and the forced internment in this barracks life had produced a vague spiritless behavior that erased the Anna she was used to.

Also, just before the earthquake, she realized she was going through the change of life. She had taken notice of the burning sensations and spotting, and keeping up her usual enthusiasm and enjoyment of caring for her family had become a burden. But not Martha. She was the one to whom she felt she could tell some of her problems because she was going through the change herself. In the Day Room, Anna and Martha found a corner sofa near the warm stove. No one was there but a young orderly who was lost in reading the morning paper.

Martha pointed at the newspaper. "Did you read where they had closed all the files on the prisoners who were dead or presumed killed in the earthquake?"

Anna frowned. "Martha, what are you talking about?"

"When the quake struck, the city prison toppled over and caught fire. It was presumed that all the prisoners inside were crushed or burned to death."

"So what?"

"So that's where that man was who pulled a gun on you. Remember? Ole somebody?"

Anna's eyes widened. "Ole was killed in the quake? . . . ." She glanced around the room to make sure no one could hear them. "Good!" she said. "That's what he deserved . . . threatening to hurt my Isabel — "

"Anna?" Martha stared at her friend. "What's come over you?"

She took a deep breath and was silent for a moment. "Martha, what am I going to do?" she said, biting her lip to keep from crying. "I'm having a terrible time. I go back and forth from physical fatigue to crying spells . . . ." It was no use. Try as she may, she couldn't hold back the tears. Anna started to sob.

Martha found a handkerchief and lovingly stroked her hand. She put her arm around her and held her close.

Finally, Anna stopped. "I can't adjust to Tent City — to getting dressed behind a blanket hung at the corner of the tent, trying to keep clean, and not having any social life. Day and night the crowds and noise are awful and the girls are gone all day. I just sit there and feel like punching holes in the canvas to open up my world, it is so lonely."

Martha tried to be helpful. "You're always welcome at our tent. Christian leaves around seven."

Anna started to tell her how going through the change added to her worries, but couldn't. She sat on the sofa like a frozen museum piece and clutched the wet handkerchief. She nodded her head as if trying to talk, but nothing came out. Her eyes became glazed, looking off to some distant object across the room.

Martha gave her a little shake but it didn't awaken Anna from her stupor. She walked across the room and asked the attendant for a glass of water. He pointed to the faucet at the end of the room. Martha took her last handkerchief and dampened it and brought it back to wipe her forehead. "Anna, wake up. I'm right here by you. Look at me, I'm your friend."

The cold cloth didn't affect her. Martha tried rubbing her neck and repeating her sentence.

Suddenly Anna broke the chain that seemed to bind her. "Was I asleep?" She stretched her arms and said, "I must have been dreaming. I always have the same dream about my mother. When she was going through the change, she used to go into deep depressions and sit in a rocking chair and rock back and forth all day. I'm scared. I dread the thought of reliving my mother's gloomy existence."

"Oh, Anna," Martha said, putting her arms around her, "don't you know how much we all love and appreciate you?"

Using the wet handkerchief to blow her nose, Anna said, "I miss Georg, but he snores at night while I am having one of those hot spells. At times like that I can't stand to feel his warm body beside me. Am I going crazy?"

"Of course not. Your body is responding to many changes. I've often felt nearly the same way about Christian, and I'm still getting over the change. Come over and visit me any time, and we'll talk." Martha held her by her shoulders and pushed her away so she could look at her face. "What about the girls? Do you hate to be around them, too?"

"You know, Martha, I just don't see them that much. I get so lonesome. Thea often works overtime at the newspaper, and Isabel and her friend Ilse have found a new youth group and spend most of their time with them. I had to work on the wharf at their age. I feel like they're wasting valuable time."

"Mary told me that Isabel and Ilse go across the Presidio to a neighbor's house outside the base. Apparently, it's a teen-age gathering place. We haven't seen much of Isabel lately, either."

"That's what adds to my worries. I'm sure I've smelled tobacco on Isabel's clothes. Once I challenged her breath. She told me it was Sen-Sen, a new kind of gum."

"I understand because when Grace was Isabel's age, she tried to smoke a corn cob pipe. She never tried that again." Martha put her arm around Anna again. "I hope Isabel won't be picking up the habits of a few loud rowdy youths. Isabel is such a creative artist but she must keep up with her sketching."

Anna took a deep breath and sighed. "I'm sorry about telling you all my problems, Martha. I do have good news. It came just at the right time."

She took the letter out of her pocket and showed her the Danish postage stamp. "It is from Tove Amorsen, Georg's cousin who lives in Roskilde, Denmark. She wrote us after she heard about our earthquake and our having to live in Tent City. She invited Isabel to come and live with her and go to school."

"That sounds great. Is she going?"

"We just received the letter which included a note for Isabel. They used to exchange charcoal sketches although Tove is nearly 15 years older. We're going to take her out to Johnny's Den for dinner tonight. We want to give her the note and talk with her about what she'd like to do."

"Anna, what do you think Isabel will do? It would be such fun for her."

"That's my problem. I want her to go but I don't want her to go. I can't think straight anymore. I'm afraid of the crowd she's with here. But what will it be like at Roskilde?"

"Maybe, Anna, part of the pain you're having with your change of life could be your fear about Isabel going away for a year?"

"How would you like to find out within three weeks that Mary would be gone for a year overseas?"

Martha sat up and looked Anna in the eye. "Anna, you and

Georg talk with her tonight. Be frank, give her time to decide. Tell
her how much you love her."

Anna felt better. "Thank you for listening. You make it sound
so easy. I seem to be divided. I don't know what's happening. I'm
anxious for Isabel's sake, and I'm anxious for me."

Isabel was curious about her parents' invitation. Thea had to
work overtime and wouldn't be able to join them. All three of them
dressed up in their Sunday best; Isabel wore a pink dress Anna had
sewn for her. Using a small hand mirror, she checked how she looked.
"Pink is definitely my color," she said as Georg waited outside
the tent.

"Let's see," he called out, fidgeting because the sun had set, the
skies were darkening, and he was hungry.

Her mother finished buttoning her new blue suit and followed
her out. Anna smiled and gave her a hug, "You are beautiful."

Isabel gave her mother a strange look. She hadn't heard Anna
say those words in many weeks.

They walked over to the military stop for an omnibus to take
them down to Johnny's Den on Lombard Street. It wasn't crowded
so they were seated right away and had a delightful time selecting
their choice of grilled fish, boiled crab, or roast beef, unlike the food
line at Tent City. Isabel wanted crab because the two times she had
been to the Embarcadero, she enjoyed cracking the legs and picking
out the white meat. Both Georg and Anna settled for roast beef.

Johnny's Den was their choice of restaurants. The dark mahogany and flickering candles made them feel as if they were at the
Palace, although Georg claimed it as the best food at lowest prices.
By the time they finished almond nut cake, Isabel began to get restless. What did they want to talk about?

"Excuse me," Anna said. "I need a glass of cold water. Maybe
two. Is it hot in here? Georg, ask the waiter. Quick." Anna hung
onto the edge of the table. After Anna drank one, then two glasses,
she calmed down so that Georg took the letter out of his pocket.
"Isabel, we came over here so we could have some time to talk with
you without all the noise at the base."

"I'm sick of that place," Isabel said.

"Here's a letter for you from Cousin Tove Amorsen. She wrote
to us, too."

Anna watched Isabel's face. She looked awestruck as she opened
the letter and read it once, then twice. Was she interested? Did she
want to go? How could they help her face the many choices of friends,

and the varying values to be met while living in the Presidio? Already the soldiers assigned to duty at the Tent City had been whistling at her whenever she walked by their barracks en route to a friend's house. But, would Roskilde be any better?

Isabel put Tove's note in front of her on the table. "Papa, does she mean she will send me a ticket, have me live with her while I finish my senior year, and help me with my sketching and drawing?"

Anna felt a hot surge roll over her again. She had tried to fight it off during dinner, but felt as if she were burning up. "Georg, please get me another glass of ice water."

The cold water helped her throat as she drank it. "Excuse me, Isabel, I feel better now."

Isabel looked surprised. "Are you all right, Mama?"

Anna smiled, "Yes, this will pass quickly. It is that part of life one learns to live with."

Georg continued his answer to Isabel's question. "Tove wouldn't offer her home and fare for your passage if she weren't sincere. She has a good job as tour guide in the Roskilde Cathedral. She's alone. Her parents have died."

"What about my Danish? I can understand you two when you speak very slowly, but my spoken Danish is hopeless."

Anna responded, "Tove always writes to me in English. She can help you. The schools offer language courses to English-speaking students."

Isabel thought a while, "I'm going to talk to Martha and Mary. She wrote a paper in our English class about Roskilde last year."

Georg leaned over toward Isabel. "We love you so very much. We'll miss you, but it would be an exciting adventure." He took a sip from his cup of coffee. "It makes me proud to have you invited to Denmark. Your grandmother lives across from Roskilde and will be happy to have you visit her."

"It sure sounds like it would be better than being stuck in this place," said Isabel.

"I'll miss setting up your easel, sharpening your charcoal, and hanging your paintings," Georg teased. "That is if you decide to go, of course."

Over the next several days, Anna and Georg wondered together over what Isabel would decide. Anna noticed that she spent more time with Mary.

"Come and take a walk with me," Isabel asked her mother one cloudy afternoon, soon after their dinner.

"Where are we going?"

"Don't worry. I want to show you something."

Isabel led the way across the Presidio. "I want to tell you, Mama, that I'm scared of going so far away."

"I felt the same way when I came to America. It is hard to be around strangers. Tove is a very caring person."

"I've thought of her as the perfect artist. I can't draw like that."

"You aren't expected to; she's more experienced. Your last sketch of the ship in full sail was beautiful."

"What if I get lonesome?"

"Isabel, you'll have friends up to your eyebrows within the first month. If there's an emergency, you can always cable us." What about my being lonesome? Anna thought. Your life is beginning. Mine is ending.

"Stop here by the Presidio fence. We go through that hole in the wire. See that house at the end of the block? That is where Ilse and I have been going to play records, eat cookies, and mix with the crowd."

"Cookies, records?" asked Anna. "Whose house is it?"

"Peter Riismoller's mother bakes us cookies and Peter has a great record collection. He's the one who smokes and some of the other fellows do too. I'm sorry how I acted. I did try a cigarette, but it was awful. I never touched another. It hurt when you didn't believe me."

Anna gave Isabel a hug and held her tight. "I've been going through some problems of my own," she said, "and find myself a little cranky. I've been unfair to you. I'm sorry. Let's stop at the Andersen's on our way back."

Martha was knitting out on the bench before her tent. "Hi," she called as she saw them approaching. "Come and visit." As they sat down on the bench, Martha asked Isabel, "What do you think about your cousin's invitation?"

Isabel smiled. "She sure surprised me. You know, I always liked her because when I was younger, Mama would send her my little drawings, and she'd send sketches back to me. I thought that she was a real artist."

"If you go, do you think you'll be able to learn Danish?"

"Tove speaks English, and I'll get a tutor or go to a language class. Mom and Dad spoke Danish when they didn't want us to understand, but I soon began to translate what they were saying."

"Sounds to me that you won't have much trouble. Have you decided yet, Isabel?"

"I'm near there. Thanks for asking the questions."

Georg and Anna would always remember June 10. They were sitting on the bench outside their tent, visiting with the Andersens, when Isabel swept up to them as if she'd just conquered the world. "Listen! I'm going to accept Cousin Tove's invitation. I'm going!" Anna gave her a hug. The decision was made. They all tried to talk at once. Georg said, "We'll send a cable to Tove tomorrow. You won't have much time to get ready." She told Georg that night, "For Isabel's sake, it is the best choice. What a difference Tove's letter made. She has a new adventure ahead."

Georg nodded his head. "I've been home so little I didn't realize her lack of purpose in being pulled into the youth group. She and Tove will become good friends. Now that she's going, I wish I had spent more time with our family. Little Isabel, how I'll miss her."

In a short period of time, they received a cable that notified them that train tickets and passage on the *Northern Star* were at the San Francisco office. The ship was sailing in two weeks, early in the morning. Tove sent a little note.

Delighted you're coming, Isabel. Fixed up back bedroom. Meet you on Copenhagen dock when Northern Star *arrives.*
I'll wear a red hat!
Cousin Tove Amorsen

Martha, Anna, Mary, and Isabel spent the next week going through Isabel's wardrobe, mending, cleaning, polishing. Isabel dug through her duffel bag. "Look! I'll even bring my old textbooks. Here are my brushes and charcoal."

Thea watched all the excitement. "Isabel, we expect you to return as the world's most outstanding artist. How about taking me along? No, I wouldn't want to go. I like my newspaper job. You better send us a weekly letter so we can keep track of you."

Tent City held a brief farewell party for Isabel with all kinds of messages given to her by the Sixteenth group to bring to their Danish family or friends. They celebrated for the trip with smorgasbord, music, and dancing.

Departure day arrived too soon for her family. Anna was fighting with herself to keep from crying or breaking down. Thea took the day off to go with them across the Bay at the first light. Georg rearranged his work schedule. He, too, looked sad and held himself in by saying very little.

Georg, Anna, and Thea took the ferry with Isabel across the San Francisco Bay to the Oakland Southern Pacific pier. Georg put her luggage on the train. Isabel started to cry and hugged her mother. "Mama, write to me."

Anna held her close. "We love you. We'll write." She couldn't say anymore without breaking into tears. This was Isabel's moment. Thea gave her a little book about Denmark. "Here's a book, a hug, now dry the tears. You're on your way to being famous."

Georg wrapped his long arms around Isabel. "We're always here to help you, honey. Write to us and have a wonderful trip." He hugged her again and helped her on the train.

They all shouted, "Bon voyage!"

Georg and Anna had never been separated from their daughters before. Anna watched the train until it was out of sight. She leaned against Georg, but she couldn't talk. Tears poured down her face while Thea held her hand.

Through water-filled eyes, Anna looked out at the gray-colored waves of the Bay which were reflecting the overcast skies of the early morning. She thought how perfectly the color of the water and skies matched her feelings — empty, cold, and alone. It wasn't that her family didn't love her and try to help. They just didn't really understand.

She turned and began the long walk back to the ferry. The three of them walked in silence for some while. Thea was still holding her hand. Finally, Anna wiped her eyes and made herself ask Thea, "How are things going for you down at *The Bien*? They certainly use up all your time."

"Mama, I like to work the late edition. Lots more excitement then. There is always a late story or a big robbery. Also, there's my friend, Lester. He and I have been working together a lot lately."

"Lester?" said Anna, scowling and turning to look into her oldest daughter's face. "Who's Lester?"

"Just a friend of mine. We've been doing some volunteer work after hours at the base hospital. But that's about over, now. They said they wouldn't need us anymore in a few days. Things seem to be settling down around the whole city."

"Is that so?" said Georg, looking puzzled, as well. "Does that mean that maybe the city's going to let me open back up without a certificate from the health department?"

Thea shrugged. "I don't know, Papa. I didn't know you were having so much trouble."

"So when are you going to let us meet Lester?" asked Anna.

"Oh, Mama. He's not that kind of a friend."

"Sounds like a nice fellow," said Georg. "We would like to meet more of your friends, Thea."

"Which days do you and he work there?" wondered Anna.

"There's no set schedule," said Thea, "but today we signed up for a few hours before work — three to six o'clock. We don't do that much: just change bedpans and run errands and things like that."

Anna nodded, deep in thought. She suddenly realized that she didn't know very much about Thea's life since everything had been drastically changed by the quake. "If I came down and saw you at work in the hospital, would you mind?"

Thea beamed. "Not at all, Mama. I would love it." They stopped and hugged.

"I love you very much, Thea," Anna said, the tears coming again as she felt the warmth of her tall oldest child. "I'm sorry if it seems I've only been thinking about Isabel lately."

"I understand, Mama. Don't worry. I love you, too."

Georg came up and put his long arms around his wife and daughter. "And I love you both very much, no matter how it may seem otherwise. Don't ever forget that, either one of you!"

That afternoon, Anna decided it was time she found out who this Lester fellow was. Maybe he was just a friend to Thea, and maybe he was a lot more. She wanted to see for herself. She remembered how it had once been with she and Georg. They had just been "friends" in the beginning, too. She couldn't believe it had been over twenty years since their first meeting.

At a little before 5:00 p.m., she made her way from the family tent down to the hospital tent that served the entire complex. She hadn't told Thea she was coming because she wasn't sure if she was up to being in a hospital, given how she was feeling. She thought she'd surprise her eldest daughter.

The moment she stepped inside, she knew she'd made a terrible mistake. The first thing that hit her was the stench. It hung in the air like a fog of anguish, clogging her nose and mouth with its putrid, vile, unceasing invasion. She fought the urge to vomit. It was worse than anything she'd ever encountered on the fish wharf in Bergen.

Anna looked side to side, up and down long rows of the rotting and dying. She had hoped to catch a glimpse of Thea, but the chorus of moans and whimpers changed her mind. Her meeting with Lester would have to wait until another day. She turned to leave. "Mama, wait. Where are you going?"

Startled by Thea's voice, Anna froze and turned slowly to face her daughter who she could now see was running toward her. Just behind her was a slender young man with rumpled brown hair and a pale, baby face. They both had on oversized, grey gowns that covered their street clothes. Blood covered the front of both uniforms. Anna wanted to run, but managed to resist the urge.

Just then, an ear-piercing scream came from one of the patients just a few feet away from Anna. She shuddered, closed her eyes, and put both hands to her ears while backing through the tent flap to the outside.

"Mama," said Thea, bursting through the tent flap followed by the young man. "Are you all right?"

By now, Anna's face had turned ash white, and she was staggering out of control.

"Mama . . . watch out!" Thea blurted as she and her male companion closed the gap. Thea grabbed her mother's hands, trying to steady her, but Anna was losing balance.

The young man, moving quickly, circled in behind Anna and put one strong arm around her back and held her shoulder with the other to hold her steady.

"Let go of me!" Anna said in a loud tone of voice. She twisted out of the young man's grip. "Just what do you think you're doing?"

"We're trying to help you," Thea said.

"I didn't ask for your help!" Anna said. "Who is this man?"

"Lester's my name . . . Lester Herbert Gray," he said, looking around for something. "Thought you was a real goner there for a minute or two, Mrs. Amorsen. Seen that look a time or two in this here hospital, ya know. Never can be too careful. Your face sure got white as a snowflake soon as that feller started yelping." Les turned completely around, still looking for something. "Can't seem to locate nothin' for ya to sit on. Lemme go inside and getcha a chair or somethin'!"

"That won't be necessary," Anna said quickly.

"Suit yourself." He looked back and forth between Thea and Anna, who obviously wanted to be alone. "Well, . . . Guess I'll be goin' back to work . . . Nice meetin' ya, Mrs. Amorsen . . . See ya later!"

Anna nodded.

"I'll be right there, Les," said Thea. "I just want to say goodbye to Mama."

"Okkie dokkie," he said, nodding at Thea. He then waved enthusiastically at Anna and disappeared inside.

"Are you sure you're all right?" Thea wondered. "You don't look well, Mama. Do you want me to walk you home?"
"I'm fine," Anna snapped. She looked down, unable to say what she was thinking.
"Why did you come?" asked Thea. "Didn't you think it would be this unpleasant?"
Anna shook her head. "I came to see you . . . I wanted to see what you did here . . . I shouldn't have come. It was a mistake. I'm sorry if I scared you." She turned to leave, then turned back and gave her daughter a brief hug. "I love you, Thea . . . and I'm proud of you." She turned and walked away.

She wished she could have found a hole and fallen into it. She couldn't believe she'd made such a fool of herself, especially in front of that ill-mannered young man. Imagine him pawing his smelly hands all over me like I was one of those patients. I'm certainly glad he and Thea are just friends.

The June fog finally disappeared. In its place came the hot July sun that filled the tents with such heat that the four sides had to be rolled up to get a breeze. Thea and Les began using their spare time to help Georg rebuild the grocery store.

Each day Anna went to the base post office looking for a letter from Isabel. She had already written to Isabel with the news that the city and federal government had reached an agreement on the reconstruction plans for their Sixteenth Street homes. Soon they would be able to move back into their old flat.

She couldn't tell anyone how lonesome she was. In an empty tent all day, Anna felt restless at night, but vowed she was going to start up her sewing group again. Yet somehow, she couldn't get herself going.

Why does this lethargy hold me in its grip? The same scenery, the constant noise, the tent which seems to wrap itself closer around me. The sun beats down and wears me out when I have a burning sensation.

She took off all her clothes and lay on her cot sweating and twisting, fighting the devil. She wondered if she could start a group again. Just wondering brought tears and feelings of hopelessness.

The one thing that brought her to her feet was the post office on the base. By late afternoon, hoping for Isabel's letter, she managed to walk over. What a wonderful surprise to find the Danish-stamped envelope.

With Isabel's letter in her hand, she headed for her favorite shade tree: a large willow with branches extending far over the lawn. Carefully she opened the letter. What would she have to say? Had she started school? Did she like living with Tove? There on the first page was a rough sketch of the Cathedral in red brick with stained glass windows. Underneath she wrote, "We live under its shadow."

Anna smiled when she finished Isabel's letter. Isabel was excited and involved already with a youth group at school and a special art class in the Cathedral. Tove was full of energy. They had just returned from a fun-fest by the Roskilde Fjord. At the very bottom she added, "I miss you."

Anna read it over once, twice, and, each time, she shed tears thinking of her little girl.

At dinner, Thea and Georg read Isabel's letter.

"It is so like her," said Thea. "Sketches, short sentences, and a quick view of her life. I wonder if she read the book on Denmark I gave her? She thinks she's a citizen already."

That night, Anna slept restlessly again. The long periods of a burning sensation were what bothered her most and left her soaked in sweat. She hated to be like that and have Georg so close. She moved over and took Isabel's cot.

Many times she felt as if she'd have better luck trying to sleep outside on the lawn. The change of life is a natural part of life, she kept reminding herself. Maybe if she repeated that ten times in her head, she'd feel better.

She made herself get up the next morning to visit with Martha after both their families had left. "Martha, how is it you always seem to be calm? You're just like me. You're going through a change of life, too."

"Anna, dear, we've both gone through a devastating earthquake. We're going through a physical change as well. It's your attitude toward yourself." Martha looked at Anna and noticed she had lost weight and lines had gathered under her eyes.

"You're right, Martha. I guess I'm also reacting to not having children around the house anymore."

"You see, you and I need to prepare for the second half of life and see what we can do."

"That sounds great, but what can we do? I came over to talk about starting another sewing circle with you, but the thought of it just wears me out."

"Why don't we start with the beginning Nordic pattern series — nothing more, simple designs, and they're fun to embroider. That isn't too big a job for the two of us."

"No, you make it sound easy. We have a number of the Sixteenth Street women who just started the class when the quake came. We could run it on the base."

"Anna, why don't I find a place and talk to a few of those women who didn't finish. Once a week, we could both share in getting the patterns ready. Come on, Anna let's start this other half of life right now."

"Martha, you are a gem," Anna hugged her. "You make me want to combat this terrible mood. I'll try — with your help."

Chapter Twenty-One

Thea's Friend

Something is wrong. Anna's eyes snap open, wide with fear. She tries to fend off the falling plaster. Her nose is filling with thick dust from all the falling debris.

Anna jumped to her feet, expecting the tent to collapse around her any moment. She was alone and the room silent. It was just another bad dream. The same dream she'd been having for over four months now, ever since that terrible morning when the quake shook their home so hard they could hardly open the door to get out. These dreams always left her feeling as if she were going to suffocate under her bed as the ceiling fell down and buried her.

She shook her head, wanting to clear her mind. I must push these thoughts out of my head, she thought, and looked at the cracked mirror hanging on the tent pole. She had to stand on tiptoes to see her pug nose, round face, and long curly brown hair with its several strands of unwanted gray. After all these years, she was just beginning to accept her stocky build; she'd even lost some weight lately. She smiled at her image because this mirror distorted her face like those strange mirrors in the fun house at Golden Gate Park.

She sat down on the cot in her tent still trying to regain her composure. She couldn't help but cringe at the image of their chimney falling, its sudden collapse onto the street shattering red clay in all directions. She closed her eyes and held her hands tight, thankful that her whole family had escaped without any of the injuries of those poor people she'd seen in the hospital tent.

How could Thea and Les stand to face that awful place as often as they had? It's a wonder they hadn't caught something working around all that filth and disease. Anna did feel a little better now that they were helping Georg instead. He was able to open the store because of them. That Les certainly did seem to be more than just a friend to Thea. They're practically always together. What a strange man that Les is!

Anna walked over to the calendar and checked off another day. She reminded herself of what she'd said to her husband earlier that morning. "Georg, please tell the contractor we want to be in by Christmas. I just can't wait much longer."

"They're working as fast as they can," Georg had replied. "Finishing work always takes more time. It won't be long."

"I spend most of my time over in the Day Room where it is warmer," Anna said. "The rain, fog, and dreary days are unbearable. We can't keep living in a tent without a stove."

Georg came over and put his arm around her. "Have patience, Anna. We're on the last stretch. We'll make it into our old apartment building by Christmas. I'll stop over there again on my way over. They know how anxious we are." He kissed her and headed out to his bicycle. He still rode to his store every day.

She thought of all the work ahead — walls to paint, curtains to sew, a garden to replant, and a kitchen to restock. She looked around their tent, angry at the news that it had been unnecessary to blow up the buildings on Sixteenth Street. All our possessions are gone, she thought, except the large trunk, a chest of drawers, and the boxes for clothes, tools, sewing patterns, and Isabel's art work stored under the four military cots. Will the city compensate us for all the things we lost due to their mistakes of judgment?

Anna paced back and forth in the small space that had been her home since April. She looked at the calendar and counted off the thirty or forty days left until they could move into their old flat. She thought about being back in her own kitchen, stirring up *frikadeller*, meat balls, or rolling out *kringler* crisp cookies. The food at the cafeteria for Tent City was sickening. Thea and Georg had told her how much they longed for her cooking.

Her mind wandered back to her immediate problem: How she was going to deal with Thea's boyfriend, Les. She wanted to hear whether Les had apologized to Thea. As far as Anna knew, the boy hadn't even said that he was sorry for grabbing her that day outside the hospital. Then, she remembered how hard he'd been working over at the store. Georg even said that he couldn't have re-opened without Les's help. He's deceptively strong, Georg had said.

"I think he and Thea may be getting serious," Georg said one night as he and Anna were falling asleep.

If we could get him to visit us, Anna thought, but this little tent isn't the place. She twisted her hands. Johnny's Den, that's it. We'll invite him to dinner and find out how he acts when he's our guest. Anna realized that if she made disparaging remarks about Les or tried to prevent him from visiting, Thea would rebel. There was no doubt Thea was enamored of him.

Anna put on a red and white sweater and wrapped a scarf around her head. She walked slowly over to the cafeteria through the thick fog thinking there has to be a way to make Thea see Les as he is — careless, lacking in manners, and out for himself. The solution, she thought, is to put him into a situation which will expose his trashy, thoughtless character.

Thea burst into the tent one night right after work, breathless and weary. "Guess what?" she blurted before Anna could respond. "The Southern Pacific transferred Les to the Salt Lake run, promoted him to supervisor, and gave him a big raise. I can't call him my peanut butcher any longer."

"What about his schedule?" asked Georg. "Is he still on the irregular shift?"

"No," Thea said, sitting on her cot. "He's on four and then off three. We'll have to plan our days so we can help you and go out to the park and visit the gardens, walk on the beach, and listen to the military band together. He'll be gone much longer on each trip, now."

"When he's off next week, why don't you two have dinner with us over at Johnny's Den? We can celebrate his promotion," suggested Anna.

Thea looked at Anna with a quizzical stare as if to ask, Why so much attention to my boyfriend? After a moment's hesitation, she said, "It depends on Les's schedule. Thanks, Mama, I'll ask him."

Several days later when they entered Johnny's Den with its dark mahogany interior and flickering candles on each table, Georg said, "You'll like the food here, Les, it matches the Palace Hotel in design but without the cost."

As they sat down to wait for their table, Les leaned forward and addressed Anna, "Hope you'll excuse me, Mrs. Amorsen, if I offended you that day at the hospital. I sorta got excited and worried that you might hurt yourself if you just keeled over and hit the ground."

Anna thanked him and began to have doubts whether taking Les to dinner would give them the chance to really size him up. She noticed his brown suit was pressed, his tie straight, and hair combed.

Those long train trips leave him too pale, she mused to herself as she gave him another quick look.

As soon as they were seated, Les took one glance at his menu and immediately closed it. "I see they got crab. That's just my speed." He signaled the waitress. "Bring me a Danish beer."

Georg, as the host, raised his eyebrows while studying his menu. "Yes," he said, "I'll have a beer too. Are you ready to order, ladies?"

Thea and Anna ordered roast beef, as did Georg. It was never served in the Tent City cafeteria.

Now the whole family can have some real meat, thought Anna. "How do you like your new job, Les?" she inquired.

"Only been on one run, but I'm the boss now. It's a lotta work supervisin' them six boys and keeping 'em going up and down them long aisles. I stock the supply chests with popcorn, candies, soda pop, and stuff."

Anna nodded her head and took a sip of water. "Do you serve liquor as well?"

"Oh, no, Mrs. Amorsen. We don't have no license."

As soon as the waitress put the dinner plates down, Les didn't wait. He quickly picked up a crab leg and picked out the crab meat with his fingers. The waitress politely put the crab picker beside his plate and poured his beer. From the look on her face, Anna thought, it was a most unusual way of eating. He stopped and drank a third of the beer in the mug.

"Say, this is a real swell feast. Sure am glad you're not mad at me any more, Mrs. Amorsen." He picked up his napkin, stuffed it under his chin and proceeded to suck the crab. "We never get no food like this on the train."

Anna watched in amazement. Even in her days in the fish stall, she never saw any of her customers sucking up the contents of a crab in such a manner.

"Who wants coffee?" Georg asked, recovering his voice.

Anna and Thea nodded their heads, but Les said, "Just make mine another beer."

Thea finished eating her roast beef, but her face recorded dismay about Les's manners. She kept her eyes averted and pretended to mix the last bite of mashed potatoes with gravy.

Anna wondered if Les was just putting on a show for them or was this the way he always ate? He'd already invited Thea to his home to have Thanksgiving dinner with his mother and Charlie, his youngest brother. As far as Anna was concerned, Les demonstrated the manners of a very uncouth young man.

Anna wished Georg would say something to indicate displeasure. Les, however, continued to wolf down his crab food dinner, completely cleaning his plate. The waitress brought coffee and beer with the menu. "What are you having for dessert?" she asked. Les immediately spoke up. "Make mine a banana split." Anna, Thea, and Georg thanked the waitress, but did not order. "We just can't eat any more," Georg said. "It was a delicious dinner."

Les drank more beer while waiting for his dessert.

Georg turned to Anna. "I've been saving a surprise. I went to our old flat this morning, and the contractor said he'll be finished right after Thanksgiving. But, we have to do the painting."

Both Anna and Thea beamed. "That's all right," said Anna. "Now I'll have a target; how many days left? Fifteen? We've really got our work cut out for us."

"It will take at least twenty days," said Georg.

Thea smiled. "Our own home again." She shook her head in disbelief. "It seems almost too good to be true."

Les's slurping of his ice cream interrupted their conversation.

"But we will still have to paint all the interior," said Anna. "Have you chosen the colors?"

"Yes, that's the contract," said Georg. "The Olsens are eager to get in the lower flat again. We'll start there. We thought we'd paint the kitchens yellow and the living room a light tan. The bedrooms need a light color — maybe pink or pale blue."

Les, finishing the last bite, pulled his napkin from under his collar, carelessly dropped it on the floor, and took a noisy swallow of the few drops left in his beer mug. "Heck, I'm a great painter. I think I'll come and help."

Anna tightened her fingers around her coffee cup. She didn't want Les hanging around, yet they certainly needed help if they were to complete the painting in time.

That night she asked Georg, "What do you think of Les?"

"Well, he certainly has no manners or social graces, but he's not afraid of hard work. Maybe he can paint. He seems to manage all right on his job, and he's certainly been a big help at the store. And, he's really strong for his size." Georg became silent. "Anna, you worry too much. Give the boy a chance to grow up!"

She didn't respond. Her plan to show Les's ungracious and crude behavior was not working. Georg accepted him as a fellow in need of some instruction on his social graces and liked Les's perseverance and good work habits. And although Thea was uncomfortable with

Les's eating habits, she had enjoyed the dinner. Besides, she had already become his steady girl.

We'll try him as a painter, Anna thought, then we'll find out about the rest of his sloppy ways and bad habits.

On Thanksgiving, they served a dry turkey plate in the cafeteria at Tent City. Anna missed a festive celebration where she could have served special recipes on her Danish Bing and Grondahl blue and white dishes. She'd even saved a few pieces and glued them together. However, with Isabel in Denmark and Thea visiting Les's family, there wasn't much need for a family dinner. "We'll have Christmas at home," Georg said, trying his best to cheer her up.

At breakfast the following morning, Anna and Thea took their time with breakfast since Thea had a holiday. "Mama, you should meet Les's mother. She is a big woman — tall with a big bust, fat thighs, and pretty blue eyes."

"I'd like to do that someday when we're settled."

"Les said his mother travels a lot because she received a train pass after his father was killed in a train accident; Les was fifteen."

"How did they manage?"

"Les's three older brothers took jobs with Southern Pacific, married, and left home. Les said he and Charlie had to finish school and also keep house."

"My, that must have been hard on the two boys with their father gone, and their mother traveling around the country."

"Oh, she was home now and then. When I was helping her in the kitchen, she looked down at her floor and told me that if I wanted my kitchen floor to shine like hers, I needed to wash it in milk."

Anna walked to the coffee urn, and poured herself another cup. Maybe that's why Les acts as he does, she thought, and felt a momentary sense of pity.

Thea wasn't through. "Mama, I haven't told you all: she's an odd cook. She put two three-inch nails in the turkey to keep the dressing inside."

"I hope they weren't rusty."

"Oh, no. They were shiny. The dinner was very good with turkey gravy for the mashed potatoes and yams. You know how I like gravy. After dinner, Les showed me the rooms he had painted with Charlie's help. They really looked nice except they used blue paint in the bedroom. Too dark."

"It sounds like you had a good time." Anna was eager to know how his manners were at home, but didn't dare ask.

Thea took her last bite and sighed, "Here I have a day off and Les has a twenty-four hour shift. I miss him already, but early tomorrow we'll be together, helping Papa at the store."

Anna didn't respond. "Wait until you find out more about this guy," she mumbled under her breath.

When Thea and Les walked into the store shortly after dawn the next morning, it was still cold and foggy outside.

"Morning, Georg," said Les, unbuttoning his heavy coat.

"Good morning, you two," he said, smiling with pride at his eldest daughter. "How was your trip, Les?"

The young man shrugged. "Too much rushin' around for my tastes," he said. He sighed and looked around the store. "You want us to keep workin' on them shelves in the back?"

Georg nodded and went behind the front counter with a pile of paper bags he'd taken from an empty wooden box. A few empty boxes littered the floor. "Keep a good ear out, would you, Thea? If things get busy, I'll probably need you up here."

"Yes, Papa." Thea gave her father a kiss on the cheek and followed Les toward the back room. Wooden boxes of unopened dry goods and packaged inventory were stacked high in all directions.

Just then, the door opened and a tall, burly man came inside. He had on a tattered sailor's navy blue cap and peacoat. His hair and bushy eyebrows were white and the odor of dead fish hung about him like a heavy cloud.

The moment Georg saw the man close the door, something foreboding and familiar about the man made him feel uneasy. "Good morning, sir," Georg said in his usual cheerful voice. "What can I get for you?"

The big man looked around the store, both hands in his jacket pockets, and didn't answer. He then began nodding his big head and ambled toward the front counter. Through bulging blue, bloodshot eyes, he stared at Georg. "Remember me?" he asked, weaving slightly. He reeked of alcohol.

Georg scratched his head and swallowed. He did remember. In the same instant fear, anger, and disbelief shot through his veins: He made two fists by his sides. "Yes, I remember you, Ole Ludeman," he said through clenched teeth, "and you'd better get out of this store, right this minute. I don't want any trouble."

"You owe me money!" Ole yelled at the top of his lungs, slamming his fist on the counter. "I want three hundred dollars. You stole my wife!"

"You are a liar, Mr. Ludeman!" Georg yelled right back. "I stole nothing from you. I'm sick and tired of you bothering me and my family. Now, you'd better get the hell out of here right now, before I have to make you leave!"

Ole threw his head back and roared. He stepped back and drew a long hunting knife from his pocket, waving it in the air. "Go ahead and try, old man," he slurred in this thick Norwegian accent. "I'll carve open that fat stomach of yours and leave your guts hanging out like you were just another over-stuffed salmon!"

Hearing the commotion, Thea came running out of the back room. When she saw Ole brandishing the knife, she froze, threw both hands to her ears, and screamed.

Georg turned toward his daughter. "Thea get out of here!" he yelled, waving her from the room.

"Oh, my God," she exclaimed, running into the back room. "Les! Les! Come quick!"

While Georg's head was turned toward Thea, Ole jumped over the counter and swung the long knife down at his victim. Georg raised his left arm in self-defense and partially deflected the blow. The knife struck him in the top of the shoulder. Ole then smashed his other fist into Georg's face, knocking him backwards. Georg hit the back of his head on one of the stacked wooden boxes and slumped unconscious to the floor. Blood was already pouring from the large wound in the top of his chest.

Ole frantically cranked the cash register handle. One of the drawers sprung open. He was stuffing cash into his pockets when Les ran into the room, carpentry hammer in hand, Thea close behind. Les immediately recognized the situation.

"Hey, you, stop," he blurted and threw the hammer at Ole. Distracted by the appearance of another man, the thief didn't react in time and the hammer hit him in the head, stunning him momentarily.

"Get help," Les ordered, waving Thea toward the front door while blocking Ole's escape route. "Your dad's hurt bad."

Thea scurried to the front door and ran down the street. "Help! Help!" she shouted at the top of her lungs. "We're being robbed! My Dad's been stabbed!"

Les then picked up an empty wooden box from where Georg had been working and held it as a shield to fend off the larger man's expected charge.

By now, Ole had regained his senses. He turned toward the younger man, the long bloody knife raised high above his head. "Get out of my way, little man!" he bellowed. "You're going to end up just like this old man! You want that?"

"You're not going anywhere, you rotten son-of-a-bitch," growled Les, crouching low. "You're going to jail . . . for a long, long time!" Ole charged. With his free hand, he ripped the box from Les and threw it bouncing and spinning onto the floor in front of the counter. He then rushed his young tormentor and swung the hunting knife down at the young man's head. Les grabbed Ole's arm with both hands and slowed the thrust of the attack, but wasn't quite strong enough. The bloody knife plunged into Les's back just below his left shoulder blade.

Les screamed in pain. "You bastard!" he yelled and kneed Ole in the crotch. Les shoved his attacker away with one hand and smashed his fist into the taller man's mouth with the other.

Still clutching the knife, Ole staggered backward and attempted to regain his balance. As he turned to reach for one of the counters, he tripped over the wooden box he'd just thrown to the floor and fell flat on his face.

Les tried to pursue the man, but felt dizzy. The room started to swirl, then everything went black. He fell to the floor, blood oozing through his shirt and running onto the floor.

When Anna awoke that same morning, the pounding of hammers and the screech of saws cutting metal filled the air. To Anna, the noise of hammers felt as if it were beating holes in her head, particularly when she could already feel a migraine headache coming on. The range of decibels from the low to the high sounded like chalk across a cold blackboard.

Anna's clock said it was seven o'clock. Later, she found out that the contractor had delivered the old city election booths to the Presidio, and workmen were now cutting them apart. They were making one-room shelters for those who had been displaced by new construction, some of which was to remodel existing buildings which had survived the quake, but were too old.

Yesterday, Anna watched them dig foundations for new buildings. Soon they would have more new neighbors. She'd even dodged a baseball thrown by teenage boys playing nearby. The thought of more neighbors and the constant noise of families and children made her stomach tight as a knot.

As she lay alone on Isabel's cot, she felt another series of heat spells rolling through her body. She tore off her sheet and see-through gown and used them to fan herself. The slight breeze helped a little, but now she needed a glass of water. The night before had not been a good one: she'd made three visits in the dark to the spigot to fill a glass with water. She just hoped she used the spigot with the "suitable for drinking" sign. The damnable heat spell wouldn't stop. She didn't know when it started; it felt like she was sitting in hell. She was certain the Sun God, Apollo, was beginning to beat on the roof of the tent. There could be no doubt about: The wrong God was stirring up trouble for today.

Anna reached for the small statue of Aditi, the Sky goddess, that stood on the trunk. Isabel had copied Aditi from a larger statue and had given it to Anna when she left for Denmark. She told Anna to keep the statue in sight because Aditi was a graceful symbol and a reminder of one's creative powers.

The gift from Isabel had surprised her mother, but Anna recalled that when she and Georg had chosen Thea Christi as their first daughter's name, the Lutheran minister had objected to the Greek word Thea meaning goddess. Anna felt she could be a Christian and still respect the Greek name for a force which motivated women.

She stroked the little statue. "Please help me get motivated and active again," she said out loud. "How does one develop creative powers and learn to use them? My greatest gift was the birth of two daughters, but now what? Martha helped me start the new women's embroidery group here at the Presidio, but I walked out. What a way to treat a best friend. Why didn't I stay with her like I promised?"

Her head was beginning to pulsate in time with the hammers. She had to get up and leave this horrible cage. It was time to get dressed and have breakfast. As she walked across the green to the cafeteria, she could hear the high-pitched whistles of tugs and the bass bellows of ocean steamers. Salty sea breezes cooled her a little; if only this heat wave would stop.

The line for breakfast twisted slowly down around the cafeteria's entrance. It took some time, but Anna finally got inside to choose her cereal and pour a mug of luke-warm coffee. She sat in the corner not wanting to be recognized and quickly chewed the cereal and gulped her coffee. She felt hot enough despite the luke-warm coffee. She stacked her dishes and left by the rear door.

Should I go to the post office box? If only Isabel would write more often. Over three months had passed and Isabel had sent only five letters. In one, she had written that she had a wonderful partner in the drawing class. He was so helpful in helping her shade her drawings. He was a little older, but was also a student.

Why didn't she tell us more? Anna thought. A few lines didn't help. Did they do the right thing in encouraging Isabel to go live with Tove? It most likely was just as well. There had been two big brawls by the newly recruited soldiers over the poor food served by the Presidio's cafeteria. One noon session ended with the tent residents fleeing out the door as the soldiers threw plates across the room. She walked over to the post office and sat under the oak tree, waiting for the morning mail to be distributed in the boxes. The picture Isabel had sent from Denmark — the one of her holding up the Aditi figure — made Anna wonder if Isabel and Tove attended Sunday worship in the Roskilde Cathedral? Isabel had only described the Cathedral with its beautiful stained glass windows. Who could blame her, Anna thought. She and Georg had not been regular members at their local American Lutheran church. Anna sighed; even Thea rarely attended church.

Stop this "what if" game you're playing, she told herself. Why do you sit here and mope? Every woman faces the same experience as she grows older. Martha told her it would soon pass, but for the past months it had been a wrestle with the devil. Perhaps I'd better take a walk under the eucalyptus trees and burn off these constantly circular thoughts.

She started out toward the ocean on the north side of the Presidio. The one thing that consoled her was the sound of the oncoming waves breaking against the cliffs. Sparkling bubbles and foaming wave tops rolled along and smashed with a vengeance against the rocks. The salt spray flew through the air and Anna stood on the cliff and inhaled deeply, trying to get cool.

The cliffs reminded her of her little Bergen home on the side of the *fjord*, peering down at the blue water below. She thought of her mother, cutting out dresses on the dining table, and then having clients climb and stand on the table while she pinned the hems. Her mother was a seamstress, but somehow found time to work in the family fish stall. Anna often wondered how Mama fed and dressed them from the pittance her father earned from his fishing boat.

Once again, Anna remembered the farewells with her family when she sailed to America. If only we could have visited Gudrun and Papa when we returned to Denmark, she thought, but Georg wanted to stay with his parents and locate a job in Haderslev. It was too far from Bergen. Dreams of bringing Papa and Gudrun to America were never fulfilled, either. She felt her anger rise at herself when she thought of how meekly she had agreed with Georg's plans.

Anna thought about Georg's riding his bike across town seven days a week. The quake had broken the windows and ceiling and shelves and bottles and left the market in a smelly jumble. To save their livelihood and keep customers, he worked day and night to put the store back in order. It was difficult to obtain lumber because everyone was rebuilding. Luckily, Georg's father had sent money to help pay for some of the rebuilding materials.

To open the market, Georg had obtained a certificate of health from the city department. Thea and Les had really helped with that — lots of hard work. Anna sighed, wishing she could have helped him as she had when she was younger and healthier. He used come home for lunch; they had talked together and shared their lives. But, no longer. He was too busy and too far away.

Anna picked up a tree twig and made two hearts in the soft sand. Maybe we can do more things together on Sunday with their old neighbors, once we get moved back into our old place. She retraced their hearts and recalled their first courting days when he came to call in his well-pressed suit, his jaunty hat, and his neatly-trimmed Van Dyke beard. What a handsome man, but he's working himself to death. He has little time to talk. He doesn't understand the effect my change of life has had on me. Isabel is gone and Thea spends all her time away from home. My life is empty. I feel useless.

She sat down on the big rock above the cliffs and watched the waves as they came rolling to shore. The water looked tempting. Why not give up? She shook her head. What am I thinking she thought. Maybe there is a letter from Isabel. I'll return to the post office and check my box.

When she put her hand in her box she pulled out an envelope with the Sisterhood's title, but nothing from Isabel. She walked over and sat under her favorite oak tree and carelessly tore it open. It was most likely an announcement of the monthly meeting, she thought, as she opened it. There in big letters was an invitation to come to the next meeting just before Christmas to receive an award from the Sisterhood for saving the treasury and the record book during the earthquake.

The truth is she had tried to put the whole earthquake scene in the back of her mind. It had been hard enough to learn to live in a tent after the city officials had needlessly dynamited their homes as a protection against the fire. The broken pieces of her Danish blue china were still in the bag in which she had collected them the night they had to move out.

I must go to Martha and apologize for my behavior and share this announcement with her, she thought. I hope she'll understand.

I'll make up for my absence if she wants me to take over the next class, providing women want to continue.

As she walked back to their tent, she kept thinking about the award and feeling good about it. Georg and the girls would be proud. She rolled up the canvas sides to let the few breezes through, combed her hair and powdered her nose. She forced a smile and then laughed at the mirror image as she put on her floppy straw hat. Somehow the sad feelings of the past hour were buried in the excitement of being chosen for the award.

Anna's headache had gone away and the heat flashes had ceased. I must go over and see Martha now, she thought. I can't stand all this noise and pounding so close to our tent. As she walked across the green, shaded from the sun by her floppy straw hat, she asked herself what she would do if she were in Martha's shoes. Would she welcome her back? Martha was her special friend. As she passed the commissary, she bought a bouquet of summer flowers for her friend.

When Anna arrived at the sewing class, no one was there. It was their regular time. Where could they be? She walked back to Martha's tent, but it was empty. She counted on Martha and the sudden feeling of emptiness returned. Finally she went to the Day Room and asked the orderly, "Have you rescheduled the women's sewing class?"

"Oh, no, Ma'am. They were assigned a bigger room to have enough space for all the sewing machines. They're in room 292 in back of the commissary."

Anna blinked. More sewing machines. How did they get them? She had tried ever since they arrived in April to obtain sufficient machines for the sewing class. She hurried back across the Presidio to find the room. Sure enough, the sound of machines could be heard. She forgot the heat as she hurried up the stairs and opened the door. To Anna's amazement, all the women stopped sewing, stood up, and clapped.

Martha ran over and gave Anna a hug. "Your requests for the machines finally came through. The machines arrived yesterday."

Anna tried to smile, but tears rolled down her cheeks. "I am so ashamed of leaving you. I felt so useless. Here are some flowers. Please, forgive me."

"Why, Anna, I know how you felt. It is good you had some time away for yourself. Now, however, we need you back with us. We have a big class."

"Yes, yes, I'll help!" Anna agreed, excitement in her voice.

Martha turned to the class, "Anna's going to help us. Back to work, ladies. Three weeks until the fashion show."

"Three weeks?" asked Anna. "Look, here's a letter from the Sisterhood. They invited me to attend the annual meeting and receive an award for saving the treasury and registry."

"That's what we're preparing for. Our class was invited to put on a fashion show at the annual meeting. I knew you were to receive the award, but don't tell the others because it is supposed to be a surprise. Want me to help you make yourself a new dress?"

Anna's head was twirling: an award, new machines, teaching classes, fashion show, and new dress. How could she handle all this? "I guess so, Martha. I'm trying to put this all together. I felt so useless and lonesome, and here you have me already involved. I need you, Martha, dear."

Later that morning when she had returned to their tent for her sewing materials, she pulled up the flaps, thankful that the autumn fog hadn't burned off yet. At least she'd be cool for a little longer before the blazing sun from this Indian summer came out and made life almost unbearable. She picked up her goddess Aditi and thought *I can be confident. I can learn to look beyond myself and control my emotional self as well as my physical self. It is not easy, little goddess, but I'll really try.*

Suddenly, she heard the sound of wheels crunching on the graveled path to her tent. Georg was the only one who made that sound. She looked her clock: 10:19. What was he doing here at this hour. She ran outside. "Georg! The Sisterhood is going to give me an award for saving the . . . ."

The two policemen stared at her for a moment. "Are you Mrs. Amorsen?" one of them finally asked. "Mrs. Georg Amorsen?"

"Yes . . . What's . . . What's the matter? Why are you here? What's happened?"

Chapter Twenty-Two

The Hospital

It was almost noon when the San Francisco Police wagon pulled up in front of Bay View General Hospital. Anna and Martha jumped out and rushed inside. Thea was waiting in the lobby. As soon as she saw them, the young woman got up and, without a word, went to her mother and gave her a long hug.

Martha stood to one side, ready for the worst.

Anna returned her daughter's hug, but didn't speak. Tears began to roll down her cheeks.

The two women were silent as they embraced, eyes closed, amid the hustle and bustle of the lobby of the busy hospital. It was as if mother and daughter had an unspoken understanding that neither would require the other to speak. Maybe if they didn't talk about it, the awful truth about Georg and Les and their wounds would go away —wouldn't exist.

Finally, the suspense was too much for Anna. She slid her arms up to Thea's shoulders and gently pushed her away to study her daughter's face. Tears were streaming down Thea's cheeks.

"How bad is it?" Anna whispered, girding herself for the worst. All during the ride from Tent City, Anna had been trying to steel herself to face the news about her husband no matter how bad. Martha kept reminding her that she couldn't be sure what the news would be and to keep her mind open, but Anna felt in her heart that this was the end of her wonderful Georg. Ole was so much stronger and mean and hateful. She was sure this was her payment from God for not having told Georg about Ole from the beginning. No matter how things turned out, she kept telling herself, all this was her fault.

As Thea swallowed and looked her mother in the eye, Martha placed an arm around both their waists.

"The doctor says they're going to be okay," Thea said.

Anna scowled. "Really?" she asked, afraid to believe.

"Barring any complications!"

Anna let out a high-pitched shriek, and as she looked toward heaven in thanks, her knees buckled. "Oh, God. Oh, sweet God!" Thea and Martha caught her as she began to sob — deep, gasping sobs. Her whole body quivered and shook, eyes blinking and darting side to side. "Oh, my God! Oh, my God!" she exclaimed over and over as Thea and Martha led her toward a chair.

The two policemen who had brought Anna and Martha came over and inquired if everything was all right. Most of those in the big lobby looked up briefly from their own private misery to stare at this stammering, middle-aged woman with wild eyes and ashen face.

Once Anna was seated on a bench, Martha hurried to the receptionist and found a nurse who grudgingly gave her a few damp cloths. She and Thea put them on Anna's forehead and the back of her neck. Gradually, the color in her cheeks began to return.

"I'm all right," Anna whispered finally, removing the cloths and sitting up straight. "I'm all right. Now tell me the rest, Thea. I want to know everything!"

Thea sat down, faced her mother, and took both her hands. She then explained about the fight and what Les had done and how she had brought the police back to Papa's store. Luckily, she knew of a doctor whose office was close to the store. "He stopped the bleeding for both Papa and Les. But, it was too late for Ole," she said. "He'd fallen onto his knife. The doctor said he was dead the moment he hit the floor."

Anna's eyes widened. "He's really dead?"

Thea nodded.

"Good!" Anna blurted. "Good! What a horrible, horrible man. And to think I was supposed to have married that animal!" She shook her head and became quiet while staring up into Thea's eyes. "Les saved Georg's life and probably yours as well."

Martha nodded her agreement.

Anna threw both arms around her eldest. "Thank God you're safe! I love you so much, Thea. I don't know what I would have done if anything had happened to you." Tears slid from the corners of her eyes and rolled down her cheeks. "I'm so sorry I've been so mean to you lately."

Thea returned her embrace. "I love you too, Mama." She began to sob. "You've been fine, Mama. Just fine."

"No, I haven't. No, I definitely have not."

"What do you mean?" asked Thea, pulling back to watch her mother's face. "What are you talking about?"

Anna shook her head and looked down at the floor. Martha handed her friend a handkerchief. "Never mind . . . we'll talk about it later." She stood up, wiping away her tears. "Where are Georg and Les? I want to see them both."

"Now?" Thea wondered.

"Now!"

"I don't think you can . . . ," Thea said, looking around the room. "The doctor was just here. He told me they've moved them to the third floor in the critical care unit. They're both still recovering from their stitches and ether."

"I don't care," Anna said. "I want to be with my Georg. It doesn't matter if he's awake or not. And you should be with your Les. Remember, he saved your father's life. He'll be expecting you to be there when he wakes up. When he's awake and out of danger, I want to see him and thank him and . . . ," She covered her mouth and tears began to flow. "I'm sorry. I'm so very, very sorry, Thea." She turned and walked away, fighting the tears, her body quivering with grief.

Martha took Thea's hand. "Don't worry, honey. I'll stay with your mother. She'll get herself together; she's just very upset. You understand, don't you, honey? You should be with Les." Martha walked away from Thea and put one arm around Anna. "Be sure and thank Les for your mother," she said over her shoulder. "You're very lucky to have such a good man love you, Thea . . . but I'm sure you already know that."

Thea nodded ever so slightly. "Thank you, Martha." She turned to walk away, tears welling up in her eyes. "Tell Mama, I'm going to be with Les. I want to tell him what happened. I don't want some policeman telling him about Ole."

Martha nodded that she understood.

Anna had covered her face and was still sobbing; she didn't see or hear Thea leave. She couldn't believe how badly she'd behaved toward her own daughter and Les.

Anna sent Martha to check the situation at the store before going to see her husband. She wanted to make sure Karl, Georg's helper, had shown up and that the store was open for business. After all, it was their only source of income. This hospital bill was certainly going to put a dent in their savings, but she was glad Thea had decided to place her father in a private room. Too bad Les couldn't afford a decent room of his own, but Thea had said his injury wasn't nearly as bad.

The harsh smell of ether stung Anna's nostrils when she entered Georg's hospital room, and her stomach knotted. She couldn't believe this man in the bed was really her husband. In addition to facial cuts and the huge bandage on his shoulder, there was an ugly bump protruding on his forehead.

Oh, Georg, she thought, what has happened to you? I almost didn't even recognize you lying there with all your wounds and bloody bandages!

His head lay to one side, eyes closed.

She leaned forward and took the pulse at his throat. Thank the Lord, his heart was still beating. She stroked his hair and held her face down to his and pressed against him. His eyes didn't open. For a brief moment, she thought he looked like a corpse. She stooped beside him and listened for his breathing.

The thought of what Georg had just gone through made her even sicker to her stomach: her wonderful, hard-working husband fighting Ole to keep their money — the money he worked so hard to provide for their whole family. Why did he have to be so stubborn? It would have been better just to give Ole the $300. But no, that was not her Georg. Her heart almost burst with love, and a tear slid down the side of her cheek.

Georg moaned and moved one arm up to his head. His eyes opened and, for a split second, she thought he could see her. She went to the sink and ran cold water over some towels, then placed one on his forehead. Again, he tried to open his eyes.

This time, she used a damp towel to wipe his face. "Oh good, you're here, Anna," he whispered. "Please help me. It hurts. It really hurts bad. Can you make it stop hurting?"

Gently, she kissed him on the cheek. "Of course, my darling. Show me where it hurts."

He placed one hand on his forehead. "It feels like my head is going to explode. Will you please get the doctor."

She ran to the hallway and called for a nurse. When one came scurrying from one of the other private rooms, Anna explained that her husband was in terrible pain and he never complained about pain and that scared her more than just a little bit because he had also asked for her to get a doctor and that was so unlike her Georg because asking for a doctor is just about the last thing in the world he would ever do, so would the nurse please hurry and find a doctor who would come and examine her husband's head right now?

The nurse was a middle-aged woman, tall and austere in her long white uniform and a cap that sat perched precariously on the top of her tightly drawn hair like it might blow away any moment. She gave Anna a long, withering stare. "Madame," she said between clenched teeth, "this is *not* a hotel. This is a hospital, and, I am not a chamber maid to be ordered about. I am a nurse. I will examine your husband, and, if he is in need of a doctor's care, I will bring a doctor, when and if one is available. Is that quite clear?"

Anna stood there with her mouth open. All she could think to do was to nod her head.

The nurse breezed into Georg's room, telling Anna to remain outside. A few moments later, she whisked out of the room, past Anna, without a word.

The fisherman's daughter then went inside and sat beside her husband. His eyes were closed, and the knot on his head had not receded. "I think she went for a doctor," Anna said.

Georg nodded.

A few minutes later a doctor appeared with the same nurse and introduced himself. His name was Dr. Svenn Larsen, and hearing Anna's accent, addressed her in Danish. She explained about Georg's pain and then watched while the doctor and nurse made their examination.

Anna had to grit her teeth when they removed the bandages, and she saw the extent of the wound in Georg's chest and shoulder. It was big and ugly — blood was everywhere and the forehead bump looked as big as an egg. She couldn't stop the tears that flowed down her face.

Georg began to move his lips. "It was Ole, Anna," he mumbled. "We had paid him all his money. Why was he so nasty? He wanted the cash box, and when I wouldn't give it to him he took out his knife and stabbed me. He was crazy."

Finally the doctor was done.

"Everything's going to be all right, Mr. Amorsen," he said. "Nurse Johnson will put on a fresh bandage for you, and then you need to just rest. There's nothing I can do for your head except prescribe something for the pain. The police say someone hit you pretty hard. Is that right?"

"Yes. He knocked me out."

"There's a new medicine called aspirin. Let's give it a try and see how it does. It should bring some relief. It may take a few days, but eventually the pain will go away by itself. I'll come back and visit in an hour or so. Is that all right?"

Georg nodded, barely.

The nurse began to redress the wound. The doctor motioned for Anna to follow him out into the hallway.

"I'll be right back, Georg," she said.

"Your husband's sustained a deep and serious knife wound, Mrs. Amorsen," Dr. Larsen explained outside. "He should stay here for a while so we can keep an eye on him and make sure that wound doesn't become infected."

Anna nodded. "What about the pain in his head?"

"I'm afraid there's nothing more I can do about that except give him a mild pain reliever. He's suffered a concussion. The only real cure is bed rest."

Anna's eyes widened. "So how long is he going to be here?"

Larsen shrugged. "Depends. If things go well, it could be just a few weeks. If there's complications, it could be somewhat longer. He's not a young man, Mrs. Amorsen. Our bodies don't recover as quickly when we get over fifty, you know."

Anna nodded and bit her lip.

"Are you going to sit with him?" he asked.

She nodded, again, wiping her eyes.

"Please don't worry yourself, Mrs. Amorsen. He's going to be fine. He's a very lucky man. That knife just missed his heart. The only thing we really need to worry about is the infection and that there are no possible complications from the blow he received to his head. You'll see. In a couple of days, he'll be yelling at me to let him go home." Dr. Larsen turned and hurried down the hall.

Georg looked like he was asleep when she came back in. "Anna, have the police come yet?" he called.

She sat down beside him and held his hand. "No, don't worry, honey. The important thing is that you're going to be feeling better in no time." She leaned over and gave him a kiss. "I love you, Georg." His tired face and listless look made her want to hug him to take away the pain.

"Don't feel so sad. I love you too, honey." He stroked her hair. "It could have been worse."

There was a knock on the door. An officer dressed in a blue uniform with a badge opened the door. "I'm Officer Devlin. Mr. and Mrs. Amorsen, please, we have to prepare a report on what happened at your store today."

"Not now," said Anna. She felt so small looking up at this tall police officer. "My husband has been stabbed and beaten and left for

dead. He's here in bed and he's in terrible pain. The doctor just left."
The policeman carried a folder with him and walked into the
hospital room, studying Georg. He could see his eyes were barely
open. "Do you know who did this to you, sir?"
"Not now!" Anna shouted. "Can't you see this man is hurt?"
"It's all right, Anna . . . His name was Ole Ludeman, officer,"
said Georg, straining to pronounce the words. "Now, I'm in a lot of
pain. Could we do this later, after I've had some medicine or maybe
even tomorrow?"
A look of confusion spread across the officer's face. "I understand. I'm sorry to have come at such a bad time, and I will come
back later. One last question, though. Since you knew Mr. Ludeman,
what about Mr. Lester Gray; had he ever met Mr. Ludeman before?"
"No," Georg said, his eyes closed. "He was just helping out
with the shelving in the back room. He's my daughter's boyfriend.
Good thing, too. Hadn't been for him, no telling what might have
happened to the store or my daughter!"
Anna closed her eyes and took a deep breath.
The officer nodded several times, first writing and then studying
his folder. "I see," he said, backing slowly toward the doorway.
"Thank you both for your help. I hope you're feeling better by the
morning, Mr. Amorsen. Thanks again. Sorry to have bothered you."
Anna shook her head and watched the officer close the door
after him. The room was silent while she collected her thoughts.
"The doctor says you need to get lots of rest, Georg. He's talking
about you being in bed for several weeks."
"What?"
"That's right."
"That's impossible! Who's going to run the store?"
"Looks like Karl, Thea, and I are going to have to do it."
Georg raised himself off his pillow. "Ouch!" he blurted, grabbing his head and falling back onto his pillow. "My God, that hurts!"
"Georg, the only way you're going to get better is to rest and
take care of yourself," Anna said. "You're just going to have to let us
do it. There's no alternative." She got up and rinsed more towels in
cold water over the sink. "Now I want you to promise you'll lay still
with your eyes closed while I keep these cold compresses on you,"
she said, whisking back over to the bed and placing the cold towels
on his forehead. "And it wouldn't hurt a bit if you were to fall asleep,
especially after they bring you that new medicine for your head pains."
"Yes, Anna," he whispered, "whatever you say."
Just then the door swung open and a young, slim nurse with

blond hair pulled tightly up into a bun breezed in, carrying a tray of medicine. The smell of sweet perfume filled the room. She too was dressed in a long white uniform and a little white cap that appeared ready to fall off.

Seeing Anna, the woman spoke in a Danish accent. "Sorry, ma'am," she said in a flat, matter-of-fact tone, "but you're going to have to leave. Mr. Amorsen needs to rest. Doctor's orders."

"I'm his wife."

"Oh, . . . I see," she said, giving Anna a long once over. "Nice to meet you Mrs. Amorsen. My name is Nurse Swamberg." She flashed a smile and opened the floor stand beside Georg's bed, looking for something. "Of course, you understand how important it is that your husband rest. Why don't you come back in a few hours? That should be plenty of time."

Anna fought a momentary impulse to say something rude, then sighed, stood up, and took Georg's hand. "You do need some rest, darling," she said and gave him a long kiss on the cheek. "I'll be back in a few hours. Maybe you'll feel better, then."

Georg nodded, eyes closed, still holding his head.

Anna left. She needed to find someplace quiet so she could think and organize her thoughts. There was so much to do.

Thea sat quietly beside Les in the hospital ward room, trying to read the morning issue of *The Bien*. Les had closed his eyes and was attempting to rest; the ordeal with Ole had left him weak and throbbing with pain. Noise and commotion filled the room: Several older men coughed constantly; others moaned and cried like children, their voices high and raw from overuse; a short hospital orderly by the name of Shawn was changing the sheets for a middle-aged man who would shout, "Jesus Christ!" each time he was moved. The man had broken both legs a few days ago when the front of an abandoned building collapsed on him as he nailed boarding up over the windows.

The nurses had already told Les he would have to leave tomorrow unless he could produce proof that he had enough money for more than one day at the hospital. Despite Thea's objections and attempts to intervene on his behalf, Les had already made up his mind that he would leave in the morning. "If worst comes to worst," he'd said, "I can always go home and stay with Mom. She'll find a place for me."

Les opened his eyes. "I just remembered," he said out loud to Thea. "I didn't tell anyone at work about my accident . . . That's terrible. They just gave me a promotion, and now this stupid stab wound might make me miss work." He paused. "Do you think you could get word to them somehow for me?"

Thea looked up. "Good idea," she said, folding the paper. "I should have thought of that. I was still thinking you were off from work and had forgotten about when you had to go back."

"Of course, I might be feeling better in a couple of days."

Thea chuffed. "Your mother and I might break both your legs, too!" she said, an impish grin on her face. "Don't you be getting any ideas about going back to work until the doctor says you're ready! Those people on the railroad aren't going to fire you for being sick. They know what a hard worker you are."

Les stared at the ceiling. "You're probably right. Still, I should warn them so they can schedule someone else in case I can't show. It's only fair, don't you think?"

Unseen and unheard by Thea or Les, Anna entered the noisy ward room and stopped several feet behind where her daughter sat, listening to Les. Anna stood there, momentarily transfixed by the commotion and anguish taking place in the rest of the ward. The smell was just as pungent this time as it had been at the hospital in Tent City, but for some reason, Anna noticed, it didn't bother her.

Thea got up from her chair. "I'll go send the railroad a telegram, right now," she said, giving Les a gentle peck on the cheek. "But, I have no intention of mentioning the possibility of a miraculous recovery . . . especially since tomorrow you're probably going to your mother's to recuperate."

"What's all this about Les going to his mother's?" Anna asked, stopping directly behind Thea.

The younger woman whirled around. "Oh hello, Mama. I didn't see you there."

"I just arrived." Anna frowned and cast her eyes on Les. "Are you so well you can go home tomorrow, Les?"

There was an awkward silence.

"Hello, Mrs. Amorsen," Les said, noticing Anna's bloodshot eyes. "How nice to see you. Is your husband all right?"

Anna nodded. "Georg'll be fine," she said, looking back and forth between Thea and Les. "Why won't one of you answer my question? Why will Les be going home tomorrow with a knife wound in his back that's barely twenty-four hours old?"

There was another short silence while Thea averted her eyes.

Finally, Les cleared his throat. "Because I can't afford to stay here," he said. "The nurses told me that unless I can prove I have enough money to stay here after today, I gotta leave."

"I see," said Anna, nodding her understanding of the situation. "The nurses *are* rather rude here, aren't they." She studied Thea whose eyes had been riveted on Les as he explained his plight. "Thea," Anna continued, "didn't I hear you say you were about to leave to send a telegram?"

Scowling, Thea looked back at her mother. "Yes." There was a note of confusion in her voice.

"Well, why don't you go do that? I want to talk to Les alone for a few minutes. Do you mind?" she said, turning to Les.

He shook his head and made eye contact with Thea. "It would be an honor," he said with sincerity. "I'm just glad we're not in a restaurant right now, Mrs. Amorsen. That way, I can't make another fool of myself."

Anna grinned.

Thea snickered and started to leave.

"Just a moment, Thea," said Anna. "I want to say something to both of you, first."

Thea spun around, more puzzlement on her face.

Anna reached out and took Thea's and Les's hands. Tears were welling up in her eyes. "I just want to thank both of you," she said, her chin quivering, "especially you, Les — for saving Georg's life. Without both of you, . . . well, I'm absolutely certain he would be dead, right this minute."

"Oh, Mama," Thea said, putting her arms around her mother, "you don't have to thank us. We're just glad we were there."

"That's right," Les said, "there's no thanks necessary. We were there, and we did what anyone else would 'a done. I'm just glad we were in the store when that nasty man came in."

"So am I," whispered Anna, "so am I . . . ." Tears were streaming down her cheeks as she hugged her daughter with all her strength. The two women stood there for a moment before Anna pulled away and wiped her eyes with one hand. "Now, you go send that telegram, sweetheart. I want to have a word with Les."

Thea opened her purse and handed a handkerchief to her mother before hurrying from the hospital room. She didn't want her mother to see her tears of hope — hope that at long last maybe her mother had come to accept the man she loved. Thea knew there was nothing she could do to overhear what was said — she'd just have to wait for Les to tell her. She walked to the telegraph office across the street from the hospital.

Les studied Anna as she sat down in the chair beside his bed, wiping her eyes. The bloodshot in her eyes was worse. "Are you all right, Mrs. Amorsen?" he asked.

Anna smiled and took a deep breath. "I'm just fine, Les. Just fine." She looked into his big, brown eyes filled with care. "Les," she began in a gentle voice, "from now on, I want you to call me Anna, and . . . I want you to always think of me as your friend . . . Always."

Les nodded. "Thank you Mrs. Amor . . . Anna," he said. "Likewise, I'm sure. I'm happy . . . to be your friend."

"No, you don't understand, Les. You've always been my friend. Ever since you and Thea became friends, you've been a real friend to her and all our family. That's not my point. What I want you to understand is that I want to be *your* friend."

He thought for a moment. "I . . . I don't know what to say. Of . . . of course, you can be my friend. I'm honored to have you ask, but you've always been my friend, ever since we met."

Anna shook her head. "No, I haven't, Les. Not at all."

"I don't understand. You've always been so nice to me."

"To your face, maybe, but not behind your back."

Les paused and carefully looked in to her eyes. "What do you mean, Mrs . . . Anna?"

She bit her upper lip, fighting feelings of shame. "I mean . . . I was . . . trying to embarrass you, make you look foolish so Thea wouldn't like you. I was not your friend, Les." She hesitated and swallowed, not wanting the tears to start. "I've come here today to ask your forgiveness and tell you how sorry I am. I was so wrong about you, Les. I've never been more wrong about a person in my entire life." She stopped, gritting her teeth and trying to make the tears stay away, but they flowed from the corner of each eye anyway. She sniffed and swallowed again. "Will you please forgive me?"

Les lay in the bed, staring at the ceiling for a few moments. The coughing and muted moans in the ward continued. By now, the orderly had finished changing the sheets for the man with two broken legs and was moving him back onto his pillow for the last time. "Goddammit," said the man, overwhelmed by the pain once more.

Les then turned back and looked at his visitor. "You know, Anna, you are very brave. I don't know if I would 'a had the guts to tell someone what you just told me." He reached out his hand and she took it. "Of course, I forgive you. Thank you for your honesty. You don't know . . . ." He paused to swallow and clear his throat. "You don't know how much that means to me."

"Thank you. Thank you for everything. Thank you for loving my daughter. Thank you for being my friend, and thank you for saving the life of my husband and my daughter, but most of all thank you for understanding the ramblings of this old woman."

Les laughed, then winced. "Old woman, indeed," he said, letting go of her hand and turning onto his side. "Listen, 'old woman,' how 'bout telling this 'old man' about your husband's condition? You said, 'He'll be fine.' What does that mean? How long will it be before he'll be up and back at the store?"

Anna smiled a broad, knowing grin. How lucky you are, Anna, she thought to herself, to have met this remarkable young man. He's like the son you never had. And how lucky Thea is to have fallen in love with such a wonderful human being. She's really much wiser than you have ever given her credit. God bless them both. From now on, Anna Amorsen, you are going to do everything you can to help them know the beautiful love you have always had with your handsome and hard-working Georg. And to think, but for Thea's quick thinking and a few inches either way in Les's back or Georg's chest, you might be at the morgue right now, mourning the death of all three. How foolish you were to be worrying about such silly things as table manners and a new house and saving china from Norway. What really matters is now.

"Anna," Les asked, "are you all right? Did you hear me?"

Suddenly, she snapped back to the present. She looked around the ward and remembered how much work she had to do. "I've got a million things to do, Les," she said, opening her purse and putting away Thea's handkerchief.

"To answer your question, the doctor says Georg will heal back to perfect health. His only worry at the moment is the blow to Georg's head. He thinks it may be a concussion. The only cure for that is rest. That will drive Georg crazy, but he'll survive." She stood up. "I don't mean to be rude, but I really have to go. I need to figure out how we're going to keep the store open. I hope you understand."

Les nodded. "Don't worry. I do understand, Anna. If there's anything I can do to help, please let me know."

She started to extend her hand, then changed her mind. She moved close to the bed, leaned over, and gave Les a quick kiss on the forehead. "Thanks for understanding, Les," she said, standing back up and watching him blush. "And thanks for loving my daughter. You and I will be seeing a lot more of each other from now on. You can count on that."

Les nodded.

Anna Amorsen turned and whisked out of the ward; by now she didn't even notice the terrible smell. She had too many things on her mind. The first thing she had to think about was how she was going to run the store and move out of Tent City without Georg or Les to help with the moving or the painting. There had to be a way. She was a Viking woman, wasn't she? She'd figure it out somehow.

Chapter Twenty-Three

Surprises

Even though Dr. Larsen advised against it, both Georg and Les left the hospital within a week. Neither had fully recovered, but serious concern about infection in their wounds had passed. Georg still had headaches, but insisted on keeping the books for the store.

Before Georg came home, Anna had to sleep alone in their tent. It was very hard for her because the image of Ole raising his knife above his head and stabbing Georg made her shiver. That same image haunted her day and night. Ole could have cut into Georg's heart, killing him or damaging him for life. How fortunate Thea and Les were there and that a doctor came so quickly. Anna realized that it might take some time for her husband to completely heal. She closed her eyes, bowed her head. "Thank you, Lord, for keeping my wonderful Georg alive."

Les had stayed several days at the hospital because an anonymous benefactor paid his bill. When Les and Thea asked Anna about this turn of events, she shrugged and denied any knowledge. She did say how happy she was to hear that Les would make a full recovery and suggested maybe the railroad had put up the money. After all, there was all that front-page publicity in the paper about Les thwarting the robbery attempt, she reminded them, especially the part about him being an employee of the Southern Pacific.

Les moved from the hospital back in with his mother where she promised to make him take the time to recuperate and rest. Thea had been spending whatever free time she had over there. She and Anna and Karl and the old owner were keeping the store open. Meanwhile, Georg had come home to Tent City. Dr. Larsen told Anna that if her husband didn't stay in bed and mend properly, he would probably contract pneumonia or worse. However, the doctor said it was desirable for Georg to take long walks in the morning, afternoon, and evening.

One night after Anna had made dinner for the two of them and washed up, she and Georg were walking across the green when she said, "You know, it wasn't until the Sisterhood balanced their own bank books that they discovered they hadn't come over to collect their money."

Georg chuckled. "By the way," he said, "where did you hide that pouch and the records you rescued? I don't remember seeing them since Isabel left. Weren't they in that big trunk?"

Anna scowled and stared at him, a far-off look in her eyes. "Now that I think of it, you're right. I've been meaning to look for them, but with everything going on at the store and sewing for the fashion show, I forgot."

When they returned to the tent, Anna took the keys for the trunk out of her little jewelry box and gave them to Georg. "Here. Open the trunk and get them out."

Anna lifted Aditi off the top and held it as Georg unlocked the trunk and reached in among the many objects to lift out the money bag. He couldn't feel it, so he started to scoop out most of the possessions and leaned way over and looked again. There was no money bag. There was no record book. "They're not here."

Anna searched frantically inside the trunk. "They must be here, they have to be. Isabel was helping put things away; I gave her the Sisterhood's things to store in the bottom of this very trunk."

"But Anna, there is nothing here," he said. "Are you sure she didn't do something else with them?"

"I'm sure she did what I asked. She didn't carry the bag around the tent. She put it away."

"Let's dump over the entire trunk." Georg suggested. "Maybe the papers and money are stuck on the side." He held up the trunk and turned it upside down.

Both watched as the contents fell to the floor. Anna pawed through legal papers, the bag of broken pottery, Thea's first shoes, Isabel's picture of the ship, a silk blouse covered with sequins, and Georg's white shirts. "I can't believe it, Georg. There's no other place in this tent to hide anything."

"I think we'd better immediately send a cable to Isabel," he said. "You can't turn over the money and the books to the new treasurer unless we can find them. You know Isabel. She may have some secret place that she put them."

"I guess you're right," Anna said. "Be sure to word it so she doesn't think we're blaming her. Isabel would never take someone else's money."

Next morning, Georg hurried off to the cable office while Anna carefully went through each article in the tent, searching for odd spaces the book and the money could have been stored.

Day after day, there was no response from Isabel. Anna didn't tell anyone about her predicament. As the Sisterhood party drew closer, she and Georg started thinking about how they could replace the money in the bag. Georg told her how their savings had virtually disappeared with payment of the hospital bill as well as the costs required to reopen the store.

One night, they lay in their respective cots, side-by-side, talking. "I could ask my father," he said, "but I still haven't paid him back the money he lent us to rebuild the store. I'm sure Isabel will cable us back any day."

"But what if she doesn't," Anna worried. "What will we do then? What if she's on vacation or the cable doesn't get through? I can't show up at that party and collect an award without turning in the books and money."

Georg nodded. "That is a problem, but, if it came to that, we'd only have one alternative: tell the truth. Everyone in the Sisterhood knows we're honest. Certainly, they would understand how it could become lost in the move to our tent."

Anna shook her head. "No, they wouldn't. People are funny about money. They always believe the worst. If we can't find the money or borrow the money before the party, I'll have to resign from the Sisterhood and refuse their award."

Neither spoke.

"Well," he said slowly, "you should at least wait till the last moment before resigning. Isabel may yet answer." He paused and turned on his side to face Anna in the dark. "In the morning, I think I'll cable Cousin Tove; she should know where Isabel is."

The days dragged on. Martha and Anna had selected the pattern for her new dress and cut it out from beautiful blue cotton cloth. Martha noticed that Anna seemed uneasy. "You seem to be so nervous lately, Anna. Can I help in any way?"

"Oh, no, Martha. I'll be fine. There are just so many things I need to do. Business at the store is almost too good because of the holidays. At least my heat spells have stopped."

"I see," Martha said, closely studying her friend. "Remember, Anna," she continued, "if there's ever *anything* I can do to help, you can count on me."

The last week before the party arrived, and there was no word from Tove or Isabel. "I can't understand why they haven't answered," Georg said with frustration. "I hope everything is all right over there."

"Well," Anna said, "Isabel may have felt it was a secret and sent her answer by letter."

"Tomorrow is the last day. If we don't hear from her, I'll cable my father. Maybe he'll be able to help."

The next day was Wednesday. Georg went to the post office early to look in the other boxes to see if Isabel's cable had been misplaced. When he finally checked in their own box, he found:

> *Georg and Anna: I have been unable to contact Isabel.*
> *She's on holiday from school and traveling with friends.*
> *I'll keep trying. Sorry.*
> > *Cousin Tove.*

Georg immediately sent a cable of his own. He was rushing to get back to his tent before Anna left for the store. It bothered him that she still wouldn't let him go back to work even though he felt fine. Only a few more days, he reminded himself.

"Georg!" he heard a familiar female voice cry out from behind. "Georg, over here."

He turned and saw Martha hurrying toward him on her bicycle. "Georg, please wait a moment," she gasped. She put on her brakes, dismounted, and came to where he was. "Thank God I caught you," she said, out of breath. "I have something very important to tell you." An impish smirk covered her face.

Anna was pacing by the front of their tent by the time Georg arrived home. "Where have you been? It never takes you this long to go to the post office and back. I was worried sick. Now, I'm going to be late to the store." She crossed her arms. "Is there any news from Isabel?"

"Just this," he said meekly, handing her Tove's telegram.

She grabbed and read it.

"I've already sent a telegram to my father," he said while she read. He went to his cot and sat down. "I even paid the delivery boy 50¢ so he'd run over here as soon as Pop sends his answer. Everything's going to be fine, Anna. We'll have the money."

She shook her head and watched him, hands on hips.

He laid back on the bed and took a deep breath. "Stop your worrying, my little *Norska*," he said. There was an unusual gentleness in his voice. "You worry too much. I give you my word: One way or another, you'll have the money to give back to them by the time of the party. You may not have the books by then, but you will have the money. You'll just have to explain to the Sisterhood what happened about the books. Eventually, Isabel will get in touch with Tove, and then we'll have her answer. Everything's going to be fine."

Anna stared at her husband. There seemed to be something different about him, but she couldn't figure out what it was. One thing was for sure: she was late. Her bus had already left; she'd have to catch a cab. She hoped Karl would tell the delivery people to unload their merchandise, even if she wasn't there. Ever since all that publicity in the paper, she hadn't been able to keep enough inventory in the store. In a matter of weeks, business had almost tripled.

"All right, Georg," she said, sighing out loud. "You're right — I do worry too much. In any event, I don't have much choice." She paused, deep in thought. "So, you're in charge of raising money for me to return to the Sisterhood. Come the night of the party if we don't have the money, I'm not going. I'll have to resign and lose all of my friends."

He studied her for a moment from his bed, started to say something, then merely nodded. "I understand," he said. "I won't let you down. Just put this whole thing out of your mind and go take care of our store. Two more days, and I'll have kept my promise to wait three weeks before going back to work. Soon as you leave, I'm going back to sleep." He sat up and started taking off his shoes. "Don't forget to give me a kiss before you go. I want to have sweet dreams of my little *Norska*."

Anna shook her head. She'd never seen him like this before. He seemed so . . . devilish was the only word that came to mind. She swished over to him, and they exchanged a quick kiss.

"Hurry home," he said as she hurried toward the opening in their tent. "I can't wait to hear how much business we've done today. We still have lots of bills to pay. Maybe you should think about working there even after I'm back at work full-time. After all, those new customers don't even know me."

She smiled and waved goodbye. "No, thank you, Mr. Amorsen. Remember, we have to get ready to move. That rental flat of ours is going to be ready next week — the week before Christmas. I want to spend Christmas day there. We're going to have a Christmas day house-warming and invite our friends."

"Yes, ma'am," Georg said, nodding and smiling.

"Mother, where are you?" Thea called as she came out of the family tent.

Early in the afternoon, on the day of the party, Anna was across the path talking with a neighbor. She hurried over to greet her eldest daughter. "How thoughtful of you, Thea, to come early to help me get ready." Anna hugged her. "I'm so happy to see you. We've had so little time together lately, except at the store."

"Where's Papa?"

"Riding his bike. I can't wait for him to go back to work. He's been driving me crazy."

"Is the blue dress that's hanging inside for tonight?"

Anna smiled and nodded with pride as a crisp breeze blew by. "You like it? Martha made it."

"It's beautiful," Thea said, looking up into the sky.

Her mother noticed how Thea's curly light-brown hair waved and bobbed in the wind. She was built like her father — slim and taller than Anna, but with deep brown eyes. Thea was the one, Anna had decided, who would one day conquer the world. She'd try anything once and made friends easily.

"I love this setting," Thea whispered, watching the wind blow leaves from the trees. "The quiet here lends a poignant depth to the beauty of the birds' songs." She began to walk down the path toward the woods. "Do you hear the breeze blowing through the empty branches?"

Anna followed. Thea and Anna's footsteps were the only sounds except for the birds. The path led them to open space which overlooked the Pacific Ocean to the west and the entrance to San Francisco Bay to the north.

"Let's sit here awhile a look at this view," said Thea. "From this distance we can see how our beautiful city is making its remarkable comeback."

Anna happily sat down on the grass; everything was so peaceful. "The new construction along Market Street is only half done," she said. "It's going to take a long time to complete."

"Look at the ocean. I love the way the big waves roll up onto the sand." Thea walked around the flat top, raising her arms as if she was saluting the sea. "Les and I went over to see the flat last week. The painting's almost done."

"I can't wait until it's finished. Is Les coming tonight?"

"Yes, but he may be late. It depends on when his train arrives. I couldn't keep him from going to work today."

"How did you meet Les?"

"The newspaper had an employee picnic in San Jose and sent all of us down by train. I met him on the train; he was selling popcorn. His father used to work on the railroads and died many years ago in a train collision."

Anna shook her head. "We need to find him a job away from that dangerous railroad." She paused. "Does he like to dance? You know we're having the Scandy band tonight."

"Well, we're not so good on the waltzes, but we have a great time with the polkas." Thea sat down by her mother and started to draw houses on the dirt path.

"Has Isabel ever written you at *The Bien*?"

"Yes, . . . she's written me now and then."

"Who is this Ben she writes about?"

"He's helping with her lessons because of her limited use of Danish. He also helps the teacher in her class."

"I'm worried about Isabel. She writes me about bike rides. We don't hear about her school work. And then she goes off on vacation over Christmas vacation and doesn't even tell her own family. Cousin Tove still hasn't been able to locate her."

Thea took a deep breath. "Please don't fuss, Mama," she pleaded. "You know Isabel has a way of always landing on her feet. I think she really likes this Benjamin Von Dietrick. From her letters and the things they do, I think he's very rich."

"He's older, Thea. I would like to know more about him."

Suddenly, Thea seemed to get an idea. "Why not let me write her and ask how she thinks she's doing in her classes, and I'm sure she will write back about Ben as well."

Anna reached over and gave Thea a hug. "Thank you, honey. What a wonderful idea." They held each other for a moment. "Already, I feel much better. It's past noon. Are you hungry?"

"This is such a beautiful place," Thea said, standing up and looking out at the ocean again. "I must bring Les up here someday. Yes, I'm ready for a sandwich."

It was still warm outside when later that afternoon Georg arrived back at the tent, puffing from his bike trip. Anna and Thea had just finished lunch and were sitting on one of the benches outside, enjoying the sun's rays.

"You'd think by now I'd be able to do this without sounding as if I were on my last breath," he said. He sat down on the other bench. "Good to see you, Thea. I'm certainly glad Karl and Oluf are taking charge of the market this afternoon. I don't want to think about a thing tonight except having a good time. Would you get me a towel, please Thea? I'm sweating like a pig."

She tossed him his towel and he wiped his face. She noticed how he was beginning to show new wrinkles. He stretched out on the bench. "Don't disturb me, ladies, just tell me when you're ready to let me inside. I need to bathe or at least wash off."

"Still no word from Isabel?" asked Anna.

"Nothing," he mumbled.

"Hope she's all right," Anna said. "Can't understand why she would go off for three weeks and not tell anyone where she was going. Sometimes, I just don't understand that girl."

Georg and Thea exchanged a quick glance. He made sure Anna wouldn't see, then winked.

She began to pace. "So, I'm going to have to tell the whole Sisterhood that I lost their books and records. I can't believe it. I'm going to feel so utterly foolish." She crossed her arms and paced some more. "You do have the money, right Georg?"

"Yes, Anna, I have the money . . . for the hundredth time, I have the money. It's in my pocket. I will give it to you when we get there. Will you please relax?"

"Everyone will understand, Mama. Most of the women in the Sisterhood are your friends and know how Isabel is and that eventually we'll find the books. Anyone who would go into a building in the middle of an earthquake to rescue them isn't likely to lose them!"

Anna continued to pace. "I know . . . I was going to tell Martha about the books and records this morning when she was eating breakfast, but decided not to in the hope we'd hear from Isabel. Now it's too late. She's already at the Officer's Club getting everything ready for the party . . . I'll just have to tell her first thing when we get there. She's going to kill me for not telling her earlier. Luckily, she is my best friend."

"That's more like it," Georg said. "If you'll just relax a little, I'm sure everything's going to turn out fine." He stood and looked into the sky. "I hate to rush you, ladies, but we're rapidly running out of time. Will you please get dressed so we can leave?"

"All right, Georg. By the way, I hung out your good blue suit and the starched white shirt with your dark shoes." She turned to Thea. "Come on, honey. Let's get ready to have a good time."

By six o'clock, the Amorsens were dressed in their very best clothes: Thea in her red and blue dress; Anna in her blue dress with its long skirt. Georg looked just like Anna had envisioned: a tall, serious-looking professor.

"Thea, where is Les?" asked Anna.

"He promised to be here. I'll wait if you want to walk on ahead to the Officer's Club."

"No," Anna said emphatically. "He's part of the family."

At that moment Les arrived, huffing and puffing. Anna smiled when she saw his new dark suit and tie with black shoes to match. His hair was uncombed and his tie needed straightening.

"Hi, folks. Just came from the train. Everybody ready for a good time? I hope they have some of that Danish beer."

"Yes, we're ready, Les," said Georg. "Why don't you come inside with me for a moment? I want to show you something."

Les shrugged his shoulders as if it didn't much matter.

Anna and Thea exchanged a knowing grin. "He'll be fine," Anna said to her eldest in a motherly tone. "It may take a while, but he'll be just fine."

When Les came back, he had combed his hair, straightened his tie, and even wiped his shoes. Georg gave him a pat on the back. "There, you look great."

Thea gave him a hug, then took his arm.

Anna walked up to Georg and tapped the bulge in his suit jacket. "Give this to Martha as soon as we get there, all right? I don't want to worry about it anymore. I'll have to find the right time to tell her about the books and records."

"Accept my arm, my dear *Norska*. Come, I will escort you to your throne." Anna smiled and wrapped her arm around his.

The Officer's Club Hall was crowded as the Amorsens entered. Georg went to find Martha. Anna was glad to have that out of the way. She smiled as she looked about the room and recognized so many of her friends. She noted that Thea and Les were to be seated at the head table about four seats from Georg.

The dinner commenced with a pledge of allegiance to the American flag which Martha carried into the room. She was dressed in a red dress, with a beautiful white sash across her chest. Next came three women carrying their country's flags — Norway, Denmark, and Sweden — and wearing their native costumes.

Anna led the women of the sewing class who were also dressed in the typical costumes of their respective countries. The Norwegians marched past wearing high-waisted skirts hanging from narrow yokes or suspenders. Each woman had a wide belt in yellow and blue. Their skirts were midnight blue with red bodices over white blouses. Some of the women wore black caps bound with colorful ribbons. Seeing her native land's colorful costumes brought an ache to Anna's heart. Her sister had never left Bergen. Over ten years ago she had married Eric Breum, her high school sweetheart, and now they had two children. I'm their aunt, she thought, and I only know them by photographs.

The Norwegian costumes also reminded her of her father who used to dress up in blue, red, and white on May seventeenth, Constitution Day. It was a day of appreciation for country and heritage, celebrated throughout Norway. Anna shook her head. Why was she living in the past? The years of catching and selling fish, and the miraculous rescue on the ship to America flashed through her mind. For some reason, she felt close to her family back in Norway at that very moment.

As the fashion show progressed, Anna and Georg paid more attention to the Danish group; Georg had taught Anna the Danish language which was similar to Norwegian. She watched the Danish women wearing red woolen blouses under a sleeveless red bodice edged with gold braid. A white apron over a red skirt with delicate embroidery added to the costume. The women wore either white tight-fitting bonnets or head scarves and matching neckerchiefs.

The Swedish group was third. They wore white long-sleeved blouses gathered at the wrists, a dark blue skirt with a green band at the hem covered by a horizontally striped apron worn with a red decorated bag. Shawls edged with red designs were wrapped around their shoulders, and embroidered caps with bows and red and white ribbons completed their costume. Anna liked her own blue dress better than any of the costumes.

Five men followed, of which Christian — Martha's husband — was one, dressed in deep blue breeches fastened below the knees with red braid and pompoms. Their waist coats, in red or green, worn over long-sleeved white shirts, were decorated with metal buttons. Tassel blue caps completed the outfits. Anna recalled her father dancing in the same costume in the square when she was a little girl. He loved to celebrate their holidays. He was always doing all he could to bring up his two daughters.

The fashion parade finished with "America the Beautiful." Pastor Neils Jacobsen then gave the opening grace. "Ours is the richness of two cultures, that of our homeland and this new land. We are here to recognize the spiritual values bound up in each of us — to recognize the strength and belief in our community and each other. For this we thank you, *Mange takk*, Our Lord, Amen."

Dinner didn't appeal to Anna. She was tense and didn't want to eat. She kept thinking about how she needed to tell Martha about the books and membership records, but she was nowhere in sight. Anna picked up her fork and poked at her *rødkål*. She thought of the many times she had helped her mother chop the cabbage or add the spice and vinegar. The fragrance reminded her of Bergen.

After dinner, Mrs. Olga Nelson, president of the Sisterhood, called the meeting to order. Following a brief reading of the minutes and a vote on accepting two new members, she introduced Martha Andersen, program chairman.

Martha, wearing the same pattern as Anna's, smiled as she stepped to the podium. She nodded at Anna. "Please, Anna Amorsen, come up here so we all can see you, and bring Georg. He's a part of this, too." Martha then moved in front of the podium, out onto the dance floor.

As Anna came up to the podium, everyone in the room rose to their feet and clapped, smiling and calling her name.

Martha welcomed Anna with a hug and waited for the applause to wane. "As is customary at our annual celebration," Martha continued with a wide grin, "it is time for the outgoing treasurer to turn over the books and records and cash to the incoming treasurer. Since I am the incoming treasurer, Anna would you now please bring me those items."

A loud cheer arose from those assembled as Anna stood there in front of the Sisterhood, frozen with fear and unable to decide what to do next. She wanted to die. She should have told Martha about Isabel and the lost books, but it was too late. Out of nowhere, Georg was handing her a cloth pouch. "Martha wouldn't take it from me earlier," he whispered in her ear.

For a fleeting second, Anna thought the pouch looked familiar, but things were moving too fast. Her only focus was what she was going to say about the missing records. Holding up the pouch for all to see, Anna handed it to Martha while the clapping and stomping reached an almost deafening roar. Tears began to roll down Anna's cheeks.

Suddenly, from the crowd, Isabel Amorsen burst toward her mother, arms extended and screaming with delight.

Anna couldn't believe her eyes as she shrieked with joy and embraced her youngest daughter. The two held each other and sobbed uncontrollably while thunderous applause rained down upon them, louder and louder. "Oh, Isabel," Anna cried into her ear, "I can't believe it's really you! I love you so much! How did you get here? This is a miracle!" She pushed her to arm's length to take another look at her long-lost daughter. For an instant, Anna felt the room spinning.

Just then, Thea came running and embraced them both, all three women now sobbed and jumped with glee. Les stood beside Georg as the two men exchanged a misty-eyed glance. Georg put his arm around Les's shoulders and patted his back. He leaned toward Les. "I think we did it," he said into Les's ear. "She looks completely surprised!"

The younger man nodded.

Gradually, the applause died. "There's still a few small matters to be resolved," Martha said for all to hear. An impish smirk hovered at the corners of her mouth while she unwrapped the money pouch. "I can easily see that this is the actual money Mrs. Amorsen has been guarding all these months.

Anna suddenly realized it was the exact money she had saved from the earthquake. Where had it come from?

"However," Martha intoned, "there's the small matter of the books and membership list."

Anna was ashen and turned to Isabel, arms outstretched, palms up. "Do you know where they are?"

Isabel smiled and ran toward the crowd. She grabbed the arm of a man who had been hidden in the crowd and brought him toward her family. He carried something under the other arm. "Mama, I want you to meet my husband, Baron Benjamin Von Dietrick."

Those closest in the crowd heard what Isabel had said and quickly shared it with those behind. A murmur spread through the crowd while a stunned Anna shook hands with the tall, smiling stranger.

The man bowed and looked into Anna's eyes. "Mrs. Amorsen, Isabel has told me of your many activities. I'm most impressed," he said, handing Anna a pouch. "It's an honor to meet you."

Anna couldn't believe her senses as she mechanically accepted the packet and handed it to Martha. She immediately recognized it as the missing books and records. Her mouth hung open as she stared in amazement at her new son-in-law.

"I am delighted to meet you, sir," she said, looking around at Georg and Thea and Les who obviously had met him before. "We've heard much about you from Isabel's letters." She studied his well-fitted suit, round face, blue eyes and blond hair. So this was the

Benjamin who helped her with her art work and learning Danish.
And now they were married?

Anna reached out and gave Isabel another hug and kiss. "Isabel,
what a wonderful surprise. You found the money and records for me
and you're here. This is unbelievable!"

Thea joined in hugging with her sister and mother.

Georg stood as if in cement. Finally, he stepped forward to shake
Benjamin's hand. "Well done, sir. Well done. You've managed to
completely surprise and delight Isabel's mother. I can't thank you
enough for making all this possible."

"You're more than welcome, Mr. Amorsen," Ben said. "It's the
least I could do after not having both of you at the wedding." The
Baron leaned closer to Georg. "When are you planning to give her
your surprise?"

Georg shrugged. "It's hard to know when's the right time. Let's
wait till she's received her awards. I just hope she doesn't pass out."

Ben smiled and waved to a couple huddled against the wall at
the back of the crowd. They seemed out of place. "Well, at least
we'll all be standing close to her."

Georg smiled. "That's for certain."

Another round of applause spread through the audience as Martha
held up the old dog-eared books and records. She then put an arm
around her friend and held up one hand for silence.

"Anna Amorsen, honored treasurer," Martha began, loud enough
for all to hear. "On Saturday, April 18, 1906, waves of earth three-
feet high swept through the landfill of downtown San Francisco.
Buildings twisted and crashed, chimneys collapsed, and fire spread
everywhere, and yet you, our own sister, took it upon yourself to
save the resources of this lodge. In recognition of your putting your
own life in jeopardy, we wish to present you with this engraved medallion. It reads as follows:

'Anna Amorsen, honored treasurer, April 18, 1906, in
appreciation of your bravery in re-entering your home and
rescuing the Sisterhood's money pouch and register of
members, we thank you and honor you for your courage.
Signed: Olga Nelson, President of the Sisterhood.' "

Martha put the gold chain with the engraved medal around Anna's
neck who started to say a few words of appreciation, but was still
crying and couldn't talk.

Anna looked around at the people, standing and clapping. How was it possible that all this was happening just for her?

She turned and gave Martha a hug, wiped her tears, and then turned to face her friends.

"My dear Sisterhood," she said in a gentle voice. "Please accept my sincere and humble thanks for this lovely gift which I will treasure all the rest of my life. I also want to thank my husband, Georg, and his three brave helpers, Christian Andersen, Hans Sorensen, and Ignacion Enaldo who so gallantly risked their lives to carry me to safety.

"I will never forget this night, and I thank you all."

The crowd yelled, some stamped their feet, and others shouted, "Hurrah for Anna!"

She buried her head in Georg's chest, crying again for joy. He wrapped his arms around her and kissed her on the forehead. "I love you, my *Norska*," he whispered.

Isabel and Thea were still hugging.

Martha held up her hand and the crowd quieted. "We're not done yet, Anna," she said, stealing a mischievous glance at her friend. "Not only are we proud and honored that you went to such extraordinary ends as our Treasurer, but on behalf of the entire Sisterhood," Martha continued, "I'd like to take this opportunity to thank you for your tireless efforts on behalf of your fellow citizens of San Francisco. As a small token of our esteem and thanks, we'd like to present you with this little package."

Martha then handed Anna a small gift-wrapped present. "I'd like you to open the it now, if you don't mind."

With hands shaking and tears running down her face, Anna ripped off the wrapping paper and opened the box. She reached inside and held up a set of silver keys. "Those keys are to your new house," Martha said, calm as can be. "It's ready for occupancy, right now."

Anna shrieked with joy, then hugged and kissed Georg, Thea, Isabel, and finally Martha. Tears covered her face.

"You don't have to wait any more for your very own house," Martha continued, "twenty years is enough. We got the city to put you at the front of the line. We decided that the least we could do was to speed up the process for you. Of course, you're going to have to make the payments, but this is your house now, Anna. No more rental flats for the Amorsen family. This is your very own home. Welcome to San Francisco, and congratulations to 'Our Woman of the Year.' "

This is what the crowd had been waiting for. They jumped and shouted and cheered and applauded. The noise was deafening. By now, Anna was emotionally numb; her mind could barely function. Everything seemed like a dream, almost unreal and disconnected from her. Tears streamed down her face.

The three bearers of the Scandinavian flags gathered their groups together and marched up to Anna and invited her to join them to march around the ballroom while they cleared the floor for dancing. The *"Aarhus Tappenstreg-Marsch,"* a Danish march, played by the accordion band expert and the drummer, caused the gathering to clap and stomp all the louder.

Anna marched in a daze. All this happening for her. She kept feeling the medal with one hand, tracing the print with her index finger. Finally, Georg joined her and put one arm around her waist. He kissed her gently on the cheek as they paraded around the room. "You were wonderful," he said. "Would you like to sit down for a moment so you can think about all this?"

She nodded absent-mindedly, and he escorted her to the nearest table and pulled out a chair for her as the band played the *"Borghild Reinlaender."* He then signaled for someone to bring her a cup of coffee. "I'm hoping that you and I can do some dancing tonight. This is a very good band, you know."

Soon couples went out onto the floor and began to dance. Georg whispered in Anna's ear, "I'm so proud of you."

Anna just sat there staring at him, shaking her head. "How long has all this been in the planning?" she asked.

He smiled. "Did we surprise you?"

"Oh, yes," she said. "You surprised me so much, I still can't believe everything that's happened." She paused and looked him in the eye. "I love you, Georg Amorsen. This is the most wonderful day of my life. I can't thank you enough."

"Don't thank me. It was mostly all worked out between Thea and Isabel and Martha. I did a little acting, but it was really their surprise for you." He paused and looked around the room for a second. "I've got to go do something; I'll be right back. I want you to stay seated, okay?"

Suddenly, Thea and Les joined them.

"Will both of you please sit with Mama for a moment?" he asked, winking at Thea. "There's something I've got to do."

The couple sat down around Anna who looked momentarily perplexed. "Don't worry, Mr. Amorsen," said Les, "we'll watch her for ya. She's got all that gold around her neck. We can't let anything happen to her now."

Everyone chuckled.

Anna turned and looked at Les and Thea while Georg walked across the dance floor to where the band was playing. He whispered something to the leader. Both watched Georg with rapt attention and pretended they didn't notice Anna's confusion.

The band immediately stopped playing, then there was a drum roll. "Ladies and Gentlemen," Georg intoned loud enough for all to hear. "Please excuse the interruption; this will only take a minute." He looked around the room as if he were a preacher waiting for his congregation to get quiet in their seats.

"For those of you who don't know me, my name is Georg Amorsen," he began, "and I have a brief announcement that concerns our Anna." He took a deep breath while couples on the dance floor crowded closer. "Over twenty years ago, Anna and I were married in Chicago. Weeks later, we moved to Denmark for more than a year until I got laid off. When my brother wrote that we should come back to North America, we barely had enough money for the trip. On the way, Anna begged me to let us stop in Norway and see her father and sister. I was young, naive, and full of myself; I told her we didn't have the time or money at that time, but one day we would come back to visit her family in Bergen."

Georg then strained to see through the lights and crowd to the table where Anna was seated. The crowd parted and made a small path to her table. Whispers filled the air. People huddled close to Anna, and the room became very quiet.

"I'm so sorry, my dearest Anna," he said, his voice quivering with emotion, "that we've never been back to visit your beautiful Bergen. I always meant for us to, it just never worked out . . . ." He cleared his throat, then paused. "But," he continued finally, "today, in honor of this special occasion and as a token of my deep love and appreciation for all you've done for our beautiful family and especially me, I wonder if you'd mind if Bergen came to you?"

As Georg said the word "Bergen," Anna looked around at two people who were now standing very close to her. She screamed as soon as she saw who they were. It was Gudrun and their stooped, white-haired father. Ben and Isabel held each of the visitors from Norway by one arm.

"Oh, my God!" Anna said, bolting from her chair and staring at them, hands on cheeks. "Oh, my God! Oh, my God! It's really you!" She broke into heaving sobs as she hugged and held her father and sister. The three of them just stood there, clutching each other and weeping uncontrollably and unashamedly. "I can't believe you're here. I can't believe you're really here," she said over and over while the whole audience clapped.

As Georg watched the commotion at the table where Anna was seated from in front of the band, Martha came up and gave him a long hug. "You're a wonderful man, Georg Amorsen," she said, pulling back to peer into his eyes. One tear streamed down his cheek. "This was a magnificent idea. Thank you for letting me play a small part in this beautiful evening. I'm sure Anna will never forget tonight for as long as she lives."

"Thank you," Georg said, wiping the tear with one hand. "I couldn't have done it without you, Martha. Anna's lucky to have such a good friend."

The band had been playing a long time before Anna knew how all the surprises of the evening came to be. It had begun with Georg. He had been quietly putting aside a few dollars a week to surprise Anna at some point with a trip back to Norway. When Martha told him about the "Woman of the Year" night for Anna, he began to think this might be the right time to spring his surprise. But, that was before he found out from Thea that Isabel had secretly gotten married and was planning to come to America for the holidays with her new husband.

Georg then wired Isabel with his idea of having she and Ben go to Norway on their honeymoon and pick up Gudrun and Anna's father. When they agreed, he wired Gudrun, and she and Isabel worked out all the details. Gudrun, Papa, Ben, and Isabel had actually arrived in San Francisco just that afternoon. That's why Les was so late. He wasn't at work at all. He'd been picking them up at the railroad station and getting them settled at his mother's house just before he showed up at Tent City. Martha and Thea had worked as a team to keep Anna distracted and not suspecting a thing. Isabel sent a note with Les that she'd hidden the money and records inside her easel. Georg taking Les inside the tent to clean his shoes and comb his hair was a complete ruse.

With each new revelation or admission, Anna laughed or shook her head or good-naturedly waved her finger at someone who had deceived her. She kept holding on to her sister and father. "I just can't believe it," she said over and over.

Finally, Georg couldn't wait any more. "Anna, would you like to dance before the band has to go home?"

She looked up at her tall, handsome husband. "Yes, Georg Amorsen, I would love to dance with you." She bounded from her chair and gave him a big kiss. "Thank you, my wonderful husband.

Thank you for such a wonderful surprise and thank you for being my husband. I love you more than I could ever find the words to say." She kissed him again. "We'll talk more later!"

The band played a *Dala Hambo* and the happy couple pranced around the floor. Everyone shouted and cheered. Anna felt the medal bouncing off her chest while tears of joy streamed down her face.

Georg began to get out of breath, but didn't want to ruin Anna's fun. Just in time, Christian Andersen cut in. "I must have my dance, too," he said. No sooner had they started to dance, when the band changed songs. "Do you like the *Lokkeren-vals?*" she asked, eyes bright with delight. "It's just a slow waltz."

"Sure, just watch me."

Dancing with Martha's husband was fun; he had so much energy. Then, Ignacio cut in. After that, Hans did a polka with her. On and on Anna danced. She loved every moment.

As the evening wore on, Isabel and Thea took turns dancing with their grandfather while Les and Georg made sure Gudrun had a good time. Like her older sister, she loved to have fun on the dance floor; Gudrun never stopped.

Anna made sure she took time to dance a slow waltz with her father. As she gingerly let him guide her around the floor, she felt as if she would burst with love and delight and joy. Twenty-three years had passed since they said goodbye on the shores of Bergen, yet she realized how little his appearance had really changed. He was a little more stooped now and he'd put on a little weight and there were new wrinkles in his leathery cheeks and at the corners of his blue eyes, but their clear piercing stare still saw straight into her heart.

"Anna," he whispered, his voice choking with emotion, "I am so proud of you. You mother would be so proud of you, too." He was silent for a few steps. "This night is one of the happiest moments of my entire life. I just want you to know . . . ." He paused to swallow. "I just want to . . . ." He stopped dancing and gave her a big hug. "I love you, Anna."

They stood there for several moments before Anna led her father back to the table. They sat holding hands side by side in silence for some time before Georg came. He studied them for a moment. "Mr. Steffensen," he asked, sitting beside him, "would you mind if I danced with your daughter for a few minutes?"

The older man nodded and smiled. "That would be just fine, Mr. Amorsen," he said, looking Georg in the eye. "Thank you for taking such good care of her for all these years, and thank you for making it possible for me to be here." He extended a gnarled and calloused hand; the two men shook hands. "You are a good man, Georg Amorsen. Now go and shuffle your legs off. I'm just happy to be here. My dancing days are a little behind me."

Georg took Anna's hand and they hurried to the floor. Only a few couples were dancing. By now, most of the others had danced themselves into exhaustion or decided they'd had enough. Not Georg and Anna. The band was playing slow tunes and Georg and Anna Amorsen spun and twirled and looked in each other's eyes until the orchestra finally had to put away their instruments. It was just like the old days.

But now it was time to go home. Georg and Anna said goodbye to everyone and made plans to get together the next day. Anna made certain the gold medal was still around her neck and that the keys to their new house were in her purse.

There was too much to say to Georg, yet she didn't know where to begin. They walked in silence. She clung to his arm and felt as if Aditi had touched her with a magic wand. It was a beautiful crisp evening with the moon shining down as they stepped outside and walked across the dew-laden grass. A gentle breeze rustled her hair. Like Cinderella, Anna didn't want midnight to come and end this most magical of nights.

She snuggled against Georg and looked up at his handsome face. How silly you were, Anna Steffensen, she thought. All these months and years you thought he didn't understand how you felt. You were the one who didn't understand. How's that for a surprise? You were wrong about Les and you were wrong about Georg, but nobody cares if you were wrong. She fondled her medallion as a tear trickled down her cheek.

At home in their chilly tent, they got undressed for bed with hardly a word. Anna suddenly felt exhausted and began to yawn, but there was something she had to do. While Georg went to the outhouse, she pulled their two cots together, then covered them with a mattress she had propped up and stored in one corner. By the time Georg got back, their new make-shift bed was made and Anna was waiting under the covers.

"Well," he said with a grin on his face, "I like this. What a perfect idea. Now we can really be warm!"

She smiled and welcomed him with open arms. She gave him a big kiss on the lips, then hugged him for a long time. "Thank you, my wonderful husband," she whispered. "Thank you for the best day of my life. I will never forget this night. Never." She hugged him again, then turned and snuggled her back up against him, taking his arms and wrapping them over her chest.

He returned her hug and gently kissed her head and cheek. They stayed that way for several minutes. "You're certainly welcome, my sweet *Norska,*" he finally whispered into the cold darkness. "I, too, love you with all my heart." The only noise he could hear was her deep breathing.

He leaned up on one elbow and saw that she was sound asleep. In one hand she clutched her gold medallion, in the other he saw the silver keys to their new home. Goodnight, my sweet *Norska,* he thought, closing his eyes. It would be his best night's sleep since leaving Denmark.

About Dr. Doris Amorsen Meek

Doris grew up with a desire to teach and received a doctorate in education at UC in 1961. She taught at SF State College in the area of teacher education, continuing her career south at SDSU. She was invited to serve one year as dean of the college of education.

In the early 80s, Doris conducted a public radio program, interviewing prominent educators at SDSU. Later she began facilitating San Diego County's Learning Channel, which resulted in her becoming host of a new program called "Senior Life Styles."

Doris named the new book *Norska: A Viking Woman's Journey* as she and Mike brought the final pages of the story together.

About Michael Tynan MacCarthy

Mike MacCarthy is an author, publisher, and ghostwriter. During the past eighteen months, he has collaborated on three other novels: In February 1995, *The Celestial Bar* sold at auction for a substantial advance; it was then released in June by Delacorte Press. *The Valise* and *The Bamboo Wall* are currently in negotiation — one for a book deal, the other for a movie deal.

Mike recently authored *The Man From Samsun*, a political action adventure, and has a suspense thriller in progress entitled *Incident at Third Base*.

For further information about this book or its authors, write or call care of:

San Diego Writers' Monthly
3910 Chapman Street
San Diego, CA 92110

Phone: (619) 226-0896

FAX: (619) 224-0530